Do You Know That I Love You

◆

Do You Know That I Love You

Boyband

◆

Mark A. Roeder

Writers Club Press
San Jose New York Lincoln Shanghai

Do You Know That I Love You
Boyband

Writers Club Press
an imprint of iUniverse.com, Inc.

For information address:
iUniverse.com, Inc.
5220 S 16th, Ste. 200
Lincoln, NE 68512
www.iuniverse.com

ISBN: 0-595-18827-3

Printed in the United States of America

This novel is dedicated to the readers of my books who take the time to contact me and keep me going with their supportive words. It is also dedicated to "Graham", one of the greatest keyboard players in the world.

Foreword

◆

For many years, the prejudiced and ignorant have worked very hard to keep gays hidden. Their greatest fear is that gays will stand up and be recognized, for if this is done, all will see not only how very many of us there are, but how much artistic and other talent is held in the hands of those who are gay. Many, perhaps even most, of the greatest artists, writers, and musicians throughout history have been gay. Without the gay population, Western culture would not exist as we know it. What would the world be like if there had been no Leonardo DaVinci? I could fill this book with the names of gay artists, writers, musicians, scientists, and more, but I think this single example will suffice. Without gays, the world would be a pitiful place.

It is especially important for gays who are in the limelight to stand up for what they are. The entire gay community, and particularly the young, need to see individuals who are gay, and who excel. Such role models have too long been hidden from us. The prejudiced have bent all their will upon keeping such role models in the dark, mainly by creating an atmosphere in which the talented are afraid to be honest about what they are for fear of rejection or ridicule. The ignorant and prejudiced should no longer be allowed to hold the most talented segments of society down. They have had their chance to make the decisions and the result has been widespread violence, drug use, and disaster. It is time for the creative influence to be felt and time that all our energies are focused on making the world safe for all, instead of attempting to discriminate against a group because of something as insignificant as sexual orientation.

It is also time we realize that such terms as "gay", "straight", and "bisexual" are nothing more than words. They are terms that are meaningless in a world that is filled with shades of gray and not black and white. We have a desire to neatly categorize everything, but the real world defies such attempts. I doubt that we will cease to use these terms in the near future, but we need to understand that no label can adequately describe any of us. Each of us is an individual and should be valued as such. It is not what we are called, but what we are that matters.

Acknowledgements

◆

I'd like to thank Ronald Donaghe and Ken Clark for all their help. Ron, for taking time out from writing his own novel, "The Blind Season", to correct my many mistakes. Ken, for giving me the keen insights of a reader and for suggesting ideas that made this a better book. Finally, I'd like to thank both Ron and Ken for all the work they did designing the cover of this book.

Chronology

"Do You Know That I Love You" is a contemporary story that takes place not long after "Someone Is Killing The Gay Boys of Verona" and some twenty years after "Ancient Prejudice Break to New Mutiny", "Someone Is Watching", and "A Better Place".

Introduction

———————————————— ◆ ————————————————

In order to save myself a great deal of time, I'd like to answer a question before it is asked yet again. That question is "Is your novel based on a real pop star, or rock group?". The answer is "No." *Phantom* is a fictional boyband and each member of the band is a fictional character. No doubt comparisons can be drawn between the characters and real life music stars. Readers may well see a bit of their favorite rock star in Jordan, or Ross, or Kieran. This is as it should be, otherwise *Phantom* would not be believable as a boyband. Those who have a deep knowledge of boybands will find accurate "inside" information, such as what it's like on an actual tour bus or how security works at a concert or autograph signing. Even if I was at liberty to reveal my sources for this information, I would not do so. Many details in the novel are real, some of the settings are real, but the events and characters themselves are fictional. *Phantom* may seem to be one boyband or another, but it is not. Jordan, Ross, and Kieran may seem like real pop stars, but they exist only in this book. "Do You Know That I Love You" is a work of fiction, not a dramatization based on actual events. If it seems real to you, then so much the better. I've done my job well.

Boyband

◆

Ralph

---◆---

"No! Not again! If I have to hear *Do You Know That I Love You* one more time I'm gonna blow chunks! I swear I will!" said Chris.

"Those are fightin' words!" I yelled, with mock-menace. Chris was my best friend and I knew he was just pushing my buttons for fun.

"Oh yeah, that's right. I almost forgot about your *disturbing* obsession for Jordan," said Chris.

I took my hand off the wheel long enough to punch Chris in the shoulder. I turned the radio up louder and Jordan's beautiful voice filled the car.

"Oh God I can't stand it!" yelled Chris covering his ears. He began screaming and moaning, but he couldn't quite keep from laughing as he pretended the music was torturing him.

"It's horrible!" he said. "I can't take it!"

"Horrible?!"

"Yeah, horrible! Awful! Like fingernails on a chalkboard! If they made criminals listen to that instead of going to jail, there'd be no crime!"

"I'm gonna hurt you later for this, you know that don't you?" I asked him. Chris only smiled.

His protests did him no good. Chris knew it was useless. There was nothing I loved more than listening to Jordan. I'd practically worn out the latest *Phantom* CD and I'd only had it for three weeks.

"How many times have they played that song on the radio anyway? They must have played it a million times already," complained Chris.

"Not quite, but it's been number one for six weeks now," I answered. Chris rolled his eyes.

"You know Ralph, I have no problem with you being gay and all, but do you have to have a thing for someone so damned ugly?" He jerked back as I took a swing at him. Chris laughed. He loved making fun of Jordan. He knew how it irritated me.

"Ugly? You'd kill to look like him and you know it!"

"Yeah, right!"

"You're just jealous because you don't have millions of teenage girls screaming for you."

"And one teenage boy," said Chris smiling. I couldn't help but smile back. There was no denying that I had a thing for Jordan. Okay, it was more than a thing, I guess it was close to an obsession. As far as I was concerned, Jordan was the most beautiful boy in the entire world.

The song ended and Chris let up on Jordan for the time being. I cut Chris some slack, and decided not to kill him for making fun of my boy. Chris and I had been through a lot together. Not many guys would have been as cool as Chris when they found out their best friend was gay. I remembered how I trembled when I told him, and how relieved I was when he told me it didn't matter to him, and that he loved me like a brother. Friends like that were rare. Chris was the only guy who was aware I was gay, and was one of only two people who knew. Denise was the other. I was nearly as close to her as I was to Chris. I was lucky. I didn't have many friends, but I had good ones.

I turned the car onto the gravel road that led toward our farm. It was a dead end, in more ways than one. It wasn't long before I pulled up in front of the house and Chris and I got out. Mom and Dad were gone, so we had the place to ourselves. We raided the refrigerator, went to my room, and turned on the radio. Chris started thumbing through my CD's.

"*Phantom, Phantom, Phantom* import, *Phantom, Phantom* import, *Phantom* single, crap, crap, crap. Don't you have anything decent?" said Chris as he flipped through my CD box. "Ah, here we are, something cool at last."

I crossed my arms and gave him a dirty look for his comment. I wasn't really mad. Chris liked to tease me, just like I liked to tease him about drooling over Julie Paterson all the time. He had it bad for that girl.

Chris put his CD on and we sat on the bed and listened. We fiddled around with a computer game for a bit, but it didn't take us long to get bored. There just wasn't that much to do. Chris turned on my little television.

"Ohhhhhh look! Your idol is on," said Chris gleefully. "I know we've got to watch this. Couldn't miss out on your dream boy now could we?"

I ignored Chris. My eyes were drawn to the screen. It was showing Jordan and the other band members coming out of some studio, being mobbed by girls.

"And you said he was ugly. Look at all those girls after him."

"Nah, they're after those two other guys. See 'em all going for that one with the long black hair."

"His name is Ross," I said. "He is pretty hot, but he's no Jordan. I wonder how many years it took him to grow his hair that long?" I was almost speaking more to myself than Chris. I'd kind of forgotten he was in the room. Some reporter started talking and I turned up the sound.

"...once called a one hit wonder, *Phantom* has become the hottest pop group on the scene with no less than three multi-platinum albums. They're been favorably compared to the *Beatles,* and looking at the scene behind me, I am reminded of the Beatle-mania that swept the country several decades ago. *Phantom* is no British invasion however, with band members coming from Indiana, Virginia, and New Mexico..."

I stopped listening. The camera had gone to a tight shot of Jordan and I was spellbound. Every time I looked at him it was the same. I couldn't imagine that anyone could be so beautiful. He could easily have been a model if he wasn't a singer, more than a model, an angel.

"You're totally hopeless," said Chris, looking at me.

I smiled at him without taking my eyes off Jordan. Despite his words, he understood me. He just liked to torment me.

"Let's go outside," said Chris.

The piece on *Phantom* ended, so I was more than willing to depart. We left the small farmhouse and I followed Chris to the barn. The barn was old, and big, built by my grandfather some forty years before out of wood and concrete block. I think it's what I liked best about the farm. Chris had a special liking for the hayloft and that's where he led me. As soon as we'd both climbed up the wooden ladder, he turned and faced me. I knew what was coming.

Chris grabbed for me, but I was more than ready for his surprise attack. I dodged him. We circled each other, looking for an opening. Chris darted in and grabbed my upper arms. We struggled against each other, lost our balance, and tumbled into the hay.

We rolled around, each trying to get on top of the other. Chris was a little stronger than me, but I had a slight height advantage and my longer arms made up the difference. Our wrestling matches usually went on until we were both breathless. Neither of us minded that, we both loved to wrestle around in the hayloft, Chris especially.

Our muscles bulged as we struggled and we got all sweaty and hot. Straw started to stick to my damp forehead. I brushed it away with one hand and it was a mistake. Chris slammed me back and got on top of me before I could stop him. Before I knew it, he had his knees on my shoulders and my hands up above my head. I was doomed.

"I guess we know who the real man is here," said Chris laughing.

"How long did it take to create this little fantasy world you live in Chris?" I asked him.

"Funny!"

"Okay, I'll let you up, weanie-boy, if…" Chris paused to think of something suitably nasty. A smile spread across his features and I knew he'd come up with something. "All you have to do is say 'Jordan is butt ugly' and I'll let you up."

"Never!"

"Oh, ve have vays of making you talk," said Chris in his best German accent, and started to tickle me. "Say it, say it!"

"I will die first!" I said laughing. He was killing me. I hated being tickled like that and he knew it. I was powerless to stop him.

"Say it! Jordan is butt ugly!"

"Jordan… is…. gorgeous!" I laughed harder than ever.

"Wrong! Try again punk." Chris tickled me without mercy. It was torture. I was writhing on the hay, twisting and turning, trying to get away.

"I'll just keep doing it. Say it Ralph!"

Chris was having way too much fun. He got so tickled with himself that he threw his head back and laughed. It was a mistake. I saw my chance. I hooked my leg around his neck and pulled him backward at a high rate of speed. He hit the hay and I pounced on him. Before he could stop me, I pinned him.

"Okay straight boy, it's payback time." I tickled him. Chris wasn't as ticklish as me, but I still found his torment satisfying. He squirmed in an attempt to free himself.

"Okay Chris, now you say 'Jordan is my favorite singer' and I'll let you up! No, I'll make it easy on you, just say 'Jordan rules' and you're free."

"Oh no! Not that! I'll never say that!"

"Say it!'

"Jordan is a girl!" he yelled as he laughed.

I tickled him harder for that, then looked down at him and smiled.

"I can see you're going to be difficult. I think it's time for trial by drool."

"No way, that is not cool!"

"You know what I wanna hear. You just better say it before it's too late."

Chris squirmed as the long line of spit grew closer and closer to his face. I could tell he was getting panicky.

"Okay, okay! Jordan rules!" he screamed.

I pulled the spit back into my mouth.

"You cut that one close," I said.

"That's disgusting," said Chris.

"And oh so effective," I laughed.

Jordan

◆

"Hey Jordan, time to get up, dude." I slowly came to consciousness as someone shook my shoulder. I opened my eyes and focused on Chad, the leader of the stage crew that traveled on tour with us.

"Seattle," he said, before I could ask him where we were. I'd asked that question so many times he'd come to anticipate it. I slept so many nights on the tour bus, and moved from one hotel room to another so often, I didn't know where I was sometimes.

"We'll be ready for the sound check in another hour. Breakfast is on the table when you're ready," said Chad.

"Thanks."

Chad smiled, closed the curtain, and left me to myself. He knew I wasn't too talkative in the mornings. I sat up in my bunk and looked at the clock at my feet, 10:30 a.m. No wonder I felt rested. I usually had to get up much earlier.

I grabbed the remote and turned on the little color television at the foot of my bunk. There was nothing on but some game and talk shows, so I turned it back off. I didn't really want to leave the comfort of my bunk. It was small, but cozy. Each of us had our own bunk on the tour bus. At the foot of each bunk was a combination TV/VCR, a phone, and an alarm clock. It wasn't a bad set up really.

I pulled the curtain back and slipped to the floor. I dressed and walked toward the front of the bus. I smiled, there was a large paper sack that said "Burger Dude" on the side sitting on the table. The sack was already open and Ross and Kieran were chowing down.

"You better have saved some for me!" I said.

"Hey, would we touch your French toast squares and cinnamon mini's? said Kieran.

"Yes."

"Well, you're lucky, we didn't get to them yet."

I pulled the sack toward me and pulled out a couple of boxes. I loved French toast squares from Burger Dude, although I hadn't been there for over two years. It was a long time since I'd been able to go out to a public place like Burger Dude like a normal boy. It was the price of fame. I took a drink of iced tea and munched on a French toast square.

"Ah man, I forgot to ask Chad to check out keyboard two, some of the keys were sticking last night," I said as I began to wake up.

"So that's what that horrible sound was, I thought you forgot how to play," laughed Ross.

"Funny man!"

"Chill Jordan, you know Chad, he'll have it fixed before you ask him," said Kieran.

He was right. Chad was more than just another stagehand. He was in charge of the instruments and treated them like his babies. He was also a whiz with the sound system. He'd gotten us out of more than a few jams, like the time the main soundboard blew just seconds into the Orlando concert. He had a new one set up almost before we knew it. Chad looked and sounded like a California surfer and said "dude" more than anyone I knew. He appeared to be a bit slow witted, but it was an illusion. I didn't know anyone as sharp as Chad. I relaxed and enjoyed my breakfast.

"Think our hotel will have a pool?" asked Kieran.

"Think we'll get a chance to use it even if it does?" said Ross. He picked up his drumsticks and started banging on the table until Kieran took them away from him. That didn't stop Ross, he just drummed with his fingers. He could never sit still for more than five seconds.

Ross was right, we had a busy day ahead. We had to do a sound check, then do the set list, and then get over to some radio station or other for an on-air interview. After that, there was a short autograph session scheduled, then it was off to a press conference, then to another autograph signing at some record store, then back to the hotel to get ready for the show at 8 p.m. Before the show, there was a meet and greet backstage at 7:15 and a few more people to meet after the concert. Somewhere in there was lunch and supper and hopefully a little time to rest. It was unlikely we'd be seeing the pool. Even if we did have time, our bodyguards were likely to nix it, especially mine. Mike watched me like a hawk.

We sat and ate and talked. Breakfast was the only quiet time of day. I enjoyed my time alone with Kieran and Ross. They shared my love of music. They kept me laughing, too, especially Ross. He was crazy. I think it had something to do with him being a drummer. Every drummer I'd known was a little wild and a bit off tilt. Ross was in a world all his own when he got behind his drum set. He gazed off into space on the slow songs like he didn't know where he was, and turned into a mass of flying hair when we kicked it up. Come to think of it, he was in his own little world most of the time.

Sometimes Ross and Kieran seemed almost like my brothers. I was an only child and had long yearned for a brother, perhaps even a sister, perhaps not. I knew there was no chance of a sibling. It wasn't going to happen. Sometimes I thought of Ross and Kieran as the brothers I never had. In some ways, we were a lot alike. In others, we were not. We sure didn't look alike, Ross had hair as black as mine was blond, and Kieran's hair was light brown. Our looks were different, but that didn't matter. What mattered was on the inside, and on the inside we were close.

I peaked out the window before stepping outside a few minutes later. There were already a few girls hovering around outside, even though it was nine hours until the concert. The windows of the tour bus were tinted, so we could see out and no one could see in. There were only about a dozen of them and I was relieved. Sometimes just getting in a building could be difficult when the crowd was large.

Mike and the other body guards, Shawn and Rod, were waiting on us just outside the bus. They looked a little like secret service men with their sunglasses and ear pieces. They also looked a little like professional wrestler's, because they were big and intimidating. I gave Mike a nod and he opened the door. The girls immediately started screaming and jumping up and down. It wasn't bad since there were so few of them, but when there was a large group, they sometimes hurt my ears.

Mike and the others often had to push a path open for us, but it was a bit calmer this time. I was just barely aware of our guards watching the girls, glaring at them to keep their hands to themselves. Even though each of us had had a bodyguard for two years or so, I still wasn't quite accustomed to it. They were necessary, however, not so much because anyone was out to hurt any of us, but because crowds could get out of hand. I'd been injured more than once by well meaning fans pressing in to get a look at me.

Kieran, Ross, and I took some time to sign a few autographs and shake hands with the girls that were hanging out near our buses. We talked with them a little bit too. I really liked talking to the fans, especially when there were only a few of them. Just talking wasn't enough for Ross, of course. He had to propose to more than one of the girls before we moved on.

"You'll have to forgive Ross," said Kieran. "We seem to have misplaced his straight-jacket again."

One girl was so excited she screamed right into my face. I never quite got used to that. Another one looked like she was going to pass out and I actually had to grab her shoulder to keep her from falling.

"Oh my God! Oh my God! Jordan touched me! He touched me!" she shouted over and over as we turned and went inside.

"Ohhhhh will you touch me?" mocked Ross when we were alone once more. "Please Jordan, you're sooooooo cute." He burst out laughing. He lived to give me a hard time. Had I been the type who tended to get a big head about things, I'm sure Ross would have taken me down instantly. He never let me take myself too seriously. Neither did Kieran, but Ross was definitely the crazy one of the group.

I wondered how long those girls had been standing out there, and how long they'd remain to see if we came back out. I'd grown used to the girls for the most part, but sometimes it was still hard to handle. Don't get me wrong, it's not that I didn't like it. Who wouldn't love getting all that attention? It's just that it got to be a bit much. In the very beginning, it was overwhelming. I just couldn't get used to hundreds and hundreds of girls screaming my name and trying to touch me. It just didn't seem real. Sometimes I didn't even feel like I was me anymore. It had grown easier with time. I enjoyed it when we got a chance to meet a few of the fans at a time. It was much better than when there were huge crowds. You just can't interact with hundreds of people at once, unless it's a concert. That's what I really loved best, the concerts, and the music.

We stepped out onto the stage. The auditorium was huge. Seattle was a major venue. It was quiet at the moment, but I knew every seat would be filled that night with thousands of screaming fans. I stepped up to keyboard two and played a small section of one of our songs. Yeah, Chad had already taken care of whatever was wrong with it. He looked over at me and smiled. I gave him a thumbs up. He was the best.

Ross checked out the layout of his drums, while Kieran fine-tuned his guitar. In a few minutes we were ready to run the sound test.

"Okay, how about 'Til I See You Again'?" I asked.

Ross started a drum beat and we began playing. The sound technicians began making adjustments on the sound boards and moving around speakers and microphones. The amount of work there was to do before a concert always amazed me. It was the stage crew that did the work, but I still found it overwhelming. Sometimes I didn't see how they did it all. It was one thing when we had several hours to set up, but it was quite another when we were rushed. I'd seen the crew throw everything together in just a couple of hours when we were running late. Chad was always there overseeing it all. No matter how tight the schedule, he made sure everything was perfect for the concert. Chad was an absolute genius with sound equipment. Sometimes I swore he could make a sound board out of toothpicks and dental floss if he had to.

I had a bit of a rough start, but then I warmed up and really got into the music. "'Til I See You Again" was one of my favorites. It was a ballad and one of our slower songs. I'd written most of it myself, but Ross and Kieran had helped out with a few parts that I couldn't quite seem to get. We all had input into just about every song, although sometimes one of us did most of the work on a particular song.

"Can you hold it a minute, Jordan?" came a voice from a loudspeaker, cutting over the music. We cut off while the stage crew did some tinkering with cables.

"Okay," said the voice from above again.

"Where we left off," I said, and we started playing.

We had to pause once more before the end of the song, and then twice during "Jump Back". After that the sound check was over. We played a couple more songs just for practice. I loved playing my music. I didn't know what I'd do if I wasn't able to perform. Sometimes my problems almost overwhelmed me, but when I played, I felt like everything was going to be okay.

Ralph

―――――――――――――◆―――――――――――――

I sat at the edge of the pond, throwing a rock at its smooth surface now and then. The waves rippled out in a great circle until they disappeared. I was bored and lonely. I wished that Chris or Denise was there. It was usually fun when they were around. The old farm could get pretty boring when they weren't, however. There just wasn't that much to do on a farm in the middle of nowhere. It wasn't even a working farm. My parents kept a few chickens, but that was it. The corn that grew in the fields was planted and tended by someone else. My parents rented out the land, rather than try and farm it themselves. Mom did have a small garden, but that was it.

It wasn't the farm that was the problem. It was about as exciting as watching paint dry sometimes, but it was something else that made me feel lonely. I couldn't even begin to count the number of Friday nights I'd stayed home. I was seventeen and I'd never dated. There was a reason for that. I didn't like girls. Even if I did, I'd probably still be in the same fix. I wasn't all that good looking. I wasn't ugly I guess, but I sure wasn't one of the hunks that made the girls drool. I was plain at best, with ordinary brown eyes and hair, and an ordinary, even somewhat pudgy build. I wasn't quite fat, but close. I sure wasn't one of those boys with a perfectly flat stomach and well-defined abs. Maybe it didn't matter. I didn't give two cents about attracting a girl, and finding a boyfriend in southern Indiana was about as easy as finding a needle in a haystack. I felt like I was the only gay boy in the world sometimes.

I reached into my pocket, and pulled out a wrinkled piece of paper. I'd been trying to write a poem earlier, but I wasn't sure I had it quite right. I read over the words again:

> *I see him in my dreams,*
> *but he's not really there.*
> *I yearn for him,*
> *look for him in every face that passes,*
> *but he does not come.*
>
> *I've waited for him forever,*
> *but he does not appear.*
> *Will he ever?*
> *Is he real?*
> *My dream boy,*
> *the one that I love?*

That's why I was lonely. I didn't have anyone, and I had the feeling I never would. I had this feeling that I was supposed to have met someone, but that it didn't happen. I felt as if I were living in a time-line that wasn't supposed to be. Something had gone wrong and I had never met the boy who should have been the love of my life. I guess that was just silly, however. I threw another stone into the pond and watched the ripples travel without purpose until they disappeared.

I lay back in the grass and felt the sun shining warm upon me. An image of my dream boy came into my mind, Jordan. I felt kind of silly about it sometimes, like some starry eyed girl, but he was my dream boy. He had been since the first moment I saw him singing on television. Actually, he'd been my dream boy even before I first saw him. He was wandering around in my mind long before I even laid eyes upon him. I was shocked when I did see him for the first time. It was as if some fictional character had suddenly stepped from the pages of a book and become real. It was as if Jordan had stepped right out of my own mind. I couldn't help but love him.

I guess that's why I had every *Phantom* CD ever made, recorded every single television appearance, and clipped every photo and mention of him out of the papers. I had a whole scrapbook of Jordan clippings, largely thanks to Denise. I was too embarrassed to buy teen magazines that were usually purchased by girls, but Denise did it for me. Whenever one came out with Jordan on the cover, she got it for me. I must have spent a fortune on those things, but I didn't care. I loved him. I could spend all day looking at him, or dreaming about him.

Phantom was on tour for the second time and Jordan was going to be in both Indianapolis and Fort Wayne. The band hadn't even come to Indiana during the first tour. Both cities were hours away, but I'd been thinking about trying to get to the concert anyway. Who knew when I'd have another chance? This could well be the only time that *Phantom* performed anywhere close. Seeing Jordan in person would be the fulfillment of a lifelong dream.

I knew I'd feel out of place, however. There I'd be, me and a few thousand screaming girls. They'd probably all wonder why I was there. I'd look like a freak. I'd probably be the only guy there alone. All the rest would be there because their girls wanted them to go. They'd probably all be looking at me like I was some kind of weirdo.

It made me sadder still when I thought about not going. I could just picture myself on the night of the concert, sitting alone in my room, knowing that I could have been in the same theatre as my dream boy, knowing I could have seen *him*, in the flesh.

I've heard that when you die, you don't regret the things you did, you regret the things you didn't do. Something clicked inside me. I didn't care what those girls thought, or their boyfriends, or anyone else. Damn it, I was going to go. This was probably my only chance to see *Phantom* in person, and I wasn't going to give it up because of what someone might think.

I got up and walked up the hill to the house. I went into my room and got onto the internet. I found one of those on-line ticket sites and searched for *Phantom* events in Indiana. Two were listed, one in Indy at the Murat and the other in Ft. Wayne at the Embassy Theatre. I clicked on the Murat link first. Indy was about two and a half hours away. Ft. Wayne was twice that far, or more. My heart fell when I saw the words "Sold Out".

I was getting nervous. I went back and clicked on the Embassy link. I was in luck. It read "On Sale". I used the form to search for the best seat possible and crossed my fingers. I was disappointed with the result. The best I could get was in the balcony, near the back. Jordan would probably look like a little action figure from that far away. I wondered for a moment if it was worth it, a six hour drive for a bad seat. The ticket was close to $30 and I'd have to get a hotel room too. I didn't even know if my parents would let me go so far away by myself. The seconds ticked by. The screen said I had only 5 minutes to reserve the seat. Since it was so far back, it was probably one of the last ones left.

It was a bad seat, but it was to see *Phantom* after all. Even just being near Jordan would be the thrill of a lifetime. I could actually be in the same room with him. That made up my mind. I made the reservation. Luckily, I had my own credit card. It only had a $200 limit, but that was more than I needed. My reservation was confirmed. I smiled. I was going to see *Phantom* live. I was going to see Jordan for real. I couldn't wait to tell Denise. I wasn't so sure I'd tell Chris.

Jordan

— ◆ —

Torque, our opening act, finished and the stage crew quickly began setting up for us. The crowd started chanting *"Phantom! Phantom!"* and even *"Jordan! Jordan!"* and it got louder and louder. I took a deep breath and felt the butterflies in my stomach that were always flying around just before a performance. I knew they'd disappear when I got out there. I was always nervous before a concert, always pumped during it, and always drained after the euphoria of it all wore off a few hours after the concert. I looked to my side and saw Kieran nodding his head up and down in time with the beat of the crowd. He looked a little tense, like he always did, but eager to go on. Ross was tapping his drumsticks together, and in the air, and on me, and Kieran, and whoever chanced to walk past. He was like a jet all revved up to blast off. He was smiling. He loved it. All of us loved to get out there and do our stuff.

Moments later, we were announced and went running onto the stage. Everyone was standing and screaming and clapping. There was a crowd of over 12,000 and they were deafening. I ran to my keyboard and jumped right into "You Don't Know", the first song in our set. My butterflies flew away, I was tripping.

The music seemed to flow into my fingers from the keyboard, or maybe it was the other way round. Either way, I felt it surge through me, like a powerful wave. I changed when I got out there and sang, I transformed into something new. I felt like I became the music. The music and I were one, there was no difference between us.

I looked into the crowd as I sang and played. Everywhere there were faces looking at me, mostly young girls, but a lot of guys and older people too. I smiled and sang. I let the cheers and screams flow over me like a wave. It was the best feeling in all the world. A lot of famous people said they didn't care for all the attention, but I didn't believe them. It was a pain sometimes, it could even be frightening, but it was impossible not to love it. I felt like I could walk on air.

We finished the first song and the screams grew even louder than before. I really think a jet could have taken off in there and no one would have heard it.

"I think you're all excited tonight!" I said into the microphone. The sound system carried my voice all over the auditorium, even above the screams of the crowd. That made them scream ever louder.

"Let's pump it up!" I said and dove right into "Rock It Down Deep". I could feel the adrenaline running through my body. It was hard to maintain contact with my keyboard, I wanted to leap into the air and run all over the place. I really felt like I could do just about anything on stage. The power from the crowd was indescribable. There was all this energy just coming at me, it was incredible. Performing is like nothing else in all the world.

We played three more songs in quick succession, then ran off stage for a set change. While the stage crew moved instruments closer to the edge of the stage, I pulled off the long-sleeved shirt I was wearing over my tank top. It was hot as blazes in there. I noticed that Kieran took the opportunity to get rid of his leather jacket. I knew he had to be burning up in that thing.

We ran back out and played "I'll Keep You Up All Night". The crowd was wild. I slowed things down a little with a ballad, then brought it down a little more. I liked to do that—pump up the crowd with some fast paced stuff, then bring it down, then drive it up again. The highs and lows made it all flow beautifully. It was such a rush!

After a few more songs, we did "Deep In The Night". I liked that one because it gave me a chance to get out from behind my keyboard. Kieran had a lot of freedom of movement. He could go about anywhere he wanted with his electric guitar, but I was kind of tied to my keyboard. Ross was the least free of all. He was stuck to his drums for pretty much the entire concert. I don't think he minded. Actually, I knew he didn't mind. He was meant to play the drums. He played the drums even when he wasn't playing them. He was always tapping on something. I glanced back and caught a glimpse of him bobbing his head up and down, looking like nothing but a mass of flying black hair. Ross was in his own little world, and it was where he belonged.

I ran to the very edge of the stage as I sang. There were fans pressed right up against it, all of them reaching out for me. I leaned down shook hands as I made my way across the stage, although "shook" probably isn't the way to describe it, it was more like "touched" hands. I tried to get to as many of them as I could, but there was never enough time. Sometimes I couldn't believe how many people were pressed right up against the stage, and they were only the beginning.

I went back to my keyboard to play a small verse, then grabbed my water bottle and ran back to the crowd. I took a swig, then showered the crowd with the rest as I sang. I leaned down and gave it to a girl who acted like it was made of gold instead of plastic. I resisted the temptation to throw it into the crowd. I'd learned that was a bad idea. It caused a lot of shoving and pushing. I'd learned that if I leaned down and handed something to one person, that no one else tried to push in and get it, well, most of the time.

I ran back to the keyboard for the end of the song. When it finished, the crowd was going crazy. We jumped right into another. When I was playing, I felt like I was in another world.

I caught glimpses of Kieran as he played his guitar. He loved performing as much as I did. He also cared about our fans as I did too. His eyes were on them often as he played. Kieran and I both tried for a lot of eye contact with the fans. When we looked right into their eyes, there was a special connection there. Kieran was smiling, happy to be sharing what he loved most, and happy to be loved for it.

Ross seemed as if he were from a different world. When the beat was slow, his mind drifted off into space. He was aware of the fans as well, however. I could see the flash of his dark, penetrating eyes as he scanned the crowd and peered into one face, then another. When the pace was fast, Ross was a wild man. He was little more than a blur. His ability amazed me. I knew I was lucky to be with him. In my opinion at least, he was the greatest drummer in the world.

Most of the time, I wasn't consciously aware of Kieran and Ross, although there was always a connection between us. They didn't seem like separate individuals when we played, but rather like another part of me. When we performed I was most aware of the fans, and the music. That was everything.

Before I knew it, we'd been playing for almost an hour and a half. Time always slipped by like that. I was drenched with sweat. My heart was pounding wildly in my chest. I was exhausted and yet felt exhilarated as if I never wanted to stop. I didn't want to stop playing. I wanted to keep on singing and playing forever. At the end of the song, I took a moment to just look out over the crowd. They loved us, they really did.

I wondered if they'd still love me if they knew the truth. I didn't let it bother me. I pushed it out of my mind, as I always did.

"I hope all you guys have had as much fun as we have!" I yelled into the microphone, not sure if even the sound system could make me heard over the screams this time. I could feel the waves of sound from the crowd, vibrating my body. "You guys rock!" The crowd screamed even louder. "We've loved being here in Seattle! Have a great night!"

Kieran and I waved to the crowd as we walked off stage. Ross ran to the edge of the stage and handed his drumsticks to a girl, then followed us. We stood off stage for a few moments, listening to the crowd scream. We caught our breaths while waiting to go back on. It was something we always did. We acted like we were finished, then went back out and did one more song. Everyone expected it. It was a tradition. After just a few moments more we ran back out to cheers even louder than before.

"There's one more song we thought we should play!" I yelled. "I think you know this one!"

We jumped into "Do You Know That I Love You" and it was wild. While Ross was doing his drum solo I stuck my hands above my head and got the audience clapping. I started playing again and clapped some too to keep them going. I loved to watch all those girls really get into it, the guys too. There were some really cute ones in the audience, guys that is. I never failed to notice them.

We finished up, ran to the edge of the stage, and shook more hands. We stood back, joined hands, and bowed. The cheers were deafening. My ears were ringing from it. We waved as we ran off stage and made our way backstage. I could still hear the screams as I sat down and took a breather.

In just a few moments, there would be about twenty members of our fan club coming backstage to meet us, get autographs, and have their pictures taken with us. We did that at nearly every tour stop. I loved it. I'd be completely drained in a couple of hours or so, but I was so pumped after a concert that I needed to calm down before I could rest. Meeting a few fans was just the thing. There was nothing like being a rock star.

*   *   *

It was nearly one in the morning before we got back to the hotel. We had to leave the next morning a little after ten, but at least I had a real bed for the night, and some privacy. Mike went through my room before I went in. It seemed a little silly to me, but he insisted on it. Sometimes he acted like I was the President or something. I thought checking my room out was a bit much. A girl did sneak in once and Mike found her hiding in the closet, but she only wanted to meet me. It was a little scary that she'd managed to get in. Mike had used the situation for an example—"It was just a harmless fan this time, but next time it could be some wacko waiting on you with a knife," he'd said. I thought he was putting too serious a spin on it all, but I guess he was right. There were some crazy people out there. Even when I thought he was taking things a bit far, I let Mike do his job. He was there to protect me and it would have been stupid to interfere with that.

"It's all clear," said Mike.

"Thanks. Have a good night."

"Good night, Jordan."

I entered my room and closed the door. I knew Mike was on the other side listening to make sure I locked it, so I did so. I heard him walk down the hall once I secured the door. I knew that either he or Shawn or Rod would be patrolling the hall all night long. Our bodyguards took turns watching out for us. It made me feel like a prisoner sometimes, but I guess it was the price of fame.

I pulled off my clothes and took a quick shower. Exhaustion was setting in, but the hot water helped to revive me a bit. I started feeling kind of depressed, like I knew I would. Once the euphoria of the show wore off that always happened to me. When I was performing my music, it was like I had no problems and nothing could touch me. I was invulnerable, immortal. Once the heady thrill of that had worn off, my problems were there waiting on me. Sometimes I almost felt like my problems were some kind of entities that sat and waited for me in my hotel room, or in on my bunk on the bus.

I thought about all those girls that loved me and it brought me instant sadness. What would they think if they knew? What would they do if they found out I liked boys instead of girls? I could just imagine what would happen if my secret got out, and it wasn't good.

It hurt when I thought about it, because I really liked all those girls, I even cared about them. I wasn't physically attracted to them, but that didn't mean I didn't like them. Thinking of how they might turn on me if they knew the truth made me feel insecure, and alone.

My eyes got watery and a tear ran down my cheek. The loneliness was hard to handle. I bet no one ever thought I was lonely, but I was. Sure, I was surrounded by others almost all the time. Sometimes it seemed like the only time I was alone was when I was asleep, but I could be lonely no matter how many others were around. I felt it most keenly when I was truly alone. That's when it hit me. If others were around I could lose myself in their company, but when I was all by myself I was reminded that I had no one to love.

I thought about all those boys in the audience. They didn't know when I looked at them that I was searching, searching for someone to love. I ached for a boyfriend, someone to talk to, someone to share my life with, and yes, someone to make love with. What I needed most of all is what everyone needed, just someone to love, and to love me back. I thought of those boys in the audience and it made my heart ache. A lot of them were there with their girls. They didn't know how lucky they were to have someone like that. Some people thought I had everything, but they were wrong. I lacked the one thing that mattered the most.

I crawled into bed and closed my eyes. I knew the best thing I could do was just close my eyes and go to sleep. That was the only way to escape my loneliness and depression. Tomorrow, I'd wake up and it would be gone. There would be a lingering ghost of it, but I'd be busy doing what I loved and wouldn't feel it keenly again until another day was nearly done.

My body was exhausted, my mind too. I let myself drift off into sleep. Maybe I'd find a boyfriend there. Maybe I could at least have what I needed while I was asleep…someone to love.

Ralph

◆

"Did you get it?"

"Of course I got it, do I ever let you down Ralph?"

"Never!" I said as Denise handed me the latest copy of *Teen Music Stars Weekly*. Jordan was on the cover. I was particularly keen on getting my hands on this issue because I'd heard it had a shot of Jordan in a wife-beater. Seeing him in a tank-top was probably the closest I'd ever get to seeing him without a shirt.

Denise and I sat on the edge of my bed, as we gazed at the cover.

"Look at those eyes," I said.

"So sexy," said Denise.

Denise shared my admiration for Jordan. She wasn't crazy over him like I was, but she thought he was hot. We spent a lot of time drooling over him together.

"I still wish you could come to the concert with me," I said.

"Can't. I just can't get off work. Everyone at the store seems to have tried to take their vacation at the same time. There's no way I can get off." Denise worked part time at the local grocery store.

"Well when I get back, I'll tell you all about it!" I said.

"Yeah, over and over and over," she laughed.

"Probably."

I turned the pages of the magazine. One read "Phantom Contest" at the top. If you answered all the questions and mailed in the sheet, you could win an autographed CD, if yours was one of the six entries picked.

"You should enter," said Denise as she read it.

"Yeah, I probably will, but the chances of winning are probably like a million to one or something."

"Yeah, but you never know."

We kept looking at the magazine. I turned another page and there it was, Jordan in a wife-beater.

"Oh man!" I said.

"Down boy!" giggled Denise, but her eyes were glued to the page as well.

"He's so beautiful," I said. "I can't even imagine looking like that."

"Sexy," said Denise.

"Definitely. Mmmmm, look at the sides where you can see part of his chest. Wow."

"I wouldn't mind pulling that shirt off him," said Denise.

"Oh yeah!" I said. "What I wouldn't give for just a picture of him without a shirt!"

"Still haven't found one huh?"

"I don't think there is one. I've searched every single *Phantom* site on the internet and there isn't a single one. This pic is the closest to it I've ever seen."

"Try not to drool on it," giggled Denise.

"I might say the same to you."

"Guilty as charged. He's so gorgeous."

"I bet he's really nice too. You can just tell, you know?" I said. "I know I go on and on about how he looks, and he is hot, but there's a lot more I like about him than that."

"I know," said Denise. I was sure she did. We'd talked a lot about how much I loved Jordan. Sometimes I just felt the need to make sure she knew I wasn't into him just for his bod and face. I guess I didn't really need another reason to be into him, but I had plenty. I was in love with him.

"Ohhhh, I like this pic of him too," said Denise.

"Which one?"

"This one," she said pointing to a photo on the opposite page. It showed Jordan, Ross, and Kieran walking away. "Nice ass."

"You're terrible!" I said.

"Like you didn't notice."

"Okay, I noticed." I smiled and we continued looking through the magazine. I was in heaven.

When Denise left, about an hour later, we were still looking at the magazine. It had a lot of *Phantom* stuff in it, more than usual, and a lot of pictures of Jordan. There was Jordan at the Grammy's, Jordan at concerts, Jordan signing autographs for fans, Jordan skateboarding, and more. I loved it.

I opened my closet and dug out one of my boxes. I had three big boxes stacked with magazines and every one of them had Jordan in them somewhere. I pulled out a few of the older ones and looked at them. He was so beautiful he made my heart ache. He was my dream boy. He'd been on my mind forever and soon I'd really get to see him. It was a dream come true.

I heard the back door open and close. I stuffed the magazines carefully back in their box and pushed it back into the closet. I kept most of my *Phantom* stuff hidden from my parents, except some of my CD's. I was afraid they'd think it odd that I had boxes full of teen magazines. They were for girls mainly. I'm sure lots of guys bought them too, but it was mainly a girl thing. I didn't want anything to make my parents suspicious. I didn't think they'd kick me out or anything if they found out I was gay, but I didn't want them to know. I didn't want to deal with it, or have to talk about it. I don't think anyone liked to discuss sex with their parents and I sure didn't want to talk about being attracted to other guys. It would be a nightmare.

$*$ $*$ $*$

"Rogers, please tell me that's not a *Phantom* sticker in your locker," smirked Adam. I hated the way he always called me by my last name.

"And what if it is?"

"Then you're a fucking girl." Adam laughed for his two buddies that were standing behind him. He rarely traveled alone. "You know only girls listen to that sissy music."

"You know Adam, I think you're jealous. Jordan could have…"

"Jordan? Oh my God, you even know their names! You are such a loser Rogers."

"I was saying," I told him "that Jordan could have any girl he wanted, but you're stuck with… Ohhhh, that's right, Angela dumped your sorry ass didn't she."

"Fag."

Adam shouldered me and walked on. I was a bit upset, but I felt I came out ahead in our encounter. I was uncomfortable that he'd seen my *Phantom* sticker, and that he'd called me fag. I did my best to keep my sexual orientation a secret. I wasn't sure what would happen if I was found out. Southern Indiana wasn't exactly known for acceptance.

I didn't let myself worry about it much. I believed that everything happened for a reason. If I was outed someday, then I'd deal with it when the time came. I had no intention of spending all my time worrying about it. I'd learned not to worry about stuff long ago. There was a time when I agonized over things like dentist appointments days before they happened. Then I realized that the worrying was the worst part. Events were usually not nearly so bad as I feared. And so, I learned to stop worrying. That took away the worst part of any unpleasant event.

I was just the opposite about things that I was eagerly anticipating. I liked to think about good things coming up as much as I possibly could. I found that it increased my enjoyment of whatever I was looking forward to considerably. The *Phantom* Concert was such an event. It was *THE* event. I found myself growing more and more excited as the day approached. I almost couldn't believe that my parents actually gave me permission to drive all the way to Ft. Wayne by myself, and to stay all night in a hotel. I had to promise to check in when I got there, and call when I left for home, but that was no problem. I guess staying out of serious trouble all those years had its advantages. I did have to pay for it all myself and it would bankrupt me, but it was worth it!

Chris walked up just as Adam and his crew were disappearing from sight.

"They giving you a hard time?" he asked.

"Trying to. Adam saw my *Phantom* sticker. I mentioned Angela."

"Ouch!" said Chris and laughed. "You are a devil." Angela was a serious sore spot with Adam. She'd dumped him and dumped him hard.

"Come on, I'll give you a ride home," I said.

"Hey, you want to go camping or something this weekend?" asked Chris, as I pulled out of the school parking lot.

"Can't."

"Why not?"

I paused. I hadn't told him about the concert.

"I'm going somewhere."

"Where?"

"Fort Wayne."

"Why?" There was a long pause. "Wait a minute…" Chris eyed me suspiciously. "No way! You aren't!" I'd told him there was a *Phantom* concert coming up in Fort Wayne. I'd talked about it, even before I'd bought a ticket. I was sorry about that now.

"Yes I am and you can just shut up," I said a little embarrassed.

"You know," said Chris, smiling wickedly, "this takes your disturbing obsession with Jordan to a whole new level. You going to try to get his autograph?" Chris began to mock me, pretending he was me. "Oh Jordan, you're so wonderful. I sleep with your picture at night…"

"Shut up Chris!" I yelled at him. I was getting a little mad. "I do not sleep with his picture!"

"You might as well," said Chris.

"I wouldn't do something like that."

"Oh yeah you would. If they had Jordan pajamas, you'd be sleeping in them." Chris laughed at his own wit, before continuing to mock me. "Oh Jordan, you're so handsome, so talented…"

"You are evil," I told him.

"What took you so long to notice?"

Jordan

◆

I sat alone in the back lounge. It was usually the domain of Ross, but he and all the others were sleeping in their bunks. I could feel the miles speeding past beneath the wheels of the bus. It was late, but I didn't feel like going to bed yet. My old fears and insecurities were keeping me awake.

I knew I shouldn't let it get to me, but I kept wondering what things would be like if the world knew I was gay. I was sure the tabloids would have a field day with it. Ross, Kieran, and I had all been in the tabloids more than our share of times. Just the month before the tabloids had printed that Ross had a serious drug problem and that the management company had spent over a million dollars to cover it up. It was a complete lie. The only thing Ross was addicted to was sugar. One of the current issues said I'd had plastic surgery when I was thirteen so I'd have a better chance at a music career. Like most of what they printed, it was a load of crap.

The tabloids aside, I did feel uneasy about harboring a secret. It would have been bad enough if I was just a normal boy, but sometimes I felt like the eyes of the whole world were on me. That was the downside of being famous. Sometimes I felt like I couldn't blow my nose without someone doing a story on it. It was almost unreal. I knew that if my secret got out, it would be a media circus. I knew there were plenty of people who were more than willing to make a quick $500 or so by telling everything they knew.

I guess I didn't have to worry too much about being found out. No one really seemed to even suspect me, and as far as evidence was concerned, there was none. I was a virgin. I hadn't had sex with anyone, much less another guy. Even if I was straight, it would have been difficult hooking up with someone. Everyone probably thought me and Kieran and Ross could have as many girls as we wanted, but the truth was we were far too visible for anything like that. Being followed around 24/7 by a bodyguard would have about made it an impossibility. Ross had hooked up with a girl once, but she was one he'd met months before and had been e-mailing forever. It took some major diversionary tactics on the part of Kieran and me for Ross to get her to his room. I wasn't sure if I approved of it or not, but that was Ross' business. I could just imagine trying to sneak a boy into my room for the night. That was a real laugh!

Actually, it wasn't sex that I really wanted. Okay, I wanted it, but what I wanted more was a boyfriend. I'd have been content with a boyfriend even if we never slept together. It didn't look like that would ever happen, however. How could I even have a chance of meeting anyone? Sure, I met a lot of guys every day, but rarely was there any privacy at all. Even if there were, it wasn't like I could ask "Hey, you looking for a boyfriend?" I knew no guy would have the balls to come up and admit to me that he was gay either. Most of the boys I met seemed like they were afraid of saying the wrong thing. A few of them actually had trouble speaking, just because I was famous. I couldn't imagine any boy having the courage to tell me he liked me in that way.

I couldn't tell any boy that I found him attractive, and no boy seemed able to tell me that he liked me either. How was I ever going to find a boyfriend if I couldn't even let anyone know I was interested?

I hated having to hide that part of myself. It made me unsure of everything. I had all these girls screaming when they saw me and telling me how awesome I was, but they didn't know the real me. Would they still be so excited over me if they knew? Not knowing that made my whole life seem fake sometimes. It made all the autograph signings and public appearances an ordeal. I loved doing that stuff, and yet it was a reminder that everything I had was an illusion. Sometimes I dreamed about just walking away from it all and being a normal, gay, teenaged boy, instead of a rock star that had to hide what was inside.

Ralph

———————— ◆ ————————

Denise walked into my room the evening before I was to leave for Ft. Wayne. I was busy packing my little bag for the trip. She acted like she could hardly contain herself as she entered. She was carrying a small wrapped package, which she handed to me.

"What's this?"

"It's a present silly."

"I can see that, but what's it for?"

"Call it an early birthday present. Now open it!"

Denise was so excited she was actually bouncing up and down. I couldn't imagine what could be so wonderful, but her mood was contagious and I began to get excited myself. I ripped the paper away and opened the box. I reached inside and pulled out a ticket. I was perplexed. It was a ticket for the *Phantom* Concert in Ft. Wayne the next night. I wondered why she was giving me one, as I already had a ticket. Then I looked at it more closely.

"Oh my God! Oh my God! How did you get this?"

My eyes practically bugged out of my head as I looked at the ticket. It was for Section C, Row B, Seat A. Row B was the 2nd row, mere feet from the stage!

"There was this radio contest two weeks ago. I was the eighth caller, I knew the answer to the question, and well, I got it. I knew you were going, so I saved this for a surprise. I just got it in the mail day before yesterday."

"The second row! That's close enough to see *Jordan* sweat!" I laughed. I hugged Denise tightly. "This is the best birthday present ever! Hell, this can be my present for all my birthdays, and every Christmas from now on!"

"I won't hold you to that," said Denise. "Besides, you know how I love to shop for presents."

"What was the question you answered anyway?" I asked her.

"They asked Jordan's birthday. I knew it since you made me listen to all his CD's that day to celebrate, and we made that birthday cake, remember? I guess you won the ticket in a way."

"Thanks so much Denise!" I hugged her again. I couldn't believe it. Second row!

I was excited just to be going to the concert, but now I could hardly contain myself. I'd thought I'd be sitting far, far away, but I'd almost be on top of the stage!

"Are you sure you can't go with me?" I asked Denise. "I've even got a spare ticket now."

"I wish I could Ralph, but there's just no way."

I was sorry she couldn't come because I wanted to share this with her, as we'd shared everything about Jordan. I didn't let myself dwell on it. Nothing could dampen my spirits. The next day I'd be setting out to fulfill a dream.

"Since you are sitting so close, I want details," said Denise. "Find out if his eyes are as dreamy in person as they are in all those photos. I expect you to come back and describe every part of his body in detail."

"I will," I laughed.

Denise and I were both so excited we could hardly contain ourselves. Denise was a real friend. She knew what this trip meant to me and she was even happier for me than I was myself. I couldn't wait to get back and tell her everything about it, and I hadn't even left yet.

*   *   *

The next day I set out early. The concert didn't start until 7 p.m., but it was a six hour drive. I stopped briefly for gas in a little town called Newberry, then again in Spencer for a burger, and once more at a rest stop before I got to Indy. Driving around Indianapolis on the interstate was quite an experience, but it really wasn't much worse than driving in Evansville. All the cars did go really fast, however. I was doing 65 and most of the other cars passed me like I was sitting still.

About an hour from Ft. Wayne, I saw a big bus ahead. I wondered if maybe it wasn't *Phantom's* tour bus. I turned up my "Do You Know That I Love You" CD and sped up a little to catch up to the bus. My heart beat faster as I grew near. It turned out to be just some chartered bus, but I was all excited. I laughed at myself when I thought about it. *Phantom* had been in Milwaukee the night before and would have been approaching Ft. Wayne from an entirely different direction. It had still been exciting thinking that it might be their tour bus, however. I was so excited about everything that I could barely contain myself.

I got into Ft. Wayne a couple of hours before I could get into my room at the Holiday Inn. It was a sizable city, and unfamiliar as I'd never been there. It wasn't too hard to find my way around with a map, however. I had plenty of time to spare, so there was no rush.

I drove right by the Embassy Theatre on my way in. It was a beautiful old building that housed the theatre, as well as a hotel. I expected it to be bigger. I didn't see how there could be much of a theatre in there. I didn't care. I was going to see *Phantom* and that's all that mattered.

On the marquee it said "*Phantom*" in letters about three feet high and "*With Special Guest Torque*" in smaller letters beneath. Just seeing the name made my heart beat faster.

My hotel was only about two blocks from the Embassy, which was great because I could just walk there. I parked the car, checked out the hotel, then had a quick lunch at the Burger Dude that was just across the street.

After lunch, I walked toward the Embassy. About a block before I got there, I saw a huge maroon bus parked by The Hilton. I knew it had to be *Phantom's* tour bus. There were even a few girls standing across the street holding signs with stuff like "I Love You Jordan" and "We Love *Phantom*" on them. I changed my course and walked right by the bus. I couldn't see inside because the few windows the bus had were tinted. I knew Jordan was probably already in the hotel, but I was excited that I was so close. In only a few hours, I'd be closer still.

I rounded the corner and walked around the block to the Embassy. It was beautiful. It looked old, like it had been built in the early 1900's and it was real fancy. Seeing *Phantom* in those big letters got me all excited. I couldn't believe they were really going to be there. I couldn't believe I'd really get to see Jordan himself. I could see why the band was staying in the Hilton. It was right across the street from the Embassy and there was even a walkway above the street that connected the two buildings.

I had some time to kill, so I took another look at the tour bus, and the girls watching it. There was a big botanical garden right next to the Embassy, so I decided to have a look at it. As I was walking toward the building, I glanced back at the tour bus. My heart fluttered in my chest and I got all excited. I thought I saw Jordan. It turned out it was only some girl that worked at the Hilton with long blonde hair like his. I knew I had to watch myself, or I'd be thinking I was seeing Jordan everywhere.

I spent about an hour in the botanical gardens. There were three big connected greenhouses filled with all kinds of plants. I especially like the tropical room with the big banana tree. That part even had a waterfall and a little pool with big goldfish in it. The desert area was great too, with all of the huge cacti.

As I was walking around, I had this little fantasy about meeting Jordan or Kieran or Ross in there. I was sure they had more important things to do than check out the botanical gardens, but wouldn't it have been something? I could just picture myself saying "hi" to them and maybe even talking for a little bit. It was only a fantasy, but it excited me.

By the time I was done looking, I could check into the hotel, so I walked back to the Holiday Inn. My room was nice, but nothing fancy. I never stayed in hotel rooms, so it was kind of cool. I didn't waste any time in locating the indoor pool. I changed into my swim suit and had a nice swim. There was also a hot tub so I got in that after I was finished in the pool. It was awesome. I'd never been in a hot tub before. I quickly named the Holiday Inn my favorite hotel.

Time was getting on, so I changed, went to another burger place for supper, then headed back to the hotel room for a quick shower. After my shower, I changed into the clothes I'd brought along especially for the concert; light blue jeans, a dressy white short-sleeved shirt, and a pale green long-sleeved shirt that was a lot sharper looking than it probably sounds. I also put on my gold chain that I wore just about everywhere. I looked at myself in the mirror when I was finished. I looked good, well, as good as I could look.

It was just six p.m., but I wanted to get down to the Embassy just to be a part of the crowd. I walked down the sidewalk, growing more excited with every step. I looked where the tour bus had been parked earlier, but it was gone. The marquee of the Embassy was all lit up. It looked like some Broadway theatre, not that I'd ever been on Broadway to know what a theatre there looked like. The biggest city I'd ever been to was Chicago and I was only there a couple of times.

I could see quite a crowd in front of the Embassy as I neared. The doors were apparently not opened yet. I got in the back of the disorganized line and stood there. I felt a little uncomfortable standing there all alone. I was relieved to see some other guys, although most of them were there with their girlfriends. I talked to a couple of girls and their mom's. I couldn't believe how lucky they were. They were going backstage to meet the band! They'd actually get to meet Jordan. I was a bit jealous, but I was so excited, and so happy to be there, that it didn't matter.

One girl's mom kept singing *Phantom* songs out loud to embarrass her daughter. It worked. It was kind of funny the way she tried to hide. I was already having fun and we weren't inside yet. There was something about being surrounded by *Phantom* fans that made me feel I was surrounded by friends. I'd been really uneasy about going to the concert. I was afraid that everyone would be looking at me, wondering why I was there. I was still a little uneasy, but everyone was cool. My excitement overrode my fear. I couldn't believe that in less than an hour, I'd be seeing *him*.

Some boys drove by in a car and yelled "Phantom Sucks". That raised a lot of fingers in the air. It was a good thing those boys didn't stop. I think the girls would have dragged them out of the car and beaten them. I would have been more than happy to help.

We kept waiting and waiting. It was past 6:30 and the doors still weren't open. Finally, at about a quarter to seven, we got inside. It was like stepping into a dream. The Embassy Theatre was absolutely beautiful, with chandeliers, marble, and painted woodwork everywhere. It wasn't just a Theatre, it was one of those old movie palaces.

I searched out my seat and was amazed at how close I was to the stage. I still couldn't believe Denise had won me a ticket in the second row. The stage was about half as wide as I was expecting, so I was really close. I thought I'd be a bit off to one side, but I wasn't. I was nearly in the exact center.

I was so excited I couldn't possibly sit still. I had some time to kill, so I searched out the restrooms downstairs. There was a huge line for the women's restroom and none for the men's. Just as I was leaving a girl came running into the men's restroom. I was glad I'd already zipped up, but I guess it didn't really matter. I was a bit shocked, but I found it funny. The line of women outside were talking and laughing about it when I came out. I told them that no one was in the men's room and that they should take it over. Several of them went rushing to the men's room door, then more followed. It was so funny. I guess I was responsible for starting a small riot.

I went back to my seat and Jordan's opening act, *Torque*, came on and started playing. The group was made up of four guys, they were young and cute and sang very well. I thought that I might like to get their CD if they had one.

I left for the lobby because I wanted to get a program and I wasn't about to miss a moment of *Phantom*. I knew there wouldn't be time later and the crowd had been so huge earlier that it wasn't possible to even get near the table. There were a bunch of people out there and only two guys handling sales, but the crowd had thinned and it didn't take too long to buy a program. I also got an event poster. I was thrilled to get it because I'd been thinking how much I'd like the one displayed outside the theatre. I didn't know they'd have any for sale.

I went back to my seat and watched the rest of *Torque*. They were awesome. I definitely wanted their CD. After they were done, there was about fifteen minutes of set changing time. It was so exciting to see the *Phantom* insignia on the drum set. The audience kept chanting "*Phantom, Phantom, Phantom.*" It was wild. The entire room seemed filled with excitement and anticipation. Finally, Jordan, Ross, and Kieran rushed out on the stage and immediately started singing. My jaw dropped open. I couldn't believe it. There they were!

Everyone stood up. The girls in the audience screamed so loud I thought my eardrums were going to bust. During the concert my hearing actually distorted for a while. I didn't care. I'd have gone deaf to hear Jordan sing live.

I couldn't believe how close I was. Kieran was right in front of me, with Jordan a bit off to the right, and Ross between them further back. I just stared at them, amazed at how close I was. I was so close I really could see Jordan sweat. Later, all of them came over to this little runway to my left. Each of them got within five feet of me. I could almost touch them.

Kieran was wearing close fitting maroon leather pants, a dark blue silk shirt, and a dark leather jacket. Ross was wearing a football jersey with the number 11 on it. Jordan was wearing khaki pants and a tan shirt. I could see Jordan's necklaces and they were the same as the ones he was wearing in the program photos.

I kept looking from Kieran to Ross to Jordan, thinking "It's really them." There was an unreal quality to it all, like a dream, and I had to remind myself that it was real and that I was actually standing just a few feet from them. I'd listened to their CD's so many times and seen them on television and video tape so often, that it was almost like I was still doing that instead of seeing them right there. I spent the whole concert looking at them, thinking how much that moment meant to me. Of course, I mostly looked at Jordan. He was so beautiful he made my heart ache. I was in love with him.

The sound was overwhelming. The screams never quite stopped and the music was so loud I could feel it. I raised my hands and felt the music vibrating them. I loved it. I was totally surrounded by the voices of Jordan and his band, their instruments, and the sounds of those who loved them. It was almost overwhelming. I'd never been to a concert before and I could see why people go. It is way beyond just listening to a CD. It's totally impossible to get that same intense sound outside of a concert. Standing there, I felt like I was inside the music, or it was inside of me. I heard it more keenly than ever before and felt it vibrating through my entire body. It was an experience that's impossible to describe.

There were two or three set changes and I sat down during them. Everyone was standing the rest of the time and I got a bit tired on my feet. I really think I could have stood there forever, however. Between sets I sat there and looked around. There were girls with *"Phantom"* written on their foreheads. Some had the name of one of the guys written on them. There were more *Phantom* shirts that I'd ever seen in my life and fans were waving pictures of the band in the air.

Kieran had taken off the leather jacket when he came back on. I thought he must be burning up in it. Jordan had taken off the tan shirt and was wearing a light gray tank top. My heart raced. I'd been excited to see him in a wife-beater in that magazine and there he was wearing one in the flesh! Jordan wasn't as skinny as I thought he was, he actually had a pretty good build. I loved being able to see the upper part of his pecs. I was drooling. Looking at him just about made me melt, and when he sang...

It was warm even off stage and I know it was hot on stage. Sweat was streaming down Jordan's face and chest. In no time at all, his light gray tank top was dark gray from the sweat. It clung to his body and revealed even more of his slim, muscular form. He was walking perfection.

I was hoping that *Phantom* would play four songs in particular: "You Don't Know", "Jump Back", "Deep In The Darkness", and of course I had to hear Jordan sing "Do You Know That I Love You". During the concert they played them all.

It was so incredible to see them actually perform "Do You Know That I Love You " at the end of the concert. I couldn't take my eyes off Jordan as he sang it. Of course, I couldn't take my eyes off him period.

I couldn't believe how many songs they performed. They started out with "You Never Know" and just kept right on going. Sometimes they barely even paused between songs. I was in heaven. I stood there gazing at Jordan, letting his music vibrate through my body, letting it touch my soul.

I watched Jordan most of the time, but I got an eyeful of the others too. Kieran was right in front of me, so I could see him the best of all. I watched Ross some too, and he was really into his drums. He was swinging his head back and forth so hard all I could see was hair. He was wild.

The crowd was playing with beach balls during the concert. There were two or three of them going everywhere, even onto the stage. It was more like a party than a concert. When Ross was up close some girls were holding up signs for him to read. He was beating on his drums, reading the signs, and smiling at what they said. He even laughed once. Jordan shook hands with a lot of the girls right on the edge of the stage several times and Kieran got really close a lot. Kieran moved around more than the others, but then he could go about anywhere with his guitar.

Kieran messed up once and started playing his guitar a little early, it was cool. There were set lists taped to the floor for all of them, saying what song to play in what order. They did some very intense songs, then brought things down with some ballads, then back up again. The lights and the smoke machine were a show in themselves. It was awesome.

I could tell Jordan was exhausted near the end. He leaned his head over and rested it sometimes, like when he and Kieran were singing into the same microphone during "Rock It Down Deep". He leaned his head on Kieran's and I could tell he was about to drop. His energy was unbelievable, however. He just kept going and going at full power. The others did too. They performed for a long time. They must have sang for more than an hour and a half. I wish Jordan would have sang forever.

Jordan, Kieran, and Ross were all a bit taller than I expected. Ross had broad shoulders and is going to be massive later on. At the "end" of the concert, Ross came to the edge of the runway and gave away his drumsticks. It looked like the concert was over, but the band came back and did a couple more songs, then joined hands and bowed.

The very last song Jordan sang was "Do You Know That I Love You". The whole concert had been a blast, but something happened during the last song that made my heart flutter in my chest. While he was singing, Jordan looked straight at me. He didn't just do it once either. He kept looking back at me. Our eyes locked and I knew he was aware of me. He was looking at me out of all those hundreds of people in the audience. I just about melted when he sang the words "Do you know that I love you" as he stared into my eyes. I felt like he really meant it. I knew it was a moment I'd never forget. If I'd died right then, I'd have died happy.

The song ended. Jordan, Kieran, and Ross joined hands and took a bow. The whole place went crazy cheering and screaming. I couldn't even imagine what it must be like to be a rock star. It must have been incredible. Jordan and the others ran off the stage. I watched them until the last possible second. I knew I'd probably never get the chance to see them in concert again. I didn't let that get me down, it was the best night in my life. I still couldn't believe it, Jordan looked at me. I couldn't wait to tell Denise.

As the crowd filed out, ushers at the doors handed everyone a big round sticker with the *Phantom* insignia on it. I knew where mine was going, on the back of my car. I walked back to the hotel in the company of those who had been to the concert. It felt wonderful to be surrounded by those who loved *Phantom* like I did, although I couldn't imagine anyone loving them as much as me. The music was still playing in my head and my ears were still ringing with it. It was magical. I couldn't believe it. I'd really seen him, and he'd seen me.

Jordan

◆

Fort Wayne was a small venue, but I liked it best when we performed for a small, intimate crowd. Of course, 2,500 wasn't exactly an intimate gathering, but I was accustomed to playing for audiences numbering more than 10,000. At some of the big venues, I couldn't even begin to see the back rows. Of course, all the lights obscured my vision. I often wondered why so many people were willing to sit so far away during a concert. Ross, Kieran, and I had to look tiny from the back rows. That's what I liked about small theatres like the Embassy, even the back rows had a good view.

Near the end of the concert, a boy in the second row caught my eye. I never failed to scope out the cute boys in the audience, but there was something about this one. I kind of felt drawn to him. It was one of those times when I wished I wasn't famous. If I was just an ordinary boy, I might have had the chance to get to know him. I could have looked for him in the lobby, talked to him, and maybe even have asked if he wanted to go and get something to eat or whatever. As it was, I'd never see him again. I found myself having warm and fuzzy thoughts about him as I looked into his eyes. I was even so bold as to actually sing to him. I think he knew I was doing it too. It wasn't the brightest of ideas. I had to keep the fact that I liked boys a secret. It wasn't too dangerous, however. I doubt that anyone except for him knew what I was doing. He probably wasn't even sure himself.

That was another problem with being famous. I knew that gay boys had it rough all over, but I didn't even have the option of being out. Most of my fans were girls. If they knew I was gay, then my career might suffer. I didn't know what I would do if I wasn't able to perform. My music was my life. The thought of losing it was unbearable.

It wasn't just me that I had to think about either. A lot of people would suffer if I damaged my image. I'd hurt Ross and Kieran, my publicist, my management company, the stage crew, my bodyguard, the theatre owners, the record company, everyone that got paid to make and sell *Phantom* merchandise, and a lot of others. Ross, Kieran, and I weren't even supposed to mention if we had girlfriends, because it could hurt record sales. I could just imagine what would happen if word got out that I was gay.

I was but one member of *Phantom*, but I knew that most of the fans concentrated on me. I know that makes me sound conceited, but it was the truth. I didn't agree with it myself. Ross and Kieran were every bit as talented as me, but that's the way things were, to many of the fans, I was *Phantom*. I couldn't afford to screw things up, not for myself, and not for all those others.

I had long ago ceased to be an individual. I was a business. Hell, I was a small empire and a lot of people would be hurt if I did something stupid. I didn't like all that responsibility on my shoulders, but what could I do? It was the price of fame. I owed those people. I owed my fans too. I knew there'd be a lot of broken hearts if those girls found out I was into boys. The way they acted around me made that obvious. I'd had girls faint just because I spoke to them. I didn't want to hurt them. I didn't want to hurt anyone.

I wanted to live my life as the real me, but I couldn't. I didn't fail to realize how good I had things. There were thousands of teenaged girls who wanted to be my girlfriend, and thousands of teenaged boys who wanted to be me. I was damned lucky to have what I did. It took a lot of work to get there, and I didn't want to screw it up. I'm not just talking about the fame and fortune either. What really made me lucky wasn't that, it was being able to do what I loved. The fame didn't matter. The money didn't matter. My music did.

It was kind of hard hiding the real me sometimes. It wasn't difficult to fool most people. When I was up on stage singing to all those girls it was easy. I wasn't attracted to girls, but that didn't mean that I didn't like them. I loved singing to them. I loved making them happy. I loved it when they got so excited. I loved it that they loved my music. I could easily sing to them as if I loved them because I did, just not in the way some of them were thinking.

Keeping my secret was harder around others, especially Ross and Kieran. They were the ones I spent most of my time with. They were my best friends on the road, and often off. They were the guys that knew me best, and saw me just about every day. I had to watch myself more around them than anyone else. I had to watch what I said, and what I did. I had to keep my eyes to myself when attractive boys were around.

I had no chance at any kind of a relationship whatsoever. I was almost never alone. Everywhere I went, my bodyguard went with me. I could just image trying to date another boy under those circumstances. I'm sure every boy in the country thought I got all the sex I wanted. The truth was, I was a virgin and seemed likely to remain one. I didn't like that thought at all. I was a teenaged boy. I needed sex. It wasn't even the sex that I missed having the most, however. I just wanted to be with someone, care about someone, and have them care about me. Sure, I had millions of fans who cared about me. I cared about them too. But I wanted just one intimate friend, not a crowd.

Sometimes it really sucked to be me. I couldn't even feel properly sorry for myself. Every time I tried, I was reminded of my fame and my money. My face was on every teen magazine on the stands, and on a lot of the others. I'd been on the covers of more than I could name. I'd done every major talk show, even the late night ones. My face was on the side of buses and on billboards. I had more money than I could spend in a lifetime. While most kids were lucky if they got $20 a week allowance, I was pulling in more than some corporations. What right did I have to feel sorry for myself?

*   *   *

After the show I was pumped as usual. I was often restless after a show and needed to do something to unwind. I should have been exhausted after a concert, but I guess my body was hyped up on adrenaline or something. After a show, I was almost as hyped as Ross seemed to be all the time, and that's saying something.

I went back to the hotel room. I felt like a good swim. I need to do something physical. I dug my swimsuit out of my luggage while I talked to Mike, my bodyguard.

"Don't even think about it," said Mike.

"Why not?"

"The hotel is crawling with girls. You wouldn't make it near the pool without getting mobbed."

I was not happy, but Mike was right. We'd had a lot of trouble even making it to the elevator. If I went out, it would make a scene. I guess I just wasn't thinking.

"Okay, okay, I'll settle for a shower instead." I pulled off my shirt and made for the bathroom.

"I'll be right outside if you need me," said Mike.

"It's okay, I know how to shower," I teased him. Mike laughed, and left the room.

I locked the door behind him out of reflex. Mike insisted that my door be locked when he wasn't in the room with me. It was one of his security precautions. It had taken me a long time to get into the habit of doing it, but I did as he asked. I tried to make things easy on Mike, most of the time. I knew I drove him crazy sometimes, the way I never really thought about my own safety. I just couldn't get used to the idea of being famous. I just couldn't get used to the idea that I needed a body-guard. Mike's position was probably a nightmare for a bodyguard, guarding a teenaged rock star. I knew he had to put up with a lot, from me, and especially from the fans. A lot of my fans saw Mike as the enemy, because he stood between them and me.

The hot shower felt good, but it wasn't what I had in mind at all. I wanted to get out and do something, something fun, something freak-ing normal for a change. It was one of those nights when I didn't want to be famous. I just wanted to be a normal boy. I just wanted to be me.

As I rinsed out my hair I got an idea. It was mischievous. I knew I shouldn't do it. I knew it would cause some trouble. In other words, it was perfect.

I dried off and picked out some clothes. The kind of clothes any boy in town might wear. I picked some jeans, a tee shirt, and a hooded sweatshirt that would hide my hair. I also grabbed a pair of sunglasses. Last of all, I went for my swimsuit. That's when there was a knock at the door. I quickly hid the swimsuit and pulled on some boxers and my jeans. I answered the door.

"Going somewhere super stud?" said Ross as soon as the door was closed again.

"Is it that obvious? I'm going out."

"Mike's not gonna like that," he said in a mischievous voice that showed he approved. Ross loved mischief.

"He's not going to know."

"You know he'll find out."

"Well, if he does it will be too late."

"What if I tell him?" asked Ross, drumming his fingers on his stom-ach.

"What if I tell your Mom about the girl you sneaked into your room in Kansas City?"

"Owwww," said Ross. He knew I was kidding. I wouldn't tell. I knew he wouldn't nark on me either.

"Seriously though, be careful."

"I'll stay out of the alley Mom."

"Hey, I just want to make sure nothing happens to the Prince of Rock and Roll. What would we all do then?"

"Shut up Ross!" I yelled. I hated it when he called me that. I think that's the main reason he did it. He wasn't the only one either, I got it from the whole crew sometimes. It was a running gag.

"At least take your cell phone."

"Okay, okay, I will. Happy now?"

"Have a good time. I'll see if I can keep Mike busy. Just give me five minutes okay?" He smiled wickedly. I almost pitied Mike.

"Sure thing, and thanks."

Ross smiled at me. He knew I was stressed and needed to get away. I wondered just what he'd do to keep Mike occupied. I knew it was better if I didn't think about it. Knowing Ross, he'd probably cause a riot in the lobby just to stir things up. That kind of thing was his idea of fun. He was a wild boy.

I'd finished dressing as I talked to Ross, so there was nothing to do but wait. I planned my escape route in my head. Soon, it was time to go. I quietly unlocked the door and peered out. There was no sign of Mike, or the other bodyguards. I slipped out of my room and down the hall. I pulled the hood of my sweatshirt up over my hair. I knew I had to hide my hair, it was my most recognizable feature.

I made it into the elevator, so far, so good. I was enjoying myself already. I felt like some kind of spy that had penetrated an enemy stronghold, obtained top-secret documents, and was now trying to escape with them. The elevator reached the ground floor and I walked out. I was avoiding the main lobby, but it was still risky. I knew the casual approach was best. If I looked like I was trying to go unnoticed, I'd undoubtedly be spotted by someone. I just hoped no one would recognize me. Luckily, there weren't many people about. I headed down the hallway to a side exit. I was just a bit nervous, but I was having fun.

I thought I was going to get spotted even before I left the hotel. A couple of girls came walking toward me. I looked the other way as they drew near and they went right on. I breathed a sigh of relief. It was close.

I pushed the door open, and stepped outside. I took in a deep breath. Freedom. I wasn't quite sure where I wanted to go, so I just started walking. My only real plan was to find another hotel with a pool, or some YMCA or something, and go for a swim. I'd be less likely to be spotted outside my own hotel. All the fans knew we were staying at The Hilton.

It felt good to stretch my legs. I looked back and saw the Embassy Theatre, now dark, then walked on. After a couple of blocks I saw a Burger Dude. I could see the people inside, talking and laughing and eating. I looked at it longingly, but I knew going in would be pretty stupid. Dropping in a fast food restaurant just after a concert wasn't a bright idea. I'd get recognized for sure. I didn't usually mind being recognized, it's just that things often got out of hand. Just up ahead was a Holiday Inn. The thought "indoor pool" came to my mind and I walked toward it.

Ralph

———————— ◆ ————————

I paced around my hotel room, too excited to sit. Music was playing in my mind, Jordan's music. My ears were still ringing with it too, with it and the screams of the fans. I wanted nothing more than to go back and experience the concert all over again. It might seem silly to some, but it was the best night of my life. I still couldn't believe I'd been so close to *him*. I still couldn't believe he actually looked at *me*.

I took the elevator down to the second floor. I'd seen some vending machines down there and I needed a candy bar or something. I stood before the machine and picked out a chocolate bar with almonds, and one with caramel and nuts. I glanced at the pool as I walked by and thought about going for a swim before I went to bed. I didn't get the chance to use an indoor pool often. It was late, but I wasn't tired.

My head was in the clouds, thinking dreamy thoughts of Jordan, as I walked around the corner. I collided with someone hard, hard enough to knock him down.

"I'm so sorry, I wasn't paying…" I fell silent. I actually couldn't speak. I know my mouth was gaping open as I stared down at the boy in the hooded sweatshirt. The hood partially obscured his features, but there was no doubt…

"Hey, it's okay. I wasn't paying attention to where I was going either. Just kind of messing around you know," he said as I gave him a hand up.

I was silent for a bit longer, it was hard to find my voice. I swallowed hard.

"I'm Ralph."

"Jordan," he said, lowering his hood.

I had no idea what to say, but I wanted to keep talking. I didn't want the moment to end.

"I just came down to get some candy bars, thought about going for a swim later."

"So this place has an indoor pool?"

"Yeah, just around the corner." I stepped back to allow Jordan a good look at the pool.

"Ah man, it's locked."

"My room card will open the door," I said hopefully. I was eager to do anything I could to please him. I absolutely couldn't believe who I was talking to.

"Hey, you want to go swimming? I actually came looking for a pool. I've got my suit with me," said Jordan.

My head was spinning. I just knew I was going to wake up at any second, and when I did I'd be pissed. It had to be a dream. This couldn't really be happening, could it? If it was a dream, I didn't want to wake up. I wanted to just keep on dreaming. Somehow I knew that it was no dream. I was actually standing there talking to *him*. Jordan had actually just asked me to go swimming with him! Oh my God!

"That would be great!" I said. "Um, want to change in my room?" I hoped he didn't think I was some kind of freak for asking him that.

"That would be cool, didn't really want to change in the pool."

Never in any span of years would I have dreamed that I'd be leading Jordan back to my hotel room. My heart was racing a mile a minute. It was all I could do to keep from telling him how awesome I thought he was. It was hard to keep myself from asking him all kinds of questions. I wanted to be cool, however. I was sure everyone bugged him about stuff like that all the time. His fans were always shoving photos at him to sign and pestering him to death. I had the feeling he was there just to get away from all that.

His pocket started buzzing in the elevator. He pulled out a small cell phone, looked at it frowning, pushed a button and put it back in his pocket.

"Just someone I don't want to talk to just now," he said.

He followed me to my room and we entered.

"You can use the bathroom," I said.

I changed into my swimsuit while Jordan was out of the room. He was back out almost before I was done. I had to fight to keep from staring. Jordan was standing there wearing nothing but his swimsuit. I'd been looking for months for a picture of him without a shirt. I'd dreamed about finding one. I'd have paid any price to see Jordan with a bare chest, and there he was standing before me. He was beautiful. He was slim and firm. He didn't have a lot of muscle, but he was beautifully proportioned, a work of art. Jordan sat down on the bed and put on his shoes.

"Ready?" he said.

"Yeah." It was unbelievably hard to speak. He was so beautiful he took my breath away.

"I've been dying for a swim. I haven't had one in like, forever," he said.

"I don't get to swim in a pool much either," I said. "We've got one at school, but we only have swimming about two weeks out of the semester. Mainly I just swim in the pond." I suddenly felt like a country bumpkin talking about swimming in a pond, but Jordan didn't look like he thought that way about me at all.

"That sounds like fun too. I haven't swam in a pond since I was real little."

Jordan was talking to me like he was just a real person. He was, of course, but all I'd ever known of him was based on seeing him in magazines and on television. All that made him seem almost unreal, bigger than life. Walking by his side, there was no denying he was real. He was as nice a boy as I had imagined. I just knew he'd be cool and kind and he was! I loved him more than ever.

A wave of sadness hit me. I loved him, but I sure couldn't tell him that. Even if I'd been a girl, he'd have thought I was just another crazed fan. Since I was a boy, he'd probably run away screaming. That didn't make me feel so good.

I was so stupid! I was living a dream come true. I was actually hanging out with Jordan. I was doing something millions of his fans dreamed of doing and I was getting depressed. I kicked myself in the ass for it, and forced myself to enjoy what was happening, rather than wallow in self-pity. I knew I'd be remembering what happened in the next few minutes for the rest of my life. I wanted to savor every second of it. I was actually with *him* and I was going to enjoy it!

I got us into the pool area and Jordan slipped into the water. I came in right after him.

"Now this is nice," he said, as he tread water in the deep end.

"Yeah."

"You staying in Ft. Wayne long?" he asked.

"No, I have to leave tomorrow."

"Me too."

"Where you from?" asked Jordan.

"Southern Indiana, about forty miles northeast of Evansville."

"I've been there, Evansville that is. I didn't get to see anything though. We were just passing through."

"There's not that much to see anyway," I laughed.

I hoped that Jordan didn't notice that I couldn't keep from looking at him. He had the most amazing eyes, and the most beautiful features I'd ever seen on a boy. He was even more beautiful close up and in person than he was in magazines. I hoped he didn't notice that I kept stealing looks at his bare chest either. I just couldn't help myself.

Jordan and I started playing around in the water, fighting and wrestling. I must admit that it was overwhelming at first touching him like that. He was someone that it didn't seem right to touch. I had to remind myself that he was just a boy, however. Sure, he was a famous boy who was on the cover of every magazine and probably had movie stars for friends, but he was still a boy. It was obvious that he wanted to be treated like any other guy, and not like a rock star. He never once mentioned who he was, I didn't either. I think he liked that.

Even though I was touching him, there was nothing sexual to it. I won't say I wasn't attracted to him, because that would be a total lie. It's just that I didn't have sexual thoughts about him. It's hard to explain, but he was too good for that. He was too important to me to be thought of like that. Not that there was anything wrong with sex, but still… I'd never had sexual fantasies about Jordan. I had them about a lot of other guys, but not him. When I dreamed about Jordan, I dreamed about just spending time with him, and maybe holding hands. I dreamed of him kissing me lightly, but that was it. I guess that meant I was really in love with him.

Just spending time with Jordan is what I dreamed about the most, and I was actually getting to do it! That thought occurred to me every now and then. Mostly, I didn't think about it. I think the most wonderful thing about being with Jordan is that it seemed I was hanging out with someone I'd known for a long time, a friend.

I never thought I'd actually get to meet Jordan, let alone hang with him, but I'd always had a secret fear about it. I'd heard stories about people getting to meet someone famous they admired. I heard stories about them being disappointed. Sometimes the real person didn't match up with the public image. I always wondered what I'd do if I met Jordan and found out he was a creep. That worry was sure gone. He was everything I thought he was, and more.

We climbed out of the pool, and into the hot tub. Luckily, we had the whole place to ourselves. I sat across from Jordan, feeling the hot bubbling water on my body. His hair was wet and sticking to the sides of his face. It reached most of the way down his shoulders. He looked quite different from any picture I'd ever seen of him, but he was no less beautiful.

What I noticed most about him was his eyes. Even during the concert, even before he looked at me, I was captivated by his eyes. They were greenish-blue, and enchanting. I could get lost in those eyes.

The sign on the wall said to only stay in the hot tub for fifteen minutes at a time, so we got out when our time was up. I could see why it was a good idea not to stay in too long, I felt a little lightheaded. Of course, that may have been because of Jordan.

We left the hot tub, returned to the room and changed, then went to the vending machine area where there were a few video games. I soon discovered that Jordan was into them big-time.

"I love these things!" he said.

"Me too. I've got a lot of computer games at home, but there's something about a full size arcade game."

"Definitely."

I really liked Jordan. We seemed to have so much in common. Of course, there were a lot of differences too, not the least of which was that he was a big rock star and I was just an average boy. That didn't seem to matter to him. I liked him all the more because of it. He was real. He didn't try to put on an act. I could tell he didn't think he was special and above me. He just thought of himself as a regular guy.

We played for a long time, and talked a lot too. We laughed and joked around. It was wonderful.

When we'd been at it for over an hour, a big guy walked up and glared at us.

"Uh oh," said Jordan. "Busted."

I looked at the guy, then back to Jordan.

"Hey Mike," said Jordan. "This is Ralph, Ralph um… You never told me your last name."

"Rogers."

"Nice to meet you Ralph," said Mike. He looked back to Jordan. He didn't look happy at all. "You shouldn't put yourself in danger like this. You know what could happen."

"You worry too much."

"It's my job to worry."

No one said anything, but I had no doubt that Mike was Jordan's bodyguard.

"I know. I'm sorry, but I just needed to get out and have some fun."

Mike smiled. Jordan turned to me.

"Well, it has been fun Ralph. I had a really good time."

"Me too," I said smiling.

"I guess I have to go," he said. "Nice meeting you."

"You too."

Jordan walked away. I just stood there and watched him go. I couldn't believe it. I couldn't believe I'd spent the night with Jordan.

I went back upstairs. I pulled off my swimsuit and hung it on the shower curtain to dry. It was only then that I noticed Jordan's own swimsuit hanging in the bathroom. The only thing I could think of at first as "Wow, Jordan's swimsuit." I picked it up and started for the door. I stopped before I reached it. I was going to see if I could catch him to return it, but I was sure he was long gone. I thought of trying to get it back to him in some other way, but I knew there was little chance of that. That was okay, I really wanted to keep that swimsuit. I didn't think he'd mind.

I sat on the edge of the bed and thought about what had happened. I smiled. I'd been thrilled to see Jordan live in concert. I'd never dreamed about anything like this. I'd just experienced the greatest night of my life. I played it all over and over in my mind so I wouldn't forget a moment of it. I was in heaven.

Jordan

◆

As the bus pulled away from Ft. Wayne in the morning, I found myself thinking about Ralph. He was just the kind of boy I wanted in my life. I'm sure he knew who I was, but he didn't let on. He sure didn't scream or paw at me the way many of my female fans did. He treated me like he would anyone else, and I liked that.

I smiled. Ralph was the very boy I'd spotted in the audience, the very one I'd been so bold to sing to. I wondered what he thought about that? I wanted to ask him when we were together, but I couldn't. If I had, he would probably have asked me why I did it, and I wasn't prepared to answer. I just couldn't. I also didn't want to mention anything about my life when I was with him. I just wanted to be me. For a few minutes at least, my dream had come true, I was just me, and not a rock star.

Ralph was probably headed back to wherever he lived near Evansville. We were headed for Nashville, Tennessee. Our next concert was in Ryman Auditorium. After that it was off to St. Louis, Kansas City, Tulsa, and beyond. I loved being on tour, but part of me wished I was just heading home like Ralph. Part of me wished I was heading home with Ralph.

At least I'd had a chance to swim, soak in a hot tub, and play some video games without being mobbed. Those were the kind of things I really missed, all those ordinary things that most people took for granted. Often, I wondered if I wouldn't have been better off if I wasn't quite so famous.

Mike wasn't happy with me at all for the stunt I'd pulled. He'd gone on and on about all the horrible things that could have happened to me. I'd pointed out that nothing bad had happened at all, but that didn't make any difference to him. All that mattered to Mike was what could have happened.

I guess he was right, but I didn't want to live my life in fear. I went around guarded most of the time like I was an armored car full of gold or something, so I didn't think it hurt that much if I slipped off for a bit of fun once in a while. I didn't say that to Mike. I knew it would have only prolonged the lecture. Most kids got bent out of shape because their parents chewed them out for pulling something. I think maybe I had it worse. I got chewed out just the same, but I was paying the guy to do it.

*   *   *

I woke up. We were nearly at Nashville. I was glad I'd had a chance to rest. I didn't get much sleep the night before. I'd been out on the prowl, then there was an hour's lecture from Mike, and then I had too many thoughts running around in my head to get to sleep. I'd barely slept at all in the hotel room, so it sure felt good to catch a few hours sleep in my bunk. In a few minutes, the bus stopped.

"Man!" said Ross when he looked outside.

We were scheduled to do an autograph signing at a local radio station. There was a huge crowd. There must have been hundreds of people there. We'd expected a good crowd, but not one quite so huge. Mike got off the bus and went inside. Shawn and Rod came off another bus and stood just outside the entrance to ours, doing their unintentional secret service imitation. Mike came back in a couple of minutes with an escort of city police for us. Without them, there was no way we could make it inside.

We stepped off the bus and were immediately lost in a sea of fans. They were everywhere, mostly screaming girls. A lot of them were holding signs. Some had photos, or tee-shirts, or calendars for us to sign. I was blinded for a moment by all the camera flashes. I lowered my eyes a little so I wouldn't be seeing spots for the next fifteen minutes. Even with the escort, girls were reaching in and touching me. I didn't mind that so much, but some of them were a little aggressive. I'd had my shirt ripped a few times by over-enthusiastic fans. Sometimes they could get a little scary, like the time one girl somehow managed to sneak onto the tour bus. We came back and there she was. It was just like the time that girl hid in my hotel room. She wasn't dangerous. She just wanted to meet us, but still it was a bit frightening.

After what seemed like forever, we were inside. We did a little on-air interview. Ross was all keyed up and I thought we were going to have to shoot him with a tranquilizer gun to calm him down. He was out of control and was even tapping on the microphone like it was a drum. Ross usually added an interesting touch to our interviews, especially if they were live.

The DJ hit us with some predictable questions that we'd heard a hundred times before.

"Do you guys have girlfriends?" he asked after a short introduction.

"We're too busy to even think about girlfriends right now," said Kieran, giving him our pat response.

"We've got the tour, then we go right into developing and recording our next CD." I said. "I don't think anyone would want to date any of us. They'd never see us."

"Do any of you have the chance to go out, on just a one time date now and then?"

"I do!" yelled Ross. "I think it's my duty to go out with fans and I never shirk my duty!" Ross was laughing and the rest of us couldn't help but laugh too.

"How about you Jordan?"

I didn't like having the question aimed directly at me, especially during a live interview. I was uncomfortable about the topic for obvious reasons.

"Well, uh, Ross here is kind of our ambassador in the dating department. He handles that kind of thing for us."

"Yeah!!" screamed Ross.

I thought I did a pretty good job of ducking the question, but it came back at me in a way I didn't expect.

"Does *Phantom* do any kind of charity work?"

"We've never done a benefit concert by ourselves," said Kieran, "but we have played at half a dozen or so."

"We also donate a lot of the props from our videos and autographed photos and stuff to organizations so they can sell them and make money," said Ross.

"Jordan, do you think it's important that you give something back to your fans?"

"Definitely," I said. "Any time we can help some charity to help others, we do our best to do it. The fans make our lives possible, so I think we have a responsibility to give something back. We do that through our music, but anytime we can do it in other ways, we definitely try."

"This morning," said the DJ, "we received a call here at the station from an individual offering to donate $25,000 to the Center for Abused Children if you'll take his daughter out on a date. So what do you say Jordan?"

Talk about being on the spot. I was extremely uncomfortable about the situation. I was accustomed to interacting with fans, but a one on one date with a girl was a frightening proposition. I didn't see how I could refuse, however. The donation being offered was considerable. If I

refused, I'd look like I didn't care about abused children. More impor-
tantly, I didn't think I'd feel very good about myself if I walked away and
deprived that center of money it probably desperately needed. What if
some kid didn't get the help he needed and ended up getting abused
more because I wasn't willing to make myself uncomfortable?

"How can I refuse?" I said. "Personally, I don't think a date with me is
worth $25,000."

"It's not worth $25!" yelled Ross. That got some laughs.

"As I was saying," I continued "I don't think a date with me is worth
that much, but I'll be more than happy to do it if it will help kids that
need help."

The interview went on. I was distracted, wondering what I'd gotten
myself into. I guess I didn't really get myself into it. It was more like I
was ambushed. I did have a choice, but my own conscience wouldn't let
me refuse.

The guy who had made the offer was actually at the record station,
along with his daughter. Just before I met him, the DJ told me he was a
well-known local businessman who had a reputation for making generous charitable donations. I didn't care for being forced into the spot I
was in, but I couldn't help but like him.

"I'm very glad to meet you," he said when we met after the interview.

"That's a very generous offer you made," I said.

"Well, a little selfish really. I know it put a lot of pressure on you, but
my daughter, Alicia, is a huge fan of yours and has just been dying to
meet you. You should see her room, it's absolutely plastered with photos
and posters of you."

"Dad!" Alicia had remained silent until that time. She was standing
off to one side as if afraid to approach me. She was positively beet red
with embarrassment. I smiled at her in an attempt to put her at ease.
She was a very pretty girl of about sixteen.

"I knew spending time with you would make her very happy, so what
does it hurt to donate a bit extra to a good cause?" he said.

"I think what you do is wonderful," I said. "Um, I hate to rush, but I have a lot of people waiting for me to sign autographs." I motioned Ben over to introduce him. "This is Ben, my manager. He can set everything up, and get you tickets for tonight's concert."

I walked over to Alicia before leaving.

"It's very nice to meet you Alicia," I said. She didn't say anything. She looked like she was almost afraid of me, and kind of like she was going to faint. "I guess I'll be seeing you soon. Until then."

"Later," she said. I could tell she was completely tongue tied around me. I'd experienced that with fans before. Some of them got so overwhelmed that they just didn't know what to say. It was kind of like they had temporarily forgotten how to speak. I could tell Alicia was thrilled to meet me. I gave her a big smile just before I left. She blushed.

I quickly made my way to the room where we'd be signing autographs. It was a lot better organized in there than in a lot of places. Ross and Kieran were already there. Everyone was already there. I hated making them all wait.

There was a long table for us to sit at and everything was roped off. The whole autograph line went through a bunch of roped paths, kind of like those found at amusement parks. The room was already filled, and the line extended outside. There were more flashes from cameras, but not as many as before.

I joined Ross and Kieran at the long table and the security people the radio station hired started letting a few fans through at a time. Mike stood behind us with his arms crossed. Shawn and Rod were out in front. I don't think they quite trusted the abilities of the security guys hired by the station. All three of them, and especially Mike, took their jobs seriously and were a little jealous of anyone who wandered onto their turf.

We had to move fast, but I took the time to say something to everyone that passed. I ignored the "one signed item per person" rule. I'd learned to sign my name really fast, so I could sign even three or four things while I was saying "hi" to someone. We had our own felt markers for signing. Most people didn't think about it, but using a regular pen was a lot harder. That didn't make a difference for most people, but when you are signing hundreds of autographs, it makes a big difference.

A few girls got so excited they screamed, but most were pretty cool about meeting us. One girl got so emotional she started crying.

"All I've ever wanted to do is meet you," she said.

I got up, walked around the table, and gave her a hug.

"It's very nice to meet you," I said.

She had a CD for me to sign and I drew a little heart and a smiley face on it. When I handed it to her, she gripped it like it was gold. She was smiling from ear to ear. I loved being able to make someone happy like that. Sometimes it astounded me that someone could get so excited over meeting me. I knew I was famous, but I didn't really think of myself like that. Even when I did talk shows, or was at big award shows like the Grammy's, I'd see famous people and want to go up to them, but I'd think, "Why would they want to talk to me?" I thought of others as being famous, not me.

My hand got tired from signing my name over and over, but I kept going. I wanted to get to as many people as I possibly could. I hated it when we had to go and there were still people in line. Those people made my life possible, they made it possible for me to do what I loved. If they didn't buy the CD's and calendars and concert tickets, I'd probably be flipping burgers somewhere. I never walked away from an autograph session until the last autograph had been signed, unless I absolutely couldn't help it. Kieran and Ross felt the same way about it as I did.

We were able to sign for everyone at the radio station, but there was no time for supper. I was used to that. Ross, Kieran, and I grabbed some junk food on the way to Ryman auditorium and scarfed it down. I barely had time to use the restroom before it was time for the meet and greet.

Ralph

◆

"So how was it?" asked Denise. I think she was almost as excited about the concert as I was. I'd called her and Chris as soon as I'd made it home and they both came over.

"It was beyond awesome!" I said.

"Uh oh, here we go," said Chris, rolling his eyes. Denise punched him in the arm. He laughed.

I started telling them all about the concert. Telling them allowed me to relive the whole thing. When I got to the part about Jordan looking right at me as he sang, Chris said "You're dreaming." I knew he really wouldn't believe what I had to say next.

"After the concert, back in my hotel, I was down by the vending machines. I turned the corner and *wham* I ran right into him! I ran right into Jordan!"

"Oh my gosh!" said Denise.

"Wait, wait, you're trying to tell us you met him?" asked Chris.

"Yeah, I ran into him, and I met him."

"You know you don't have to make up stories," said Chris.

"I'm not! We talked. We went swimming and played video games and hung out. It was the best night ever!"

I told them more details. Denise looked amazed. Chris looked skeptical.

"So where's his autograph?" asked Chris.

"I uh, didn't get one."

"You're telling me you spent all that time with him and you didn't get his autograph? You? 'Mr. totally obsessed with Jordan', didn't get his autograph?"

"I didn't think about it."

"Uh huh," said Chris.

"Really! I got something else though." I showed them the swimsuit Jordan had left behind.

"His swimsuit? You're a sick puppy Ralph," said Chris snickering.

Chris wasn't convinced at all. I was a little hurt that he didn't believe me, but I guess it did sound more than a little fantastic. I probably wouldn't have believed it either if I was him. Denise acted like she believed it, but I wasn't sure if she did or not. She was nice enough to act like she believed me, even if she didn't, so it was hard to tell.

I suspected that both of them were thinking I was feeding them a big line to see if they would buy it, so I could laugh at them for being gullible. Denise in particular seemed to be waiting for me to tell her I was kidding. Chris looked more like he just thought I was making it all up to be impressive.

"Well if that really is Jordan's swimsuit, which I doubt, I bet you'll be sleeping with it every night!" Chris laughed. I was a little embarrassed. I actually had thought about sleeping with it.

*   *   *

After the reactions of Denise, and particularly Chris, I sure wasn't about to tell anyone else about hanging out with Jordan. If they didn't believe me, no one else would either. Besides, I didn't like to talk about how much I liked Jordan around anyone at school. I knew they'd start calling me "queer" for being so into a boy, no matter how famous. I knew some of the guys at school probably listened to his CD's secretly, but they'd never admit it.

My friends might not believe me, but I knew what had really happened. I sat down at my computer after Denise and Chris left and wrote about it all. I tried to put in every little detail about my whole trip, and especially about hanging out with Jordan, so I wouldn't forget. It was the greatest night of my life and I wanted to remember it always.

I put Jordan's swimsuit on top of my dresser where I could see it everyday. Every time I looked at it I smiled. I had actually met him, my dream boy.

Jordan

◆

Our schedule was extremely tight, so Ben scheduled my "date" with Alicia shortly after the concert. I rushed from the meet and greet to grab a quick shower at the hotel. I was always drenched in sweat after a concert and I didn't think Alicia would appreciate having supper with a smelly boy. Even if it didn't bother her, I didn't want to smell myself during supper.

I put on some dressy clothes, then rushed downstairs with Mike on my heels. We avoided the lobby and main entrance and went out a side door instead. Even so, there was a small crowd lingering around the limo that was sitting there waiting. As soon as I stepped out the door, camera flashes started going off and girls started pressing in on me. There were only some thirty or so. I didn't think it was cool just to rush past them, even though I was in a hurry. I borrowed a pen and started signing whatever they poked at me while I talked to them and answered questions. Mike stood right beside me watching like a hawk. He was cool about letting people near me when the group was small, but he still watched every move they made.

When I'd signed something for everyone, I told the little group that I really had to run because I was late already. They were really cool about it, although I knew they didn't want me to go. The fans could get pretty demanding sometimes, but I found that if I was considerate of them, they were of me. They knew I'd taken time out to talk with them and sign things when I really didn't have the time, so they didn't fuss when I stepped into the limo and we sped away.

The driver took us to Alicia's house. It was freaking huge. I didn't know they had mansions like that in Nashville. I got out and went to the door, followed by Mike, of course. Alicia was waiting on me inside, all dressed up and looking extremely beautiful.

"I've made reservations for you and everything has been taken care of in advance," said Alicia's father. "Just make sure you don't keep my daughter out too late young man."

"Dad!" said Alicia embarrassed. Her father was smiling. I knew he was joking.

"I won't sir," I said.

We walked to the limo and the driver followed the directions provided by Alicia's Dad.

Alicia was obviously very excited, but extremely nervous and ill at ease. To be honest, I was quite ill at ease myself and wasn't feeling my most cheerful. I felt extremely awkward being on a date with a girl, even though it wasn't exactly a real date. It's not like I'd see Alicia again after tonight.

"This is my bodyguard, Mike," I said. "He's here to make sure you don't attack me."

Alicia looked frightened and confused.

"It was a joke," I said.

"I'm sorry," said Alicia, "it's just that I don't know what to say."

"Say anything you want," I told her.

"But you're…you're Jordan."

"I'm a guy, just a guy. I'm just like the boys at your school."

"No, you're not. You're Jordan."

I didn't know how to react to that.

"It's just that… I've listened to all your CDs over and over. I've gone to your concerts. I've read all about you and watched you on television.

I've been a fan of yours forever. I don't know… I'm just afraid I'll say something stupid."

"Alicia, just be yourself. So what if you say something stupid? I say stupid things all the time. Mike could tell you a lot of stories about that."

"A whole lot of stories," said Mike smiling. Alicia smiled too, but she was obviously still very nervous.

"Just treat me like you would any other boy," I told her.

"I can't do that."

"Why not?"

"Because you're a rock star. You're famous. You're Jordan."

I wasn't getting anywhere with her at all. Alicia couldn't get past the fact that I was famous. I really wondered if she liked me for me at all. I felt like she was excited over me just because I was famous. I didn't like that. Alicia was a nice girl, but I had the feeling she wouldn't even talk to me if I was just an ordinary boy. That put a definite strain on our conversation. One thing I didn't like was people who liked me only for my fame, people who wanted to be around me just so they could brag about it. I hated fakes. That is something that I hated about being famous. I couldn't really tell who liked me for me, and who just wanted to be near me because I was on magazine covers.

Maybe I was looking at things the wrong way with Alicia, however. Maybe she was one of those girls that were so obsessed with me that they couldn't act normally when I was around. It seemed unreal, but I'd actually had girls faint when they met me. For my part, I couldn't imagine how anything about me could lead to fainting, but it sometimes did. I found it frightening.

Alicia did seem pretty overwhelmed by being with me. Maybe she was like those girls who fainted. I guess I could understand her being uncomfortable around me. I wanted to set her at ease, but she seemed determined to keep me from doing so.

Our limo drew some attention when we pulled up at the restaurant and it quickly turned into a mob scene. The timing couldn't have been worse. Alicia was already nervous and then she had to deal with a big crowd pushing in on us. There were even some flashes from cameras. Did people just walk around with cameras all the time or what?

I smiled and said "hi" as Mike pushed us into the restaurant. I didn't try to stop and sign autographs. The crowd was growing faster than seemed possible and it was the type of situation that made Mike very nervous. He knew he couldn't possible watch all those people, or adequately protect me from them if it was necessary. I was glad when he got us inside. I wasn't bothered by being pushed around too much, but I knew it was upsetting Alicia.

"Is it always like that?" she asked as we were being shown to our table. Even inside, everyone was looking at us.

"Not always, but often. I don't get out much." I told her.

Mike stayed several feet back from our table, but Alicia was very aware that he was watching us.

"Is it like you thought it would be?" I asked her. "Going on a date, just you, me, and my bodyguard?" I smiled. She smiled a little too.

"He makes me nervous, watching me all the time," she said.

"Well, if it helps, he isn't really watching you. He's watching anyone who gets close." I stopped short of telling Alicia that Mike feared I'd be assassinated. I didn't think she'd appreciate that kind of humor. I didn't want to make her even more uncomfortable.

When Alicia's dad said he taken care of everything, he wasn't kidding. We didn't even have to order, although the waiter did ask if we wanted something different instead of what had been arranged.

It was much more tame inside than it was outside, mainly because reservations were required to get in. Even so, people kept coming up to our table. They were all very polite, but Alicia seemed to have a hard time getting used to it. I found it distracting myself, but I was accustomed to it. Since I was not at ease being on a date with a girl, I didn't mind it too much. In a way, it was a relief, as it gave me something to do besides just sit there.

Our lobster came and we started eating.

"How can you stand it?" asked Alicia.

"I like lobster," I said. I'd understood what she meant, but I was making a joke, a joke Alicia didn't get.

"No, I mean everyone looking at you, everyone watching you, even while you're eating."

"I just don't think about it much," I said. "People are looking at me wherever I go."

"Doesn't it bother you?"

"Well, there are times when I'd rather just be left alone, but it's part of the job, you know? I don't really mind it most of the time."

"I bet you'd rather be somewhere else, than here with me," she said.

"Why do you think that?"

"Well, you aren't really here because you want to be. My dad pretty much bought you for me. It's kind of embarrassing."

"You make me sound like a male prostitute," I said. I was trying to be funny, but it wasn't working at all.

"No, no, I didn't mean it like that at all!"

"I know Alicia. I was kidding. Loosen up. Listen, if I didn't want to be here, I wouldn't be. I could have said 'no' to your dad."

I wasn't being completely honest with her. The truth was, I didn't want to be there. It didn't have anything to do with Alicia. I was just very uncomfortable being on a date with a girl. It wasn't going well either. Alicia seemed to take everything I said the wrong way and we were being continually interrupted. It was all because I was famous and, at the moment, I wished I wasn't.

I did my best to be pleasant, but the rest of supper was as uncomfortable as the beginning. Alicia could not relax around me and everyone in the restaurant was making me feel like I was some kind of animal in a cage at the zoo. They were all very polite, but they were watching every move I made. I didn't mind that when I was onstage, or signing auto-graphs or something, but I started feeling very self-conscious sitting there with Alicia. Of course, a great deal of that feeling was generated by Alicia herself. She talked so much about how she'd be uncomfortable if she was me that I was getting uncomfortable. If I'd been eating with Ross or Kieran or anyone else I knew, people looking at me wouldn't have bothered me at all, but being observed on a "date" was becoming uncomfortable.

I was beyond relieved when I took Alicia home then climbed back into the limo. It had been a most unpleasant date. I was keenly aware that everyone noticed I was with a girl. I felt pressured. It was like every-one was watching me, just waiting for me to start dating. I felt like they were trying to force me into being something I wasn't. I knew I was being stupid. No one was trying to force me into anything. I was getting stressed out, however. It was all beginning to be too much. Too many people were depending on me. Too much was going on. I felt like my life was spinning out of control. I yearned for a little normalcy, something to anchor me, something to make me feel normal again. I sat in back of the huge limo, wishing I could just be a normal boy, at least for a while.

Ralph

———————————◆———————————

I walked down the hill, and just kept on walking. The euphoria of meeting and spending time with Jordan was wearing off. It's not that the time I had with him had become less special, but where do you go from up? The most wonderful time of my life had come, and gone.

What was really getting to me wasn't that, however. My short time with Jordan was something I'd always remember, always treasure. It was a reminder of what I didn't have, and that got to me. I always tried to appreciate what I did have, instead of getting down about what I didn't have, but sometimes it was hard. I'd met Jordan and he was just as wonderful and beautiful as I'd always imagined. I loved him more than ever. That was the real problem right there. I loved him, but he probably didn't even remember me. I knew I'd go on loving him forever. What kind of life was that, loving someone who I'd spent a couple of hours with once?

The memory of Jordan was strong in my mind; his scent, the way he laughed, the funny things he said. I wanted to be with him so bad that it hurt. I felt like he was a friend that had been ripped from my life. I knew it was silly. I knew I'd only spent a couple of hours with him, but I couldn't help but feel that way. I missed him as if he was my boyfriend, and it hurt.

As much as I treasured meeting Jordan, and spending time with him, I wondered if it might not have been better if we'd never met. The memories of him were tormenting me. Tears were actually rolling down my cheeks because I missed him. Why was I made to love someone I could never have?

Jordan

◆

Another night on the bus, more interviews, more photo shoots, another concert, another night in a hotel, it just kept going and going and going. After a while, the faces of the fans begin to blur. They ceased to be recognizable as individuals. Another autograph signing, more photos, more questions—my life was like a stuck record, repeating the same verse without end, over and over until I thought it would drive me mad. I woke up in the mornings with no idea where I was, or where'd I'd been. Sometimes I couldn't even remember what month it was, let alone day. Every hotel room looked exactly the same. It was all getting to be too much. I was getting edgy and irritable.

Ross and Kieran kept me going. They got me though the first half of our tour. There was a whole month until the second half began. I didn't know how I was going to get through the month ahead, however. Our manager and publicist had each crammed it full, just when I needed to get away from it all the most. We were scheduled to do television and radio appearances, one after the other. There were autograph signings and press conferences and promotions. On top of all that, there were meetings scheduled with executives from our record label. When I looked at our schedule I didn't see how I'd even have time to breathe, let alone rest. I wanted to scream.

I wouldn't even have performing to release the tension. A weird collection of scheduling conflicts had forced us to split the tour in half, with a month in between. That meant no concerts, and, with the tight appearance schedule, no chance to do any kind of performance. Usually, when I was all tensed up and at my wits end, I could sing and sweat out all my troubles. The size of the crowd didn't matter. As long as I could get up there and do my thing, whatever was eating at me was forced away. In the next month, I'd be lucky if I had the chance to even touch my keyboard. Signing autographs for the fans would be fun, but it wasn't the same as performing. My heart belonged to the music. I needed it. I didn't know how I could make it through the next few weeks without it.

And then it happened, the straw that broke my back. I was sitting with Ross in his hotel room, talking to him, when Kieran came in with a grim look on his face. When he saw me, he quickly hid something behind his back. He looked upset and I couldn't help but be curious about what had made him that way. Kieran was not one to get upset easily.

"What's wrong?" asked Ross.

"Um, oh…nothing," said Kieran. It was obvious he was lying.

"What have you got behind your back?" I asked.

"Nothing," said Kieran.

"Come on," I said. "You're definitely holding something back there."

"You don't want to see," he said. He sounded as if he was almost ready to cry.

"Show me." I told him. He just stood there, as if afraid to move. It was several moments before he spoke.

"I guess you'll end up seeing it anyway," he said slowly, handing Ross and me one of those nasty tabloid papers.

"What did you buy that piece of crap for?" asked Ross, but then he saw what I did. The bold letters just reached out and hit us, like a brick upside the head.

JILTED BY JORDAN
TEEN TAKES OWN LIFE

A fifteen-year-old girl committed suicide after meeting pop star Jordan, lead singer of the rock group Phantom. "She was so thrilled to meet him," said her tearful mother "but he was rude and even laughed at her when she told him she was in love with him. He's a cruel and heartless person."

Heartbroken Elizabeth, barely fifteen years old, waited until her parents had gone to sleep, then overdosed on sleeping pills. Her parents found her dead in her room in the morning, the hit song "Do You Know That I Love You?" playing over and over on little Elizabeth's CD player.

"He killed her as surely as if he'd shot her," said Elizabeth's mother. "Because of him, my baby is dead."

Jordan could not be reached for comment...

I couldn't read anymore. I burst into tears. It was too much.

"Dude, come on, you know it's not true!" said Ross as he put his arm around my shoulder and pulled me to him. I was too upset to even speak.

"You know it's just a lie," said Kieran. "Like last month, when they said you got that girl pregnant."

"What if it is true?" I asked, still crying.

"Oh come on, Jordan," said Kieran. "When have you ever been rude to anyone in your whole life? When have you ever laughed at a girl when she told you she loved you? It's bullshit and you know it."

"But what if?" I asked. "What if she met me and misunderstood somehow or something? What if I laughed about something else and she thought…" I burst out crying some more. I simply couldn't stand the thought that some girl had killed herself over me.

"Jordan, you know what that tabloid is like," said Kieran. "This is the same paper that claimed we were all aliens a few months ago. You can't believe anything they print."

"They probably made the whole thing up, all of it!" said Ross.

What they said made sense. I usually didn't pay any attention at all to what the tabloids said about me, but something about this story just got to me. Maybe if I hadn't already been stressed out it wouldn't have affected me so much, but it did get to me. I couldn't take it.

Ross and Kieran tried their best to cheer me up, but it was hard for them to get even a smile from me. I knew I'd probably never even met that girl, and if I had I certainly wouldn't have treated her badly. It pained me to think that it could be true in even some small way. No doubt there were those I had hurt, even though I had not meant to do so. I tried to be polite and kind, but I wasn't perfect. There were days when I was in a bad humor, and days when I just didn't feel like smiling and talking to everyone. I was just a boy, but everyone expected so much of me. I felt like the least little thing I did could lead to disaster. Maybe this time it had.

I returned to my own room. I needed to be alone to sort things out. I thought of what everyone who read that horrible story would think of me. Many would think it ridiculous and discard the whole thing as mere stupidity, but many would believe it. Too many people were willing to believe anything, especially if it put someone in a bad light. I didn't worry about that sort too much, but I wondered how many other people would think it was true. I didn't need that kind of pressure just then. It was too much.

My thoughts kept going back to that girl. What if? What if she really had killed herself over me? If it was true, then it would have been better if I was never famous, if I'd never sang at all. I wanted to make people happy. I didn't want to bring them pain. I felt cursed. My actions could cause such pain, without me even meaning it, without me even knowing. It was too high a price to pay. If feeling the rush of fame at a concert led to the death of an innocent girl, then it wasn't worth it. I suddenly felt like my life was built upon the suffering of others. I wasn't thinking straight, but that was what I felt just then. The price of fame was just too high.

*   *   *

Ross came into my room a bit later than night. I was sitting on the edge of the bed, thinking depressing thoughts. For once he wasn't smiling and tapping his fingers as if they were drumsticks. He looked concerned.

"You aren't thinking of doing anything stupid, are you, Jordan?"

From the way he looked at me, I knew just what he meant.

"I'm not suicidal. I'm upset and I've had enough, but I'm not ready to end it all just yet."

"You are thinking of doing something though, aren't you?"

He was right. I was turning something over and over in my mind. There was something I needed to do. If I didn't, I'd go crazy and end up downing a bottle of sleeping pills myself. I pulled my bag from its place and started stuffing it with clothes.

"Going somewhere?" asked Ross.

"I can't take it anymore," I said to him. "I can't. It's just all too much. I just wanted to play and sing, but it's all become so big, it's all out of control, and now this. Maybe it isn't even true, but it doesn't really make any difference if that girl killed herself over me or not. If she did… I just can't bear the thought. Even if she didn't… I can't take all this responsibility. I can't take everyone depending on me. I can't take people getting hurt because my smile isn't big enough when I look at them, or because I don't have enough time to talk to them. I just want to be me again."

Ross made no move to stop me. He could have easily called for Mike, or the other bodyguards, or Kieran, or any of the crew. I think he understood what I was feeling. He knew I was doing what I had to do.

"You will come back, won't you?" asked Ross. I looked at him long before answering.

"I'm not sure. I just need to go. I might come back. I might not."

I knew there was more I should say, but my future was so uncertain in my own eyes that I couldn't begin to tell Ross of it. There was a month before the second half of tour. Maybe I'd be ready to return by then, maybe I would not.

"I'm going to miss you," said Ross.

"And I you."

"Be careful," he said.

"Tell Kieran…"

"I'll explain," said Ross.

"Tell no one else."

"I'll keep your secret," he said. "You know you're going to need my help to get out of here."

I hadn't thought of that, but he was right. I wasn't thinking very clearly at all.

"I'll tell you what, Shawn said none of us should go to the lobby because there's a big mob of girls down there. They've found us again."

"No surprise there."

"There's lot of reporters too, because of…"

"No surprise there either."

"I'll ditch Shawn. He'll panic and get Mike and Rod. That will give you a chance to slip out of your room. I'll go down to the lobby, and well… just be myself."

I actually smiled for a moment. Ross being himself would create havoc. He'd turn the lobby into a circus in seconds.

"Be careful," I said.

"Hey, I really don't mind if those girls rip my shirt off. I kinda like it," he said raising an eyebrow. "Maybe it will give the press something else to talk about too."

Ross had a devilish look in his eye and I wondered what else he was thinking.

"Thanks Ross," I said and hugged him close. He was like a brother to me.

"It's what I'm here for," he said. "You just be careful, and if you get in any trouble, you call me, you hear?"

"I will, Ross."

"I love you, man."

"I love you, Ross."

Ross departed. I grabbed my baseball cap and sunglasses and paced around the room. I knew he'd act fast, but I had to give him a few minutes at least. I was more nervous than I had been in a long time. This wasn't simply slipping out for a bit the way I did in Ft. Wayne. I didn't even know where I was going, or what I was going to do. All I knew is that I had to get away.

I slipped out of my room. I avoided the elevator and hit the stairs instead. When I made it to the first floor, I could hear a commotion in the lobby. It sounded just a little like a riot. Ross was doing his stuff. I could just imagine him being mobbed by fans and reporters.

There was a hitch in my plan. The stairwell opened into the lobby. I couldn't get out that way. Well, I could, but I'd be walking straight into the chaos created by Ross. There was another exit, but it was a fire exit. The bar on the door said an alarm would sound if I pushed it. I thought for a few moments. The seconds were slipping away. I slipped on my cap and glasses. I took my chances and pushed the fire door open. An alarm sounded all right, but I doubted it added much to the confusion in the lobby. I ran for it just in case. I didn't know how much time I had before someone showed up.

I hit the ATM before heading for the bus station and withdrew a wad of cash. I didn't want to be traced through my withdraws. I didn't want to be found. I needed to get away, at least for a little while, maybe longer. I just couldn't take it anymore. The pressure was too much. I couldn't take all those people depending on me. I couldn't stand the sameness of my life. I couldn't stand being Jordan anymore.

Ralph

◆

"Ralph, there's someone here for you, out front," said Mom, poking her head in my room.

"Who?" I wondered who would be asking for me at the door. Chris or Denise would have come right in, and they'd have used the back door. No one else ever stopped by.

"He said his name was Jordie or Jordan, something like that."

I looked at my mom a bit shocked, but it couldn't be. I almost laughed at myself for even having the thought for a split second. Mom took my look for one of non-recognition.

"Blond hair, about your age, very polite, nice looking boy. He's on the porch." I swallowed hard.

"Thanks, Mom," I said, and got up from my desk.

It couldn't be, it just couldn't. I started to get a little angry. This was some sick joke that Chris had dreamed up. It had to be. It just felt like his handiwork. I was more than a little frightened as I crossed the living room. I was also already making plans to pound Chris the next time I saw him.

I opened the front door and stepped out onto the screened in porch. My heart caught in my throat. It wasn't a joke. Jordan was sitting on the porch swing. This had to be a dream. I closed my eyes and opened them again. He was still there.

"Hey," he said, "remember me?"

Remember him? Was he kidding? I was reeling in shock. I didn't know what to do or say. I did decide that I wasn't dreaming, but the whole situation seemed so unreal. It was the kind of thing that only happened in movies. It was kind of like that one where Julia Roberts dropped into that travel bookstore owned by Hugh Grant. This was real, however. He was really there.

"Of course," I said. I was too shocked to say more.

"I guess you're wondering why I'm here. I'm sorry to just show up like this, but I wasn't sure what else to do."

"How did you even find me?" When we parted, all he knew was my name. I hadn't given him my address, or phone number, or email address, or anything. I never even considered it. I never thought he'd want it.

"I have a few connections. I had you tracked down through the hotel."

That made sense.

"Are you okay?" I asked. I was afraid he was in some sort of trouble. He looked a little lost.

"Yeah. I'm okay. I just needed to get away." From the way he looked, I wasn't quite sure he was telling the truth. Something seemed to be bothering him.

I felt awkward as I stood there. I noticed he was carrying a small travel bag.

"Um, you want to put your bag inside and we can go for a walk or something?" I was stumbling through uncharted territory. What were you supposed to do or say when a rock star showed up on your doorstep?

"Sure."

Jordan followed me to my room and set his bag on the bed.

"Nice room," he said. I was sure he was just being polite. I could just imagine where he must live. Our house was probably a dump compared to it. He looked around. I was suddenly very nervous, even frightened.

My CD's were prominently displayed and practically every one of them was one of his. He looked at them, and smiled.

"I like your music," I said. It was the first time I'd acknowledged who he was. There was no denying that I knew. "Actually, I love it." He smiled sweetly and nodded his head slightly.

"Thanks. So how about that walk?"

We left the house, walked across the yard, and on past the barn.

"You know I've never been on a farm before," said Jordan.

"Well it's not too exciting. Not what you're used to I'm sure."

"That's not necessarily a bad thing," he said. We were silent for a few moments as we walked down the hill.

"Why are you here?" I asked. "Not that I'm not glad you're here, it's just…unexpected."

"I guess it is that," he paused. "I don't know. I had to get away from things, you know? It was getting to be too much. I was so tired of it all."

"Tired of being famous? Tired of having everyone love you?" I didn't really understand.

"It's just… That night I spent with you, swimming and playing video games and all, that was the first time I got to do things like a regular guy in—forever. It was the last time too. I know you probably think I'm just a whiny brat or something, but my life sucks sometimes. I mean, I just want to go to the freaking mall without being mobbed!"

I'd never really thought about it like that. I'd just thought of the glamorous side of fame. I'd never stopped to think that it might be anything other than a dream come true.

"I can understand that."

"You can?"

"Yeah. I guess it would blow if people bugged you everywhere you went. I think having people ask for your autograph and everything would be cool, but I guess it could get to be too much."

"Exactly. Don't get me wrong. There's a lot about being famous that rocks, really rocks, but sometimes…"

Jordan trailed into silence. I looked at him as we walked along a stream. I could tell he was stressed out. I could read the tension in his body. That couldn't be good for him. If he was older, I'd say he was a prime candidate for a heart attack or a stroke. He looked at me, then quickly looked away again. Tears had welled up in his eyes.

"What's wrong, Jordan?" I asked. We barely knew each other, but I loved him. I felt like I'd known him all my life.

"You probably already heard about, about that girl?"

"No." My breath caught in my throat. If he told me some girl was having his baby it would destroy me. I was so in love with him.

"Some tabloid ran a story, said a girl killed herself over me…" he trailed off, quietly sobbing. I put my hand on his shoulder.

"Those papers just print lies," I said. "I never read them. If it's in a tabloid, you know it's not true."

"Maybe. I hope you're right. You aren't the first person to tell me that. Even if it is just a lie, I get all these letters, all these emails from girls just begging me to send them an autograph, or write to them. I can't possibly get to them all. How many of them have I hurt by not writing them back?"

"You can't put all that on yourself," I said. "I imagine you must get hundreds, or thousands of letters. How could you answer them all?"

"I shouldn't have just run away like that," he said. "I'm so stupid."

"Hey, it's your life," I said. So he had run away, I thought to myself. Things must have been bad for him to run. I was worried about him.

"Yeah, but a lot of people depend on me. I'm letting them down."

"Well, I'm no expert on this kind of thing, but I'd say you had to do something. Otherwise you'd just snap or something some day."

"Probably."

I looked at him. He was beautiful. He was the same Jordan I'd idolized forever, but he was a real boy, with real problems. Maybe I couldn't even completely understand those problems, but I loved him and I wanted to help.

"Why don't you stay here for a while?"

"Won't your mom and dad mind?"

"Nah. School's almost out, we'll just tell them that yours is already out for the summer or something. We can like fake a call to your parents and act like they said you could stay here for a while. We can work it out. I know Mom and Dad won't mind."

"I don't want to impose," he said.

"Are you kidding? I want you here. It'll be great, and I'm not just saying that because you're famous. I like you, even without all that." Jordan smiled. I think he could tell I was sincere. I think it meant a lot to him. There was a sadness about him that made me want to hold him and tell him everything would be okay.

"To be honest, I guess I was hoping I could stay here. When I left, I headed straight here, although I wasn't quite sure what I was going to do."

"Let's go talk to Mom," I said.

"Okay, but one thing…" said Jordan, "You can't tell anyone I'm here, okay? You can't tell anyone who I am."

"Hey, give me some credit!" I said. Jordan smiled for a moment. It was good to see him smile, even if it didn't last.

Jordan

———————— ◆ ————————

Ralph's parents were really nice. I felt kind of bad lying to them. I couldn't tell them the truth, however. Luckily, they didn't recognize me. They were older than most of my fans, but I had a lot of fans their age. If they'd realized who I was, the whole thing would have been over before it began.

Ralph's house wasn't very big, so I'd be sharing his room while I was there, and his bed. It was a double bed, but I was still pretty uncomfortable about sleeping with him. It wasn't that I thought he'd try anything with me, not at all. To be honest, I think I'd have liked that. I was afraid that being so near another boy would be hard on me. I really liked Ralph. To be honest, I was quickly developing a crush on him. I think I'd have liked him as a boyfriend. He was funny, and kind, and fun, and sexy. I liked his dark brown hair and found his brown eyes downright dreamy. He had a decent build too. Sleeping near him wouldn't be easy. He was too attractive, too desirable. I wondered if I'd be able to sleep at all. I was also afraid that he'd find out I was attracted to him. What if I got excited lying so close to him and he noticed? I couldn't afford anyone finding out I was gay. It would destroy everything.

I tried not to worry about it. I'd learned long ago that it wasn't wise to worry about all the bad things that could happen in life. If I allowed myself to do that, I'd always be worrying about something or other. Instead, I tried to enjoy myself. I was living on a farm in Indiana. There were no crowds, no hotel rooms, no pushing fans, no reporters, no hassle. It was all quiet and peaceful. I felt like I could be a real boy again.

Ralph was at school the next day, so I had a lot of time to myself. I loved spending time with Ralph, but after the life I'd led, a little solitude was welcome. Mrs. Roger's fed us the best breakfast ever – biscuits and gravy, bacon, and toast made with homemade bread. Even the jam was homemade. I couldn't stop eating. I told Ralph's mom how good it was over and over and I meant it.

While Ralph was gone I wandered around the farm. I explored the big old barn near the house. It even had a hayloft. I'd never been on a farm before, so it was all new to me. I walked around the fields, and along the stream that we'd walked beside the day before. I enjoyed the freedom of just walking alone. There was no one wanting my autograph, no bodyguard, no one – just me.

*   *   *

"How do I look?" I asked Ralph.

"Like you're in the wrong century." He laughed. "You look great."

We were getting dressed for a dance at Ralph's school. I was looking forward to it. When he'd asked if I'd like to go, I started to tell him I couldn't possibly, but then he explained it was a costume ball to raise funds to fix up the auditorium. I jumped at the chance then. A costume ball was perfect. I could go and have fun and no one would have any idea who I was.

Ralph was dressed up as a zombie. I was going as a vampire, not a Dracula type vampire, but more like Tom Cruise in "Interview With A Vampire". Ralph had a costume that was just perfect. He had some clothes he'd worn to a rendezvous and they were just right to turn me into a creature of the night. At first, I didn't know what in the heck a rendezvous was, but then he explained it. Every year, a bunch of people got together at Vincennes and dressed up just like they did in the

Revolutionary War days. They even had mock battles and everything. Ralph said he went sometimes with his uncle.

The costume was pretty cool. There was a shirt with puffy sleeves, a vest to go over it, and pants that Ralph said were called britches. The pants only reached to a little below my knees. I think they were supposed to be like that, but I wasn't sure. There was even one of those triangular hats. Ralph found me a "Lone Ranger" type black mask that covered the upper part of my face. We put my hair back in a ponytail. When I looked in the mirror, I couldn't even recognize myself. The fake fangs made me downright frightening.

I was excited as we walked toward the high school gym. It reminded me of the days when I went to a regular school, instead of having a tutor. I was a little nervous as well. It had been a long time since I'd interacted with other kids in any kind of normal way. I wasn't sure I could handle it. I was sure going to try. I wouldn't have given up this chance for anything.

We stepped inside and loud music flowed over me. The sound of voices filled the air. There were kids standing all around talking. Some were even dancing. It was wonderful.

A pretty girl, dressed as a princess, came walking toward us. By instinct, I was ready for her to scream and ask for my autograph, but then I remembered that she didn't know who I was. I relaxed.

"Hey Denise," said Ralph.

"Hey," she said. She looked at me.

"This is um…my cousin from Arkansas…um."

"Chad," I said, smiling at her. "Ralph can never remember my name. It's such a hard one to remember." Denise laughed.

"I don't suppose you dance?" she asked. "I can never get Ralph to dance."

"As a matter of fact I do," I said.

Denise pulled me away. We began to dance. Ralph headed for the refreshment table.

"So you're just visiting?"

"Yeah, I'm spending part of my vacation here. School's out for the year where I come from."

"Not a very exciting place to come."

"I like it. Besides, it's fun hanging around with Ralph."

"You know, you look familiar. We haven't met before have we? Have you stayed with Ralph before?"

"No, we haven't met. I'd have remembered a girl as pretty as you. This is the first time I've stayed with Ralph's family. It's quite a trip out here."

She gazed into my eyes as if searching for my identity. I half feared she would figure out who I was. I was glad the mask was covering a good deal of my face.

I enjoyed myself more than I had in quite a long time. At last, I was doing something normal. I was dancing. No one knew who I was, no one cared. I was just another guy at the dance.

Denise and I danced a couple dances, then joined Ralph near the refreshments. I got Denise and myself something to drink.

"Hey Chad, this is my friend Chris," said Ralph. "He's my best friend."

"You have others?" asked Chris as if he was shocked. Ralph punched him in the shoulder.

"Chris thinks he's a comedian," said Ralph.

Chris shook my hand firmly. He was dressed like Tom Sawyer, with a straw hat, and even a corncob pipe.

We stood and talked for a bit. I liked Denise and Chris a lot. Ralph had some cool friends. I enjoyed just standing there talking to them. A new song started and I stiffened. It was "Do You Know That I Love You".

"Oh man, not the fag music," said a boy not far away. Ralph glared at him.

"Easy Ralph," said Chris leaning over and whispering to him. "We all know about your disturbing obsession for Jordan, but there's no reason to punch Miles out." Ralph turned as red as a beet.

"Shut up Chris!" said Ralph.

Chris ignored him and spoke quietly to me as if he were telling me a secret, but loud enough to make sure Ralph could hear. "Personally, I think Jordan might be a girl, but Ralph here loves his music."

Ralph looked ready to kill Chris on the spot. I was kind of amused, although I didn't like being compared to a girl. I felt bad for Ralph. I didn't like him being embarrassed like that.

"Well, everyone has their own favorites," I said.

"Yeah, but not everyone has a scrapbook filled with Jordan clippings." Ralph turned even redder than before. I didn't know how to defuse the situation, so I asked Denise to dance with me again. I could hear Chris and Ralph getting into it as we walked away.

"Chris is kind of a jerk, isn't he?" I said.

"He's pretty nice really. He just likes to give Ralph a hard time. Don't be down on him too much, Ralph usually gives as good as he takes. So, how long will you be staying?"

"Um, I'm not sure really."

"Well I hope I'll have the chance to see you again." Denise looked into my eyes. If I wasn't mistaken, I think she really liked me. That made me smile. It had been a long time since anyone had liked me just for me, and not because I was Jordan.

I got a little worried. Denise looked as though she might even have a crush on me and that was bad news. I guess there was a disadvantage to just being a regular guy. It allowed others to get close to me. As Chad, I had to deal with that, as Jordan, I did not. I still liked being able to just talk and dance with Denise. It was refreshing to spend time with a girl who didn't scream when she saw me.

At the end of the next dance, a girl came up and asked me to dance with her. Chris came and took Denise. She looked a little disappointed, but didn't say anything. During the evening, I danced with quite a few girls. Most of them asked me, but I worked up the courage to ask a couple of them. It made me feel good that they wanted to dance with me. I liked being Chad.

There were some way cute boys at the dance too. It was hard to see what some of them looked like, because of their costumes, but a lot of them didn't have their faces covered. My mask allowed me to do some looking without it being noticeable. I'd always been very, very careful about checking out other boys. I couldn't take the slightest risk of being found out.

Sometimes, I just wished I could hold a big press conference and announce that I was gay. Sometimes I felt like I was being a traitor to other gay boys by not doing so. I was famous. I had influence. I knew I might be able to help boys like me if I came out. There was too much riding on my career for me to take such a risk, however. What if I told the world I was gay and no one bought my CD's, or came to my concerts? I'd put a lot of people out of work, and ruin my own career. I had reasons for keeping my secret, but sometimes I still didn't feel too good about it.

I noticed a boy looking at me during the dance, and he was pretty cute. He was dressed as a punk rocker and had blue hair standing straight up. I think the natural color of his hair was probably light blond, as I couldn't see how he'd get it that shade of blue if his hair was brown, red, or black. He was dancing with a few girls, but he was looking at me a lot. I thought I could read a certain hunger in those eyes that I sometimes felt within myself. I had a little daydream about him and me going to a dark corner and making out. I was usually more the romantic type, but sometimes I just thought of pure physical contact. I was a virgin and at times I wanted nothing more than to be rid of my virginity. At other times, I was glad I hadn't had sex yet. I had a dream about meeting someone special, and experiencing my first time with him. It might seem old fashioned, but I really thought one should only make love with someone they loved. It was quite different from what the press said about me sometimes. Of course, the tabloids always started rumors that I'd slept with some girl or other. They were wrong on all counts.

I looked over at Ralph. He was dancing with Denise, despite what she'd said about never being able to get him to dance. He looked like he was having a pretty good time. He looked at me a lot, but I guess that was only natural. After all, I was famous and he alone in the gym knew who I really was. Ralph was a great guy. He was cute in his own way too. He wasn't one of those guys that I saw and immediately thought "Oh yeah!", but he was an attractive boy. He had the kind of good looks that became more apparent as time passed. He was kind and a lot of fun to be around too. I was beginning to wish he was looking at me for the same reasons as the boy with the blue hair.

I grew a little sad that I couldn't reveal myself to Ralph. He knew my true identity, but he didn't know the real me, no one did. I couldn't take the risk with him, not even if I thought he had the same feelings. For that, I was sad.

I looked again at the cute punk rock boy. I began to be seriously tempted to hook up with him. Maybe I couldn't have love, but at least I could get a little action. Even if it was nothing more than making out, it would be a whole lot more than I'd ever done in the past. I began looking back at him, letting him know I was looking, and that I knew he'd been looking at me. The more I looked at him, the more I wanted him. Part of me wanted to take him right there on the dance floor.

I couldn't believe how brave I was being, or was I merely being stupid? I was taking chances just by looking that I'd never dared before. Sure, I'd looked at lots of guys during concerts, but the crowds were so packed that no one could tell who I was looking at. What I was doing at the dance was something quite different. It was more like flirting.

I looked at the boy with blue hair. I wanted nothing more than to just rip his shirt off and run my hands over his chest. I wanted to open his pants and… Damn, I needed someone to throw a bucket of ice water on me or something. I had become a total horn-dog. What was I thinking? Was I actually thinking of getting it on with some boy I didn't even know just because he was cute? That wasn't me. I wanted more than just sex.

I smiled at the boy with blue hair, knowing that none of what I'd fantasized about would come true. We'd never met, never talked. I didn't even know his name, but I was glad our paths had crossed. In the space of a few moments we'd had a sort of relationship, and it had allowed me to learn something about myself. Maybe it was more like confirming something I already knew. My body had needs, desperate needs, but I wasn't about to become some kind of boy-slut to satisfy them. I knew deep down that what I really craved was love.

Ralph

———◆———

My head was in the clouds. The hours I'd spent with Jordan after the concert in Ft. Wayne had been the highlight of my life. I'd have remembered those hours with pleasure for years and years and been thrilled with that short span of time. I had so much more than that now that I could hardly believe it. If someone had told me that I'd be hanging out with Jordan on a daily basis, that he'd be living at *my* house, and sleeping not only in *my* room, but in *my* bed, I'd have told them they were nuts. It was beyond belief, but it was all happening, it was real.

Part of me felt a little guilty, like I was taking advantage of Jordan in some way, but I wasn't. I knew that I wasn't just hooked on him because he was famous. What I felt for him was much more than that. If everyone else forgot about him and he never sang or recorded another CD again, I'd still love him. I loved him for him, and not because he was famous.

There was a negative side to the whole thing that I couldn't ignore. I was jealous. At the dance I felt jealousy rise in my heart, every time he danced with a girl, even when it was Denise. I wanted Jordan for myself. I wanted him to be my boyfriend. I didn't want him dancing with girls. I didn't want him dancing with anyone, except me. I kept my eye on him the whole dance, not to spy on him, but just so I could look at him. I noticed a boy looking at him, and for the first time wondered if there was another boy like me at school. I saw the look in that boy's eyes, the one with the blue hair, he wanted Jordan. It made me want to stalk over and punch his lights out. Jordan was mine.

I had to laugh at myself, even though it wasn't funny. I guess I really was obsessed with him. I was getting jealous when I didn't have a snow-balls chance in hell with him. Jordan liked me, but that was no guarantee that I could have what I wanted with him, not in the least. Who was I kidding? He had thousands of girls lusting after him, millions. He could have any of them he wanted. They threw themselves at him. Who knew how many he'd already had? Jordan was a really nice guy, but who could resist the constant temptation of sex when it was right there for the taking? He'd probably already had sex more than I would in my entire life. What did he need me for? He'd probably gag if he even suspected I was attracted to him. It probably wouldn't matter that I was in love with him. I was another boy and that alone would probably make him sick, regardless of my feelings for him.

I was pissed at Chris. Why did he have to say that in front of Jordan? Why did he have to say I had a disturbing obsession for him? Of course, he had no idea that it was Jordan standing there, but still. I wondered what Jordan thought about it. He probably thought I was a stalker or something. But no, he knew I wasn't. I was still put out with Chris, some best friend!

Having Jordan around was the best, but it caused me exquisite pain the likes of which I'd never experienced before. I felt like I was being emotionally and physically tortured.

Sleeping next to Jordan at night was pure bliss, and pure hell. I yearned to take him in my arms and hold him close. I ached to touch his beautiful body. Sometimes he was pressed right up against me. Sometimes I felt his breath upon my naked skin. It was nearly more than I could stand. I always tried to sleep facing away from him, to hide my obvious arousal.

Every morning, when the sheets fell away, I was delighted and tor-mented by the sight of his bare chest. Before I'd met him, I'd searched long and hard for even a photo of Jordan without a shirt, and now I saw his bare chest everyday, in the flesh. It was wonderful, and terrible. It was like I was dying of thirst and someone was holding a glass of water in front of me that I could never quite reach. It was maddening, and yet, I wouldn't have given it up for anything in all the world.

Jordan didn't realize how very close I came to just jumping on him. He was driving me out of my mind. There was something keeping me from that, however, and that something was love. Before we'd met, I'd always had romantic thoughts about him, but never sexual. He was too good for that. He was more than just some guy to fantasize about, much more. Now, being so close to him, I couldn't help but desire him, but even so the feelings I had for him kept me from acting rashly. I didn't want to mess up my chances with him by moving too fast.

Ha! What chance did I have? Chance? That was a joke. There was no chance. Still, I did have something with Jordan, something very valuable—friendship. We were friends. I could hardly believe it, but we were friends. Friends could love too. I wasn't about to mess that up, not for anything, and certainly not for a chance at physical pleasure that was nothing more than an illusion anyway. The physical pleasure would last but a short time, a friendship could last forever. What was mere sex when compared to that? I smiled. I was far from having what I really wanted, but what I did have was pretty damned incredible.

Jordan

---------------- ◆ ----------------

It was Saturday morning. Mr. and Mrs. Rogers were gone, so me and
Ralph fixed our own breakfast. It wasn't nearly as good as that prepared
by Ralph's mom, but it was still better than just about anything I'd ever
had. It was real food.

After breakfast, Ralph ran into town for a bit. I stayed back because I
didn't think it wise to be seen. I was in Ralph's room when I heard the
back door open. I thought he'd returned. I walked into the kitchen and
stopped dead in my tracks. It wasn't Ralph, it was Denise.

She looked at me in shock. I could tell she couldn't believe her own
eyes. She knew what she was seeing, but her mind rejected it.

"Oh my God!" she said. "You're…. but you can't be! How could… Oh
my God!"

I thought to myself "Oh shit!". I hadn't planned for anyone to see me,
for anyone to know who I was. It seemed that ship had just sailed.

"Oh my God!" she repeated, gaping at me with her mouth open.

"Denise," I said, "you can't tell anyone I'm here."

"What are you doing here?" she almost shouted, still in utter shock.
She didn't seem to notice that I knew her name.

"I met Ralph when I was in Ft. Wayne, ran into him you might say."

"That was true! He wasn't lying? We thought he made all that up
about meeting you!"

"Nope," I said. "I think you better sit down Denise." I pulled out a chair for her. She looked like she was about to faint dead away.

"You know my name?" She'd finally noticed.

"I should. I danced with you last night. We talked remember?" She looked more shocked still, if that were possible.

"I can't believe that was you! I can't believe you are you!"

"I'm pretty sure I am me," I said, close to laughing.

"What are you doing here, in the middle of nowhere?"

"That's a long story. Let's just say I'm on a little vacation."

"No one is going to believe this!"

"You can't tell, not anyone," I said. "Please." I looked at her, turning on the charm. It wasn't necessary.

"Oh, no, of course not. I didn't mean… Of course I won't say anything."

"Thanks."

Ralph came back just then and I thought he was going to die of shock when he saw Denise sitting there, and me talking to her.

"What are you doing here?" he almost yelled.

"Nice to see you too," she said. "To be honest, I dropped by to see your cousin. He's looks an awfully lot like a certain famous singer without his mask! Cousin huh!?" I couldn't help but smile a bit, even if Ralph was in a bit of a fix.

"I'm sorry, but we couldn't tell you."

"You, of all people, should know how well I can keep a secret." I could tell Denise was a little put out with Ralph. I wasn't sure what she meant by her words, but I sensed they had a lot more meaning than they seemed to have.

"You can't tell," he said.

"We've already gone though that. The secret is safe with me," she said. Ralph visibly relaxed.

"You're a great dancer," said Denise, looking at me. The tone of her voice frightening me a little. It was the tone of voice of a girl with a crush. My life was getting complicated.

"Thanks, you're not so bad yourself."

"Well, now that you're here, you might as well hang out with us," said Ralph.

"How could I refuse such a charming invitation?" said Denise. I laughed. Denise and Ralph together were quite entertaining.

Ralph took us out to the barn and got out cane poles. We followed him to the pond down the hill and went fishing. I hadn't been fishing in so long I couldn't even remember the last time. I'd never been fishing with a twelve foot cane pole before. It was relaxing to just sit and talk and watch the cork float upon the water.

"Gosh, you must know all kinds of celebrities," said Denise.

"He doesn't want to talk about that stuff," said Ralph.

"It's okay," I told him.

"Have you ever met Tom Cruise?" she asked.

"Yeah, I visited the set when they were filming 'Mission Impossible 2'. He is a really nice guy."

"I can't believe you know Tom Cruise!"

"Well, that would be taking it a bit far. I've met him, but I wouldn't say I know him. It's not like he comes over for dinner." Denise smiled.

"Have you met Devon Sawa? He's such a cutie."

"Yeah, I've met him, and he is a cutie."

"Hey!" said Ralph.

"Just not quite as cute as you Ralph," I said.

"Now I know that's a lie, but thanks," said Ralph, smiling.

"How about Rosie O'Donnel?"

"Duh!" said Ralph. "He did her show! Five times!" I laughed at Ralph's expression, and his tone of voice.

"Sorry, but I don't know everything about him like you," she said. Ralph gave her a look that clearly said "shut up". I knew Ralph had all my CD's. I wondered how big of a fan he was.

"Rosie is the best," I said, to break the tension. "What I like best about her is that she's so common. I mean like everyone knows her, but she just thinks of herself as a regular person you know. I was so nervous being on her show the first time, but after I met her it was all cool."

"Oh, you must know all the music guys!" said Denise with great excitement as the thought occurred to her.

"Have you met the Backstreet Boys?"

"Yeah. I went to one of their concerts and met them backstage. They're cool."

"How about Nsync?"

"Yep."

"98 Degrees?"

"Yes."

"The Moffatts?"

"Yeah, I've met them a few times. They are way cool."

"Oh! How about Hanson, do you know Hanson?"

"I've met them. I wouldn't say I know them."

"You know you look kinda like Taylor, he's soooooo cute. I bet he's really nice."

"Geesh," said Ralph, rolling his eyes.

"Yeah, all three of them are really nice."

"Why don't you just ask him who he hasn't met?" asked Ralph. "I think it will save time." I smiled. Denise ignored him.

Denise kept throwing names at me and I kept telling her things about those I knew, or had at least met. Ralph rolled his eyes a few times, but didn't say anything more. I usually didn't like questions like Denise was asking, but she was cool, so it was okay. It was kind of fun watching her get so excited.

We had a really great day. We must have sat by that pond for hours. I only caught one fish the entire time, and it was a small one. I didn't care. It didn't matter. I just enjoyed being there.

Ralph

———————◆———————

I'd planned to keep Jordan's presence a major secret. I knew he didn't want to be disturbed and I sure didn't want to share him with hoards of people. I could have made myself very popular by letting word out that I knew Jordan, but I wasn't about to do that to him. I was his friend. I wasn't exactly being selfless, however, I wanted him all to myself. Mom and Dad had to know, of course, but they weren't a problem. To them, he was just another boy. They didn't know he was famous. I hadn't planned to tell Denise, but she managed to find out all by herself so I couldn't help that. I was determined that no one else would discover Jordan was my houseguest, but I hadn't reckoned with Chris.

Chris arrived without warning one afternoon just after school, which wasn't surprising because he regularly dropped by unannounced. I usually didn't mind. I was almost always delighted to see him. This time it was different. This time Jordan was in my bedroom messing with my computer and I didn't want Chris to discover him.

"You want to catch a movie or something?" he asked. "I'm bored."

"I, uh... I'm kind of busy," I said.

"I've noticed that. You've been very busy the last few days. What have you been up to?"

"Nothing, just... you know."

I thought Jordan would be as quiet as he could, but I could hear him in my bedroom. I was sure Chris could too, so I talked to keep him from hearing. He interrupted me.

"What's going on back there?" he said.

"Oh, um… Mom is just cleaning…"

"I saw your parents on their way to town as I was coming in," said Chris suspiciously.

I wasn't nearly a good enough liar to make up a convincing story quickly. It probably wouldn't have been of use anyway, Chris was already suspicious and had caught me in a lie. He suddenly grinned.

"Have you got company Ralph? You have a boy back there?"

I knew what he was thinking. He had a devilish look on his face that made it plain he thought he'd walked in when me and some boy were making out on my bed. "If only" I thought for a moment. Chris made for the bedroom. I grabbed his arm and pleaded with him.

"Please Chris! Don't go back there. Please…"

He wasn't listening, however, my pleading only made him more determined to find out what I was hiding. I thought about tackling him, but it wouldn't be of much use. He'd find out anyway. I held my breath as I rushed into the room on the heels of Chris.

Jordan was playing a computer game. He had headphones on which explained why he hadn't been more quiet. The motion of us entering caught his attention and he turned. His eyes grew wide when he saw Chris, but not nearly so wide as those of Chris himself. He sputtered like an overflowing coffeepot.

"You're… You… I… But…" Chris seemed to have lost the ability to put two words together. He sputtered and gaped and stood there open-mouthed.

Jordan pulled off the head phones. I looked at him apologetically. He shrugged with his eyebrows and smiled slightly. It seemed he was enjoy-ing the predicament of Chris. I'd told him all about my best friend, and the things he'd said about him, and about the way he gave me trouble for listening to *Phantom.* Jordan had a devilish look in his eye that matched the one I'd noticed in Chris earlier.

"So you're the one who doesn't like my music," said Jordan with a frown. I had to fight to keep from laughing. I knew Jordan was toying with Chris, playing with his mind.

"I, uh… it's fine really, I…"

"And I believe you said I was ugly," said Jordan scowling.

"I was just kidding."

"And you said I was a girl."

"No, I tried to make Ralph say that. I didn't say it." Chris was looking very distressed.

"Funny, I could have swore you said you thought I was at girl, at the dance."

"Uh…" Chris was squirming. I loved it.

"You think I'm weak, don't you?"

"No, no, not at all!"

Jordan stared at him. I was surprised he could be so menacing. Chris looked like someone who had gotten in way over his head. Jordan finally cracked a smile, then we both broke out laughing.

"You're right," Jordan said to me. "He is a lot of fun."

Chris looked out of sorts and even a bit stupid as we laughed. He recovered soon enough and it wasn't long before he was smiling. He still couldn't seem to believe that Jordan was sitting there, even though he could see him plain as day. I suspected that Chris thought he was dreaming.

The three of us had a long talk and Chris finally seemed to understand that Jordan was really there, and that he wasn't dreaming. He still seemed quite overwhelmed by the whole thing. I guess that shouldn't have surprised me. I was delighted to see Jordan take the wind out of his sails. If I lived to be a hundred, I'd never forget the look on Chris' face as Jordan went off on him.

*   *   *

Chris was a bit embarrassing. He was so obviously impressed with Jordan's fame that I was afraid Jordan wouldn't like him. I feared that Chris was acting like the very type of fan that Jordan was trying to avoid at the moment. Chris had done a complete about-face and practically fawned over Jordan. It was obvious as well that he'd listened to his music much more than he let on. Chris obviously had a *Phantom* CD or two hidden away somewhere. I fully intended to torment him about it later. I'd pay him back for riding me so hard and I'd love it.

We went out and walked around, Chris still making himself ridiculous by asking stupid questions. We found ourselves in the loft of the barn. I loved the smell of the hay and Jordan seemed to like it too. He eyed Chris for a moment.

"I'm told you like to wrestle. You wanna?" asked Jordan.

Chris looked mildly afraid. I was sure he was remembering all the times he'd called Jordan a wimp. I'm sure he figured I'd told Jordan all about it, which I had. Now he was facing him, something he never thought he'd have to do.

Jordan had an aggressive, almost hungry look on his face. I think he wanted to see if he could show Chris up. I didn't know if that was such a good idea. I knew that Chris was quite a good wrestler. I couldn't imagine that Jordan was much good. I doubted he'd ever wrestled in his life.

"Me? Wrestle you?" asked Chris, as if the idea were outlandish.

"What's wrong? Afraid of getting your butt kicked?" smiled Jordan.

"Yeah right!" said Chris. For a moment at least, he had turned back into his old self. "Okay, pretty boy, you are on."

I feared what would happen if Chris won, and I really figured he would. I knew I'd have to hear about it forever if he beat Jordan. I didn't see any way I could keep them from wrestling, however, so there was nothing for me to do, but watch.

They circled one another, Chris with a superior look on his face, Jordan with a look of concentration and determination. I hoped that

Jordan wouldn't get hurt. I knew Chris wouldn't intentionally hurt him, but it wasn't difficult to get hurt without anyone trying to do damage. I could just imagine Jordan getting his arm broken or something. Then there would be thousands of girls upset because he couldn't play. I had a quick daydream about a hoard of girls chasing me down as if it were my fault. Then I had a vision about them running Chris down and pounding on him for it. I liked that a lot better.

Chris reached in and got a good hold on Jordan. It looked like it was going to end before it truly began. I was amazed when Jordan twisted his way free, and more amazed still when he came back at Chris and threw him down. As I watched them grappling, I learned that Jordan was a good deal stronger than I'd thought. Chris was learning it too. Jordan also seemed to know a considerable amount about wrestling. I'd always pictured him as sensitive, quiet, and not very athletic. He was sensitive, and quiet, but it seemed he was athletic too.

It was exciting to watch Jordan and Chris rolling around in the hay, each trying to get the best of the other. I think what I enjoyed most was watching the look on Chris' face as it dawned on him that Jordan was not an easy mark. The boy he had called a wimp and compared to a girl was whipping his butt. Chris was outmatched. I wasn't quite sure how Jordan was managing it, but he was clearly in control. I bet Chris never thought that Jordan could beat him. I bet he thought there wasn't the slightest chance of that. Jordan was teaching him otherwise.

Chris was using all his tricks, and giving Jordan quite a hard time, but Jordan hung in there and kept going. Maybe it was Jordan's determination that kept him in control. Maybe it was his desire to prove something to Chris, and maybe himself too. Whatever it was, it was working.

I couldn't help but get a little aroused watching Jordan and Chris wrestle. I'm sure most boys didn't want to think about it, but two guys wrestling was kind of erotic. The struggle, the heavy breathing, the bulging muscles, all of that and more made wrestling sexually stimulating. I was getting more excited than I wanted to watching Jordan and Chris go at it.

Within a few minutes' time Jordan had Chris pinned and there was no escape. Chris tried his best to free himself, but it wasn't going to happen. He had been out-wrestled. Chris finally surrendered.

"Not bad for a pretty boy, huh?" asked Jordan smiling.

I was absolutely delighted to see Jordan defeat Chris. Chris knew it too. He groaned as he looked at me, knowing he'd never hear the end of it. He wouldn't. I was ecstatic. It was the gift that kept on giving.

Jordan

◆

Chris had to leave about six. I could tell he didn't want to go, but he had some appointment and couldn't miss it. I wasn't entirely sad to see him go, because he was a bit of a pain. He was nice enough, however, and I had thoroughly enjoyed trouncing him in the hayloft. Ralph could talk of little else when Chris had left. It made me smile.

"So what do you want to do now?" asked Ralph.

"How about dinner and a movie?" I said.

"Are you serious? What if someone sees you?"

I'd forgotten I was famous. Spending time with Ralph and Chris made me feel so much like a normal boy that I'd forgotten I wasn't. I'd forgotten I couldn't just go places like normal people. It was wonderful!

"I've got my baseball cap and sunglasses," I said.

"You really want to risk it?"

"Yeah." To be honest, I was beginning to get a little bored. I hadn't been staying on the farm long, but there wasn't much to do.

"Okay."

"So where can we go?"

"Evansville has the best theatres," he said. "And there will be big crowds, less chance of you getting recognized."

"Cool, you drive, I'll pay," I said.

"I don't want you paying," said Ralph.

"Hey, with the price of gas, I'm probably coming out ahead. Anyway, it was my idea. Besides, I'm paying!"

"All right, all right," said Ralph.

I wore my sunglasses all the way down to Evansville, just in case. We got there a bit before seven, just in time to catch a movie. I put on my baseball cap as we got out of the car. I felt a little foolish, but the disguise was necessary. While we were standing in line to get tickets, I heard some boy say "Who's he think he is, some movie star or something?". I pretended I didn't hear, although I was tempted to take off my hat and sunglasses and shock the hell out of him. I wasn't about to actually do it, but the thought brought a smile to my lips. I didn't take off the glasses until we were sitting and the lights were dimmed.

I liked sitting there with Ralph. I found myself having warm, fuzzy thoughts about him. I wished that he was my boyfriend, and that we were on a date. It wasn't like at the dance, when I was lusting after the blue haired boy. There was more to what I was feeling than that.

I allowed myself a little fantasy, a fantasy of settling down on the farm with Ralph. He could be my boyfriend and we'd live there and grow corn or something. I nearly laughed. I could just see myself trying to farm. The only corn I'd ever touched was in a can.

After the movie, I was hungry, starving was more like it. We hadn't eaten much lunch it was a little after 9 p.m.

"There a Burger Dude anywhere around here?" I asked.

"Yeah," said Ralph. We got in the car and drove off. It didn't take us long at all to get there.

"So you want to go through the drive thru?"

"Nah, let's go in."

"Are you sure?"

"Yeah."

I knew it was risky, but I hadn't been inside a Burger Dude in so long I could hardly remember what it was like. Sometimes I dreamed of Burger Dude.

I put on my hat and sunglasses again. It was dark and I could barely see where I was going. The girl at the counter looked at me oddly when I ordered. She probably thought I was some kind of freak.

We sat down at a booth and I dove into my Double Burger Dude Burger.

"Mmmm this is good," I said.

"You really like Burger Dude don't you?" I knew Ralph had probably read about my Burger Dude habit in some teen magazine. It had been mentioned more than once.

"Oh yeah, I love it. I have stuff from here all the time, especially French toast squares and cinnamon minis for breakfast. It's always cold by the time I get it. It's not the same warmed up in a microwave."

We ate and talked and it was wonderful. Again, I found myself forgetting that I was famous, and that I couldn't walk around in public like everyone else. I received a harsh reminder when a girl right near us screamed and pointed.

"It's Jordan! It's Jordan!"

"Oh shit," said Ralph. His words were echoed in my mind.

Almost instantly, our booth was surrounded. The girl kept screaming my name and more joined her. The place was packed and it seemed like everyone was suddenly at our booth. Some of the girls in the rear were pushing to get a better view.

"Is it really him?"

"It can't be him."

"Oh it's him, look at his hair. It's Jordan!"

Girls were pushing paper napkins and pens at me, wanting me to sign. They were all telling me how wonderful I was. Even the girl that had taken my order had come out and was trying to get to me.

"We've got to get out of here," I said to Ralph.

He looked ready to charge into the crowd to make a path, but I held him back. I got up, abandoning my supper. I knew we couldn't just push our way out. Besides, that would have been rude. Instead, I started signing napkins and whatever they pushed at me as I edged toward the door. Ralph stayed close by me. He looked frightened. I think he was afraid they were going to hurt me. I'd been in such situations before. I knew how to handle it. Those girls were my fans, they wouldn't intentionally hurt me.

My sunglasses got knocked off. I heard a crunch. A flash blinded my eyes. Someone had taken a picture. Why was there always a camera somewhere near me? My hat got knocked off too. I didn't even try to retrieve it. I knew I'd likely get trampled. I kept signing, kept edging toward the door. I kept answering questions, saying I was just in town for the night. Girls were looking at Ralph, wondering who he was. They were even pushing napkins at him to sign. I think it scared him.

We got closer to the door. "Get the car," I mouthed to Ralph. He understood. The girls got more aggressive. They were touching me, and Ralph. He pulled away from me to go from the car, but his shirt got torn before he could escape. They let him go and concentrated on me. I kept signing, kept talking, kept smiling. The manager was staring. I'm sure he couldn't wait for me to get out of there. Stuff was getting pushed around, mostly me. I felt my shirt rip, half my chest was bare.

"I'm sorry," I said. "I really have to go." I pushed my way out, hoping I wasn't being too rough.

Ralph had made it to the car, he backed it out and zipped up to me. I flung open the door and hopped in. He took off and we lost ourselves in heavy traffic. He kept looking in the rear view mirror, but we'd lost them.

"Man, they really messed up your shirt," he said.

"Looks like you're popular with the girls too," I said, pointing out his own torn shirt.

"That was scary," said Ralph.

"Yeah, they can get out of hand. That's why I can't go out in public like that and why I don't go anywhere without a bodyguard, usually."

"Man," said Ralph. "I guess being a rock star has its disadvantages."

"It sure does," I told him. "It was stupid going in there, just stupid, but it's been so long… I was hoping no one would notice me." I felt a wave of sadness flow over me. All I wanted was to eat a hamburger like a normal boy, but it seemed I couldn't even do that.

Ralph looked at me. I could tell he felt sorry for me. It wasn't a look I was accustomed to seeing. It made me feel more close to him. I wished that I could open up to him and really talk about things. He was a boy that I could be intimate with, and love. I realized at the moment that I already loved him. What was I going to do?

Ralph

$\blacklozenge$

It was late when we returned, but neither Jordan nor I felt much like going to bed. Jordan had spoken little and I knew he was lost in thought. Instead of going inside, we walked down the hill and along the stream.

"You're upset," I said.

"Yes, and no," answered Jordan. He looked at the bright moon overhead, then back at me. "Sometimes, I get really tired of being me. Sometimes I wish I could go to the mall, or go out and have a burger without anyone bothering me."

"I can imagine that must be tough. Well, perhaps I don't quite have to imagine it," I said, fingering my torn shirt.

"Sometimes it's just too much. I have all these people depending on me. And then there are all the fans, and everything they lay on me. I don't even feel real sometimes," he said. I started to speak, but Jordan's spoke again. "The weird thing is, I'm starting to miss it, not everyone depending on me, but I'm starting to miss what I left behind. Music is my life. It's what I am. I don't know what I'd do if I couldn't write songs and perform. I think I'd die."

"It's helped me a lot, your music," I said. Jordan peered at me in the darkness. "Sometimes I feel very alone, or sad, or both. When I'm feeling like that, I listen to one of your songs and it makes me feel better. It's like you are there with me, keeping me company, telling me that everything will be okay." I hoped I wasn't telling Jordan too much, but he meant the world to me and I wanted to help him. He turned to me.

"You can't even imagine how much hearing that means to me," said Jordan. "That's what it's all about really. That's what I've always wanted, for something I sing to make someone smile, or help them in some way."

"Well your music does that for me, and I'm sure I'm not the only one." I had a powerful desire to go on, to tell Jordan how I really felt about him. I couldn't make myself do it. I didn't want to ruin what had become a very dear friendship. Besides, I wanted to help Jordan, and not tell him about my problems.

There was a certain tenseness to Jordan that made me wonder if there was more. If there was, he did not speak of it. I nearly asked him, but I knew he'd tell me if he wanted. I didn't' want to be too nosy. After all, he was sharing things with me he'd probably never shared with any-one before.

I knew one thing that was eating at Jordan, one thing that was defi-nitely not a secret. He'd mentioned it to me more than once himself—the girl who had taken her own life, because of him, or so the tabloids said.

"Jordan, even if... even if that girl really did kill herself over you, which I seriously doubt, just think of all those you've helped. Even if that one really bad thing did happen, there's so much more good. There are times when I've really felt like tossing myself off a cliff or something because I felt so bad, but I didn't, because you were there for me. You weren't there physically, but you were there with me through your music. It gave me something to hold onto when I needed it the most. It made me feel like someone cared about me. I know I'm not the only one either. I can't be. And, you're going to think this is just stupid, but there was this one time... I really, really thought about killing myself, but I didn't do it. I didn't do it because I got to thinking how I wouldn't be here when your next CD came out."

Jordan didn't speak, but he smiled at me. I could tell what I said meant a lot to him. I knew he was in pain, and I wanted to help him.

Jordan was beautiful in the moonlight. He looked like some prince with his golden hair and handsome features, but there was never a prince with such beauty as his. Jordan had a beauty that wasn't just on the outside, but came from the inside too. He was a beautiful soul, so caring and loving and kind. He would have been beautiful even if his features were ugly and his body malformed. Jordan had the kind of beauty that counted, the kind that came from within.

Jordan

◆

Some time away from my hectic lifestyle was giving me a new perspective. It allowed me to take a step back and look at things in a new way. The truth was that I was beginning to miss my life. I missed my fans, I missed the attention, but most of all, I missed the music. The handful of days I'd spent with Ralph had been some of the best in my life, but I was beginning to feel out of sorts. It was almost as if I were experiencing some kind of music withdrawal.

Ralph wasn't home from school yet, and I remembered that he had a guitar in his room. I was sure he wouldn't mind me borrowing it, so I took it out on the porch. The guitar wasn't my instrument, but Kieran had taught me and I could play pretty well. Ralph's guitar was way out of tune. I could tell he didn't use it much. I had it back in tune in no time and began playing a bit.

As I played around with the guitar, a new melody began to form in my head. It was peaceful and soothing. I tried it on the guitar and began to rearrange it. I smiled. I was songwriting again. It felt good. I lost myself in the melody, and refined it, bringing out of it the feelings that it had begun to invoke. In less than an hour I had something. It wasn't anywhere near a complete song, but it could be a part of one. Writing songs was like that, it often came in bits and pieces. Sometimes the lyrics came first, from a thought or a feeling, or even something someone said. Sometimes a chorus developed, that demanded a melody and lyrics to give it voice. And sometimes the melody came first, as it did on this day. Sometimes, even the title came first. Writing a song was like assembling a puzzle, with pieces that could come from anywhere. It could happen in a million different ways, but it was always wonderful and beautiful.

I remembered when we'd written "Do You Know That I Love You". Like most of our songs, it was a cooperative effort by Kieran, Ross, and me. The main lyrics came to me when I started thinking about some of the boys that had crossed my path, boys that I could well have fallen in love with. I didn't tell the others where the idea came from, or what it was really about, but that was the beginning of it. As we worked with it, I noticed that a bridge section that Kieran had written for it was a better chorus than the chorus. The bridge we ended up using was written for an entirely different song. After we'd taken out the original bridge, Ross came up with the idea of using a bridge we'd written weeks before, but ultimately discarded. It was perfect for "Do You Know That I Love You". Writing the song wasn't easy. We had to manipulate and twist it all around to make everything fit, to make each part work with the others, but it had come together at last. It was the whole creative process that I loved, whether it was just me, or me, Kieran, and Ross putting it all together.

As I sat there on the porch, I felt the love of music flowing through me. Writing music was an act of creation. It was a way of giving voice to feelings and ideas that couldn't be expressed with words alone. Music was something that came from your heart, your mind, and your soul. Music was something that could change people's lives. I knew that I was very lucky to be a part of all that.

I found Ralph's tape recorder and made a tape of the melody I'd worked out. Someday it would find its place. Someday it would become a part of a song and millions of people would listen to it, and be affected by it. Maybe it would bring them happiness such as it brought to Ralph. Maybe it would chase away sadness and loneliness as it did for him. I smiled to myself as I recorded it. I was sitting alone on the porch, but I was doing something that would ultimately touch millions.

I smiled, but the smile soon faded from my lips. I was lucky to live the life that I did, but something was missing and I knew what it was. I needed someone in my life, someone to share it with. Sure, there was Kieran and Ross, and I guess countless others too, but I couldn't share myself with them in the way I so desperately needed. I craved a more intimate sharing of thoughts and feelings that I had so far not dared to share with anyone. I wondered if I could ever dare. The price of gaining the desire of my heart might well be the loss of all that I loved. Still, I couldn't help but yearn for it.

I thought of Ralph. Had some act of fate brought us together? Was there meant to be something between us? Sometimes, when I looked at him, I saw a sense of yearning that I felt in my own heart. I saw caring, perhaps even love in his gaze, and I knew it was more than mere admiration. At least I thought I knew it. I feared that perhaps I was merely seeing what I wanted to see. He had become a close friend in such a short time that there had to be some special bond between us. I felt something for him more than fondness. Was it love?

I felt that I did love him, but I wasn't sure. I'd never been in love, didn't really know what it was like. How could I know? I smiled thinking of Ralph as I sat there. He was funny and witty and kind. I felt like I could tell him just about anything. I wondered if maybe I shouldn't share with him something I'd never shared before. If I was that brave, then maybe, just maybe, I'd know what I was feeling inside. The prospects frightened me. I might well find something other than what I sought. In an effort to reach for bliss, I might lose all that I had. My thoughts of Ralph brought me happiness, but it was bittersweet. I almost felt like I'd become lost in a song.

Ralph

◆

"Ralph? Are you okay?" I had no idea Denise was near until she spoke.

I was sitting by the edge of the pond, staring out at the still water. I didn't answer. I knew I couldn't steady my voice enough to answer. Denise came closer. She kneeled down by my side. I looked at her, tears still flowing from my eyes.

"Ralph, what's wrong? I know you've been sad these past few days. What is it?"

I didn't answer. I just cried a little more. It was all so hopeless.

"I'd think you'd be happy. I know how much you like Jordan and he's here, he's actually your friend. Something has happened that I wouldn't have thought would happen in a million years. You're actually friends with Jordan. I thought you getting to see him at the concert would be the closest you'd ever get, but look at you now." She smiled at me.

"Maybe it would have been better if that's as close as I got, at the concert. Maybe it would have been better if we never met."

"Why? What's wrong? What's happened? Did you two get into a fight? Has he turned out to be a jerk or something?"

"No, no, that's just it. He's as wonderful as I ever thought, even more so. He's fantastic, he's awesome!"

"So what's the problem?"

"I love him."

"Well duh," said Denise. I looked at her. It wasn't the response I was expecting.

"You knew?"

"At the risk of repeating myself, duh, of course I knew. You've got every freaking CD he's ever made. You have every picture, every article. You've got video tapes filled with him."

"It's more than that," I said. "I'm not just some obsessed fan. I'll admit, I'm obsessed, but it's more than that."

"I know it is Ralph," said Denise. "I've seen the way you look at him. I see how happy you are when you're with him, and how sad. I know you love him."

"That's the problem see? I love him. I'm in love with him, but he's a big time rock star and I'm nothing. Fuck, I'm gay and he's got like millions of girls after him. I told you about the other night. I told you what happened. I told you how we got mobbed."

"Yeah."

"He doesn't want me, not like that. He's got all those girls after him. Hell, even if he was gay, he could have guys way cuter than me, way better built. He could have movie stars or models. He could have guys I could only dream about. And he's rich. And he's famous. What the hell would he want with me?"

"But he does want you Ralph," said Denise.

I looked at her. I thought she must be out of her mind.

"Yeah, right! Has he told you that? Huh?"

"Well, no, but I know it just the same."

"How can you possibly?"

"Because I'm a girl."

"Huh?"

"Because I've seen the look in his eyes too. I've seen how he looks at you. I've seen how happy he is around you, and how sad. He's just like you Ralph. He may be famous and all that, but he's just a boy, a boy in love—with you."

I sat and gazed at Denise. I couldn't believe her words. I wanted to believe them more than anything, but it was just too impossible to be true. Even if I thought it might be, it was too much to hope. The pain would be too much to bear if I let myself believe. It would hurt too much if I was wrong.

Denise could read my thoughts and feelings in my eyes. She knew what was going through my mind, without me once mentioning it.

"You're scared Ralph, scared of rejection, afraid that someone like Jordan can't possibly love you, but I tell you he does. I just know it."

"And if you're wrong? Do you know what that would do to me? Do you know how much that would hurt? I've dreamed about him forever and he's everything I always thought he'd be, he's everything I always wanted. He's the one Denise, I just know it. He's the one, you understand me? If I take a chance and he tells me he doesn't love me, or pushes me away, what then? What do I do then? There would be nothing left, nothing. It would be far better to never know."

"Would it?"

"Yes."

"You're a coward," she said. I looked at her angry and hurt.

"I know you can't help but be afraid, no one could. It's not a bad thing, but think about it Ralph. You are afraid to tell him how you feel because you are afraid of the pain of rejection. But how do you feel now? Aren't you in pain now? Do you really think the pain you are feeling is going to go away? Do you really want to keep tormenting yourself because you're too afraid to take a chance? And what about Jordan? I tell you he feels the same. He's in pain too, just like you. If you love him, you can't let him hurt like that. Even if you don't believe he's in pain, you should have the balls to put your neck on the line to help him, just in case."

I sat there pale-faced. I'd never had a dressing down so intense before, and yet I knew that Denise did it because she loved me. Her words hurt. I was embarrassed, even a little humiliated, but I wasn't angry with her. This wasn't easy for her either, but she wasn't taking the easy way out. She was doing what she thought best for me. What's more, she was right.

I was miserable, and it would go on and on as long as I allowed it. What if she was right about Jordan? What if he was feeling the same? I couldn't bear to think of him in such pain. Denise was right. I had to take the chance, if for no other reason than to end his suffering. I did love him. Even if I was wrong, I had to do it. Denise made me see that I was wallowing in self pity, and thinking only of myself.

"How can I ever work up the courage to tell him?" I asked.

"That you'll have to figure out by yourself," said Denise. "But you'd better hurry, because you're only going to have about ten minutes to do it."

"Why?" I asked, suddenly frightened.

"Because I'm going right now to tell Jordan you need to talk to him." Denise got up and started walking up the hill.

"But!" I said.

"No time for that," she called back.

"But!" I repeated.

"No time for that either! Think fast!" said Denise, and kept on walking.

I stared at the back of her head. I didn't know whether to yell at her, or run and hug her, or just plain run away. I swallowed hard, and shook in terror.

Jordan

♦

I didn't hear anyone coming. If I had, I would have turned off the monitor. Denise was standing there before I knew she was in the house. My face turned red. I was looking at shirtless pics of cute boys. It wasn't like the site was pornographic or anything, but I knew she had to wonder what the hell I was doing. She could see what I was looking at clearly. There was no denying it. I was screwed.

"Well I guess this makes things easier," she said.

"Huh?" I was totally confused.

"Ralph's down by the pond. He needs to talk to you."

"Oh, okay." I paused. I thought about trying to explain why I was looking at an internet site of shirtless boys, but I knew I couldn't explain it away. "Please don't tell anyone." It was all I could think to say.

"I won't Jordan. I wouldn't do that to a friend." I smiled.

"Thanks." I cut the internet connection and turned off the browser. The boys disappeared. I stood and made for the door. Denise grabbed my arm as I passed.

"Ralph has something important to tell you. If you... Just be kind to him okay?" I was more confused than ever.

"I will be. I like Ralph, a lot." There was something to Denise's smile. I knew there was meaning there, but I couldn't figure it out.

"What's this about?" I asked.

"I think Ralph needs to tell you that, but I think everything is going to be okay."

I was more confused than ever. Denise grabbed me again and hugged me, then released me and smiled.

"Now get going!" she said.

"Yes Ma'am."

I walked down the hill, faintly afraid of what Denise might be thinking of me, cursing myself for my own stupidity and lack of control. She didn't seem in the least upset, however. She seemed more like…happy. It was rather odd. She was being very mysterious too. She acted as if me looking at boys was nothing, and she just wanted to send me on my way. I was perplexed.

I also wondered what was up with Ralph. He'd been acting moody, and now this. I didn't have long to think about any of it. It didn't take long to walk to the pond. When I got there, Ralph was pale. He looked scared, and nervous. When I looked at his hands they were trembling. It didn't make sense. Denise had given me no indication he was in such a state.

"Ralph what's wrong?" I was worried about him. I couldn't imagine what could be so terrible. I knew I'd help him in any way I could, however, no matter what it was. I wanted more than anything to take him in my arms and tell him that I loved him, and that everything would be okay. I couldn't bear to see him suffering so.

"I'm so afraid of losing what I have with you, of losing you," he said. He was crying.

"Ralph, you're not going to lose me. We're friends, close friends." I wanted to say more, but I just couldn't. I was too afraid.

"Close friends break up over stuff like this," he said. "You're my friend now, but when I say what I have to say, you may hate me."

"I could never hate you," I said. My mind was reeling. I wondered what could be so bad that it had Ralph this worked up. It sounded like he'd killed someone, or molested some little kid or something, but I knew Ralph could never, would never, do anything like that. Whatever he'd done, I'd stick by him, even if it was something unthinkable.

Ralph was crying. I could read the pain in his face. Tears were welling up in my own eyes. I cared about him so much. I couldn't bear to see him hurt like that. I put my hand on his shoulder.

"Ralph, I'm here. I'm your friend. I care about you. Just tell me whatever it is. I'm here for you."

He looked into my eyes, searching. He looked like he was ready to scream. He was on the brink.

"I love you!" he blurted out, as if he had to force the words out quickly or not say them at all. "I'm gay and I love you and I want you to be my boyfriend. I've always loved you." I was shocked. Ralph looked at me, pleading with his eyes.

"Please don't hate me. Please don't leave me. I'm so afraid of losing you." He was sobbing. He was writhing in emotional pain.

I hated to see Ralph suffer like that, but I couldn't help but smile. My smile came from a happiness inside me, a happiness that came from knowing that I could quiet all Ralph's fears, a happiness that came from knowing that the impossible had happened.

"I love you too, Ralph."

Ralph's head jerked up and he gawked at me. He looked like he couldn't believe what I'd said.

"I love you, Ralph." I repeated, peering into his beautiful brown eyes. He just stared for several moments. It was like he just couldn't comprehend. I wrapped my arms around him and Ralph bawled into my shoulder. He hugged me tight. His tears were tears of relief. I knew what they were. I was crying them too.

After a while, Ralph took his head off my shoulder and looked into my eyes.

"You're serious right?" he said. I laughed a little.

"Of course I'm serious. I wouldn't say something like that if I didn't mean it."

"Denise was right," he said quietly.

"Huh?"

"Just a few minutes ago, before she went to get you, I told her that I loved you. I told her I was afraid you'd hate me if you knew, but she said I didn't have anything to worry about. She said she'd seen the look in your eyes, and knew that you loved me too. I couldn't dare to believe it, but she was right." He was smiling at me. He hugged me tightly.

"I'm so happy," I said. "You don't know how much I've wanted to tell you how I feel about you. I'm so glad you had the courage to do it. I don't know if I could have ever worked up the nerve to tell you."

"Let's not worry about that," said Ralph. "We both know now, and that's all that matters." He paused. "Jordan, will you be my boyfriend?" I smiled at him.

"Yes, Ralph, I will." I felt a little sappy, like I was in one of those movies where a guy asks a girl to marry him and it gets all corny. I didn't care, though, I really didn't. I'd feared I'd live my life without real love, and suddenly the boy that I loved told me that he loved me. I couldn't have been more happy at that moment. I pulled Ralph close and kissed him gently on the lips.

Ralph

◆

The next time I saw Denise, I was going to give her a big hug. I owed her and I knew it. If she hadn't pushed me and interfered, who knows how long it would have taken me to express my feelings to Jordan? I suspected that I'd never have been able to do it. I'm sure I would have decided to do it sooner or later, but deciding and actually doing it were two totally different things.

I was so happy I was walking on air. Even the guys at school noticed. Some of them thought that I must have a girl. How wrong they were. I wished that I could tell them why I was so happy, but I couldn't for more than one reason. I wasn't about to tell them I had a boyfriend, and I couldn't tell them about Jordan period.

My life was a dream. Jordan and I spent every moment together we could. Mostly, we just did the same things we'd been doing the whole time he was staying on the farm, but we did a few others things too. I loved holding hands with him as we walked. We could do that in the seclusion of the farm. As long as we were out of sight of the house, there were no prying eyes. I loved holding Jordan close and kissing him too. We kissed a lot, long passionate kisses full of hunger and desire. Kissing Jordan made my head spin.

Jordan and I could have done a lot more, especially since we slept in the very same bed. We decided not to rush things, however. We had plenty of time and we wanted to do everything just right. I must admit that part of me wanted to have sex with Jordan so bad I could hardly stand it, but I was content to just hold him close and kiss him. The rest could wait. There was something romantic, sexy, and arousing about waiting. I knew it would be that much more special when we finally did make love. Who says teenaged boys only think of sex and have no self control?

*   *   *

"We've got a *BIG* problem," said Denise, almost before she was in the door.

It was Saturday morning. Mom and Dad were out shopping and Jordan and I were fixing a late breakfast.

"What?" said Jordan and I almost at the same time.

"This," she said, handing us a supermarket tabloid. Right on the front it read "JORDAN KIDNAPED".

"Shit!" said Jordan.

"Look inside," said Denise.

"Oh fuck," I said. There, as clear as day, was a picture of Jordan and *me*, side by side, in the Burger Dude. Denise took the paper back and read part of it.

> "...Jordan was last seen with a teenaged boy in Evansville, Indiana, hundreds of miles from where he disappeared. Authorities are not yet certain whether or not the boy is connected with the kidnapping. A ransom note demanding $100 million dollars has allegedly been received by Jordan's management company..."

"What a load of shit!" I said.

"Well consider the source," said Jordan. "They're always printing up lies about me, but this..."

"It's not just them," said Denise. She took us into the living room and turned on a news channel. It wasn't long before Jordan's face popped up on the screen. His disappearance had hit the national news. Jordan sank down on the couch and buried his head in his hands.

"I'm so stupid," he said. "I should have known I couldn't just walk away."

Mom and Dad picked just then to come back. Jordan's face was the screen, but it didn't matter, they already knew.

"You two have some explaining to do," said my father. He wasn't in a good mood at all. We followed him and Mom back into the kitchen and sat down at the table. Denise stood over to the side.

"What were you two thinking?" asked Dad.

"It's my fault," said Jordan. "Ralph didn't even know I was coming here. I just kind of showed up. I had to get away. It was all getting to me. You don't know what it's like."

"No, I don't, but I know you can't run from your troubles son, and now you've caused a whole lot of people a whole lot of trouble."

"Yes sir."

Jordan looked out the window, as if expecting to see squad cars surrounding the house or something. It wouldn't have surprised me too much. How long would it take before the authorities tracked Jordan down? I could just picture a swat team training automatic weapons on the farm house.

"I've got to put an end to this," said Jordan. He went to the bedroom and came back with his cell phone. I didn't even know that he had it. "I've had it turned off," he said in answer to my unspoken question. He dialed a number.

"Hey, it's Jordan," he said. I kind of wished I could hear the other end of the conversation. "Chill dude, I'm fine. No, I wasn't kidnapped. I'm staying with a friend. No, no one is making me say that. Okay, okay. If it will make you feel better fine, but I'm telling you nothing is wrong. I just had to get away for a while. I'm sure they are upset, but tough, it's *my* life! Okay, yeah. I'll call you back after that. No, I'm not leaving the phone on. All right. Bye."

"My manager," said Jordan. "Um, I hope you don't mind, but he wants me to call the state police and have them come here, just to be sure you're not all kidnappers and were forcing me to say that stuff."

"I'll call," said Mom, and dialed 911.

Jordan dialed another number with his cell phone.

"Hey, Ross. It's Jordan…" He walked into the other room as he spoke and I couldn't quite tell what he was saying. He was back in just a few minutes.

"I'm really sorry about all this," Jordan said to Dad. There was no doubt he was sincere.

"Come with me," said Dad. He took Jordan outside and I saw them walking down the hill. I wondered what Dad was saying to him.

*   *   *

"You okay?" I asked, after Jordan had returned from his walk with Dad, and the state police trooper had departed.

"Yeah."

"What did he say, Dad that is?"

"He was pretty cool about it all, not too happy, but we talked and I think he understood. It was kind of a Father/son talk. I hope you don't mind me borrowing your dad."

"No," I said laughing, "any time." "Um, what about your dad Jordan? Shouldn't you call your parents or something? Won't they be worried?"

"No. I'm not sure where my mom is, probably on some beach somewhere." I had the feeling they weren't close. "My dad died before I was born. He…killed himself. I don't think he even knew about me. I wish I could have known him."

I pulled Jordan to me and hugged him. I'd always thought his life was perfect, but he was just like the rest of us. He had problems, pain, and worries. I couldn't imagine having never known my own father, and being so distant from my mother. It must have made Jordan feel very alone sometimes. My heart ached for him and I hugged him closer, letting him know that he'd never be alone again.

Jordan

———————— ◆ ————————

One thing I noticed about Ralph's parents was that they didn't act any different after they found out I was a famous rock star. To them, I was the same old Jordan that had been staying with them for a few days. It really didn't matter to them. I liked that. I liked it a lot. The only thing Ralph's mom ever said about it was "I just can't imagine." That made me laugh.I was glad that Ralph's parents didn't toss me out on my ass after they found out what I'd done. They were upset and had a right to be. They were pretty cool about it, however.

Poor Ross, I'd been thinking about him a lot. I knew I'd put him in a tough spot. He must have been going crazy when the whole "Jordan Kidnapped" story broke. There he was, with all hell breaking loose, and he couldn't say anything. I should have made it a point to call him every day, just in case he needed to talk to me. I just wasn't thinking. I'd talked to him a lot in the last day, however. He was cool about everything. When I apologized, all he said was "No problem dude." It was a typical Ross comment.

My time with Ralph was coming to an end. I had to go back, and soon. In just a week *Phantom* would be starting the second half of the tour. I had run away because I couldn't take it, but I'd quickly come to miss some of the very things I thought I couldn't take. I almost couldn't believe it, but I missed my frantic schedule. I missed Ross and Kieran, but that was no surprise. I expected to miss them. I didn't expect to miss everything else. Hell, I even missed the tour bus and the hotel rooms, and the paparazzi. What I missed most of all was the music. I was dying to get my hands on a keyboard. My time on the farm had made me remember what it was all about—the music. I didn't know what I'd do if I couldn't perform. I was itching to get back to it, to the crowds, to the screaming girls—all of it. There was nothing else like it, doing exactly what I loved to do, and being loved for it.

What had really sent me running was the story about that girl committing suicide because I'd rejected her. That had pushed me over the edge. I'd been trying to tell myself that it wasn't true, that it was just like the rest of the garbage those tabloids printed, but I couldn't quite shake it. It was always there, in the back of my mind, tormenting me. I didn't say much about it to Ralph, but it was eating at me.

Only a few hours after the whole "Jordan Kidnapped" debacle, Kieran called me with the best news I'd ever had in my life—it had been made up, all of it. Our management company and our record company were both suing the tabloid that had run the story. According to Kieran, the tabloid was disavowing responsibility and claiming to be just as shocked and outraged as everyone else that it wasn't true. The tabloid's position was that one of its reporters had fabricated the story on his own and had even presented fake source material to the editors. That could have been true I guess, but I really doubted that the tabloid ever bothered to check sources. It didn't change anything. What they did was wrong. It hurt me and a lot of people. I couldn't even begin to describe the pain and anguish it had caused me. I was relieved beyond measure to find out it wasn't true. I knew it couldn't possibly have been true as written, but I feared some girl had killed herself over an imagined slight and it was difficult to live with that hanging over my head. There were people who would still believe the story. They'd believe my management company or someone was discrediting the reporter and covering it all up to save my career. I didn't care what they believed, however. I knew now that it wasn't true and that's all that mattered.

*   *   *

With the suicide story proven false, I was more eager than ever to get back to my life. Not all was well, however. As much as I wanted to go back, I didn't want to leave Ralph. I loved him. It might seem silly to love someone I'd known such a short time, but love him I did. I knew it wasn't just a passing phase either. It wasn't because he was the first boy with whom I'd been able to have a relationship. There was something special about him. He was the one. Somehow, in my heart, I knew it.

I was torn. I couldn't live without my music, it was a part of me, it was me. I couldn't live without Ralph either. No matter what I did, I was screwed. How could I go back to my old life if it meant leaving Ralph behind? How could I not go back? I felt like I could never be happy again, because I couldn't be in two places at once. I couldn't be on the road, and on the farm, at the same time.

I knew Ralph was thinking about the future too. He was happy for the most part, but there was a sad edge to him. I know he was trying to hide it, but I know he was worried about what was going to happen. He knew I couldn't stay there forever and he had to be wondering how he was going to fit into my life. I didn't know the answer, but one thing was for certain. I was determined that he would be in my life, no matter what.

I wasn't nearly as skilled at hiding my feelings as Ralph. I moped around and it didn't take Ralph long at all to notice it. Actually, saying he noticed it instantly would be nearer the mark. He didn't wait long to confront me about it either.

"Spill it," he said as we were walking along the stream again. I loved how he could be so direct. I told him what was on my mind. He started talking to me about it, but as soon as the words began to come from his lips, I began to ignore him. My mind was racing. I'd thought of something. I had a wonderful idea. I interrupted him in mid-sentence.

"Why don't you come with me?" I asked. I was almost jumping up and down with excitement.

"Come with you?"

"Yeah, on the road."

"But…"

"Come on, it's perfect! School's out. You've got the whole summer don't you? Just think of all the places you can see. And we'll be together!"

Ralph didn't look very happy. It brought me down immediately.

"Ralph, what's wrong?" I asked.

"My parents would never let me do that."

"Why not?"

"Because they're… parents."

"We can at least try."

"And if they say 'no'?"

"Then we're no worse off than we are now. It's worth a shot. I'll do the talking. I can be very persuasive."

"This I gotta see," smiled Ralph.

"You would like it though? Right?"

"Oh heck yeah! It would be awesome, beyond awesome! I just don't want to get my hopes up. It'll hurt that much more when you go if I do."

"Don't be so pessimistic," I said. Ralph smiled wanly.

It was a few hours before we had a chance to talk to Ralph's parents. I was more nervous than I'd been in a long time. It was easier standing in front of a crowd of thousands, than to sit at the kitchen table and talk with them.

"Go on tour with you?" asked Ralph's mom when I broached the topic.

"Yeah, Ralph could travel with me, on the tour bus. He'd get to see all kinds of places. We'll be traveling all over the country."

"I don't like the idea of him traveling around unsupervised," said Ralph's mom. I actually laughed.

"Unsupervised? No way. More like over supervised. I have a personal bodyguard whose job is to do nothing but supervise. Ross and Kieran each have their own bodyguard too. All three of them watch over us.

Then there's my manager, and my publicist, at least one of them travels with me all the time. Then there's the stage crew. Wherever we go there will be security. Ralph couldn't be better supervised or guarded if he was in one of those armored trucks. He'll be watched every minute, just like me." I think I made some headway with that argument.

"I don't know," said Ralph's dad.

"Please Dad," said Ralph. "Jordan will be going to Los Angeles, New York, and all over! I might never get the chance to see some of those places. And you've been saying how I need to get a job. Jordan said I could work with the stage crew and help him at autograph signings and such." Ralph's dad looked at me, asking with his eyes if the job was legitimate.

"If he can't come, my management company will have to hire someone else. We're short a man," I said, and I wasn't lying. "Listen, I can call up my management company and you can ask anything you want. I know you can't just let Ralph go without thinking it over, but talk to my manager okay?"

Ralph and I worked on his parents for quite a while longer, describing the advantages for him, and me, and pointing out how safe he would be. We weren't lying about anything. He would be well supervised. He'd always be with someone. Life on the road was not private. I was hoping Ralph and I could manage some private time, but that was another matter.

It all went better than I'd hoped, and way better than Ralph had feared. I got my manager on the cell phone and handed it to Ralph's dad. Ralph and I went outside and let them talk. I'd already called my manager before and told him about the idea, and how much I wanted Ralph to come with me. I told him I thought it would help me deal with all the stuff that had caused me to run, and it would. I even hinted that I wouldn't come back if Ralph didn't come with me. My manager was in my corner. He had to be. If I didn't return, he was out of a job.

Ralph and I took our time walking around. When we got out of sight of the house, we joined hands. It felt so good to hold his hand. I'd always envied the guys that could hold their girl's hand, and the guys that could hold their boyfriend's hand even more. Out in the fields, there was no one to see us.

I knew my time with Ralph might be very short. I really needed to head back as soon as possible, but I didn't want to go if I'd be leaving Ralph behind. I tried to think positively, but I knew that things might not work out like I wanted.

I'd been thinking a lot about something, but I was afraid to mention it. So far, Ralph and I hadn't done anything more than make out. Some of our make out sessions were pretty hot and heavy, but we hadn't gone any further. If Ralph did have to stay behind, I wondered if maybe we shouldn't take things further, before I left. I definitely wanted to go beyond what we'd done. That was an understatement if there ever was one. Sometimes, I just wanted to… Well, you know.

Ralph and I stopped and kissed at the far edge of the fields. His lips were warm and moist, his eyes beautiful as I looked into them. I loved him with all my heart. I came within a hair's breadth of speaking my mind about our physical relationship, but I held back. I'd wait and see what happened, and what Ralph's parents decided. If he couldn't come with me, then I'd approach him, maybe.

We walked on and I wondered what I'd do if Ralph's parents wouldn't let him come with me. I could call him every single day, but it wouldn't be the same. After the tour was over, I could even fly in to see him a lot, but there would be no time for that during the tour itself. Once the second half started, there would be no chance to get away.

We walked back the way we'd come. We were standing in the kitchen of the farmhouse again almost before we knew it. Ralph's parents were sitting there. His Dad looked at us and said one word.

"Okay."

"You mean it!?" said Ralph.

"Of course I mean it. I wouldn't have said it if I didn't mean it," said his Dad with a touch of a smile.

"Yes!" said Ralph. "Oh yes!"

Ralph

◆

The world had gone crazy, or maybe hell had frozen over. Not only had I actually met Jordan, and become his friend, and his boyfriend, but my parents had said "okay" to me traveling with him for the entire summer. Each event seemed less likely to take place than the one before, and yet it had all happened.

Once the decision had been made, we moved quickly. Jordan called his management company and they had things set up for us in a flash. We were scheduled to depart in only two days.

We used what time we had left on the farm to our advantage. Jordan explained that we'd have very little time alone once we left. That didn't surprise me. I knew it would be hectic. Jordan and I spent as much time alone together as we could manage. A great deal of that time was spent hugging and making out. I considered the possibility of taking things further, but there was something so romantic and exciting about waiting. I never thought that it could be true, but not having sex was sexy. I knew that when the moment finally came, it would be beyond awesome.

We spent some time with Denise and Chris too. I wouldn't be seeing them for nearly three months and I'd never been parted from them for so long. We hadn't even left and I was experiencing a bout of homesickness. The truth was, I'd never been away from home for any extended period of time. I was already missing my parents, and my friends. The thought of not going didn't even occur to me, despite the homesickness. I wasn't about to miss out on what was to come for anything. I did make an effort to appreciate my last few days on the farm as best I could. It seemed a much nicer and more interesting place now that I knew I was soon to leave it.

Denise was thrilled beyond belief that I was going on tour with *Phantom*. She could not have possibly been happier for me. I loved Denise. She was the most selfless person I knew. It often amazed me how much pleasure she could derive from the happiness of others. Her own life hardly seemed to matter to her. The kindness she showed others rewarded her, by coming back to her. By being happy for others, she was made happy herself. I couldn't think of anyone who deserved it more.

If I'd been a straight boy, I think that Denise would have made a good girlfriend. We probably would have not dated even then, however. We had such a wonderful friendship that it was best as it was. Dating would have messed things up. There was no real reason to even think about it, because I wasn't straight and would never be, and I had the best boyfriend ever!

I knew I'd miss Chris. He was my best friend. I shared a lot of things with Chris and we always had a good time when we were together. He'd been more entertaining than ever lately. I found it very hard not to laugh when I was with both him and Jordan. Before I met Jordan, Chris had done nothing but poke fun at him, and at me for liking him. Chris probably came up with more *Phantom* and Jordan putdowns and jokes than anyone, and he hurled them all at me without mercy. He'd done a quick about-face when he actually met Jordan. I could tell he was in awe of him. Chris couldn't quite get over the fact that Jordan was a famous rock star. I'd seen Jordan shake his head when Chris was fawning over him, as if to say "Oh please!" Sometimes I felt like smacking Chris in the back of the head, but Jordan was patient with him, probably because Chris had such great entertainment value. Jordan took an almost sadistic pleasure in taunting Chris. All the putdowns and jokes Chris had hurled at me in the past were coming back to haunt him. Time after time he turned red and then apologized profusely, until he noticed that Jordan was smiling. I was delighted.

I knew Jordan found Chris to be a pain at times. Chris was too obviously impressed with Jordan's fame. Jordan might have quickly grown tired of him, but he knew what a good friend he'd been to me. We were both hoping the Chris would calm down with time. One day he even brought a camera and started snapping pictures. I got him alone and told him to knock it off.

I actually had to walk away to keep from laughing when Chris brought a picture for Jordan to autograph. It was just too funny. The boy who had ridiculed Jordan had become an adoring fan. Jordan was very kind to him, however. He even told him, he'd get tickets and backstage passes for him and some friends when the tour came back to Indiana. Chris seemed a different person from the one he was on the day he had tried to make me say "Jordan is a girl."

*   *   *

I looked out the terminal window at the 747, still unable to believe that we'd be taking off for Los Angeles in just a few minutes. I'd never been on a plane before, much less a big one, much less in first class. I was overwhelmed.

Jordan wasn't trying to disguise himself anymore. He did wear his baseball cap and sunglasses until we got on the plane, but he took them off after we got on. Some girls recognized him and were so excited I thought they were going to pee their pants. There were only four of them. Jordan spoke to them in a low voice and they calmed down. One of them was actually crying. Another one kept jumping up and down. Jordan stopped and signed autographs for them as the stewardess showed me to our seats. Five minutes passed and there was still no

Jordan. I was beginning to get worried. Maybe those girls had kidnapped him or something. It was about time for us to take off and he still wasn't there. I guess I didn't need to worry, he was on the plane after all.

"Sorry," he said, as he plopped down in the seat beside me.

"No problem." I told him. "It must be tough being so wonderful." I snickered. Jordan punched me in the shoulder.

"Think you're funny huh?"

"Yeah!"

He laughed.

I was nervous as our plane taxied out, and more so as it took off. I wasn't scared, just nervous. I didn't see how such a big piece of metal could fly, but it obviously could. When we got in the air, I was fine. I looked out the window and everything got smaller and smaller.

It didn't seem to take us any time at all to get to O'Hare in Chicago. We had to switch flights there. There wasn't a nonstop from Evansville to L.A. That wasn't surprising.

Jordan's bodyguard met us as we got off the plane. Man was he built, and big. I had the feeling he could rip my head off with his bare hands if he took a notion to do it. He gave Jordan a scowl, no doubt for sneaking off, but then a smile.

"Sorry," said Jordan coyly.

"Sure you are," said Mike.

"Well, I'm not sorry for going, but I am sorry for any trouble I caused you."

"I'd have done the same if I was you probably. Just don't do it again, ever, or you'll get me fired! You know how I love my job guarding the Prince of Rock and Roll."

"Shut up! You know I hate it when you call me that!" said Jordan.

"Yes I do," said Mike. "It's part of your punishment for ditching me. So behave or you'll be hearing it a lot more." I could tell Jordan and Mike had an interesting relationship.

"Prince of Rock and Roll huh?" I asked with a devilish grin.

"Don't you start!" said Jordan. I learned later that it was a nickname Ross and Kieran often tormented him with. I filed away the name in my mind for possible future use.

"You guys met briefly in Fort Wayne, but Ralph, this is the secret service. Mike, this is my friend Ralph."

If I hadn't known better, I might have actually believed that Mike was a secret service man. He looked like one, right down to the ear-piece. He was awfully big, however, like a professional bodybuilder or something. I felt small compared to him.

Airport security picked us up moments later and it was a good thing. At first our passing just turned a few heads, but pretty soon a small crowd was going along with us. It turned into a big crowd within seconds and we could barely move. I was afraid it was going to be the whole Burger Dude fiasco all over again, except on a much larger scale. Flashes from cameras started going off and I got blinded and couldn't see for a bit. Security pushed me along and kept me from falling on my face. Girls were reaching in and trying to touch Jordan.

Jordan was smiling and saying "hi" to people. He was shaking outstretched hands as he passed. It didn't seem to bother him at all. Then again, I guess he was used to it. It was all new to me. I couldn't imagine living like that. I guess I wouldn't have to imagine it. When I was with Jordan, I'd be living it.

I looked around in a bewildered state as I was pushed along. I must admit, I kind of liked it. It was almost like being famous myself. A lot of girls were looking at me. I bet they were wondering who I was. Maybe they thought I was a new band member. I even overhead one say "That boy with Jordan is cute." I liked hearing that, even if I didn't agree with her.

We got to board the next plane before anyone else. I think airport security thought it was easier that way. I already knew Jordan lived a life quite different from my own, but my experience in the airport really brought the point home. It was funny, but in the short time I'd known Jordan, I'd come to think of him as just a regular person. Sometimes I forgot he was a rock star. When I did remember, my life seemed unreal. How was it possible? I was dating the boy on all the teen magazines. Talk about weird.

If I thought Chicago was wild, it was nothing compared to L.A. The plane didn't pull up to the terminal. Instead, they brought one of those big flights of stairs up to it. Me and Mike got off with Jordan. Some guy was waiting for us at the bottom of the stairs. He shook Jordan's hand, then followed us.

There was a huge crowd behind a chain-linked fence screaming and yelling. Some of them were holding up signs saying things like "I love you Jordan!", "Phantom Rules", and "Jordan Kicks Ass". There were more camera flashes, but they didn't bother me because we were out-side.

My eyes got big when I saw the big limousine waiting for us. It was huge. I got in behind Jordan. I'd never seen a back seat that big before. It wasn't just a backseat, it was two backseats facing each other. It was like a lounge or something. There was even a television and a DVD player and everything. Jordan opened a small refrigerator and tossed me a soda.

"This is Ben, he represents me for my management company," said Jordan as we pulled away.

"You must be Ralph. Nice to meet you."

The guy seemed likeable enough, but he'd barely introduced himself before he turned back to Jordan.

"Your publicist is waiting at the hotel. I've scheduled a press confer-ence for you at 8 p.m., the press is clamoring for a statement on your disappearance. I've also scheduled an autograph session with Ross and Kieran tomorrow morning at 10. Now, we need to go over what you're going to say about this whole kidnapping situation."

"I've missed you too," said Jordan with more than a hint of sarcasm.

Ben kept rattling on about this and that. It didn't take me long to tune him out. He was all business, and boring.

I felt a little out of place. Everyone was paying attention to Jordan, and I wasn't sure he even knew I was there. I was beginning to wonder if all this was such a good idea after all.

Jordan

———————— ◆ ————————

I thought everyone would be pissed because I'd run off, but no one said much about it, except that I'd better not do it again. Of course, I'd let Ross know I was going. Without his help I couldn't have accomplished my getaway in the first place. He'd told Kieran, so the two that really mattered had known all about it. I hadn't been completely thoughtless when I ran away either. I did run for it during the break in our tour. I knew the management company was probably sweating it, okay, they were probably having a cow. If I hadn't come back, things would have been a mess, but I did come back. I wasn't even gone that long. It seemed longer, but it was only a few days.

I think most of those around me, and particularly the management company, were afraid to say too much about my disappearance. I think they were afraid that if they pushed me too far, or gave me too much crap about it, that I'd disappear again, and for good. They'd be screwed then. I'd undoubtedly get my ass sued off if I violated my contract, but the management company knew they'd come out looking like a big, evil corporation picking on a teenaged boy. They also knew my fans would turn on them. No one had anything to worry about, however. I wasn't sorry I'd ran, but I realized it was a rather immature thing to do. There were better ways of dealing with problems. If the pressure got to be too much again, I'd find a better way to handle it. My short time away from my usual life gave me a better appreciation for it. I'd learned that I missed many of the very things that had stressed me out. No, I wasn't going to run again. Besides, with Ralph at my side, I could handle anything.

My publicist was the most understanding of all those around me, except for Ross and Kieran of course. When we met her in my hotel room, she didn't seem to mind at all. She was all excited over the publicity prospects.

"You can't buy publicity like this," she said excitedly. "It was brilliant. You were on all the network news broadcasts, satellite, and cable news programs—all of them! Plus radio and newspapers. It would have cost millions if we had to buy all that. The concerts are selling out faster than ever and two restaurant chains are wanting *Phantom* for commercials."

My publicist was definitely good at her job. Listening to her made me feel guilty, however. I hadn't run for publicity. The way I saw it, I didn't need any more. My face was already on the cover of every teen magazine all over the world. Sometimes I felt like my face was on everything. I was amazed that everyone didn't get sick of looking at me. No, I hadn't run for publicity, but I hadn't thought much about anyone but myself when I did it.

My manager had told me the *Phantom* hotline had received hundreds of calls from crying girls all upset over my disappearance. Some of them were even getting together in groups to go looking for me. There were postings in all kinds of internet newsgroups saying I was dead, that I'd been killed in a plane crash, that I'd been killed in a car wreck, and even that I'd been gunned down outside my hotel room. What got to me was the letters and emails from girls all hysterical with worry over me. There were thousands of them. It was all out of control. I'd never thought that I'd be causing so many people so much pain. The truth is, I hadn't thought at all. I just ran. It was selfish of me.

*   *   *

The conference room of the hotel was absolutely stuffed with reporters when I arrived for the press conference. As soon as I stepped into view, the room exploded with camera flashes. Lights from video cameras blinded me. There were shouted questions, but I ignored them. I took my place behind the podium and just stood there looking at them. When the room quieted a bit, I spoke.

"Before taking any questions, I'd like to make a statement," I said. "The rumors that I was kidnapped are false. I don't know how the rumors got started, but there is no truth to them whatsoever. The rumors of my death, by various means, are obviously also false." That got a few laughs, but it wasn't a humorous occasion.

"What has happened, is simply a misunderstanding. I felt the need to get away from my hectic life for a short time, and did so without adequately informing my management company. I was never in any danger. My 'disappearance' was nothing more than a short vacation.

"I want to thank all the fans that have expressed concern over my 'disappearance'. I can't possibly answer the thousands of phone calls, letters, and emails, so I wanted to say 'thank you' now. I can't tell you how much I appreciate your concern, and your love.

"I also want to apologize to my fans that were worried by the rumors. I have no control over rumors, but I do bear responsibility in that I departed in such a way that it led to the rumors. For that, I am truly sorry. I care about all of you deeply. You make my life possible, and I can't bear the thought that my actions have brought you pain. So once again, I apologize to my fans and hope that all of you understand."

The statement was difficult, but it was the easy part. The questions came next and I found it hard to answer many of them.

"It has been said that your disappearance was nothing more than a publicity stunt. What is your response to that?" asked a reporter.

"That is absolutely false. I left because I was under a great deal of stress and greatly disturbed by the tabloid story that a girl took her own life because of me. I simply felt I had to get away. My departure was not

planned in advance and neither my publicist or management company
knew anything about it."

I knew a lot of people wouldn't believe me. They'd think that's just
what it was, a publicity stunt. I didn't like them thinking that, but I
couldn't do anything about it. I'd made my choice when I ran, and now
I had to take my medicine.

"What do you have to say about the tabloid report that a young girl
took her life because you rejected her, now that it has been proven
false?"

"The tabloids have a long history of printing exaggerations and
sometimes outright lies about me and others. I don't mind it so much
when they claim I'm an alien, but reports such as the one about the girl
are irresponsible and damaging. That story brought me a great amount
of personal pain and anguish. I can't even express how angry and upset
I am over the falsified story."

"Is it true you are suing the tabloid over the story?"

"My management company is suing the tabloid on my behalf. I have
nothing to do with the process myself. No amount of money can make
up for what that story put me through. I'd like to make a personal
appeal to my fans to not purchase such tabloids. If no one buys them,
they won't be able to publish stories like that anymore. So please, stop
buying them."

"There is a rumor that you are secretly dating actress Julia Landry. Is
it true?"

I hated questions about my love-life. Anything I said made me feel
like a liar. I certainly couldn't answer that the rumor wasn't true because
I was dating Ralph.

"I'm a great admirer of Julia Landry, but we are not dating and have,
in fact, never met."

"Would you date her, if you got the chance?"

"I don't think such a relationship would even be possible. Our schedules wouldn't permit it. Besides, I'm sure Julia Landry has better taste

than that." Some of the reporters laughed. I often tried to joke myself out of questions about my dating habits.

"Are you dating any girl at the moment?"

Damn, the dating question just would not go away. It pursued me like the Hounds of Hell.

"I'm in the middle of a concert tour right now and have a busy schedule. I don't even really have the time for this press conference, much less for a girlfriend."

There were a lot more questions, many about my "disappearance" and a great many others besides. A lot of them were about really meaningless stuff, but I was accustomed to those. They were a lot easier to answer than questions about girlfriends.

I apologized to my fans again at the end of the press conference. I knew I'd caused a lot of them pain, and for that I was sorry. I should have thought more about the consequences of my actions before taking off like I did. Had I done so, I would have realized what would happen. I wasn't thinking straight when I'd taken off. If I had been, I'd never have done it.

I left the press conference feeling drained and very unhappy with myself. I'd done something stupid that had caused a lot of pain. I wasn't about to do that again. Like it or not, I wasn't a private person, I belonged to my fans. I couldn't do something foolish like that without hurting them, and that I did not want to do.

That evening, I was on all the news programs again. I didn't intend to watch, but my publicist dropped in just before time for the news to begin in L.A. I had looked forward to spending some time alone with Ralph, but there was no chance of that. My publicist kept flipping through channels, practically squealing with delight. She was especially excited by the fans reaction.

"They love you," she said. I was so embarrassed I wanted to crawl under my chair. It was worse because Ralph was there to hear it.

I was so glad when my publicist left and we had a little time alone. We didn't have much time, it was past eleven and I had to get up early, so did Ralph.

"I guess you think I'm a big jerk," I said to him.

"Why would I think that?"

"That," I said, pointing to the now blank television screen. "I really didn't think everyone would get so upset. All those girls…" I was on the verge of crying. Ralph came over and held me and petted my hair.

"Hey, hey, you didn't know. You didn't mean to hurt anyone."

"Yeah, but I didn't think about it at all. It was just me, me, me. I didn't have a right…" Tears were rolling down my cheeks.

"Of course you did."

"No, I didn't."

"Hey," said Ralph, taking my chin in his hand and making me look at him, "those girls would understand if they knew. They'd be cool with it."

"How do you know?"

"Because I would," Ralph told me. He didn't speak for a moment to let the meaning sink in. "Listen, if you'd gone somewhere else, and I heard about you being missing, and I would have, I'd have been upset. Okay, I'd have been real upset. I'd have cried and worried, just like them. But it would have all been cool when I found out you were okay. The relief would have been worth it. And if I knew the whole story, I'd have understood."

I was feeling a little better despite myself. For the moment, I felt that I needed to feel bad. I guess I wanted to punish myself for what I'd done.

"It wasn't that bad Jordan. You did the best you could. When you found out that everyone thought you'd been kidnapped, how long was it before you acted? Huh? You were on that phone as fast as you could get there. You weren't thinking about yourself then, you just did your best to keep everyone else from worrying."

"I'm sorry I did it. It was stupid," I said.

"I'm not sorry," said Ralph. He looked into my eyes. "I've always loved you. That night we spent together in Ft. Wayne was like a dream, a dream come true. You have no idea how happy I was just having that night to remember. Spending those few hours with you was the best thing that had ever happened to me. Even if I hadn't run into you at the hotel, even if I'd just seen you at the concert, that would have been the best thing ever. When our eyes met, and you were singing "Do you know that I love you" I really felt like you were singing it just to me. I'd have remembered that forever."

"I was singing it just to you," I said, smiling shyly. Ralph smiled back.

"What happened in Ft. Wayne was the best ever, until you showed up at my door. I couldn't believe it. I never thought I'd see you again, but there you were. I'm not sorry you ran at all, because you ran to me. I love so much Jordan! I'm so happy when I'm with you." Ralph hugged me close. I hugged him back and told him how much I loved him too. I never meant any words more than I did those.

It felt so good to be in Ralph's arms. I knew I was the luckiest boy in the world, and it had nothing to do with being rich or famous. I was lucky because I had Ralph. Some people lived their whole lives without finding love like that. I had more than I deserved and I knew it. It made me determined to help others as much as I could. I knew there was a lot I could do that I hadn't done before. That was going to change. My talent was a gift. My fame and fortune all came from that. I'd tried to use it to help others before, but I was going to do a lot better job of it from now on. Ralph had made me a better person and I loved him all the more.

Ralph

———— ◆ ————

I woke up the next morning, still in my clothes, on the couch with Jordan. It was about half past six. I shook Jordan awake and told him what time it was. Just moments later, Mike entered with a Burger Dude bag.

"Breakfast. I hope you like this stuff." Mike said to me.

"Oh yeah! Thanks."

"I'm gonna grab a shower," said Jordan, and rushed for the bathroom after grabbing a French toast square.

I sat and talked with Mike while I ate.

"So you're going on tour with us?" said Mike.

"Yeah, Jordan says I'm going to be kind of a personal assistant, kind of a gopher."

"Maybe you can start going to Burger Dude for the guys then."

"Sure," I said. "I want to help out however I can."

"You're not after my job, are you?" asked Mike. At first I thought he was serious, then I noticed his grin.

"Like I could do your job! All those fans would just push me over."

"The trick is to look mean and intimidating," said Mike.

"I don't think I could manage that," I told him.

"Just don't show fear." I couldn't tell if he was serious or not this time. "Hey, I have to take care of some security details for the signing, nice to meet you, Ralph."

Mike hadn't been gone for more than a few seconds before Ross and Kieran burst into the room. I was a little overwhelmed. I was used to seeing Jordan, but not them. The first thing I thought was "There's the guys from *Phantom!*", like it was a total surprise to see them. Then I remembered whose hotel room I was sitting in, and that I was about to join the *Phantom* road crew. It was still kind of surreal.

"Call security, it's a crazed fan!" yelled Ross and hit the floor when he saw me.

"Shut up Ross!" said Kieran. "You'll have to forgive Ross, his mom dropped him on his head a few too many times when he was a baby."

"She liked to watch me bounce!" said Ross. I'd heard Ross was wild, but he was quite an experience in person. He acted like he'd just eaten a five pound bag of sugar. He tapped his fingers on the table, or the chair, or Kieran, or me almost constantly. I could see why he was a drummer.

"I'm Kieran."

"Ralph."

"You're here to replace me aren't you!?" yelled Ross so loud I was sure the whole hotel could hear. "I knew it! You're a drummer! Jordan went out and found a new drummer! Ohhhhhhhhhhhhh!"

"Sit down hyper-boy," said Kieran. I couldn't help but laugh.

"You have NOTHING to worry about, believe me," I said to Ross. "I'm going to be Jordan's assistant, probably yours too."

"Oh, okay, so I'd like a dozen donuts, some chocolate milk…" said Ross as if placing an order. Kieran just shook his head.

"What?" said Ross as if he had no idea he was acting crazy. Jordan came out of the bathroom just then, wearing nothing but a towel. Ross whistled.

"Hey sexy!" Ross yelled. "I missed you!" He ran across the room and clasped Jordan in a bear hug, practically knocking his towel off.

"Run out of Prozac again?" asked Jordan, but he smiled. I could tell he was glad to see him.

"I see you guys have met Ralph."

"Yeah," said Ross, "he said he was going to be our new slave… I mean assistant."

"*My* assistant, thank you very much," said Jordan.

Ross made a gesture behind Jordan's back, as if to say Jordan was getting a big head. Jordan caught him at it and punched him in the arm.

"See what I have to put up with?" he said to me.

Jordan dressed, then sat down and ate his breakfast. Ross tried to steal one of his French toast squares, but Jordan slapped his hand.

"You've already had yours," he said laughing.

Ross settled down and Jordan filled the guys in on what I'd be doing I could tell I was going to like spending my time with Ross and Kieran. I was already having fun. I wonder what everyone at school would think if they knew I was hanging out with *Phantom* for the summer. I was almost sorry school was out so I couldn't go back and tell them.

Before I knew it, it was time to go. Ben, the manager, stuck his head in the room and everyone scurried for the door. I was hard pressed to keep up. Minutes later, we were in another big limousine and headed for the local radio station for a signing. Jordan, Ross, and Kieran had probably done it a million times, but it was my first. I was especially excited because it was my first real day as Jordan's assistant. I'd be sitting at the table with the guys, taking whatever the fans wanted signed, and handing it off to whomever sat next to me.

Ross never shut up the whole time we were in the limo. He was a bundle of nervous energy. He kept tapping his fingers on things. He tapped and tapped and tapped. He never stopped. He also kept flinging his hair back, trying to keep it out of his face. He had the longest hair of all three of the boys. It came down well past his shoulders.

There was a big crowd outside the radio station, well more like huge. The signing was being done in the parking lot and it was filled. There was a roped off area where the boys would be signing, and doing an interview. The autograph line was already full. It was set up with ropes so that the line zigzagged back and forth. There was tons of security.

I was deafened by the screams as we got out of the car. There was just a short distance to walk before reaching the roped off area, but it wasn't easy getting there. Everyone was pushed in so close I was afraid I'd get lost. I grabbed onto the back of Jordan's shirt and let one of the security guards push me along. I was kind of glad that I wasn't famous.

There was a long table with a banner across the front that read "*Phantom*" where the boys would be signing. I made for it as the guys went over to another table with microphones where'd they be doing the interview. I was glad to be out of the center of things for the moment. I placed the box I'd been carrying on the table and began to set out several markers for the guys to use.

"Do you know *Phantom*?"

I turned toward the voice, it belonged to a girl about thirteen right near the front of the line.

"Well, yeah," I said.

"Is Jordan really as nice as he seems?" she asked. "I can't imagine he wouldn't be." She was so excited she was bouncing up and down.

"Oh yeah, he's really nice," I said. I was glad I could give her the answer she wanted. I don't think she'd have liked it at all if I'd said any different.

"I got here at 5 a.m. this morning," she said. "I just had to meet *Phantom*, especially Jordan, he's soooooo cute!"

"Well you will." I told her. My grasp of the obvious was magnificent, but I didn't quite know what to say. It had never occurred to me that I'd be talking to any of *Phantom's* fans. I wasn't accustomed to being on the other side of the fence. It was a whole new world.

"I'm Christine," she said.

"Ralph."

"Um, Ralph…" she said, beckoning me to come closer. I stepped over to her and she whispered. "Do you think you could do something for me. I feel a little silly, but…" She had me lean in closer until her lips were almost touching my ear. "Could you get some of Jordan's hair for me?" she whispered so quietly, I almost couldn't hear her. She leaned back and turned positively red with embarrassment. "I can't believe I just asked you that," she said, clapping her hand to her mouth. She was so cute and funny.

"I'll see what I can do." I told her.

It wasn't long before the interview was over and the boys came and sat down. As the DJ explained how the signing would work, I walked up behind Jordan.

"Hold still," I said. "I need to get something."

"What? Ouch!" said Jordan. I'd pulled a few strands of his hair.

"Something for one of your fans."

"I think you liked doing that," he said, rubbing the back of his head.

"Yes I did." I smiled wickedly.

"Just don't do it too often. I don't want to end up bald!"

I went back to my seat. The security guard at the head of the line started letting the fans come up a few at a time. Most of them were so busy staring at the boys that I had to remind them to give me what they wanted signed. Christine was one of the first there. When she handed me a CD to have signed, I gave her the few strands of Jordan's hair that I'd snatched for her. She positively squealed with delight.

I was sitting next to Kieran and handed him photo after photo, as well as CD's, calendars, posters, and shirts. They just kept coming. I was glad I didn't have to sign all that stuff. I just knew my hand would get a cramp.

The boys were signing fast, trying to get to everyone, but they took time to say a few words to each fan. I could hear Kieran quite clearly. Some of the girls just about fainted when he spoke to them. I could see why, Kieran was a real cutie. Being a rock star didn't hurt either I'm sure, but I think the girls would have still fainted just because of his looks.

Where I was and what I was doing dawned on me as I sat there. I almost couldn't believe it. Only yesterday I was on a little farm in

Indiana, and now I was in Los Angeles at an autograph signing with *Phantom*. I was doing the kind of thing I'd read about in magazines. Had someone told me a few weeks before that I'd be handing Kieran photos to autograph, I'd have told them they were crazy.

After we'd been there about an hour, a little girl, about eight or nine, was wheeled up in a wheel chair. Her mom told me she had MS and cancer. It seemed so unfair that a little girl like that would be afflicted with either of those things, let alone both. It broke my heart.

When Jordan saw her, he got up, walked around the table, and kneeled down so that they were eye to eye.

"You're Samantha right?"

"Mommy, he knows who I am," said the little girl, then looked back at Jordan. "You know who I am."

"Of course, you wrote me didn't you? You said you were coming."

The little girl smiled sweetly and she reached out to Jordan. He gave her a big hug and kissed her on the cheek. Kieran and Ross came around and took time to give her a lot of attention. They both gave her a kiss on the cheek too. They all signed a photo she'd brought and I saw that Jordan drew a little heart by his name. No one waiting in line seemed to mind in the least. The little girl had the biggest smile I'd ever seen when her mom wheeled her on her way. I noticed that Jordan had tears in his eyes as he walked back around the table. I loved him more than ever.

I asked him later about the little girl's letter. I knew he couldn't possibly read all the mail he got. He told me that someone handled all of *Phantom's* mail, and forwarded special letters like Samantha's. Jordan's manager had handed him the letter not long before they started signing. Letters like that were one of the things I'd be handling during the tour.

The time for the signing was going fast, but there were still a lot of people left. The security guard at the head of the line closed it off. The fans weren't happy. Jordan leaned back and spoke to Ben, his manager, who went over and spoke to the security guard. He started letting people through again. Everyone cheered. Jordan motioned to me and I came over. He gave me instructions. I walked in front of the table and waved both hands in the air.

"They've got to go in twenty minutes, so we've got to move fast!" I yelled. "When you get up here, keep it moving!"

I went back to my seat and started handling photos as quickly as I could. The minutes ticked by, and the line grew shorter. When twenty minutes had passed, there were only about fifteen people left in line. The boys shifted into high speed and signed the last few pieces, then we all ran for the limo, literally.

Jordan

———————— ◆ ————————

"Where are we going now?" asked Ralph.

"Photo shoot. Ben here sees to it that we never have a moment to spare," I said, shooting Ben a look.

"You'd have had plenty of time, if you hadn't run off into the blue," said Ben.

I could tell he wasn't happy about what I'd done at all. It was the first time he'd really said much about it, but he was fuming under the surface. I guess I couldn't blame him. My disappearance hadn't cost the management company, or anyone else, any money, but it would have if I hadn't come back. The second leg of our tour was scheduled to start in just days. I knew Ben had probably been on the verge of insanity with worry, not so much over me, but over all the concerts he'd have to cancel. The financial loss would have been staggering.

"Well I'm back from the blue," I said.

We made it into the photographer's studio without any fuss. Our session was scheduled with such short notice that no one had time to find out about it. As a result, there were no fans waiting to besiege us. That was fine by me. I loved the fans, but sometimes it was hard to get things done because of them.

I'd been through photo sessions before, but it was all new to Ralph. He leaned against the wall and watched as Andre', the photographer, started positioning us. Ralph had an amused look on his face. I'm sure he was glad it was us and not him in front of the camera. I stuck out my tongue at him. I was wise enough to do it before the filming started.

Andre' was quite an experience. He was French and had a thick accent that made him difficult to understand now and then. There were times when I thought he was speaking French. He kept snapping photos, saying "beautiful" and "marvelous". A lot of photographers used those words. I wondered if there was a photography school somewhere that taught them that kind of thing. The way Andre' said "Super" almost made me laugh. It was just too funny.

"Now Jordan," said Andre', putting me in the center, "I want you to put your hands behind your neck and look down, but look up at the camera. Kieran, turn to the side and give me a sexy look. Ross, you stand on the other side of Jordan and face him, but look at the camera, look sultry. Jordan, I need more expression—show me…desire. Now angle your head down more, but look natural."

I had to fight to keep from laughing. Andre' was posing us as if we were contortionists, but then wanted us to look natural. I glanced at Ralph for a moment. He was about to lose it. I looked quickly away. If I didn't, I knew I'd bust out laughing. Andre' took shots from various angles and positioned us again.

I kept count and we changed clothes fourteen times. Andre' went through roll after roll of film, shooting us as a group, and individually. I had a chance to talk with Ralph while Andre' was concentrating on Ross.

"So what do you think?" I asked.

"I think he's a nut case," whispered Ralph. I laughed.

"We had one in New York that was much worse."

"Not possible," said Ralph.

I looked at Ralph and wanted very much to kiss him. I knew that would not do at all. We weren't exactly alone and I couldn't risk the slightest hint of suspicion. The tabloids would just love to get a story like that. I could see the headline "JORDAN CAUGHT IN HOMOSEX-

UAL SEX ACT". That's what they'd write, if anyone caught me kissing Ralph and they found out about it. The tabloids would blow it all out of proportion. If we got caught kissing, the papers would make it sound like we were going at it like nobody's business. I knew they'd probably find out if I kissed Ralph in public. Those tabloids paid such big money for stuff like that that someone was bound to talk. I wondered just how much they'd give for a photo of me making out with Ralph.

It was so unfair. I loved Ralph. He was my boyfriend, but I couldn't tell anyone, couldn't so much as touch him in public. What made it worse was that I was always in public. Our opportunities to be alone together were definitely rare.

If I'd had a girlfriend, I wouldn't have had to worry quite so much. At least there wouldn't be a big scandal if word got out. I would have had to keep even a girlfriend secret, however. My manager and publicist were together on that one. Kieran, Ross, and I had been told to never confirm that we had a girlfriend, as it could damage our fan base. Most of our fans were young girls, and we might lose some of them if we said we had a girlfriend. I didn't like being told what to say and not say. I especially didn't like having to keep secrets because we might lose a few fans. I owed the fans a lot. They were the ones who bought the CD's, and the concert tickets, and everything else. If it weren't for them I wouldn't be able to do what I loved to do, and I'd never lose sight of that. Still, I didn't like having to hide things because of what the fans might think.

I felt like a bit of a hypocrite standing there with Ralph. I had all these high ideas about honesty and yet I was living the biggest lie of all. I didn't have to lie about not having a girlfriend, but I lied every time I made a comment that made it sound like I was interested in girls. I was careful never to say anything that could pin me down, but I knew the impression I was leaving. I was allowing others to believe what they wanted to believe. That was its own kind of lying. I wondered what all my fans would think if they knew.

"Jordan, we need you, babe," said Andre'.

I didn't have time to think more, but I had a much harder time smiling for the camera. Andre' didn't seem to mind. He liked the serious look too.

Andre' stepped up to me and started pulling my shirt over my head. I jerked it back down.

"What are you doing?" I asked him, in a not too friendly tone.

"You have a very nice torso Jordan, we need to show it off."

"No."

"No?"

"You heard me. No shirtless shots."

"Okay," pouted Andre'.

I didn't want to be filmed shirtless. It wasn't that I was ashamed of my body or anything, although I did think I was too slim, but I wanted to be taken seriously as a musician. Too many members of boy bands pulled their shirts off at the drop of the hat. I sometimes wondered if they were models or musicians. I intended to keep my shirt on.

Andre' kept shooting roll after roll of film. We were in there over six hours. To say that I was glad when we were done was an understatement. I could tell the others felt the same. Ross was practically swinging from the rafters by the end. Staying in one place for more than a few minutes was about more than he could take. He was running around getting into all kinds of mischief. Despite everything, he never failed to make me laugh.Andre' was probably glad to see him go.

Ralph

◆

I followed Jordan out of the hotel to see the tour bus sitting there. It was the very same one I'd seen in Ft. Wayne, what seemed like a life-time before. There were two other buses sitting there too, almost identical to the first, but both dark blue instead of maroon.

"There's three buses?" I asked no one in particular.

"Yeah," said Kieran, "we have way too big a road crew for just one."

I put my luggage in one of the lower compartments along with everyone else, then stepped onto the bus. As well as myself, Jordan, Kieran, and Ross, there was also Mike. Jordan told me that sometimes various others rode along too, but for now it was just us.

"Now for the grand tour," said Jordan. "This is the front lounge." He indicated a small area near the front. "We usually hang out here most of the time."

I looked around. The front lounge was part lounge, part kitchen. There was a table with built in booths, a sink, fridge, microwave, toaster, and coffee maker. There was also a television with a VCR, and satellite dish hookup. It was surprisingly roomy, but then again, the bus was pretty big.

"Here is the bathroom," said Jordan, showing me what looked more like a closet in a corner of the lounge than anything else.

"And this," said Jordan, opening a sliding door at the rear of the lounge "is the sleeping area. There's twelve bunks in all. This one is yours, right under mine."

"I like to think of mine as a coffin," yelled Ross from behind.

The bunks weren't very big. I'd say about six feet long and two wide. I wondered how well I'd sleep in mine.

"And finally," said Jordan, "is the back lounge."

The back lounge had a couch, table, television, VCR, DVD player, stereo, Playstation, Playstation II, and all kinds of video games and DVD's. Like the rest of the bus, it was awesome.

"Ross thinks the back lounge belongs to him," said Jordan in a conspiratorial whisper.

"I heard that!" yelled Ross. "And it is mine!"

"Let's head back up front," said Jordan, rolling his eyes. Despite the claims of Ross, Mike sat down in the back lounge and started watching television as the rest of us departed.

We sat down at the table with Ross and Kieran just as the bus began to pull out. I couldn't believe it, we were actually on our way. I remembered when I'd walked by this very bus when I was in Ft. Wayne. I couldn't see in the windows then and now here I was inside! It all seemed like one big adventure.

Our first destination was Dallas, which was a very long way from Los Angeles. We'd be traveling pretty much non-stop, however, and a lot of the miles would pass while I was asleep. Traveling in the bus was a lot different than traveling in a car. It was hard to tell we were even moving most of the time. The front lounge seemed more like it was part of a house than a bus.

"Time for some Risk," said Kieran.

"You do play Risk, don't you?" asked Ross.

"Um, sure," I said.

"You can't ride the bus if you don't play Risk," said Ross. "It's the rules."

Kieran set the board on the table and everyone grabbed pieces. I got stuck with yellow, which I didn't mind too much. Kieran and Ross quickly allied themselves, so I hooked up with Jordan. Between us, we controlled most of North and South America. It was obvious that all three of the boys were expert players. I knew I was up against some tough competition. It had been a while since I'd played, but I did pretty well, especially with a few suggestions from Jordan.

We talked while we played, and sipped on sodas from the fridge. I'd always wondered what it was like on the *Phantom* bus. I guess this was it. Kieran and Ross were pretty much regular guys. Well, not Ross, I guess, he was more like a regular guy hyped up on sugar. He laughed in an evil voice every time he knocked out one of our armies.

"In your face, Ralph!" he yelled as he wiped me completely out of Brazil. I'd always thought Ross couldn't possibly be like he was on stage in real life. I was wrong. He was just as crazy in person as he was performing. I knew it was going to be quite a ride.

We played for over two hours and then, quite suddenly, Kieran and Ross broke through our outer defenses. It didn't take them long to destroy me and Jordan after that. Our empires collapsed. Kieran howled with delight and Ross actually got up on the table and danced.

Ross and Kieran retired to the rear lounge, Ross to play video games and Kieran to work on a song he'd been fiddling with. Jordan looked quickly around, then leaned over the table and gave me a quick kiss. He sat back and smiled.

"I like it more with you here," he said.

"It seems pretty nice even without me." I told him. "I really like Kieran and Ross. Ross is a nut."

"You're not telling me anything new. Just wait until you see him after he's had chocolate."

"I'm excited about Dallas," I told Jordan.

"It will be a blast! I miss being up there on stage to much!"

"I don't think I could handle it," I said. "I mean, thousands of people looking at you, hanging on everything you do…"

"It's such a rush, Ralph. You wouldn't believe the energy. There's all these people screaming and clapping and it's all directed at you. It's intense. It's like… Well, I don't know what it's like, but it's an incredible feeling." Jordan was beaming. His eyes were all lit up.

"Hey, want to help with the set list?" he asked.

"You mean the songs you're going to play?"

"Yeah. We set up what we're going to play, and in what order, before the concert. We also write down a few things we want to say, and who's going to say it when."

"Sounds almost like a script."

"Well, kind of, not really though. Most of what we say is just spontaneous, and sometimes we decide to throw in songs we didn't plan to do. We just kind of go with it."

"You going to sing 'Do You Know That I Love You'?"

"You think they'd let us live if we didn't?" Jordan laughed. "We always do that one."

"Ever get tired of it?"

"Not really. Sometimes I'd like to do something different, but we get to do a whole lot of songs every concert, so I get to do a lot of stuff. So what would you like to see if you were going to the concert as a fan?"

"You've got to do 'Deep in the Darkness'. I love that one."

"I wrote it," Jordan smiled. "most of it anyway. Ross and Kieran added a touch here and there, but it's mainly mine. All of us have a hand in every song." Jordan wrote down the title.

"Make sure you do 'You Don't Know'. That one is awesome!" Jordan wrote that song down too. We sat and came up with a whole list.

"I'll see what Kieran and Ross think of this later," he said, setting the list aside.

We talked some more, then grew quiet. Jordan started answering a few letters. I went to my bunk and dug my portable CD player out. I returned to the front lounge, put on the ear phones, and laid back and closed my eyes listening to my "Do You Know That I Love You" CD. Occasionally, I'd open my eyes to look at Jordan, as if to reassure myself that he was really there. I'd listened to that CD so many times back on the farm, before I'd met Jordan. Sometimes I liked to dream that I was with him. Listening to the music on the bus with my eyes closed almost made me feel like I was back in my room, pretending I was with Jordan. I don't think I'd realized how lonely I was back then. It was only now, when I was no longer alone, that the contrast became apparent. I finally opened my eyes and kept them open. I was almost afraid it would all slip away if I didn't keep a tight hold on it.

*   *   *

I undressed and crawled into my bunk. Jordan was just above me, and both Ross and Kieran were just across the aisle. Mike wasn't far away. We all said "goodnight". Ross screamed it of course and broke into a wild rendition of "Rock It Down Deep" until everyone told him to shut up. I laughed and pulled my curtain shut. Laying in my bunk with the curtain drawn was about as much privacy as could be found on the bus. Within just a few minutes I could hear Ross snoring slightly. He must have been tired to fall asleep so quickly. I had the feeling he ran flat out until he just ran out of steam and collapsed. He was intense like that.

The bunk wasn't big, but it was comfy. There was a little TV/VCR combination at my feet. If I sat up, I could watch whatever I wanted in my own little space. There was also a Playstation, and even a phone. The bus had everything. At the moment, all I really cared about was the bunk itself. It had been a wonderful day, but I was tired. The gentle rumble of the bus sounded almost like wind. Jordan had told me how he liked to lay in his bunk and pretend that it was raining or snowing just outside, and that the wind was blowing. It made him feel all comfy and safe inside his little bunk. I let myself imagine it was raining outside too. I drifted off, almost thinking I was dreaming my life, instead of living it. If it was a dream, I didn't want to wake up.

Jordan

---◆---

I was so close to Ralph, and yet I might as well have been a million miles away. We had barely a moment alone on the bus. I fondly remembered the days when we could walk hand in hand on his farm. I looked forward to when we could go there once more, but there were months ahead before that. We'd be touring all over the south, then up along the east coast, then back into the Mid-west. Who knew where we'd go from there. New venues were always being added, and schedules changed. Nothing was certain on the road.

We pulled into Dallas mid-morning, a whole day before the concert. We would actually have some spare time for once. We needed it for practice. I intended to hit the keyboard as soon as the crew got everything set up. Kieran, Ross, and I made for our hotel rooms. It would feel good to sleep on a bed that wasn't moving for once. Ralph went off with the crew. He was eager to see how setting up for a show worked.

I'd have been happy to have Ralph along, even if he wasn't my boyfriend, even if I didn't know him. He was always ready to help with whatever needed done. Even Ben remarked on how valuable he'd become. Valuable or not, it didn't matter. I loved him.

I caught a shower, then allowed myself a few minutes to veg out in my room. I liked to stay busy most of the time, but it felt good to just do nothing sometimes. I liked to clear my mind and just let it rest, before I rushed onto whatever was next.

I didn't have long to rest. I had told Chad to come and get me as soon as things were set up enough that I could do something with my keyboard. It seemed like no time had passed at all before he was knocking on the door.

I liked Chad a lot. He was in his late thirties, but he seemed like he was about sixteen. He was almost as filled with energy as Ross, and he was a whiz with anything to do with sound equipment. He had blond hair, even longer than mine, that he usually wore in a ponytail. I loved the way he said "dude" all the time. He said "dude" about as often as Ross tapped his fingers on something, which is saying a lot.

I knew we were lucky to get Chad. He'd been working with one rock band or another since he was in his late teens. He was a man unlike any other. It seemed he'd always gone his own way, and had always done his own thing. I think he loved working with instruments and sound equipment as much as I loved music.

Most people thought Chad was a little high on something when they first met him, but that was just Chad. I'd learned as he traveled with us, that he was reluctant to take so much as an aspirin if he had a headache. I asked him why once and he told me he'd had some really bad experiences with drugs when he was younger. It had messed him up and he still wasn't quite right because of it. He didn't seem to want to talk about it much. Doing so actually seemed to cause him pain, so I didn't press. Chad acted kind of odd at times, but I didn't think he was messed up. I thought he was brilliant. He was like an older brother, and had given me good advice on a lot of things. I should probably have talked to him before I ran.

                    *   *   *

I walked out onto the stage. The auditorium was like a vast cavern. Even though the crew was crawling all over the place setting things up, the room seemed empty. I looked out at the hundreds of empty seats.

Tomorrow night they'd be filled, but at the moment the place seemed almost haunted.

I saw Ralph helping to move Ross' drum set. He looked like he was having a good time. I walked over to my keyboard and put my hands on the keys. I almost felt like hugging it.

I started playing "Deep in the Darkness". It was a ballad and I liked its slower rhythm. It was also a song that played well without guitar or drum accompaniment. It was even better with Ross and Kieran playing along, but I liked the sound of it with just the keyboard. I didn't sing it for the moment, I just played. I loved playing the keyboard. It had been too long.

I hadn't forgotten how it was done. Like riding a bicycle, I jumped right back into it. Actually, I was far better on a keyboard than a bike, although I was rather fond of my four-wheeler.

I could feel the music moving through me. It was far more than mere sound. It spoke to me. Even without words, it was poetry, filled with meaning and emotion. I felt it wash over me like a physical force. I smiled. This was what I loved. I loved playing for a crowd even more, but it was the music that mattered. Even if I'd been all alone it wouldn't have made a difference. Music was my life.

The melody that had come to me as I sat on Ralph's porch came to me once more. I worked it out on the keyboard until I had it down like I remembered. As I played it, it began to grow. I found a bridge for it as I stood there, and began working it. Some lyrics came to me. They weren't quite right, but I tried variations until they began to gel with the music. It was far from a finished song, but it was beginning to come together. When Kieran and Ross had some time, I'd get them to work on it with me.

I played and played, not even aware of the crew moving around me. I just stood there, moving in time with the music. I drifted off into my own little world. I didn't even notice when Ralph came up to watch. I actually jumped a bit when I stopped and he spoke to me.

"That's beautiful," he said.

"Thanks."

"I've always loved your music," said Ralph. He leaned close and whispered "Of course you're not bad looking either." I smiled. He went on. "Whenever I was feeling lonely, I just put on one of your songs and it made me feel better. It made me feel like you were right there. I think that's why you're so popular. Even when I didn't know you, I felt like I did. I don't think you'll ever know how much your music touches people."

I could feel my face growing hot and red. I was embarrassed by his words.

"Thank you," I said. "That means a lot to me. I think the most important thing for anyone to do, is to try to make things better for others. It doesn't matter what you do, just so it makes some little difference, just so it makes someone happy or helps them in some way. So, hearing you say that, and knowing that you mean it, well, it makes me feel like my life's worthwhile."

"It looks to me like you'd feel it's worthwhile already." said Ralph.

"Well, I do, but still... I have plenty of people telling me I'm great, or that they love me, or whatever, but not many say something like you've just said."

"I think I understand," said Ralph.

"You know, Ralph, you do for me what my music does for you, just by being my friend," I leaned in close and whispered, "and my boyfriend." It was his turn to blush. I smiled.

"Okay, let's get this show on the road!" yelled Ross as he walked onto the stage. He had his drumsticks in hand, and was already beating them on imaginary drums.

"We are on the road, Ross," said Kieran, who arrived just after Ross.

"Good," said Chad, "glad you dudes are here. We need a sound check."

Ross and Kieran walked to their instruments and did a quick check to make sure all was in order. We each played a bit separately, then together, then sang a cappella. While we were doing so, a group of about twenty or thirty very small kids entered the auditorium with a few adults. They rushed right to the edge of the stage, whispering and pointing, but obviously being very careful not to interrupt us. I learned a bit later that they were from a day care center, run by a cousin of one of the crew.

"Let's try 'Do You Know That I Love You,'" I said.

"Ohhhhh, I've heard that," whispered one little girl loudly just before we began.

We performed the song, stopping once or twice so Chad could make a few adjustments. I smiled at the little kids as we played and sang. They seemed very excited to be there. I liked having them there. Sometimes an audience of just a few was the best audience of all. When we finished, I walked over to the edge of the stage. Kieran and Ross joined me.

"I'm Christine Baker. Chad arranged for us to get in. I hope it's okay," she said.

"No problem," I answered.

"It's Jordan!" said a little girl, very excited. She couldn't have been more than six. There were some older kids there, but none were over ten. They were all quite a bit younger than our usual fans.

"And what's your name?" I asked the little girl. She was so shy she wouldn't answer, so Christine did for her.

"I think Angelina's a very pretty name," I said. The little girl went pink.

"I'm Alex, can I have your autograph?" said a boy of perhaps nine. He wasn't shy at all.

"Certainly," I said. "Hey Ralph, could you get us some photos to sign? Check with Randy, tell him we need about three dozen." Ralph ran off to get photos.

"These boys are musician's," said Christine, the teacher, "Do any of you think you'd like to do that when you grow up?"

"I would!" said Alex. "I wanna be a drummer!"

"Oh yeah!" said Ross. "He's the smart one! Come up here dude and I'll show you my drum set."

Alex clambered up onto the stage and followed Ross. It wasn't long before he was banging on the drums. Kieran and I answered questions. I could tell some of those kids had no idea who we were, while others did without doubt. A handful even had *Phantom* tee shirts on. They were cute little kids.

Ralph came back with photos and we all signed one for each of the kids, and the adults too. I had a feeling a lot of those photos would end up all crumpled on the floor, but it didn't matter. Angelina grasped hers with obvious delight. Seeing her so excited made me smile. We played another song for them, talked to them a bit more, and then they left. I really enjoyed talking to them. They had some pretty intelligent questions for such little kids.

Ralph

— ◆ —

"Here, you'll need this," said Jordan, as he hung a backstage pass around my neck. "This is a blue one, it will get you in anywhere. Don't lose it or security won't let you pass, even if they know you."

"Got it," I said.

"I've got to go change. Things will get hectic in a few minutes, so I probably won't have time to talk until after the concert. I'll see you in a few minutes, then I guess I'll meet you on the bus. We're pulling out right after the show's over." Jordan disappeared almost as soon as the words were out of his mouth.

I stepped off the stage and walked past the empty rows of seats. It was relatively quiet for the moment, but I knew how loud it would get in a few minutes. I remembered the concert in Ft. Wayne fondly. I almost couldn't believe I was on the verge of another concert, with a backstage pass around my neck no less.

I walked out into the lobby and could see a great mass of people waiting to get in. Most of them were young girls, but there were guys too, and older people. A lot of people thought all of *Phantom's* fans were teenaged girls, but they were wrong. Most were teenaged girls, but there were plenty of others. Good music was good music.

I walked up to the head of security and asked him to get the group with passes for the meet and greet. One of the local radio stations had a contest and the winners got free tickets and a chance to meet the band

before the show. Jordan put me in charge of it. Chad had always handled it before, but he was really needed for other things, like handling
last minute adjustments to the sound equipment and so on.

It wasn't long before a little group of about twenty assembled inside,
all wearing purple *Phantom* tags that gained them entrance to the meet
and greet session. All of them were girls, except for three guys. The guys
seemed just as excited as the girls, but they did a better job of holding
still. I wondered if the boys were just fans, or if they had a deeper attraction to Jordan or Kieran or Ross. I could just imagine how thrilled they
were in any case. The security guard left them with me. The people
watching through the doors looked envious.

"Hi," I said. "I'm Jordan's personal assistant." I felt rather proud of
myself saying that. "I'll take you back to meet the band in just a few
minutes. You'll all get the chance to talk with them for a bit, then we'll
do some photos and they'll sign you all autographs. I need you to put
your addresses on these cards so I can mail you the photos we'll take." I
handed out address cards.

"They're really back there?" asked one girl, all excited. I thought it
was kind of a silly question, but I guess she was so overwhelmed she
didn't quite know what to say.

"Yeah, Jordan's in the dressing room and I think Kieran and Ross are
too."

There were more questions and I must admit I felt kind of important
answering them. I definitely liked this part of the job.

"We'll have about twenty minutes, then the guys will have to go and
get ready for the show. I'll take you to your seats when the meet and
greet is over, they're right down front."

I led the little group down the aisle in the auditorium. Just as we were
stepping onto the stage, people began to enter and take their seats.

"Watch out for the cables," I said as I led them backstage. We were
there in moments.

"Ohhhhh look! It's Kieran!" screamed a girl, right into my ear.

Kieran smiled and walked over. He could smile. He could still hear out of his right ear. Ross showed up in just a few moments and Jordan wasn't far behind him. I managed to get my little group into a line so the guys could all shake hands with them. It was fun to watch them all so excited. I know I would have been if I was them.

Next we shot a big group photo, and then I took more photos of smaller groups with the band. By the time that was done, our time was growing short. I got out photos for the guys to sign. They quickly signed them and personalized them too. There wasn't a lot of time, but Jordan, Kieran, and Ross were all really nice to their little group of fans. They let them take all kinds of photos as they talked to them.

I wondered what it would be like to be adored like that. Jordan had tried to explain how it felt to me, but mere words weren't up to the task. I'd learned that there was a lot more to it than signing autographs and performing too. Being a rock star looked pretty incredible from the out-side, but the more I learned, the more I understood that it wasn't all fame and fortune. Still, it definitely didn't suck.

"I hate to say this, but time's up. The guy's have to get ready for the show. If you'll follow me, I'll show you to your seats." I felt a bit like a villain ending the meet and greet, but it was my job.

I had a little trouble getting a couple of the girls to follow me, but Jordan and the others disappeared in the other direction and that made it easier. The auditorium was getting packed as we walked along the edge of the stage. Security checked each person in my group to make sure they really belonged in the seats down front. I left them there and went backstage.

In just a few minutes *Torque*, the opening act for *Phantom*, ran out on the stage and started playing. They were awesome. I hadn't had the chance to meet any of them yet, as they'd only arrived earlier in the day. They would be riding on one of the tour buses, so I was sure I'd get to know them. I knew their names already. Allen was the lead singer. He didn't play an instrument, but he had a fantastic voice. Scott played the keyboard, Nicky the guitar, and Jimmy the drums. All of them had short, dark hair and looked like they could be brothers. None of them were related though, except Allen and Nicky, who were cousins.

Torque really got the crowd revved up. It wouldn't surprise me at all if they were on their own tour soon. They were that good. I thought they weren't quite on the level of *Phantom*, but then again, I was a little biased.

Before long it was time for *Phantom* to take the stage. I was almost as excited as I had been when I was just one of the crowd. It was almost like I didn't know Jordan or Kieran or Ross personally. It was almost like I hadn't played Risk with them, hung out with them, and set fire to the microwave trying to make smores with them. As they ran out onto the stage, I actually caught myself thinking "Oh my God, it's Jordan!" I laughed at myself.

I still couldn't believe I was Jordan's friend, much less his boyfriend. My life had become a dream. I wondered what I'd done to deserve such a wonderful life. It must have been in a past life, because I couldn't think of anything deserving of something so wonderful in this one. I was almost afraid that something terrible was going to happen, and that I had it so good now because I was being allowed some happiness before my life was destroyed.

I pushed the negative thoughts from my mind. The guys were doing "Chamber of Secrets" and there was no way I could even think about being pessimistic during that. I let myself be carried away by the music. It brought me happiness standing there just off stage the same way it had back when I was listening to it home alone.

I wondered what it must be like standing up there in front of thousands of people, with all of them screaming your name. Even standing off to the side, I could feel the energy that Jordan had talked to me about. I couldn't imagine what it would be like having all that directed at me. Part of me very much wanted to feel it. Who wouldn't want to stand in front of a huge crowd and have them go nuts like that? I knew in my heart that I wouldn't want it for long. I didn't see how Jordan and the others did it. I think I would have loved to be as famous as them for maybe a couple of weeks, but then I'd want to go back to just being me. I knew there was no going back, however. Jordan and Kieran and Ross would be famous to the end of their days. There would come a time when they weren't on the cover of every magazine and on every talk show, but they'd always be famous. I think I was happier being me, standing a bit off to the side. Fame was great, but it could be too much of a good thing.

Jordan

◆

Sweat poured off my body as I sang and pounded out "Jump Back" on the keyboard. I loved ballads, but I loved fast, intense songs even more. I couldn't help but throw myself into a song when I got going. I became consumed with it, obsessed by it almost. I was like that even when I was alone, but add in Kieran, Ross, and a few thousand screaming fans and I became a wild boy. It was a powerful experience.

The song ended, and the screams swelled to deafening proportions. I raised my hands in the air for a few moments and just let the feel of it all wash over me. I heard a few artists say they didn't really like being famous, but how could they not?

One of the beach balls floating around in the crowd made it up on stage. I gave it a good underhanded punch, like I was serving a volleyball, and sent it flying back. I loved concerts, it was like a huge party with a few thousand friends. Standing there, it was hard to even remember why I'd run from it all.

Kieran sang the lead in the next song and it was one of the few that didn't have many keyboard sections. I was free to walk around a bit, as long as I made it back to my keyboard at the right times. I ran up to the edge of the stage and loads of girls, and a few guys, extended their hands, reaching for me. I bent down as I sang and clasped hands with girl after girl. One didn't want to let go and just about jerked me off the stage. I saw the security guard near start to go after her, but she released my hand, looking embarrassed. She didn't mean to nearly pull me down, she just got overly excited. I winked at her.

I made my way down the stage until it was time to rush back to my keyboard. I made it just in time. I knew I would. I was good at timing. I never missed a beat. I listened to Kieran as he sang another solo section. He had a beautiful voice, and great talent. I watched the girls in the crowd as he sang. Some looked at him with love in their eyes. The press sometimes acted like I was *Phantom*, and that Kieran and Ross were nothing more than backup. I knew they couldn't be more wrong. Our fans knew it too. I wasn't naïve. I knew I was the most popular, the most visible, but I didn't let myself think for a minute that Kieran and Ross weren't important. I tried not to let anyone else think it either.

I wanted to get the crowd really worked up for the next song, so I ran up near the edge of the stage again and clapped my hands over my head. A bunch of the girls in the audience started doing it too and more joined in. I ran back and forth across the stage getting everyone going. Just about everyone was doing it. I ran back to my keyboard and started in. I loved it when the crowd got into it, and became a part of it.

The clapping died out a bit, so I put my hands over my head and got things revved up again. I danced around behind my keyboard as I played and sang. Of course, that was nothing new. I never could hold still while I was performing.

I was burning up, even though I was in a wife-beater. It was soaked with my sweat. I was tempted to just pull it off. The lights were hot and I moved around so much I might as well have been running a marathon. As soon as the song ended, I took a big swig from my water bottle, then dumped most of the rest over my head. I took what was left and slung it out over the crowd. I moved along the edge of the stage again. A boy took my hand and I realized when I pulled it away that he'd put a note in it. I'd had notes given to be before, but never from a boy.

Ross broke into a drum solo, so I had a few moments to take a look at the note. It read,

I know you probably think this is sick since I'm a boy,
but I love you Jordan. I just wanted you to know—
Courtney

I looked into the crowd where the boy was standing. He was still there and there were tears in his eyes. I wished I could walk over to him and tell him I understood, and that all was cool. I couldn't do it, however. Even if I hadn't been performing in a concert, I just couldn't do it. I smiled at him and I think he understood that I didn't think he was sick. It made my heart ache that there were boys out there that thought they were sick because they loved another boy.

Nearly two hours after we'd started, Kieran, Ross, and I joined hands, took a bow, and ran off the stage. I was practically panting. The stage crew was already moving onto the stage as we ran off. We had another concert the very next night and a long way to travel. I grabbed a quick shower, then sought out Ralph. He was helping to move equipment. He didn't have to do that of course, but I think he liked it.

I was usually hyped up after a concert, but this time I was subdued. Ralph picked up on it right away.

"What's wrong?" he asked.

"Not here," I said, looking around. "Lets talk on the bus."

We sat down in the front lounge a few moments later. I didn't know how much time we'd have alone, so I started right in. I needed to talk to someone, and that someone was definitely Ralph.

"There was this boy in the audience. He gave me a note." I said, handing it to Ralph. He looked up at me when he'd read it.

"That's sad. You know, that boy could almost be me. If I'd given you a note before I knew you, it might have said that."

"That's what bothers me." I told him. "Why do we have to feel so bad because we like boys instead of girls? What's wrong with it anyway? I don't see anything wrong with it. You know some boys even kill themselves because of it. My dad…" I grew silent and looked at Ralph in fear.

I'd said something I hadn't meant to say. Now that I'd said it, however, I couldn't quite remember why I'd wanted to keep it a secret. Maybe I'd kept it a secret so long it had become a habit. There was no reason to keep it from Ralph, no reason at all.

"I told you my dad killed himself, when he was our age," I said. Ralph nodded. "I didn't tell you why. He had a boyfriend. His parents found out, kicked him out of the house. He couldn't take it. He overdosed on some pills."

"Your dad was gay? How's that possible?" asked Ralph. I just looked at him for a moment.

"Gay guys can have kids you know. You or I could do it."

"Sorry, guess I just wasn't thinking," said Ralph. "I bet your mom wasn't happy when she found out."

"No, it broke her heart. She told me all about it one night when she was real upset. They were dating when she found out about him. She'd had her doubts. They'd only had sex once and he didn't seem to want to do it even then. She said she was furious when she found out about him, but then it wasn't long before he killed himself. His boyfriend did too. I think that made Mom understand that he didn't try to hurt her. She loved him, still does."

"Damn, that's hard," said Ralph.

"Yeah. He was just about my age when he died. Mom says I look just like him. His name was Taylor."

Ralph looked at me with compassion in his eyes. I loved him for caring about me so much. I didn't know how I'd lived without him all those years.

"I can't help but feel that if things had been different, then maybe my dad would still be alive. I miss him and I never even knew him." Ralph took my hand and held it.

"That boy," I said, "he thought he was sick because he loved me. Why does he have to think like that? Why do any of us? What if he ends up killing himself like my dad? It's just all wrong. I wish I could do something."

Ralph looked at me closely, he knew there was more.

"What are you thinking Jordan?"

"Well… I'm famous. I've got more money that I could spend in ten life-times. I could do something and no one could really hurt me. I feel like maybe I should. That gay youth magazine you loaned me even said something about it. It said there had to be gay guys in at least some of the boy bands. It said one of them should have the courage to come forward and admit it. Maybe if I did, gay boys wouldn't think so badly about themselves. I don't mean to sound conceited, but look at me, look what I've done, look at what I am. I'm gay and I'm all this Maybe if I went public, it would make a difference."

"That is a lot to think about," said Ralph.

"I know. I've always been so very careful to hide that side of myself. Well, you know. I feel like a big coward though. I'm hiding when maybe I could do some good if I didn't. Who knows? Maybe some of those boys wouldn't kill themselves if they knew I was gay too. That boy…when I read his note, then looked up and saw the tears in his eyes, saw the pain, it just…hurt. I felt like I should go over and talk to him, but I couldn't. I was just too afraid."

I grew silent. I was so upset I began to cry. Ralph took me in his arms and held me. I was glad no one came in and saw us. Thinking that made me feel even more miserable. Why did I have to be such a coward? I felt like I was standing by while I watched others suffer, when I could do something to stop it. Everyone had a reason for living. I'd always thought mine was to make people happy through music, but maybe there was more. Maybe the music was only the beginning.

Ralph

◆

I held Jordan as he cried onto my shoulder. He was a sensitive boy, and, at the moment, he felt like he had the weight of the world on his shoulders. Perhaps he did. When he settled down a bit, I took his head in my hands and kissed him gently on the lips. He responded, and opened his mouth as we kissed. He needed me just then. He needed to be held and loved. We kissed deeply, our tongues entwined.

It was a terrible mistake. Ross and Kieran picked just that moment to walk in. I didn't know why we hadn't heard them coming, but it mattered little. They were there, and they had seen.

Jordan took one look at them and ran for the back lounge, crying. He was already upset, and now this… Kieran and Ross were so shocked they just stood there. I froze. I felt like a deer staring into the lights of an oncoming car as I sat there. I really wanted to run too, but there was no where to go.

"Dude," said Ross shocked. "Were you two making out?"

"That's none of your business," said Kieran, although he was clearly shocked too. It was a needless question really. There was no doubt about what we'd been doing.

"We uh… No," I said.

"But you were kissing," said Ross.

"Ross!" hissed Kieran through clinched teeth. The door to the sleeping area slid open and Jordan stepped out, eyes red, tears still in his eyes. Everyone looked at him.

"I kissed Jordan," I said. "He didn't..."

"We were kissing," said Jordan. He gave me a look, letting me know I didn't have to lie for him.

Ross looked angry and hurt. I'd never seen him look like that before. I'd never seen him act so serious before either. He was always the crazy one, the one who laughed and screwed around without fail. He wasn't doing any of that now. He just stood there, shocked, angry, hurt, and accusing.

"Ralph is my boyfriend," said Jordan. He swallowed hard. I knew what courage it took to speak those words.

Kieran nodded. Ross turned on his heel and stalked off the bus. Jordan leaned against the wall, looking like he was going to fall. Kieran guided him to a seat.

"He'll be okay," said Kieran, nodding in the direction Ross had gone. Jordan peered at Kieran with his intelligent eyes.

"You knew, didn't you?" he said, as if he'd just worked it out in his head.

"I suspected," said Kieran quite seriously.

"Are we obvious?" he asked.

"No, just something in the eyes, and you seem happy. Your little vacation didn't seem enough of an explanation for that."

"You knew I was gay?" I could tell Jordan was forcing out the words.

"Suspected," said Kieran.

"Do I seem gay?"

"I don't know what seeming gay would be," said Kieran. "It's just that I've seen you look at boys sometimes. I've seen interest in your eyes. It isn't there when you look at girls. I know you like girls, but not like that."

"So are we cool?" asked Jordan, almost fearfully.

"We're cool," said Kieran. He leaned down and hugged Jordan tight, letting him know that nothing had changed. Jordan cried a little more, with relief this time. My own eyes filled with tears.

"Ross isn't cool with it," said Jordan, looking very worried.

"He'll come around. He's just…a little hurt and….jealous," said Kieran slowly, as if he were saying something that he didn't know if he should say.

"Jealous? You mean he's…." began Jordan.

"Not exactly," said Kieran.

"Then what?"

"I think you'd better let him tell you that. I've said too much already."

Jordan looked very sad.

"Hey, Jordan, it will be okay," said Kieran.

Jordan smiled at him sadly, and at me. He left the front lounge and stepped off the bus, in search of Ross no doubt.

I looked at Kieran. He was always quiet. He was sensitive, and kind. There was a lot going on behind those sensitive eyes, however. Kieran figured things out. Kieran knew things no one else did. He was the keeper of secrets.

Jordan

◆

I found Ross back in the dressing room, pacing back and forth. He looked up when he saw me. He didn't seem angry. He didn't seem anything. I indicated that we should sit down.

"Surprised?" I asked quietly.

"Shocked," he said. He wasn't drumming his fingers. It worried me.

"You're mad at me, aren't you?" I asked.

"No," said Ross, shaking his head. "It's just…"

"Do you like girls?" I asked him.

"Oh yes! Very much!"

"But?"

Ross looked away. It was the only time I'd ever seen a look that even approached shyness on his face.

"I kind of…" Ross trailed off in silence. "I'm kind of…"

"It's okay Ross," I said. "It's okay. Just tell me."

"I don't think I understand it enough to tell you."

"Try."

"Well, I like girls. I'm not lying about that. I *really* like girls. Boy do I like 'em." The tone of his voice almost made me laugh. "I'm not gay and trying to cover up. Not that there's anything wrong with being gay. I like girls. It's just that I… Well, I like you too. I mean, it's stupid really. I like girls. I think about them all the time, but then I think about you. It's not even sexual, I think. I just… Sometimes I feel like I've got this crush on you or something. You're so handsome, and your voice is so beautiful… It just…confuses me."

"You know we'll always be friends," I said. Ross smiled.

"You think I'm bi?" he asked.

"I don't know, maybe, maybe not."

"I don't know either. I did some stuff once. Well, a couple times, but I think all guys do that. I don't think about boys like that, but sometimes… Well, I'll just say it, sometimes I feel like I want to kiss you. It's nothing more than that, and that's the truth."

I took a calculated risk and leaned over and kissed Ross delicately on the lips. He looked at me thoughtfully, then smiled sweetly.

"That was…wonderful," he said slowly as if he was savoring our kiss. "But I still like girls." He said the last part more to himself than me. He looked back at me. "I'm kind of screwed up huh?"

"Like that's news." I laughed softly. Ross laughed too. "I think you're just fine Ross. You're crazy, but you're not crazy, if you know what I mean."

"Thanks," he smiled again. "So, Ralph is your boyfriend?"

"Yes." I paused for a few moments. "Jealous?"

"Just a little. I'm happy for you though. You really like him, don't you?"

"Oh yeah." I took Ross by the hand and peered into his eyes. "I like you too. We'll always be friends."

"Yeah, we will, won't we?" It was a statement, not a question. Ross sat silent for a few moments. "This is good," he said at last. "Yeah, this is good, it makes things easier. I love you, and I think the crush or whatever it is comes from that maybe. Maybe you're just such a good friend that I'm getting confused about things. I mean, where's the line between friends and more than friends? Anyway, now that it's out in the open, maybe I can handle it better. I can't promise not to be a little jealous, but we're cool."

"So am I a good kisser?" I asked him mischievously.

"To be honest, yes," said Ross, turning red.

"So are you. The girls you meet are lucky."

"Thanks," said Ross.

"Give me a hug," I told him, and he did.

          *   *   *

I lay in my bunk that night as the wheels of the bus turned somewhere beneath me. I felt a lot better about things, and understood them more clearly. I think the real reason I'd run away was that I felt so alone. I didn't even realize it then. I thought I ran because I just had to get away. I thought I ran because of that horrible story about that girl. Maybe I wasn't running away from something as much as I was toward something, or someone. Maybe in my heart I knew I needed Ralph. I think I was meant to meet him. I don't think it was an accident when our eyes locked at that concert in Indiana. I don't think it was an accident that I ran into him in the hotel later that night. It certainly wasn't an accident when I'd gone to him when I ran. We were meant to be, that's all there was to it. The chain of events was just too strange and unlikely to have happened on their own.

I sure never guessed about Ross. Of course, I still wasn't completely sure what all that was about. He wasn't sure either. We were cool though, and now that things were out in the open, we could be there for each other. I had a feeling it would make our friendship stronger.

I felt good. My boyfriend was sleeping in the bunk just beneath me and I had two good friends sleeping near. It had been a tough night, but all had worked out for the best. Maybe everything happened for a reason.

I thought about Courtney, the boy at the concert. I wished I could have talked to him. I wished I could have let him know that everything was okay, and that he was too. I hoped everything worked out for him. I felt really bad that I hadn't done something for him when I could have.

True, it was during a concert and I couldn't exactly stop the whole thing and talk to him, but I could have motioned Ralph or someone over and had them bring him backstage. I'd missed an opportunity to make a difference. Who knew how I could have changed his life? The opportunity was gone, lost forever. I'd let it slip away from me and it was gone. It was my loss, and worse, it was Courtney's.

*   *   *

No one awakened me the next morning. I woke up to find the bus still moving. I got out of bed and found Ralph fixing toast for Kieran and Ross, who were sitting with bowls of cereal and glasses of orange juice in the front lounge.

"Look, it's sleeping beauty," said Ross.

"Shut up," I said sleepily.

"Ohhh, is the Prince of Rock and Roll grumpy this morning?" teased Kieran.

"Shut up!" I said louder.

"His highness is a bit gruff," said Ross smiling.

"We're running behind schedule," explained Kieran. "We had to stop last night for a repair to one of the other buses."

I nodded. I hadn't even noticed that we'd stopped during the night. That wasn't all that surprising. I was a sound sleeper on the road.

Ralph handed out toast, and got me some juice and cereal.

"Such a cute couple, aren't they?" said Ross with a smile. Kieran smiled too. "So um, have you guys done it yet?"

"Ross!" yelled Kieran. Ralph and I looked at each other. It felt rather weird to have our relationship discussed openly.

"Well have you?" asked Ross. He was obviously back to his old self. He was even drumming his fingers on the table.

"Well, no…" I said.

"Still number one!" yelled Ross, who had long been very proud that he was the only one of us who wasn't still a virgin. "So why not?"

"That's personal," said Kieran. He looked as if he'd like to punch Ross on the nose.

"We're just waiting for the right time," I said.

"It's always the right time for love," said Ross loudly. "Unh unh!" This time Kieran did hit him, just on the shoulder though.

I was a bit embarrassed and hoped I wasn't turning red. There was a tinge of red to Ralph's face. Ross did raise an interesting point. What were we waiting for, other than some privacy?

Kieran successfully steered the conversation onto how we'd have to rush when we got to the next venue. There would be precious little time for anything. Of course, it was the crew who would be pushed the most. It took a lot of time to set up for a show. I didn't mind the hurried pace myself. I was used to it. Life on the road wasn't always easy. It always seemed that I was rushing someplace or other. This was no different. Besides, I had far bigger worries on my mind.

Ralph

— ◆ —

I woke up not knowing where I was. Well, that's not quite true. I was on the tour bus. I just didn't have any idea where it was. There had been a concert the night before, but for the life of me I couldn't remember what city it was in. There was another concert in two days, but I couldn't remember where we were headed to either. Everything kind of blurred together. One city looked much like the next. The hotel rooms were practically identical. Even the auditoriums and theatres started looking the same after a while. Don't get me wrong, I'm not saying I was bored. Being on tour was the most exciting time of my life. I just wished I could remember what freaking state I was in.

Jordan had seemed a little edgy since Dallas. I don't think anyone else could pick up on it, but then no one else was as close to him as me. There seemed to be an edge of fear to him, but I wasn't at all certain what it was about. I was always worried that some lunatic would bring a gun to a concert and start shooting, but Jordan never worried about stuff like that. The one time I mentioned it, he just said "What are we going to do, run everyone through a metal detector?" I knew he wasn't worried about some lunatic attacking him, but I had no idea what was eating at him.

It was still early, but I got up and got some juice from the fridge. I sat and tried to figure out where we were. I'd been sitting there about ten minutes when Jordan walked in.

"You're up early," he said.

"So are you." Jordan was usually the last to get up. He wasn't exactly a morning person.

"Hey, where's the next concert?" I asked.

"Um, Boston, why?"

"Boston! That's right. I couldn't remember."

"Welcome to my world," said Jordan as he looked at me.

I got up from my seat and hugged him. It felt so good to have him in my arms again. We'd had a great deal of difficulty finding any time alone. Even when we were staying in a hotel, there was precious little time. We were afraid to sleep in the same bed for fear that someone would catch us. Ross and Kieran knew now of course, but it would be kind of hard to explain me in Jordan's room in the middle of the night, or first thing in the morning, if his manager or publicist, or anyone else walked in. The whole crew knew we were friends, but they had no idea we were anything more than that. To most of them, I was just Jordan's assistant.

I didn't dare share a room with Jordan. That would have raised eyebrows. He usually had his own room. If there was a shortage of rooms, then Kieran and Ross shared with him. Me sharing with him would have raised too many questions. Even if we had shared a room, we would have been so tired when we got there that we wouldn't have been able to do anything. Most nights, I fell asleep before my head hit the pillow, and I'm not exaggerating. It really happened. I'd start to lay down and that was it. I couldn't even remember my head making contact with the pillow. Sharing a room wouldn't have helped with anything, except to put us in danger of being found out. No, it was far better that I shared with Chad, the guy in charge of all the stage hands.

"They're at it again," said Ross as he walked into the front lounge.

"Ah! They're like rabbits!" said Kieran, who was right behind him.

Jordan and I just smiled. It was a relief that Ross and Kieran felt comfortable enough with our relationship to tease us. I was a little surprised that Kieran was joking around. He'd been laying into Ross the night before when he was asking personal questions. I guess this was different. These weren't questions, they were just crude, locker room comments. I thought they were funny.

"I wish we were like rabbits," said Jordan. That raised a few eyebrows, including mine. It made me want to kiss him right then and there, and do a few other things besides.

Jordan walked up and spoke to the driver, then returned shortly after. I hoped the driver hadn't heard anything, but that wasn't likely. Besides, he'd probably have no idea what we were talking about even if he did.

I didn't mind Ross and Kieran walking in on us. All we were doing was hugging after all. However, it was an example of how little privacy we had and made it painfully clear that not much could happen between us. A simple hug or kiss was a big risk. Anything more was out of the question.

Jordan and I had decided to wait until the time was right, but I wasn't sure how much longer I could wait. I was a teenaged boy and I had needs. Of course, I was a virgin, so seeing that those needs had never been met, I supposed waiting a bit more wouldn't hurt. I wondered how much longer I'd have to wait. Where this kind of waiting was concerned, a day seemed like a year.

There was a certain thrill to the anticipation. Just thinking of what Jordan and I would someday be doing was arousing beyond belief. Just thinking of what he looked like naked was pretty exciting too. I'd seen him shirtless. I'd seen him in a swim-suit and in just his boxers, but that was it. I was yearning to see more. The anticipation was enjoyable, but I just hoped I wouldn't explode or something before we got our chance.

I had no idea when that chance would come. We wanted to wait until the time was right and it seemed that it couldn't possibly be right during the tour. That meant waiting the entire summer. That was a long, long time to wait for something I wanted right now!

The bus turned, then stopped. I didn't think we were in Boston yet. We weren't. When I went to a window and looked out, I saw a Burger Dude sitting there. It was clear what Jordan had talked to the bus driver about. Jordan joined me at the window and smiled.

"Hmm, I was hoping to get out, but it looks like there's too many people. You mind?" he asked me.

"Of course not, what do you want?"

I knew the answer before the words were out of Jordan's mouth. He wanted French toast squares and cinnamon minis. That's what he always wanted. I took a pad of paper and wrote down what everyone wanted, including the bus driver. Jordan handed me way more cash than I'd need and I left the bus.

I drew some looks as I stepped out. The bus wasn't marked, but it obviously wasn't an ordinary bus. It didn't look like a commercial passenger bus and it was way too big for some kind of recreational vehicle. It had a very expensive look it to too. It would have drawn more attention if the other buses had stopped too, but they had driven on.

A couple of girls were looking at me as I placed a rather large order. They were whispering to each other. I stood back once I'd placed the order and they edged up to me. I had little doubt they were *Phantom* fans.

"Hi," said the blonde girl.

"Hey," I said.

"We saw you on television, didn't we?" she asked. I wasn't ready for that question. I was expecting her to ask if it was the *Phantom* bus parked outside or something like that.

"Um, I don't think so." I told her.

"Yeah, I'm sure it was you," said her friend. "You were walking with Jordan and talking, coming off the bus, out in California I think." She looked meaningfully at the bus through the window.

"Well, I didn't know I was on television, but I guess it was me you saw."

"That is *Phantom's* bus out there then, isn't it?" she asked quietly, so as not to draw attention.

"Yes." I whispered back. Both girls practically squealed with delight, but tried to keep from drawing attention at the same time.

"Is *he* on there?" the blonde one asked. I considered lying, but I didn't really like to do that, and I didn't see any reason to do so. I had no doubt she was talking about Jordan.

"Yeah," I said. "He couldn't come out because he'd get mobbed and we don't have much time to spare."

The girls were practically jumping up and down.

"We're going to the concert in Boston!" said one.

"Do you think you could get us an autograph?" said the other.

The order was ready. I went to pick it up.

"Um, tell you what," I said. "You wait here, and I'll see what I can do. I'll be right back. I promise."

I could tell they would rather have come with me, but luckily they were too polite to press. I had the driver wait for a moment. I dumped the bags on the table, grabbed up what I needed from a drawer, and walked back out to the girls, who were standing just outside the doors of Burger Dude.

"Oh my God!" they both said when they saw what I was holding. "Those are…"

"Backstage passes," I finished for them. "I've really got to run, but you show up at the concert an hour or so early, show those to security, and you can come back and meet the guys then. I'm sure they'll be happy to sign autographs for you."

The girls grabbed me and kissed my cheeks. "I've really got to run!" I said, and dashed back to the bus. It took off moments later.

"I thought you liked boys," said Ross as I entered to find everyone already chowing down.

"Cheating on me huh?" said Jordan laughing. Everyone had clearly been watching me from the bus.

"Hey, I didn't ask them to kiss me," I said.

"They were pretty cute," said Ross. "Maybe they need a ride?"

"Down boy!" said Kieran.

"You'll get your chance to meet them. I gave them backstage passes."

"Way to go Ralph!" said Ross and gave me a high five. Kieran rolled his eyes.

"I think they're mainly after Jordan," I said.

"They always are," said Ross mournfully.

"Not always," said Jordan.

"Most of the time, and you don't even like girls!" said Ross. "It's so unfair!"

"I like them. I just don't want to date them." Jordan smiled. "I'll try to point some in your direction."

"He does need all the help he can get," said Kieran.

"Hey!" yelled Ross, practically jumping on the table. He was laughing, however, and hyped up as usual.

"You guys can just shut up, I'm still number one! Yeah!" Ross flexed his arms over his head like he thought he was master of the universe or something. His slim muscles bulged. He put his arms down and started playing an air drum. I loved Ross.

Jordan

———————— ◆ ————————

I pulled Ralph to me and kissed him. The Boston concert was just getting ready to begin and we were alone for the moment in a short hallway backstage. We were nearly at the end of the tour, and the summer, and we still hadn't found time to be alone together. To be honest, I didn't know how much longer I could stand it. I was so aroused when I was around Ralph that I couldn't even walk right half the time.

Kieran and Ross ran interference for us and we were able to grab a few minutes here and there, but that was it. I enjoyed even the fleeting moments. A quick kiss or hug felt so good coming from the boy I loved. Just being near him made me happy. I hugged him close and kissed him again.

"What the!?" said a girl loudly as she rounded the corner with another girl and found me and Ralph with our lips locked. Kieran and Ross picked just that moment to turn the other corner.

"He's a fag," she said to her friend. She looked straight at me. "You're a fucking fag!" She threw her concert program to the floor, turned on her heel, and walked away cussing and calling me horrible names. Her friend gave me a nasty look and followed her. I burst into tears. I'd never had anyone call me names like that before. I'd never had anyone yell obscenities at me.

Tears filled my eyes. I couldn't believe how much mere words hurt. Someone took me in his arms and held me. It was Ralph. Kieran and Ross closed in protectively and put their hands on my shoulders.

"Oh God," I said. What I'd feared most had happened. I'd been discovered. Those girls had seen me, making out with Ralph. I was terribly shaken up. I kept thinking to myself "what now?"

The chant of "*Phantom! Phantom!*" and "*Jordan! Jordan!*" came from the auditorium. Chad stuck his head out into the hall.

"Guys, are you ready?" he said. Kieran and Ross looked at me, concern showing clearly on their faces.

"You going to be okay?" asked Kieran. "Can you go on?"

I nodded my head "yes", not yet able to speak. I was still too choked up. The truth was that I didn't know if I could do it or not. I didn't know if I could sing. Kieran and Ross walked a bit up the hall and waited on me.

"I'm so sorry Jordan," said Ralph.

"Not your fault," I croaked out. I looked into his eyes. "I love you."

"I love you too," he said. I could tell he was worried sick over me. The chant of "*Phantom! Phantom!*" and "*Jordan! Jordan!*" was growing louder. I had to get myself under control. I felt like I'd been hit upside the head with a brick. The looks on those girls faces, the words they said… I hugged Ralph again then walked up to Ross and Kieran. I took a deep breath and calmed myself. I nodded at Kieran and Ross, and we ran out onto the stage.

I was deafened by the screams. It was a small theatre, but there were still two or three thousand fans in the audience. I didn't waste a moment. I knew I couldn't let myself think. I just prayed that when I opened my mouth, I could sing. I looked at Ross and nodded. He started the beat with his drumstick, and we went straight into "You Don't Know".

As soon as my hands hit the keyboard and I opened my mouth, I felt the music flow over and through me. It reminded me of who I was, and what I was there to do. The faces of those girls were etched in my mind, but there were hundreds of other faces before me—smiling, cheering. I needed those faces just then. I needed their support. I was never more appreciative of my fans than at that moment. I let their cheers, and the music, carry me away.

*   *   *

After the concert, I asked not to be disturbed, and locked myself in the dressing room. I had to think, alone, away from everyone. Now that the cheering crowds were gone, I was left with my thoughts about what had happened.

I should have known it would happen sooner or later. Perhaps I did know. Perhaps I'd even taken chances so it would happen. Ever since that boy had given me that note in Dallas, I'd felt guilty. I knew that gay boys suffered, and I knew I could do something to help them. I just didn't have the balls to do it.

I never realized how bad it hurt to be on the receiving end of a hateful stare, or to have nasty things said about me. Sure, I'd heard "Phantom sucks" yelled plenty of times, and stuff like that, but nothing that was so personal. I'd always feared it, always known it would hurt, but not like this. It had to be at least a hundred times more painful than I'd feared.

I wasn't just wallowing in self-pity. I was thinking about all the gay boys out there who felt the same pain. For the first time ever, I felt their pain, and it was nearly unbearable. No wonder so many thought so poorly of themselves. No wonder many of them even killed themselves. I'd had just the slightest taste of it and it had hurt me beyond what I thought was possible.

I cried, but I wasn't really crying for me. I was crying for Courtney in Dallas, and for all the others, and for the girls too. I was crying for my father, and his boyfriend. I was crying for everyone who was different and was ridiculed for it. The world was such an unfair place.

I thought about how lucky I really was. I had both fame and fortune, but that's not what really made me lucky. I was lucky because I had good friends who supported me, who cared about me even though they knew. I was lucky because there was a boy who loved me, that I loved too. The fame and money weren't really important, they were nothing compared to what I had with Kieran and Ross, and most of all with Ralph.

There was too much pain in the world, too much suffering. Gay boys, and girls, suffered more than their share. I couldn't change the world, but maybe there was something I could do to make it a little easier for those who needed help the most.

Ralph

———————— ◆ ————————

I could have slept in the morning after the Boston concert, but I couldn't sleep. I was too filled with worry over Jordan. I'd seen the look on his face when that girl called him a fag. I'd seen the pain. I'd seen the strain on his face as he ran onto the stage. And then, after the concert was over, he'd locked himself in the dressing room and wouldn't come out. He only did so when it was time to go and had gone straight to his bunk. He'd stopped only to tell me that he loved me, and to give me a quick goodnight kiss. I was suffering because he was in pain. I loved him more than anything, and when he hurt, so did I.

I got up and walked into the front lounge. It was always our meeting place. The lounge was empty, so I grabbed a carton of chocolate milk from the fridge and sat down at the table.

I don't know how long I'd been sitting there before Jordan slid the door open and entered. I looked up. He looked worried, serious, and determined.

"How are you?" I asked. There was a long pause before he answered.

"I've been thinking about something," he said. "There's something I've been thinking about doing, and well, the time has come and I'm scared. I don't know what's going to happen."

Just then Ross and Kieran came stumbling in.

"You know, some of us like to get some sleep around here," said Kieran. "And you're usually one of us," he said to Jordan.

"Have a seat," said Jordan. "I was about to discuss something with Ralph, but it concerns you too."

Kieran and Ross both looked suddenly serious. There was something in the tone of Jordan's voice that was a little frightening. I feared the words he would speak next.

"We have something to discuss with you as well Jordan," said Kieran. "Ross and I talked about it. What happened last night, it doesn't have to be that bad. You know how the tabloids are always making up stuff about you. Well, if those girls get something going, we'll just all act like it didn't happen. We can hide…"

"I'm done with hiding," said Jordan with a tone of finality. "I appreciate what you guys are trying to do, but I've been giving it a lot of thought and I've decided that it's best that I be honest about what I am."

Jordan told them about the note the boy named Courtney gave him in Dallas and how it hurt him to think that boys like that thought poorly of themselves, just because they were gay.

"Last night," said Jordan, "when that girl called me a fag, I couldn't believe how much it hurt. That's the first time anyone has called me something like that, but there are boys out there who have to take that every day of their lives. Everyone's got these stupid ideas about gays. They seem to think we're all weak, effeminate, child molesters, who wear dresses or something. Someone needs to show those people what being gay is really about. I've thought a lot about this, and I think I'm meant to use what I've got to help others, to help gay boys like me. This probably makes me sound conceited, but if some of those gay boys out there see me and know I'm gay, then maybe they'll think better of themselves. Maybe some of our fans will change the way they think about gays too."

I waited for Ross to make a crack about Jordan being conceited, but he didn't. He was taking what Jordan said very seriously.

"You know this will make things harder for you," said Kieran. "I know you want to change things, but you're going to be hearing a lot more stuff like you did last night if you go public."

"I know," said Jordan. "I know it may be rough. I know I'm not going to be able to change the world, but it's worth some pain if I can make a difference. Besides, I've got good friends to help me through it." He looked around at us all. I took his hand and held it.

"I can't make this decision all alone, however," said Jordan. "It effects you guys too. I'm not naïve. If I come out, it could hurt CD and ticket sales, and everything else. Some of the fans are going to walk away. I'm not worried about what the record company or our management company thinks, but I'm not going to do this without your approval."

"I think it's your decision," said Kieran. "It's your life. I want you to do whatever you think is best for you."

"I think you should do it Jordan," said Ross. "If some fans walk away just because you're gay then who needs them? We don't need them if they're that shallow."

"Thanks guys," he said, then turned to me. "Ralph, this is going to effect you as much as me. It probably won't take the press long to find out you're my boyfriend." He let the implication hang. I knew it was up to me to make the next move.

"I can handle it," I said.

"What about your parents?"

Fear struck my heart. I refused to let fear rule my life, however. If Jordan could be open, and let the world see he was gay, then surely I could do it too. I swallowed hard before answering. I paused. I wanted to make sure I meant what I said before speaking the words. Yes, I did mean it. It was time.

"It's time I told them anyway. It' s not really fair not to tell them. Besides, how could they not approve of me having the cutest boyfriend in the world?" I laughed softly, but I was nervous. Telling my parents I was gay was something I'd thought about, and feared. It was time to tell them. I wasn't ashamed of being gay and keeping it secret made it seem that I was. I needed to live my life out in the open, and not in hiding.

"Hmm," said Ross, scratching his chin. "I was just thinking..." Everyone looked at him. "When Jordan announces he's gay, all the girls will know he's unavailable. That means more will go for me!" He placed a heavy emphasis on the "me" and we all pounded him for it. It helped to break the tension.

"You're so conceited!" said Kieran to Ross. "Besides, I think we all know they'll be after me." It was Kieran's turn to be punched. It wasn't long before we were all punching each other. It's a wonder someone didn't get a black eye while we were wrestling around. Our horse play was brought to an end when the bus stopped in front of our hotel in New York City. I looked out the window and saw a tremendous crowd. I wondered if we'd even be able to make it inside.

Jordan

———————————— ◆ ————————————

I walked into the big conference room with what felt like a rock in the pit of my stomach. I'd done dozens of press conferences, but this one was different. I was about to do something that would change my life, and no one but Ralph, Kieran, and Ross knew what was coming.

Kieran and Ross looked calm enough as they sat on either side of me, but then again they weren't going to be announcing something that would shock the entire world.

The room was packed. There was usually a big crowd of reporters, but I told my publicist to let the word out that something especially newsworthy would be coming out at the conference. I neared laughed at my own choice of words, but I couldn't. I wasn't telling even my publicist what was going to happen. The truth was, I wasn't sure what was going to happen. I knew what I wanted to say, but had no idea how I'd be saying it.

The press conference started out calmly enough. There were all the usual questions, and others that I could easily have predicted.

"What will you be doing when the tour is over?" asked a reporter I recognized from one of the teen magazines.

"We'll be taking a little time off," said Kieran "then we'll begin work in the recording studio on our new CD".

"Jordan, is it true that you're planning to cut your hair?" asked a reporter from another teen magazine.

"I'm always amazed that anyone would care if I cut my hair or not," I said. "But no, I don't plan on getting it cut, at least not enough that anyone will notice."

While I was answering, I saw the reporter from "Wild Celebrity Gossip" staring at me. I knew what was coming. He shouted out his question next.

"Jordan, what have you to say about the rumors that you were caught engaged in homosexual acts prior to the Boston concert?"

The whole room went silent. "Wild Celebrity Gossip" was well known as the gutter press, but apparently most of those present thought their star reporter had gone too far this time. Security moved toward him, but I waved them off. Every camera in the room was pointed at me. I could feel Ross and Kieran stiffen beside me, and see Ralph watching me with compassion.

"The information dug up by "Wild Celebrity Gossip" is usually about as far from the truth as it's possible to get," I stated. "Last week I believe you had me fathering two illegitimate children during the tour, or was it three?" Most everyone in the room had a laugh, at the reporter's expense.

"In this case, however, you aren't entirely wrong, although your choice of words leaves much to be desired," I said. The room went silent again. "You are no doubt referring to the incident backstage when two of my fans walked in on me kissing my boyfriend."

There was stunned silence for a few moments, followed by a flurry of questions coming from every direction. The whole room exploded with activity. Camera flashes filled the room with blinding light and cameras were shoved into my face. Some reporters were already running from the room in an attempt to get the story out first. My manager tried to pull me away, but I refused. I stood and said nothing until the room quieted.

"So you are saying that you are gay?" asked a reporter.

"Yes. A lot of people have a funny idea about what it is to be gay," I said, while cameras and tape recorders were trained upon me. I was keenly aware that my words would be heard by millions. I intended to make them count. "All it really means is loving someone of the same sex. That's it. I've kept the fact that I'm gay a secret for a long time, partly because I was afraid it would hurt my career, partly because I was just afraid. I recently came to realize, however, that by hiding the truth, I was acting like someone who was ashamed of himself. I have nothing to be ashamed of, except that I did not come forward sooner."

There were more questions, but I waved them off. The reporters grew relatively quiet again. They wanted to hear my words. They knew they had a hot story.

"There are thousands of gay boys out there, and girls. We are your sons and daughters, sisters and brothers, aunts and uncles. We are your family and friends and we deserve to be treated with the same dignity and respect that all deserve. There are many out there who put us down, spread lies about us, and hate us for what we are. What we are is human; caring and feeling, and the insults and obscenities hurled at us hurt. Last night, I got my first taste of that when a girl called me "fag", simply because I was kissing my boyfriend. I realized for the first time how much words can hurt. Well, I'm not living a lie anymore. If there are those who want to hurl insults at me because of that, then I pity them. I'm going to live my life as I've always done and continue making the music I love, for I haven't changed. I'm the same Jordan I've always been, only now you know a little more about me.

"Lastly, I'd like to say something to Courtney, the boy who handed me a note at the concert in Dallas. I'm sorry I didn't have the courage to talk to you and admit that I was gay too. There is nothing wrong with you Courtney. I think you were very courageous, and I hope that I will have the opportunity to speak with you."

I turned from the microphone and smiled at Ralph. He walked over to me and we hugged, while camera flashes lit the air. Photographers were practically killing themselves to get a shot of us hugging. Ralph was obviously my boyfriend, and they wanted to get a shot of us together. Kieran and Ross got up and joined me and Ralph. They patted us both on the back, then we made our way out of the crowded room. I'd had enough questions for one day.

Ralph

--------------- ◆ ---------------

I could tell Jordan was nervous just by looking at him. He hadn't said much on the way back from the press conference. I knew he had a lot on his mind. He'd just done something that would change his life forever and there was no taking it back.

"I don't know about you," I said as we sat in the hotel room, "but I hate this waiting."

"Me too," said Jordan. "I keep thinking of what may happen. That's just it, you know? Right now what I said at that press conference is being sent out everywhere and I don't know what's going to happen because of it. There are so many possibilities. I'm not saying that I'm afraid either. I am a little afraid, but not like I thought I'd be. It's just the not knowing. So many different things could happen. I feel like… I feel like I don't know anything about life at all. I feel like I don't know what to expect the next time I walk out that door. It's like the whole world could even be different, you know?"

"I think I do. Everything has changed. Nothing will be predictable anymore, at least not for a long time."

"Exactly. I used to know what was going to happen, more or less. I mean, when I stepped off the bus, there would always be girls holding signs, people cheering, wanting my autograph. Then there were usually some punks that would yell "Jordan sucks" or some shit like that, but that was okay too. I knew it was going to happen. Now I don't know."

"But you're not sorry you did it?"

"No, I'm not sorry at all. Looking back, I know I should have done it a long time ago. I should have stopped hiding, but I'd always hid that part of myself so it was just easier to keep on doing it."

"That's kind of why I haven't told anyone about me either," I said.

"I guess you won't have to now," said Jordan.

"That's for sure! I bet some people who know me are going to keel right over when they see me with you on television, and in the magazines and papers. Of course, the bigger shock may just be that I know you."

Jordan smiled.

"I want you to know something, Jordan," I said seriously. "I love you because you are you, not because you're famous. I'd be lying if I didn't say it's as cool as can be to be the boyfriend of the lead singer of *Phantom*, but it's you I love. It's great that you're such a wonderful singer, and so famous and all, but I'd love you if you weren't any of that. I know that's easy for me to say since we'd probably never have met if you weren't famous and all that, but I love you, just for you. Damn, I don't think I'm explaining all this right."

"I understand just what you mean," said Jordan. "You didn't have to tell me that. I already knew it. Do you think I could love you like I do if I believed otherwise? There's no way. I know you love me. I can feel it." He smiled, and we kissed.

"Jordan," I said slowly, "not that I think it will happen, but if you lost everything, couldn't sing and all that, I'd still love you."

"I know you would," he said. "Just like I'll always love you."

Something both surprising and wonderful happened as we sat there and talked. We kept getting interrupted by different members of the crew dropping in. Normally, such interruptions wouldn't have been such a good thing, especially so many of them, but this was different. Whether they said it or not in words, they were all dropping in to let Jordan know that they were cool with his sexual orientation. They were letting him know that their relationship hadn't changed, or at least had-n't changed for the worse. More than one even remarked on how proud they were of Jordan. I think they realized why Jordan publicly announc-ing he was gay was such a big deal. I think they knew that it would give a big boast to gays everywhere. I know what it would have meant to me if I was further removed from the situation. If we'd never met and I found out about Jordan, my self-esteem would probably have shot through the roof on the spot. If someone that awesome was gay, then maybe there was something pretty awesome about it. There were a lot of totally cool gays, but most of them hid. Jordan was one of the very first to come out and say "Look at me. Here is what I am, and I'm gay."

I smiled as Chad walked in the door. He didn't just speak a few kind words to Jordan, he pulled him up off the couch and hugged him.

"I'm real proud of you dude," he said. "If more dudes like you came forward, us gay guys wouldn't have so many problems."

"You're gay?" I asked.

"Yeah, born that way you know." he laughed. "I just wish you were around when I was your age, Jordan. Maybe my parents would have understood me a little better. Maybe they wouldn't have tried to change me. Maybe I'd have seen them sometime in the last twenty years."

It was clear that Chad had quite a story to tell. Someday I hoped to hear it. I think the words he spoke gave Jordan a lot of courage. I think it made Jordan see, more than ever, what a wonderful and important thing he'd just done.

"Dude, you want to talk about anything, you come and see me. That goes for you too," said Chad, looking at me.

Jordan smiled, as did I. Chad departed just after that, but he left us feeling even better than we had before. He was yet another cool gay "dude".

Everyone on the crew was cool with Jordan being gay. The only per-son who didn't like it so far was his manager. I watched his face at the press conference as Jordan made his announcement. He looked like he was ready to shit a brick. He stalked off before Jordan was even finished, talking on his cell phone.

He came in as we sat on the couch together. He didn't look happy at all. He looked at Jordan like a father who was very disappointed with his son.

"Why did you do that Jordan? What were you thinking? Do you know what this will do to *Phantom*? You've cost us millions!" Jordan eyed him coolly.

"I did something I should have done a long time ago," he said. "This is what I am, and I'm not ashamed of it."

"I don't have a problem with you being gay, but did you have to announce it to the whole world? Do you know how many fans you'll lose because of this? Do you know what this will cost us?"

"Do you know how many gay boys kill themselves because everyone is down on them? Do you know how much I may have just helped them?" Jordan shot back. Ben shrugged it off like that didn't matter.

"This is about business, Jordan. You are a business, that's all. The only thing that matters about you is how many posters and calendars and tee shirts your pretty face will sell. The only thing that matters is how many CD's those little adolescent girls will buy because they think you're cute. You are a product, a product that is damaged now and will be damned hard to sell."

I was so mad I couldn't see straight. Jordan was angry too, but he kept cool.

"I'm a person," he said.

"You are what we made you," said Ben.

"Get out," said Jordan.

Mike had appeared at the sound of angry words. He opened the door just as Jordan said "Get out." Without hesitating, he grabbed Ben firmly by the arm and pulled him away.

"We'll just see how you feel when the record company dumps you and all that *Phantom* merchandise ends up in the clearance bin," said Ben as he was jerked bodily out of the room.

"Jordan, don't listen to him," I said when Ben had gone. "He's wrong. He's wrong about everything."

"Don't worry about me," said Jordan, turning to me . I was surprised to see a smile on his face. "His opinion isn't going to get me down. All his kind cares about is money. Did you hear what he said?—'You are what we made you?'. Me and the guys already had two gold records before our management company came looking to sign us."

"Do you think your record label will dump you?"

"To record companies, music is a business. They'll only dump us if our records don't sell, and that is up to our fans. I think we've got better fans than that. Don't worry, everything will be okay."

It was kind of funny that Jordan was the one comforting me. It was as if our roles were reversed.

Mike stuck his head in the door.

"You okay?" he asked.

"I'm fine," said Jordan. "Thanks." It was clear from the tone of his voice that Jordan's gratitude was deep and heartfelt.

"Don't mention it. Guarding the Prince of Rock and Roll is my job." He smiled. Jordan threw a pillow at him as he ducked out into the hall. As soon as he was gone, Jordan turned back to me.

"Even if it all goes bad, it's okay," said Jordan. "What's important to me isn't being famous, it's being able to write my music, and perform it. Me and the guys started out singing anywhere we could, anywhere someone would listen to us. In some ways, those were the best days of my life. If I have to go back and sing at county fairs and store openings, then that's what I'll do, because it's not about being famous. It's about the music, and I'll always have that."

I hugged Jordan. I was very proud of him. I wished that all his fans could see him just then. I knew they'd be proud of him too.

Jordan

◆

There was no meet and greet before the concert. That had been arranged long before I made my announcement, however, so it's not like the fans just decided they didn't want to meet me. The meet and greet was scheduled for after the concert this time. We set it up that way occasionally. I didn't know whether I was glad or not. In a way, I wasn't ready to come face to face with fans who had probably just learned I was gay. Then again, I'd be stepping out in front of some 2,500 or so fans in just a few minutes, so it might have been a good thing to get the reaction on a small scale before I was hit with it full force.

Torque was already performing and the crowd seemed as into the music as usual. I couldn't' help but wonder what would happen when I ran out. Part of me wanted to run in the opposite direction instead. I'd be lying if I said I hadn't considered grabbing Ralph and running back to his farm. That was just nerves. I hadn't considered it seriously. If I was going to hide from my life, I'd have just kept on hiding, instead of announcing to the world that I was gay.

I always had a certain sense of anticipation before a concert, a nervousness that made my stomach feel funny. That feeling was intensified more times than I could count at the moment. The seconds ticked by as *Torque* sang and I wondered what awaited me on that stage. The crowd was as big as ever. It was sold out. That was good news. At least the fans hadn't thrown their tickets to the ground and stomped away when they heard about me. I knew they'd heard. It was plastered all over the evening news.

The size of the crowd made me hopeful, but was frightening at the same time. I had no idea how all those people would react to me. I was half afraid that I'd be pelted with rotten tomatoes and garbage when I ran out. I was half afraid that girls would be holding up signs that said "We Hate Jordan, The Fag Boy", or something like that.

I remembered the letters and emails I'd read. I remembered all the girls I'd talked to, hundreds of them. I felt I could expect them to under-stand, but I didn't really know them. I often felt like I did, just as they probably felt they knew me, but, when it came right down to it, I didn't know them. I had no idea how they would react. I knew a lot of them would be disappointed. It had to be hard to find out that the boy you had a crush on wasn't interested in girls. Then again, it wasn't true that I wasn't interested in them. Girls were awesome! I loved them! It's just that I wasn't attracted to them, and wasn't looking for a girlfriend.

I tried to calm my nerves and trust in my fans, but it was hard. The unknown is always frightening, and I was facing a big unknown. I guess it was better that my first concert after the announcement was in New York City, rather than some smaller town in the Midwest. Not that I'm knocking the Midwest. It was pretty cool. At the very least it had one awesome feature—Ralph. It's just that I thought the New York crowd would probably be more accepting.

Ralph stood by my side. That was one thing I had to help me. Ralph was holding my hand, comforting me with his very presence. We'd never dared hold hands where others could see us before, but everyone knew about me now, about us, so there was no reason to hide it. I turned and looked at him. He hugged me.

"Just remember, Jordan, no matter what happens, I'll always love you."

I felt his love as if it were a physical force flowing through me. Who knows? Maybe it was. No matter, it strengthened me regardless. I did care about what was about to happen, but if I came back covered with garbage and pursued by "boos", Ralph would still be there waiting on me. He'd still love me, and that's all that really mattered.

Torque finished. Allen, Scott, Nicky, and Jimmy ran off the stage to a tidal wave of cheers. They greeted Ross, Kieran, and me with high fives the way they usually did. I was so nervous I was practically shaking. The others knew what a hard time I was having. They understood. I'm sure it was hard for Ross and Kieran too.

"It will be cool, Jordan. 'You Don't Know' first okay?" said Ross.

I nodded, but didn't speak. I couldn't trust my voice to hold steady. I appreciated his words. I appreciated the thought. I was glad he'd reminded me of the opening song too. It would be on the set list taped to the floor, but in my state, I didn't know if I'd remember to read it. I didn't know if I'd be able to remember anything.

"*Phantom! Phantom! Phantom!*" the crowd began to cheer. My fear and nervousness rose with the sound level.

"*Jordan! Jordan! Jordan!*"

My heart jumped in my chest. I'd heard my name chanted like that a hundred times or more, but this time it was different. I let myself hope that it meant things had not changed for the worse.

"You ready?" asked Kieran. The chants were growing louder.

I nodded my head, my eyes a bit wild with fear. This was going to be even harder than I thought. Ross and Kieran ran onto the stage. I turned and gave Ralph a quick kiss, took a deep breath, then turned to face my fate. I ran out onto the stage and was greeting by a chorus of cheers.

I didn't start playing immediately like I usually did. I just stood there and looked out at all the faces. They kept screaming and shouting my name. They were smiling and happy. Girls were holding up signs. I read some of them as I stood there. They read "We Love You Jordan!", "Way To Go Jordan!", and "Gay Boys Are Hot!". There were more, and they all said about the same. There wasn't one putting me down. There wasn't one that I'd feared.

Somehow, even with all the screams, I heard a boy shout "faggot!". I couldn't tell where it came from, but I found out pretty fast. There was a commotion in the audience where a group of girls were pounding on the boy that had yelled. I would have laughed if I wasn't afraid that someone would get hurt. Security was on top of it. They rescued the boy and took him out. I almost felt sorry for him. He was getting pelted with things thrown at him. It's a good thing security was escorting him because I think the crowd would have hurt him. I knew I'd have to deal with boys like him, but it sure looked like he was the exception and not the rule.

I heaved a huge sigh of relief and smiled, holding my hands above my head. I was smiling and crying and I could feel the tears flowing down my cheeks. The screaming grew louder and they were cheering for me. I mouthed the words "thank you" because I knew there was no way they'd hear me. I ran back to my keyboard and broke into "You Don't Know." I was crying with relief as I played.

I knew everything was going to be okay as I sang. It all felt right. Everything was so normal it was odd. I wasn't naïve enough to think that there would be no trouble, but I knew that it was all going to work out. It was even better than it was before. There was no more guessing, no more wondering. It was all out in the open, and my fears had not been realized.

*   *   *

I don't think I'd ever had quite so much fun at a concert. It was a blast. For the first time ever I felt like I had nothing hanging over my head. I could be the real me. When it was over, I wasn't even apprehensive about the meet and greet. I knew there could be trouble, but it was okay. I could deal with whatever happened. Most of my friends and fans were sticking with me. The ones that didn't could just go on their way.

Ralph brought a group of some sixteen girls and four boys backstage for the meet and greet. They were the winners of a local radio contest. This was the very first time ever that I'd be up close to any fans after coming out.

All the girls, and the boys, were looking at me as Ross, Kieran, and I signed autographs for them, but there was nothing unusual in that. I was most keenly aware of the boys, because I was interested in their reaction to me. If they were straight boys, and chances are they were, I wanted to see if they'd be cautious around me, or withdraw if I got close. I detected none of that, however.

I turned and smiled at Ralph as I was signing. He smiled back. He looked happier than even I did that everything was working out so well. Just looking at him made me feel good inside.

"I saw you on television," said one of the girls to Ralph. "Um, I hope this isn't being rude, but are you um…"

"This is Ralph. He's my boyfriend," I said, answering her question. She smiled.

"Could I have your autograph too?" she asked Ralph.

Ralph looked a little shocked by her request.

"Well, uh… sure, if you want it."

"I can't believe this," said the girl, turning to her friend. "I'm going to be the only girl with Jordan's autograph, and his boyfriend's!"

"Oh no you're not!" she said, then looked at Ralph. "Will you sign mine too?" By the time he was done, Ralph had signed several times. I could tell he wasn't expecting that in the least.

We took photos. It was near the end of the tour and we didn't have to rush to the next stop, so we had more time than we usually did. Ross, Kieran, and I even had time to pose with each of the fans. A couple of the girls asked if they could have a photo with just me as well. One of them leaned over and whispered in my ear as we waited for Ralph to get a shot of us.

"I think your boyfriend is really cute," she said. "I wish I was him." I smiled.

"Yeah, he is, but you're pretty cute too," I said. She blushed, and smiled.

Not one of the boys acted like they had a problem with me being gay. Instead, they seemed eager to shake my hand and talk to me. When Ross offered to take everyone on a tour of the bus, one of the boys lingered behind.

"Jordan, could I uh… get a picture with you and your boyfriend?"

"Sure," I said smiling at him. "Jon right?" I asked, trying to recall his name from signing it.

"Yeah," he said, smiling.

I called Ralph over and we stood on both sides of Jon. He put his hands over our shoulders and we all smiled at the camera. Kieran took the photo for us. Jon stood there a bit awkwardly after the photo had been taken, nervously shifting his weight from one foot to the other.

"Jordan, I just… wanted to say 'thank you,'" he said. Somehow I knew he wasn't talking about the photo, or the autograph. He looked into my eyes. "I'm gay too." He smiled. "I never told anyone that before, well, no one but my best friend. I think I… I think I can now, because of you." I smiled at him.

"That means a lot to me, Jon."

"Hey!" called one of the other boys, who was obviously Jon's friend. "He's already got a boyfriend, Jon." Jon turned as red as a beet.

"Shut up, Leo," he said through clinched teeth.

"He has a crush on you," said Leo, taking great delight in embarrassing Jon.

"Well he is kind of cute," I said to Leo. Jon turned redder still and smiled at me shyly.

"Don't mind Leo," said Jon. "Hockey player, too many pucks to the head. He's crazy. He even likes girls."

I laughed.

"Thanks," said Jon and shook my hand.

"Nice meeting you, Jon."

Jon and Leo went to catch up with the others. "I can't believe you told him that!" said Jon as they dropped out of sight.

"Looks like I've got competition," said Ralph after they'd gone.

"No one could ever replace you," I told him. I pulled him to me and kissed him on the lips to prove it.

Ralph

────────── ◆ ──────────

I was beyond relieved with Jordan's reception in New York City. I think I was as nervous as he was at the beginning of the concert. I stood just offstage crying, but they were tears of joy. I was so happy to see his fans support him when he needed them the most. They really cared about him, and accepted him just as he was. There were exceptions of course. That was to be expected, but on the whole, they loved him. Finding out he was gay didn't change that. I'm sure a lot of those girls were disappointed, but I think about all of them realized that their chances of having Jordan for a boyfriend would have been pretty much non-existent even if he was straight. After all, there were tens of thousands of them, and just one of him.

I thought about what a wonderful thing this was for gay boys everywhere. At last we had someone totally awesome to look at and say, "Look at him, he's awesome and he's gay!". Jordan was like the new poster boy for "Gay and Cool". What he'd done would help us all.

In the days that followed the New York press conference and concert, Jordan's homosexuality was big news. It was all over television and the newspapers. His coming out had stirred up a big controversy and I wasn't far from it. Jordan and I made no attempt to keep our relationship a secret and pretty soon I was in the press along with him. If I'd have thought about it beforehand, I'd probably have been terrified, but I was rather enjoying the attention. Paparazzi were actually taking pictures of me, and literally begged for photos of Jordan and me together. We stopped and posed for them. It was rather nice being famous myself, but I was happy that it probably wouldn't last. I could have a few moments of fame, then I'd fade into the background once more. I was glad. As much as I enjoyed the spotlight, I knew I wouldn't want to remain in it for long.

I was nervous about what my parents would think when they found out about me. There was no doubt they'd find out. They probably knew by now. Anyone who watched television, listened to radio, or read a newspaper knew. My parents would have to be living in a cave not to have discovered I was gay.

I didn't call them as I had been doing all along. I just couldn't bring myself to do it. I expected them to be accepting, but I knew it would be hard for them too. I just didn't know what to say to them. I just couldn't make myself pick up the phone and call. There weren't many days before I'd see them in person anyway. The tour was quickly drawing to a close.

*   *   *

Jordan and I quietly opened the door to our hotel room and peeked out. The coast was clear, so we slipped out of our room and made for the elevator. One of the bodyguards was always patrolling the hall, but whoever was on was gone for the moment. We moved quickly. The bodyguard would surely be back in mere seconds.

We made it to the safety of the elevator and punched the button for the ground floor. I looked at Jordan and smiled. Both of us were wearing only shoes and swimsuits. We were making a 2 a.m. run to the pool. The hotel we were in had a big pool outside and we knew no one was likely to be around at this time of the morning.

We reached the pool without meeting anyone. It was dark around the pool, but the pool itself was lit by lights within it. It was beautiful.

Jordan dived in and I followed. Jordan had a special love for pools. He loved to swim and just mess around. We both swam a few lengths then started wrestling in the water. The wrestling led to kissing and soon we were standing waist deep making out in the moonlight. I bet the paparazzi would have killed for a shot of us just then. I didn't care if one did manage to photograph us. Jordan and I loved each other and there was nothing wrong with us making out.

We swam more, and made out more. I thought about the time we'd swam together in the pool in Ft. Wayne. I was thrilled beyond belief to just be with Jordan then. I never dared dream that he'd someday be my boyfriend, and that we'd be making out in a pool.

We quite thoroughly enjoyed ourselves. It was wonderful to have a bit of privacy. It was worth giving up some much needed sleep. I knew it would cost us both the next day, but it was worth it.

Jordan

◆

I felt the music vibrating my entire body as I practically pounded on the keyboard. Kieran was giving new meaning to "loud" with his electric guitar and Ross was just about drowning us both out with his drums. I couldn't take my eyes off the keyboard to watch him, but I knew he was a mass of flying hair and drumsticks. We were performing "New York Nights" and it was one of our most intense songs ever. It was four and a half minutes of pure volume and energy. It required us all to play and sing our hardest to bring it off, but it was an experience in itself. It was a new song that we'd played for the very first time in New York City itself, in Madison Square Garden no less. That seemed fitting. As I looked out at the crowd, I could see it was popular in Indiana too. The cheers when we finished it were more deafening than ever.

I stood there panting, practically gasping for breath. I was drenched in sweat, but that wasn't unusual. I just stood there for several moments, taking it all in. It was the last concert on our tour and I wanted to savor it.

"You guys are crazy!" I shouted to the crowd. They cheered and screamed. "For this next song, we need you guys to clap your hands over your head like this. Yeah, that's it!" I ran to center stage and got close to the edge. "And, while your clapping, sway from side to side," I said as I demonstrated. "Then when I start, I want you all to jump up and down like this." I was bouncing on the stage. I felt so full of energy that I felt I could do it forever. "Yeah! You guys rock! Now start clapping, and swaying. Yeah, keep it up!" I ran back to my keyboard.

"One, two, three, four!" I yelled and we started playing. The audience was really into it. They kept swaying and clapping in time to the music. It wasn't just Kieran, Ross, and me making the music, it was all of us. I started jumping up and down and hundreds of fans followed. It was awesome beyond belief. It seemed almost impossible to have so much fun, and it was all the more wonderful because every single person was experiencing it, not just me.

"Ohhh yeah!" I shouted. We kept going. It was a night that I wanted to last forever.

Ralph

$\blacklozenge$

I couldn't believe the last concert had ended. I was sitting backstage with Jordan while the crowd was thinning out in the auditorium. Jordan was absolutely glistening with sweat. I'd toweled his face, but it didn't seem to make any difference. He was psyched. He fairly glowed with happiness. I looked up and was consumed by happiness myself.

"Denise!" I yelled and ran to her. It felt like I hadn't seen her in forever. I knew she was at the concert, along with Chris and a couple of his friends. I'd sent them the tickets and backstage passes myself. I hadn't seen them before the concert, however, and there was no way to pick them out while it was going on.

Chris was there too and I gave him a big hug. He seemed overwhelmed by being backstage, but immensely pleased with himself.

We all walked over to Jordan, who stood up and gave Denise a hug.

"Hey Chris," he said. Chris beamed and puffed out his chest. His friends were standing there watching, impressed that he really knew Jordan. Chris was pretty impressed with himself too. The look on his face was so comical that I had to fight to keep from laughing.

"Hey guys," said Jordan. "How'd you like the show?"

"It was awesome!" said Chris. I smiled to hear these words from someone who once said he'd hurl if he had to hear "Do You Know That I Love You" one more time.

"This is Matt and Gil," said Chris, indicating his buddies. I knew both of them, but not well. Even though we were all friends with Chris, I'd never hung out with them.

Matt and Gil were both pretty shy and hardly spoke a word. I think meeting Jordan had them speechless.

"Phone super stud!" yelled Ross as he came towards Jordan with a cell phone. Jordan stepped away and I introduced everyone to Ross. Chris was at the height of his glory. He was eating up every minute of it. Kieran came over and I left Chris and his buds to talk with them while I stepped to the side with Denise.

Denise had to hear all about the tour, and my relationship with Jordan. I couldn't cover all that territory in a few minutes time, but I did make a start. She was as happy for Jordan and me as she could be. That didn't surprise me in the least. I thanked her again for getting us together. If it hadn't been for her, neither Jordan nor I would probably have ever worked up the courage to be honest about our feelings. I was so happy, and it was all because of her.

Jordan came back a few minutes later, smiling brightly. He was even more cheerful than he had been when he'd left, if that were possible.

"You'll never guess who that was," he said. I looked at him for a moment with no idea. "Courtney," he said.

"The boy from Texas?"

"Yes!"

I knew how Jordan had regretted not talking to that boy. Courtney had haunted Jordan ever since the concert in Texas where Courtney had passed Jordan a note. Courtney calling made everything seem complete.

"I got his number," said Jordan. "When things settle down after the tour, I'm going to meet him in person."

I could just imagine how excited Courtney must be about that. I had a mental picture of him jumping up and down with joy somewhere in Texas. Jordan seemed pretty excited about it himself.

There was a limousine waiting outside. Jordan invited Denise, Chris, and the others to come back to the hotel room to hang out. Chris was so excited I thought he was going to wet his pants. I'd have no end of material to torment him with when I was back home. I almost couldn't wait.

We ordered pizzas and had a big party in Jordan's room, which was a suite this time because Jordan knew everyone would end up hanging out there on the last night. Ross and Kieran were there, of course, as well as Chad, and Allen, Scott, Nicky, and Jimmy from *Torque*. Everyone from the crew was there too. The place was packed. Chris almost couldn't handle being in the same room with two rock bands. He just kept staring at them like he couldn't believe it was all real. He was totally starstruck. I'd definitely have to use that against him in the future.

Matt and Gil seemed nearly as overwhelmed as Chris. I noticed they watched Jordan and me together, especially when Jordan draped his arm over my shoulder or I brushed his hair out of his face. I could tell they didn't know quite how to take us, two boys having a relationship was a new thing for them to see up close. I think it made them a touch uncomfortable, and yet it didn't seem to bother them too much. They weren't the least bit unfriendly to either of us. I just hoped the reception I received from my other classmates would be as cordial when the new school year started. Perhaps it would be, perhaps Matt and Gil were a sign of things to come.

We partied long into the night, then the limo took my friends back to their own hotel. Jordan and I were sharing a room, but we were too tired to do more than give each other a quick kiss before we fell asleep. It had been the same every night since New York, but the waiting was nearly over.

✶   ✶   ✶

The day after the last concert, the tour buses headed back to L.A., but Jordan and I stayed behind. We bid everyone an affectionate goodbye before they left, except Mike, he was staying with us. Tour or no tour, Jordan always had a bodyguard. Being shadowed by Mike was an inconvenience at times, but I was glad he was there. So far, there hadn't been any incidents, except with Jordan's manager, but who knew?

We stayed the night in a big, fancy hotel. Jordan got Mike a room right next to ours and promised we wouldn't leave our room all night, if he wouldn't disturb us. Mike smiled slyly as he agreed. I think he knew he had no worries about us sneaking out. Jordan and I had plans and they involved staying right in our room. We weren't going anywhere.

Our room had a big hot tub, with mirrored walls and so many plants it looked like we were in a jungle. Jordan ordered our supper from room service for later, and had some soft drinks sent up immediately. As soon as they arrived, we took them with us to the hot tub.

We watched each other a bit shyly as we took off all our clothes. It was the very first time either of us had seen the other naked. We didn't have long to look at each other before we slipped into the water, but Jordan was… beautiful. I was intoxicated by his beauty as he sat across from me. His eyes held me spellbound. He had the most amazing greenish-blue eyes. They'd always captivated me.

We sat in silence. There was no need for words between us. We just enjoyed one another's company. I marveled at our surroundings. I could just imagine what it cost to rent that room for the night. The expense was doubled really, for the room Jordan got for Mike was every bit as luxurious. It was sure nicer than any of the other rooms we'd stayed in. The others were nice enough, but they were just ordinary hotel rooms. This one was different.

Nice as it was, the room didn't really matter. All that mattered was that I was with Jordan. It made me feel very secure to know that I'd love him even if he was poor. There was no doubt about it. Even if we were just barely scraping by, I'd love him just as much.

I was a little nervous as I sat in the hot tub with Jordan. I wondered what he saw in me. He was a rich and famous rock star, while I was just a boy from Indiana. I wasn't even that good looking, or built. Jordan could have guys that made me look downright pathetic. My looks didn't matter to him, however. He loved me for me, just as I loved him for him. I knew it was easy for me to love him for him, because he was beautiful, but I knew I'd love him even if he lost his looks. Beauty fades, but love does not. No matter how Jordan might look in years to come, he'd always be sweet, kind, compassionate, and loving. Those are the things that counted, not his looks.

I was nervous for another reason too. We hadn't said so much in words, but I knew that tonight was the night. We'd known each other for months, but we'd never slept together. Well, we had, but that was only sleeping. We hadn't made love. We'd hugged, and made out. We'd held each other close and let our hands roam a bit, but we'd never made love. We'd never had the privacy. The time had never been quite right. I was amazed that we'd been able to wait so long. I knew I was about to explode and I was sure that Jordan was too. All that waiting would only make it more special and the waiting was nearly over.

I looked at Jordan, and his eyes met mine. He smiled as if he could read my thoughts. I could tell, just by looking at him, that his thoughts were nearly the same as mine. I loved him so much it hurt.

"Our supper will be here soon," said Jordan.

We both stood and dried off. I watched Jordan as I dried myself. His body was a work of art. I wanted to pull him to me right then and there, but I knew I hadn't long to wait. We both slipped on luxurious robes that the hotel provided. Jordan looked so sexy in his that it made my heart beat faster. Soon our supper arrived.

Jordan and I were both the burger and fries type, but it was nice to have an elegant dinner together. The table was covered with a white linen cloth and two tall white candles stood between us. We each had crab legs, and a large lobster tail with butter to dip it in and lemon to squeeze on top. I couldn't remember the last time I'd had lobster. There were also more shrimp than we could possibly eat. For desert, there was a beautiful cherry cheesecake that looked too good to eat.

Jordan showed me how to crack the crab legs open and how to squeeze lemon over it to give it an even better taste. We sat and talked and ate, enjoying each others company to the fullest.

"Are you nervous?" I asked.

"About what?" said Jordan mischievously.

"You know about what, about later, about us being together."

"A little."

"Me too." I paused. "I've never done anything like this before. I guess I'm afraid I won't be any good." Jordan smiled.

"I was thinking the same thing, that I might not be any good, but it doesn't matter you know? I just want to be with you."

"But you do still want to do it?" I said. It was my turn to smile mischievously.

"You have no idea how hard it's been for me not to jump on you and start ripping your clothes off," he said. Jordan always seemed so sensitive and romantic that his words surprised me a little. It was a pleasant surprise.

"The feeling is mutual," I said. We gazed at each other over the lobster, each of us with a hungry look that had nothing to do with food.

We continued to eat and talk quietly. Jordan told me about a new song he had running around in his mind and I gave him a few ideas for it.

"You know it's funny," he said "but I never really stop thinking about music. I'm so lucky to be able to do what I do."

"I think it may be contagious," I said. "I have no desire to perform like you. I'd be scared to death. But I do like working on songs with you. There's a poetry to it you know? It's like telling a story, and more."

"Exactly," said Jordan. He gazed at me with love in his eyes. "What do you say we save this desert for later?"

I nodded. I seemed to have lost the ability to speak. We slowly arose from the table and walked toward the bed. Jordan had the sweetest smile on his lips. If I hadn't loved him already, I'd have fallen for him on the spot. We stood facing each other, shyly gazing at one another. Jordan reached out and ever so slowly pulled the belt of my robe loose. I know I turned a little red, but I felt safe with him. He gently pushed the robe off my shoulders and let it fall to the floor.

I trembled slightly as I untied the belt of Jordan's robe. My eyes drank in his beauty as his robe slipped away from his slim form. Jordan pulled me to him and we embraced. It felt so good to be in his arms. I felt loved like never before. We stood there and kissed while we allowed our hands to roam free. Our breath came faster and our hearts raced. I was consumed by desire. I loved him so much it hurt. I was glad we had waited. I was glad I'd remained a virgin, until this night.

Several moments later we sank naked onto the bed. Jordan held me in his arms and we kissed. For the first time in my life, I made love, and it was the most wonderful experience of all. The sex was beyond description, but it was the love that overwhelmed me. Everything we did that night, and long into the morning, was an act of pure love. I felt like I'd waited forever, but I was glad I'd waited, and not wasted my first time on mere sex. What Jordan and I had went far beyond physical pleasure, but the physical pleasure was exquisite. It felt so good I didn't know if I could stand it.

I awakened the next morning with Jordan in my arms. It felt so good to have him beside me. I just lay there and held him while I watched him sleep. He was so beautiful that I couldn't imagine anyone, or anything, being more beautiful. I gazed at his naked body, drinking in his beauty, realizing it was but a reflection of his soul. He awakened and gave me a sleepy "Good morning."

"I don't know about you," I said. "but I'm still tired."

"You should be exhausted," said Jordan with a wicked grin. "You were an animal last night. Just the kind of wild I like." He kissed me.

"I'd give you a gold medal for your performance if I had one." I told him. Jordan snuggled up against me with his head resting on my chest. We lay there for a long time like that, just enjoying the closeness.

After a good, long while, Jordan looked up into my eyes with a mischievous look in his own.

"Again?" I asked smiling.

For answer, he climbed on top of me and we made love until past noon. We were definitely making up for lost time. Both of us had been right too, it was worth the wait.

*   *   *

Jordan and I flew to Evansville later in the day, with Mike coming along of course. Mike smiled when he saw us together. Both Jordan and I blushed and I'm sure Mike knew just what we'd been doing all night and all morning.

Jordan's management company had a car and driver waiting on us at the airport and we soon arrived at my parents' farm. It was definitely the first time a limousine had pulled into that driveway. I would have been looking forward to the expression it would cause on my parent's faces, but I had other things on my mind.

I was more than a little apprehensive about the welcome we'd receive. It's not that I thought my parents would disown me or something, but it was the first time I'd seen them since they'd found out I was gay. No doubt they knew that Jordan was my boyfriend. The rest of the world sure knew. It was therefore awkward to walk up to them with Jordan at my side. I loved him with all my heart, however, so that is where he belonged.

My parents came out of the house as we were unloading our bags. I was a bit shaky as I looked at them, but Mom came and gave me a great big hug. Dad wasn't far behind her. My parents did something then that set my mind at ease. Each of them went to Jordan and hugged him too. I nearly cried. I knew that everything was going to be fine.

They ushered us inside and insisted that I tell them all about my adventures over the summer. I'd written and called them time after time, but there was still much to tell. Perhaps it was because Mike was there, but they didn't mention that they knew I was gay, or that they knew Jordan was my boyfriend. I think they would have asked about my summer first in any case, to put me at ease and let me know that my sexual orientation wasn't the most important thing to them. I was their son, and they loved me. I was a very lucky boy.

After we'd all had a long talk, and some supper, Mike said he'd like to have a walk around the farm. He was from Los Angeles and had never been on one before. I think his real reason for going outside was to give the rest of us a chance to talk alone. I'd noticed on the tour that Mike was very good at keeping out of the way. He had a great respect for Jordan's privacy, and for mine. He was grimly serious when it came to Jordan's safety, but he tried to be as unobtrusive as possible.

Mom, Dad, Jordan, and I all sat around the kitchen table. My parents looked serious, but understanding.

"I guess you know, don't you?" I said, stating the obvious.

"We kind of knew already," said my Father, which took me by surprise.

"We could sense it, and we're not quite as dumb as you think we are," he said, smiling.

"Are you okay with it?" I asked, slightly fearful.

"Ralph, we love you, you are our son," said Dad. "Perhaps we'd be happier if you were interested in girls and would someday give us grandchildren, but we know this is what you are."

"You've always been a good son, Ralph," said my Mom. "We couldn't be more proud of you." I smiled.

"I guess you know Jordan is my boyfriend too," I said. I took Jordan's hand and held it in my own. My parents gazed at us, but their look wasn't disapproving. I knew they were somewhat uncomfortable, but they tried not to show it. I think they could tell that we loved each other very much.

"We know," said Dad, "and he's quite a boyfriend." Jordan smiled. I did too. It made me feel very good to have my parents approve of Jordan so much.

"He's the best in the world," I said. Jordan turned red with embarrassment.

Our talk turned to other matters. Everything felt right. My parents had acknowledged my sexual orientation, and my boyfriend, then they had gone on. It told me that they knew being gay was just a part of my life and not all that there was to me.

*　　　　　*　　　　　*

I called Denise and Chris the very next morning and they spent the entire day with us. Chris smiled when he saw me and gave me a hug, even though he'd seen me just a few days before. He was a bit hesitant to hug Jordan, but it wasn't because Jordan was gay, it was because he was still in awe of him.

"Your obsession has gone to a whole new level," said Chris. It wasn't a put down. He was smiling. I knew he was happy for me.

It was as fine a day as it could be. I was amazed that all had worked out so well. Jordan had even had a call from his management company, apologizing for Ben's behavior. They were giving Jordan a new personal manager, one they assured him would be a whole lot nicer. There was some talk of Ben being assigned to manage a dog that did television commercials, but I suspect that was only a joke.

Mom made a big picnic lunch and we all sat outside at a long table covered with red and white table cloths. Jordan and I sat side by side, of course. I felt so comfortable and happy. Every single person at the table accepted Jordan and me just as we were. They knew we were gay. They knew we were boyfriends. They were happy for us. It was the way it should be and it was wonderful.

After lunch, Jordan asked Chris if he wanted a wrestling rematch. Chris turned a bit red and declined. He was no doubt remembering how Jordan had kicked his butt the last time. I saw the mischievous look in Jordan's eyes. He knew Chris wouldn't want to wrestle him again. He'd asked merely to remind Chris that he'd beat him.

It was a wonderful day, even though we didn't do anything exciting in the least. It was over all too soon. I felt like time was just slipping between my fingers.

I wondered how things would go when school started. Things would certainly be different. I was oddly unafraid, however. I think that was due in large part to Denise and Chris. I knew I had at least two good friends who would stand by me. I thought of Matt and Gil too. They went to my school and they seemed pretty cool about it all. Having everyone know that I was Jordan's boyfriend would be an interesting experience. I was actually eager to see how it all went.

I wondered about me and Jordan. I was due back in school in just over a week, and he was heading to L.A. to begin recording his new CD. Our time was running out. What would become of us?

Jordan

———————— ◆ ————————

Ralph and I sat at the edge of the pond, occasionally tossing in a stone to make great ripples in the water. We were discussing our future.

"I don't know," said Ralph. "I want to be with you of course, but I've got a whole year of high school to finish."

"The thought of being away from you for even a day is painful," I said.

"I don't think my parents would like it very much if I wanted to come with you. The summer was one thing, missing my senior year is another." I tried not to let the sadness I was feeling show on my face, but I don't think I was successful.

"You know," I said, "one thing I've missed is being a normal boy. I've never been to high school, not a day. I've had tutors since I was in the eighth grade. I'm not sorry, but I kind of feel like I've missed out on something. I hate to say this... I can't believe I'm going to say this..., but I think it might be best if you finished high school here. I could get you tutors if you came with me, but it wouldn't be the same."

Ralph looked at me. I hoped he didn't think I was trying to get rid of him. I wanted what was best for him, even if it meant I couldn't be with him for a while. He smiled, and I knew he understood.

"I think you're right," he said, sadly. We sat there for a few moments in silence. Sometimes doing what is right is painful. My heart ached so I was afraid I'd start crying.

"It won't be that bad." I told him, finally. "We can call each other all the time. I'll come and visit. I'll fly you out to see me. It's only a year, well, nine months really. After you graduate, you can come with me. We'll travel together. There will probably be another tour next summer, then who knows? I wouldn't mind getting a place like this," I said, gesturing at our surroundings, "a quiet little farm somewhere, or maybe just a cabin in the woods where we could be alone and be together when we aren't busy on the road."

"I like the sound of that," said Ralph. I took his hands in mine.

"I mean it Ralph. This isn't one of those 'we'll keep in touch' things that people say and don't mean. I'm not letting you get away that easy."

I pulled him to me and kissed him. I knew the coming months would be difficult. I was already missing him and I hadn't even gone. I knew we'd get through it, both of us. It was a lot better having a boyfriend far away than not having one at all.

Ralph

———————— ◆ ————————

I sat by the pond alone, remembering just a few short days before when Jordan and I sat there and discussed our future. It had been so much easier talking about being away from each other then. I didn't know if I could bear it now. He had departed only hours before and I was miserable. A tear slipped down my cheek and fell onto the grass.

I looked beside me. He had been sitting right there not so very long ago, his beautiful eyes peering into mine. I loved him with all my heart, and what is more, I knew that he loved me. How could I make it through the coming months without him? How could I even make it through this day without him? I wanted more than anything to pack my bags and join him in L.A., but I knew the decision we had made was right. How I wished that the right decision would have left us side by side. I couldn't alter reality, however. Life was like that. You didn't always get things just the way you wanted. I knew I was lucky, so lucky I didn't have the right to complain, or feel sorry for myself. My dream had come true. I was in love with Jordan, and he was in love with me. That thought brought a smile to my lips, even though my heart still ached for him.

I jumped as my pocket started making an odd beeping noise. I smiled brightly and pulled the cell phone out of my jeans. There was only one person it could be—Jordan.

"Hey babe," said his sexy voice.

"Jordan, I love you."

"I love you too Ralph. Miss me?"

"So much it hurts."

"I know exactly how you feel. We'll get through this, Ralph. We just both need to keep busy, and call each other a lot. It will get easier. You start school tomorrow and I start working on the new CD."

"Yeah. Where are you?"

"I'm on the way to the house Ross, Kieran, and I have rented. We're going to work there, put some songs together."

"No more hotels for a while, huh?" I smiled.

"No way. I can't wait for you to come out here and stay. I haven't seen the house, but Kieran said it has a pool and everything. We're even setting up a little recording studio to work on our songs. It's going to be sweet."

"I can't wait to come out either, but I'm more interested in you than the house," I said.

"I'll have my own bedroom," said Jordan mischievously.

"Don't get me excited," I said. Jordan laughed evilly.

"I won't, because I'd get me excited too."

"It's good to just hear your voice," I told him.

"It's good to hear yours."

We went on talking and I felt like he was right there with me. I knew the phone would be my lifeline to Jordan. He said he'd call me often, and I knew that I could call anytime I wanted. We really would speak to each other every single day. I was glad of that. It was something I could hold onto.

I don't know how long we talked, but it was half an hour at least. We kept right on talking until Jordan arrived at his temporary home. We told each other "I love you" and hung up. His words echoed in my mind. Maybe I could make it after all.

I let my thoughts shift to the next day. Sitting there pitying myself because I wasn't with my boyfriend wasn't going to help the situation.

In fact, it would make it much worse. I forced myself to remember that anticipation could be the worst part of something unpleasant. Thinking about being parted from Jordan would only serve to make me miss him more. It would only increase my pain. The best thing I could do was keep busy and enjoy talking to him on the phone every day.

The opening day of school was mere hours away. When it had been a bit more distant, I'd been looking forward to it, but now that it was before me, I was apprehensive to say the least. I wasn't scared exactly, I was just facing an unknown. I'd never been popular at school. I'd never been anything. I was just another face in the crowd, one of those guys that no one really thought about much. I just kind of blended into the background. It wasn't necessarily a bad thing, but I knew it was about to change.

There weren't any openly gay boys at my school. Southern Indiana was kind of backward. I don't think the gay boys feared they'd get beat up or something, although maybe they would, but no one had ever come forward and said "I'm gay." I'm sure there had to be gay boys there. I knew that a few guys were suspected, but no one knew for sure. When I stepped into school the next day, I'd be the only openly gay boy in the whole school. I had no plans to announce it, but I hardly needed to do so. Anyone who didn't already know (if there was such a person) would undoubtedly be informed before the first day was done.

I didn't know how anyone would react. Would I be avoided and shunned? Would I be harassed? Would people look at me like I was a freak? How would Chris deal with the fact that everyone knew I was gay? He'd known it for a long time, but now everyone else knew too, and they knew he was my best friend. How would it affect him? How would it affect us? There were tons of questions, and no answers. I felt as if I were walking into total darkness, with no idea of where I was going, or what was before me.

And then there was my relationship with Jordan. Everyone in school would know he was my boyfriend. How would they react to that? How would the fact that I was dating a rock star be taken? The reaction of my classmates to that was a complete unknown. I had nothing to guide me. There sure wasn't a book in the library called *A Guide for Boys Dating Rock Stars* that would help me. I didn't have any experience that would guide me in the slightest. If anything, it was a greater unknown than how my classmates would react to me being gay. It was nearly too much to face.

*   *   *

I walked into school alone. It was a day unlike any other. I felt as if every single pair of eyes was peering at me. That wasn't quite the case, but it was uncomfortably close. There were whispers as I passed, and sometimes giggles. Every face that looked in my direction had its own story to tell. Most showed curiosity, but there was disbelief, jealousy, anger, awe, shock, surprise, happiness, and sadness too. It was as if every possible emotion was on display, or at least it seemed that way to me. My head was spinning and I couldn't quite be sure of my own thoughts and feelings, not to mention those of others. I felt as if I were moving through an alien landscape, instead of the school I'd attended for years.

Denise greeted me and I was comforted by her presence. She was a familiar element in an unfamiliar world. She could not stay with me forever, however, and soon I was left alone again to wander about confused. I found my way to my new locker and worked the combination.

"You're him right? Ralph?"

I looked up at the sound of the voice. It was a boy I did not know. He had a most serious expression on his face. He was younger than me, but taller and broader. He had thick muscles that showed even through his shirt. I grew a little afraid. Well, maybe more than a little. I knew that boy could beat me senseless if he wanted.

"Yeah, I'm Ralph," I said, wondering what was to come.

"Cool dude, I'm Jacob," a toothy grin replaced his serious look and he shook my hand. "Hey listen, I know we don't know each other, and this probably isn't cool to ask, but my girlfriend has this like total obsession with your boyfriend."

I gave him a very odd look. I was blindsided by what he was asking. I thought maybe he was going to hit me in the face, but he was asking for a favor instead. Jacob took my look to mean something other than it did.

"Not like physical…" Jacob rushed to explain. "She thinks he's cute and all, but she knows he's taken, and she has me. She just really idolizes him. She makes me listen to his music all the time, not that I don't like it. But anyway, I was wondering, if it's not too much to ask, if you could, like, get me an autograph to give to her."

I smiled. I nearly laughed. Here was this big athletic jock, who could mop the floor with me, nervously asking if I could get him an autograph. He towered over me, but I could tell he was almost scared of me. It was kind of amusing. One thing I really liked about it was that he didn't seem to care in the least that I was gay. He was just hoping I could help him score some points with his girl.

"Um, yeah, sure. I'll call Jordan later and he can probably mail me one or something."

"Oh thanks dude!" said Jacob. "I really appreciate this. Beth will like faint when I tell her."

"No problem," I told him. He shook my hand again, then went on his way.

I stood there a little dumbfounded. While we were on tour, I was used to girls asking me if I could get them an autograph or something from Jordan or Ross or Kieran, but I hadn't even thought about a big jock at school asking me, even if it was for his girl.

Throughout the day, I got asked for Jordan's autograph by a lot of girls. There got to be so many I had to make a list. I hoped that Jordan wouldn't mind. Just after I'd finished lunch, I had a whole group of girls around me, asking for Jordan's autograph and asking me all kinds of questions about him. I was glad that I'd experienced what it was like to be famous when I was with Jordan, because it had prepared me for what I was going through now. It was almost as if I was famous myself. I guess I was in a way, even if it was just for being Jordan's boyfriend.

While I was surrounded by girls in the cafeteria, Adam walked up and sneered at me. I'd never liked him. He was, quite simply, a jerk. One of his buddies was with him, like his own little bodyguard. There were usually two. I guess the other one was out beating up grade school kids or something.

"I always knew you were a fag, Rogers."

I knew I'd be hearing shit like that. I thought it would bother me more. I guess it just didn't mean much coming from Adam. Like I said, he was a jerk, so his opinion didn't count for much in my eyes.

"And you're a loser, Adam. I have a boyfriend and you're nothing but a jerk. Who comes out on top, huh?"

I could tell by the look on his face that he didn't like that at all. I knew I'd probably be getting my ass kicked in a few moments for what I said, but it was better than just sitting there taking his crap. The girls around me were eyeing Adam angrily.

"You like all this attention, don't you, Rogers? You probably let that rock star fag of yours screw you just so you could say he did. You…"

It was one thing for him to call me a fag, it was another for him to call Jordan one. Fag didn't mean gay. It took "gay" and perverted it into something horrible. It was a filthy insult and I wasn't going to let Adam abuse my boyfriend by calling him that. I grew so enraged so fast that I didn't even think before I acted. If I had, I probably wouldn't have done what I did. I didn't think, however, and before he knew what hit him, I'd jumped up and sent Adam flying with a powerful right cross.

I almost couldn't believe what I'd done. Neither could Adam. He landed on his ass and just sat there looking up at me. A trickle of blood was coming from the corner of his mouth. I stood there trembling with rage, ready to start pounding him if he came after me.

"Don't ever call my boyfriend that again!" I told him.

Adam actually looked frightened. Even his lackey didn't make a move toward me. I was breathing hard, holding my arm back for another punch. Everyone in the cafeteria was watching. The girls around me looked ready to pound Adam too. I was so furious I was hardly aware of it. Mr. Chamberlain quickly walked over and stood there looking at us. He didn't say anything, just motioned for us to follow him with his finger. He escorted us to the principal's office.

I cooled off considerably while I sat there. Adam looked at me out of the corner of his eye now and then. He was angry, but seemed even more afraid. I was a little frightened myself, because I'd never been sent to the principal's office before. I was more angry than anything. I didn't take kindly to someone insulting the boy I loved.

Mr. Zachary called me in first. I sat down in front of his desk as he looked through my file. Finally, he spoke.

"So tell me what happened Ralph."

"Adam came up and insulted me. He called me a fag. I told him he was a jerk. He insulted me again, then he insulted my boyfriend, so I hit him in the face."

"We don't approve of students attacking each other," said Mr. Zachary.

"Yes sir."

"You don't seem sorry that you did it," he said.

"I'm not sorry. He deserved it. Nothing would have happened if he hadn't come up and insulted my boyfriend. I'm not going to lie and say I'm sorry I did it, because I don't want to lie."

"I see," said Mr. Zachary, picking up my file again. "Your record is quite clean, not an incident since Kindergarten. Your grades are fairly good. The comments from your teachers positive. I don't get the feeling you are a trouble maker. Do you think you could refrain from attacking Adam again if we let this go without a suspension or detention?"

"As long as he doesn't insult my boyfriend, sir."

Mr. Zachary looked at me appraisingly. I couldn't believe I was being so calm and collected. I couldn't believe I was mentioning that I had a boyfriend so casually.

"I certainly wouldn't want to insult him," he said, smiling ever so slightly. "I'll have a talk with Adam. I would appreciate it, if there is a next time, that you come to me instead of punching Adam in the face."

"I'll try sir," I said.

"You may go."

I breathed a sigh of relief as I left the office. I was very proud of the way I'd handled myself. I actually liked Mr. Zachary and I think he respected me. Later in the day I found out he'd given Adam a lecture on courtesy, and a detention. I had the feeling Mr. Zachary thought Adam was a jerk too.

More girls came up to me between classes, and after school. It seemed like whenever I wasn't in class, I was fielding questions about Jordan, or *Phantom*, or what it was like hanging out with the band. I kind of liked the attention. It was also kind of a pain. I was beginning to wish things were the same as the year before, but I guess it was the price I had to pay for having Jordan as a boyfriend. It was a price I was more than willing to pay. Jordan was worth any sacrifice.

I didn't have to take much crap from anyone, other than Adam at lunch. I did hear stuff like "queer", "fag", "fairy", and "pillow-biter" mumbled as I passed sometimes. I could never quite tell who said those things, but I guess it didn't matter. I knew there were people out there who would be down on me because I was gay. I was just glad no one was giving me a really hard time. I knew it could happen.

*   *   *

The next day at school was a lot like the first, except there was no scene with Adam. He was giving me a wide berth. I think my aggressiveness of the day before had caught him off guard. It was probably a good thing it happened. A good part of the school had witnessed me punching Adam in the face. I'm sure they had little difficulty figuring out what it was all about. What I'd done would probably save me a lot of trouble. Guys who were thinking about giving me a hard time about being gay might think twice now, since they knew they might get a fist in the face for it. I wasn't a violent person, but I would defend myself. I guess I wasn't really defending myself, however. I hadn't punched Adam when he called me a fag. I didn't hit him in the face until he insulted my boyfriend.

Things were just a bit calmer the second day. Lots of girls, and some guys, were still coming up to me asking questions about Jordan, and *Phantom*, and asking if I could get them an autograph. It wasn't as hectic as the day before, and for that I was thankful.

Just after school I found myself in a nearly deserted hallway. I was ever so slightly edgy. It wasn't like I lived in fear or anything, but I felt like I was in one of those scary movies, in a part right before something bad happened. I could almost hear the creepy music. I nearly jumped when someone walked up behind me. It wasn't a crazed killer with a big knife, however, or even a bully all ready to pound me. It was just a boy who didn't seem particularly threatening. I figured he was another *Phantom* fan wanting to talk.

"Hey. I'm Lance," he said, extending his hand.

I shook it. He looked familiar.

"Ralph."

"Yeah, I know."

As I looked at him, who he was dawned on me. I hadn't recognized him right away because his hair was blond. The last time I'd seen him, it was bright blue. He was the boy at the costume party who kept checking out Jordan.

"I didn't know you were gay," he said.

"Well, it's not always wise to go around announcing things like that."

"Oh, I know. It makes it real hard to find someone."

We kept talking. I expected Lance to start asking questions about Jordan. The way he was looking at him at the dance, I was sure he had the hots for him. He didn't even mention him, however. It took a long time for me to realize it, but the hungry look in his eyes finally made it apparent, Lance was interested in me. More than that, I was quite sure he wanted me. It was a whole new experience for me. No guy had ever looked at me like that before. It kind of made me feel good about myself. It was kind of creepy.

"My parents are going to be gone all evening," said Lance, pointedly. I didn't say anything. "Think you'd like to come over? We could…do something." It was abundantly clear that "something" meant sex.

"Um…uh… I can't. My parents expect me home. In fact I may already be in trouble for being late." It wasn't the truth, but I just didn't know what to say to Lance.

"Oh," said Lance, clearly disappointed. "Well, sometime when you have time, I'd *really* like to get together." The emphasis he put on "really" made it clear he was desperate for sex.

Lance just about devoured me with his eyes. He looked hungry. He looked like he wanted nothing more in all the world than to just start ripping my clothes off.

"Okay, well, I really have to go," I said. I left as quickly as I could without being rude.

I thought about Lance on the way home. He knew I had a boyfriend and he'd all but asked me to come home with him and have sex. Actually, he had asked that, he just hadn't stated it clearly. Something within me was aroused by it, but I found it distasteful. Lance didn't even know me, and he wanted to have sex with me. The fact that he knew I had a boyfriend made it even worse. Why did he want me so bad, anyway? I wasn't exactly a stud puppy. Okay, I wasn't a stud puppy at all.

Was it just because he knew I was gay, and he didn't know any other gay boys? Was it because I was Jordan's boyfriend and he wanted to have sex with the boy who had made love to Jordan?

I couldn't figure Lance out. I didn't really like the way he was so focused on sex. I mean, there's nothing wrong with sex, but I'd experienced sex with someone I loved. That transformed sex into love making, which was a far more wonderful thing. Lance didn't seem to know that, and I felt a little sorry for him. I think he was a very lonely boy. Maybe he was just looking for love after all. I think a lot of people got love and sex confused, but they weren't the same thing.

Jordan

◆

"Dude!"

Ross greeted me at the car by hugging me, then putting me in a head-lock so he could use my head as a bongo drum.

"I missed you too Ross," I said, when he released me.

Ross made himself useful by helping me and Mike carry my bags into the house. It was a nice house, big and roomy, with lots of windows and light. When I stepped inside, Kieran hugged me, too, causing me to drop my bags.

"How's Ralph?" he asked.

"Beautiful."

"Nice place you picked out," I said to Kieran. The management company had really done most of the work of finding us a place to rent, but Kieran had made the final decision for us.

"Yeah, real cozy, just us, Chad, and the bodyguards. It has seven bedrooms. Come on, I'll show you yours."

Kieran led me into a nice sized bedroom with a beautiful view of the pool.

"Oh man," I said, looking at the pool below.

"Yeah, I thought you'd like that. It's the main reason I picked this place."

"Good job."

"Let me show you the studio," said Kieran.

We dropped all my stuff, then headed to the "basement". It wasn't like most basements. Almost one entire wall was glass looking out onto the pool.

"Dude," said Chad, when he caught sight of me. He gave me my third hug of the day.

"Looks like you've been busy, Chad."

"Sure thing, dude. I haven't started on the recording equipment yet, but other than that, she's all ready to go when you guys wanna play."

I walked over to my keyboard and played around with it a bit. I smiled.

"I can hardly wait to get started," I said.

"You're a workaholic Jordan," said Kieran.

"Guys, I've been working on this new song. I have some cool stuff worked out for it, but I want to see what you guys can do with it." I glanced out at the pool. "But maybe after a swim."

"You should have got a house without a pool Kieran. We'll never get anything done," said Ross.

"Like you care," said Kieran. Ross just smiled.

"I'll get my suit on, unless you wanna go nude," said Ross.

"Get your suit," I said. "I'm scared of small things." Kieran laughed. Ross laughed with him for a moment, but then he figured out what I'd meant.

"Hey! It's not small! Here, I'll show you!" Ross started to pull down his shorts right then and there.

"Uh, no, that's okay Ross," I said quickly. "I believe you. You're huge." Ross laughed and ran upstairs, drumming on the banister with his fingers along the way.

"Maybe we should have him sedated," I said to Kieran.

"Do they sell Ritalin by the case?" he asked.

"Come join us." I told him.

A few minutes later, Ross, Kieran and I were all swimming in the pool. It was hot out, but then that was to be expected in August in L.A.

It was beautiful and the sunlight made the water sparkle. It was perfectly clear and I could see right to the bottom. The pool was nice and big, with diving boards and plenty of room to swim laps. Of course, what I liked to do most was just fool around in the water.

Ross started a water fight with me and Kieran and it turned into a wrestling match. Kieran and I had to gang up on Ross. He wasn't much taller than either of us, but he was quite a bit stronger. He had broad shoulders and a thick chest and it was hard to handle him. He sent me under a few times even with Kieran and me going after him at once. It felt so good to relax after the hectic weeks of the tour. I just wished Ralph was there with us.

After several minutes of rough and serious horseplay, we calmed down and lazily floated around in the water. It felt good to just let my body drift while the sun beat down upon me. I definitely needed some sun. I'd had precious little time to be out in it all summer. Except for a few days on Ralph's farm, I hadn't been able to get out in the sun much at all. I was pale and felt like I was totally lacking a tan. I didn't tan too well in the best of situations. It was the curse of being blond. Kieran had a pretty good tan, and Ross was tanned beautifully, although they didn't get any more of a chance to get out into the sun than I did. Guys with dark hair had it easy.

Kieran got out after a while and left Ross and I to float around. Ross, as always, had a lot of excess energy, so he swam a few laps now and then before returning to lazily float on the surface. After a bit, we got out some inflatable lounges and lay back on them as they floated around the pool. They were really cool. I liked being able to sit up while still having my lower half mostly under water.

I closed my eyes and did nothing but feel the sun on my chest. I loved the warmth of the sun on me. It was a sensation I felt all too infrequently. I was compensated for that in a way by enjoying it all the more when I could feel it. Life was like that sometimes. I found that when I didn't get to do something I liked very often, that I enjoyed it all the more when I did. When I couldn't get enough sleep, I slept better. There was an elegant balance to it all. Someone who got to hang out in a pool all summer probably didn't appreciate it a tenth as much as me.

I opened my eyes and caught Ross gazing at me. He looked away a bit guiltily. In a fleeting moment, I read his eyes. I knew what he was thinking. I knew what he was feeling. It was crystal clear that he wasn't over the crush he had on me. He'd not mentioned it once since the time we'd spoken of it, right after he and Kieran had walked in on me and Ralph making out. I hadn't mentioned it either, but I'd been pretty sure he was still having trouble dealing with it. There was no doubt in my mind about it as we floated on the water with the sun shining down upon us.

Ross looked back at me, his face flushed with embarrassment. I worked my lounge closer to his and took his hand.

"It's okay Ross," I said.

Tears welled up in his eyes and he slowly shook his head "no." He started softly crying. I slipped off my lounge and pulled him to me. We stood chest high in water as I held him. He sobbed into my shoulder. After a bit, he pulled away and we both swam to the edge of the pool and sat there with our legs in the water.

"I didn't want you to know," said Ross, clearly meaning he didn't want me to know that he still had feelings for me, feelings more than friendship.

"Ross, we're friends. You don't have to hide anything from me. We're here for each other, no matter what."

"But I know it makes you uncomfortable. You have Ralph and I know you love him. You don't need me…wanting you." He looked at me. He was very uncomfortable expressing his feelings.

"So this is more than just a crush?" I asked.

"Yes. No. I don't know. I'm so screwed up." He paused for a long time. "You know how I told you I like girls? And that I didn't go for guys, except for you?"

"Yeah."

"Well, it's true. I thought when we talked before that everything was going to be cool. That I could handle it all. It's not been so cool though. I can't keep from… Sometimes when I see you I just want to… I've spent a lot of time wondering if I'm not really bi, but when I look at other guys, it's just not there. It doesn't matter how good they look, I just don't want anything with them. There was even this boy during the tour…" Ross paused as if he didn't know if he should continue.

"Go on," I said.

"Well, I slipped out of my hotel room in the wee hours of the morning. I couldn't sleep and I had this chocolate attack and there wasn't any. So I went out looking for a vending machine or something. I met this boy when I was getting my chocolate bar. We started talking. He was exceptionally good looking, really athletic and all that, but he didn't do anything for me, you know? Anyway, his eyes were roving over me. I could tell he was all nervous. We'd been talking for like half an hour and he started talking about sex, just general stuff. Then finally he told me if I wanted a blow-job, he'd give it to me, no strings attached. He said he'd do anything I wanted, and let me do anything to him I wanted. I mean, there was this really good looking guy for the taking, but I just wasn't interested. I didn't get aroused at all or anything. I have all these thoughts about you…" Ross grew silent for a moment and blushed again. "I could have had him if I wanted, but I didn't want him, you know? I ended up telling him that I just didn't swing that way. He got kinda upset and apologized for even suggesting anything like that. I told him it was cool and that I didn't have anything against gays. I just wasn't like that myself."

"So you had your chance, and you passed on it," I said.

"More than that. I just wasn't interested at all. I have like no attraction to guys, except for…you. I mean if you'd let me, right now I'd… Forget it. I shouldn't be saying that."

I didn't know what to do, or what to say. Ross was very attractive with his long, black hair, handsome face, and nicely muscled body. I had to admit to myself that I was a bit aroused with him sitting there by me. It was a dangerous situation. I was afraid something would happen that shouldn't. Ross needed me. I loved him and I wanted to be there for him, but I just couldn't. I loved Ralph. He was my boyfriend and I wanted to spend my whole life with him. I couldn't make love with Ross, even just once. I couldn't cheat on Ralph like that. I felt miserable, and even a little selfish, withholding what might have helped Ross, but I just couldn't do it.

Ross sobbed gently and I took him in my arms again. I could hold him. Ralph wouldn't mind. He would have done the same. I kept Ross in my arms until he stopped crying, then released him and wiped the hair from his face.

"I do love you, Ross. You are my friend, and I consider you my brother."

I leaned forward and pressed my lips to his. I kissed him deeply, giving him as much of what he needed as I possibly could, without going too far. He gazed at me when our lips parted.

"I love you too, Jordan, so I won't ask what I want to ask. I know you are in love with Ralph and are really happy for the first time in a long time. I wouldn't do anything to mess that up. I wouldn't do that to you, or to Ralph."

I hugged him again, then we went inside. I thought about Ross as I changed. I didn't know what I could do for him, except be his friend. Maybe that would be enough. I didn't understand his attraction to me, when he wasn't attracted to any other guy. Maybe there was just some intense, spiritual connection between us that made him feel that way. I felt very close to Ross. Maybe his attraction to me was something other than it appeared. Maybe it's not what he really wanted, but just what he thought he wanted. Maybe what he really craved was simply my love. That I could give him, willingly, gladly, and without guilt. I'd make sure Ross knew that I loved him. I'd said it, but words were often not enough. I'd make sure to show him whenever I could, and then maybe he'd be okay.

Ralph

---◆---

Life at school was completely different from the previous year. Life at home was about the same. I found myself looking at photos of Jordan in magazines while I listened to his music. I watched video tapes of him and dreamed about him, just as I had before we'd met. A few things were different. My Phantom calendar and a couple of Jordan posters were now on my walls, instead of hidden away in the closet. I also had a lot of pictures displayed that had been taken during the tour, mainly of Jordan, and me and Jordan together, but some others too. My life at home was much the same as always, but boy had things changed in the last few months. Had anyone told me a year before what my life would be like now, I'd have thought they were crazy.

I was glad I could talk to Jordan on the phone. I didn't know if I could make it without hearing his voice. I was still worried about our long distance relationship. I didn't know much about relationships at all, but I knew a long distance one was supposed to be hard. I could see why. I needed to touch Jordan, to hold him, to be with him, but I couldn't. With him so far away, a lot of my needs went unfulfilled, and I'm not just talking about sex. If sex was the only problem, I could have handled that. There was so much more, though. The few months that were spread out before me seemed like centuries.

Things calmed down at school pretty fast. I got harassed some daily for being gay, but it wasn't all that bad. Mainly I got a lot of attention because I knew Jordan. Luckily that calmed down. I think everyone realized that I'd be around for the whole school year, so they didn't have to corner me right away to get Jordan's autograph or find out about him. I was definitely a lot more popular than I had been, but most of my new "friends" were just there because I knew someone famous. I didn't let it go to my head. My real friends were still Denise and Chris, just like they'd always been.

*   *   *

"I guess your boyfriend doesn't care so much about you after all," said Adam gloating.

I was eating lunch with Chris and Denise, and a few girls, when Adam slapped a tabloid down on the table right in front of me.

"Shit!" said Chris.

"Oh it can't be!" said Denise.

Everyone was staring at the front page, including me. There was a picture of Jordan, kissing Corey Thomas, the teen heartthrob, right on the lips. There was an article with the photo.

ROCK STAR IN LOVE TRIANGLE WITH TEEN IDOL

The worlds of music and movies collided when pop star Jordan was discovered kissing teen idol Corey Thomas in a remote corner of a public Los Angeles park. "They were just kissing," said Myra Elkens, who provided the above photograph, "but they were really going at it. It was disgusting."

The two teen stars might well have been "just kissing" in public, but it's rumored that much more goes on in private. Jordan, the lead singer of Phantom, made headlines recently when he publicly outed himself after a backstage homosexual scandal. He has been seen numerous times with his boyfriend, Ralph Rogers, but apparently Jordan's Indiana farm boy didn't satisfy him and the pop star went in search of a new fling. It didn't take him long to find one in Corey Thomas, teen television and film star.

The management companies of both stars could not be reached for comment, but undoubtedly they would not shed light on the current scandal. Hollywood and the music industry both have a long standing tradition of turning a blind eye to the private lives of their stars. As long as Jordan and Corey are bringing in the big bucks, it's doubtful that their management companies will care what they do behind closed doors, or in parks.

One wonders about those left in the wake of the two young stars sexual escapades. What of Corey's girlfriend, Sandra Parker. and Jordan's boyfriend, Ralph Rogers? Undoubtedly the lives of these two were crushed when they were dumped by their famous boyfriends...

I just sat there in utter shock. I knew I'd be crying soon, but for the moment, I was just too shocked for it. It was just as well. I didn't want everyone to see me cry. Denise was looking at me with an expression of shock and disbelief. Chris looked more worried than he ever had before. Adam was gloating.

"I guess you aren't so hot now, are you gay boy? He dumped your sorry ass!"

Chris whipped around and grabbed Adam by the throat.

"Shut—the—fuck—up!" he growled menacingly. It wiped the smile off Adam's face for the moment. He departed, but left me with the paper.

I got up slowly, mustering every ounce of control I had to keep from bawling. I walked straight out of the building to my car.

"You shouldn't drive when you're this upset," said Denise as she followed me.

"I need to be alone," I told her. I appreciated her concern, but I didn't want anyone near me.

"Let me drive you home, then you can be alone. Please, you can't drive when you're like this."

I slid over to the passenger side and tossed her the keys.

"When you need to talk, I'm here for you," said Denise.

They were the only words spoken on the drive home. Denise knew I wasn't ready to talk about it. She knew I had to work it all out for myself. I just sat silent in the passenger side, tears streaming down my cheeks. I just couldn't believe it. I couldn't believe Jordan would do this to me. He'd only been gone a few days…

When we got home, I got out of the car and started walking. I didn't even look back. I knew Denise understood. My tears came faster as I walked. By the time I reached the pond and sat down, I was bawling. Nothing had ever hurt me so badly in all my life. I was sure Jordan had loved me. I felt it. I knew it. He was so sweet and wonderful and beautiful. He was my dream come true. He was the best friend I'd ever had. He was my boyfriend. We were going to spend our lives together. What had happened? And how did it happen so fast? It was unthinkable. It just could not be.

I looked at the paper I was still holding. There it was, as plain as day, Jordan kissing Corey Thomas. It looked like a deep kiss too. I wondered what else they'd been doing. Thinking of Jordan with another boy tore me apart. I bawled even louder.

When I'd calmed down a bit, I thought about the whole situation more. I'd always wondered what Jordan saw in me. I wasn't handsome or built or famous. I was just an ordinary boy. I'd wondered why he picked me instead of some movie star. I couldn't believe it, but it looked like he'd gone out and got himself one.

Why did he lead me on so? Why did he tell me he loved me and that he wanted us to be together forever if he didn't mean it? Not for sex surely. If he was just using me for sex, then we wouldn't have waited for months before doing it. If he just wanted sex, there were tons of other boys he could have had, boys way hotter than me. Was it all just some sick mind game? That didn't make sense either. I knew Jordan. It just wasn't like him. He couldn't, wouldn't do this to me. There it was though, in black and white.

I was hurt, and beginning to get angry. Did Jordan think he could just use me, play with me, and then discard me like some kind of toy? Was that all I was to him? More and more of my pain turned to anger. I pulled out the cell phone I always carried and called Jordan.

"Hey Ralph," he said when he answered.

"Just tell me one thing," I said. "Did I mean anything to you at all?"

"What are you talking about?"

"I know you kissed him Jordan."

There was silence on the other end.

"Did I mean anything to you Jordan?"

"I love you, Ralph."

"Then why did you kiss him? What else have you done? You've haven't been gone a week and you're already cheating on me. I feel like I don't even know you now!"

"Ralph, it's not what you think."

"You really had me fooled. I really thought you loved me."

"I do love you, Ralph. I thought you'd understand…"

"Understand!? I'm your boyfriend Jordan, and you go and start making out with another boy? I'm supposed to understand that? Maybe things are different with all your rock and movie star friends, but that's not how I see a relationship. Where I come from, you can't have a boyfriend and then fuck every boy you see."

"You are being unreasonable," said Jordan. I could tell he was getting angry.

"Unreasonable? Me? You are the one who cheated on me, Jordan. Why didn't you just have the balls to tell me if you didn't care about me, instead of pulling this behind my back? I feel like I don't know you, and you know what? I don't want to know you."

I hung up. I was so angry I was shaking. I let the phone drop to the ground and started bawling. I felt like my whole life had come to an end.

Jordan

———————— ◆ ————————

I let the phone drop from my hand. Tears welled up in my eyes. Ross and I had been sitting quietly alone working on a song when Ralph called. I'd been so happy to hear from him, but then...

"What's wrong?" asked Ross.

I cracked at the sound of his sympathetic voice and broke down in tears. Ross crossed the short distance between us in a flash and held me in his arms. It was a good, long time before I could stop crying.

"He knows," I said.

"Knows about what?" asked Ross.

"About us."

"Us? There isn't an us, not if you mean..."

"He knows we kissed."

"How the hell could he know that? No one knows that."

"Well someone does. Someone told him."

"Well I sure as hell didn't and you didn't."

"How could he have found out? The only ones who were even here besides us were Kieran, Chad, Mike, Shawn, and Rod. Even if they did see, none of them would have told Ralph. It doesn't make any sense."

"No one would have reason," said Ross, then he grew quiet. I looked at him. "Jordan, I did not tell him. Before you start thinking I did or something, I want to promise you I didn't. I wouldn't do that. The only person who would have a reason to tell him is me, but I didn't do it. I wouldn't do that to get Ralph out of the way so I could have you. I swear, Jordan."

Ross seemed frightened that I'd think he was the one who told Ralph. He was the only one with any real motive, as he himself had pointed out. I hadn't even thought about it yet. Now that he'd brought it to my attention, I realized why he was scared. I did not suspect him, however. Ross would just not do something like that.

"I know you didn't do it, Ross. I trust you."

"Thanks," he said. He was almost in tears himself.

"But who?" Neither of us had the answer to that.

"Shit," said Ross, looking at his watch. "I'm supposed to meet Kieran to help him pick out a new guitar. You want me to call him and cancel?"

"No. No, you go ahead. I need to be alone to think anyway."

"You sure?"

"Yeah."

"Well, we'll be back a little later. You call me if you need me and I'll come running."

"Thanks, Ross."

As soon as Ross left, I went to my bedroom, lay down, and cried. I didn't think. I just cried. I felt like my heart was broken. I don't think I'd ever been so miserable before. I felt like my whole life was ruined.

I never thought Ralph would be so hurt by me kissing Ross. If I had even suspected it, I wouldn't have done it. I was just trying to be there for a friend. Why did this have to happen? I' reached out to help someone I loved. Was that wrong? It was only a kiss. How could it cause so much harm?

Ralph's words came back to me. They had cut into me like a knife. I knew he was hurt, but he was being unreasonable. He had said some pretty hateful things to me. He hadn't acted like the Ralph I knew at all. He'd pretty much come out and called me a liar. He'd accused me of doing things I had not done. He'd all but called me a slut. I was still torn up inside, but the anger I'd felt when he was saying those things to me was returning. He had no right to go off on me like that, not for simply helping a friend who needed me. How could Ralph act like that? I wouldn't have believed it if I hadn't heard it with my own ears.

I was hurt, angry, and miserable. Everything had been so wonderful, but then Ralph had to call and destroy it all. He'd even said he didn't want to know me. He'd hung up on me. The boy I thought loved me with all his heart had dumped me. It hurt so bad I couldn't stand it. It made me so angry I couldn't see straight. I lay in bed and cried a river of tears.

When Ross and Kieran returned later, I wouldn't come out. It grew dark and still I stayed on my bed, squirming in emotional pain. The one person who I really thought loved me didn't. I couldn't take it. How could I go on?

Ross knocked on my door later and I let him in. I sat up in bed and he sat on the edge near me. I knew he was worried sick about me.

"I'm so sorry, Jordan. This is my fault. If it wasn't for my crush on you, I'd never have got all upset, and you'd never have kissed me to make me feel better. I've ruined everything for you. I'm so sorry."

"It's not your fault, Ross. You didn't mean for this to happen. No one could have predicted it. I sure didn't. I kissed you because I wanted to, because you are my friend and you were hurting and you needed to be loved. I do love you Ross and I couldn't take seeing you suffer so. This is not your fault. If it is anyone's, it's mine, or Ralph's."

Ross was so upset over me that his eyes were glistening with tears. If I hadn't known before, I would have known then that he loved me.

"I thought he loved me, Ross, but now he says he doesn't even want to know me. I thought we'd be spending our lives together, and now I'll never see him again. I thought he loved me, Ross, I thought he loved me."

I started crying all over again. Ross pulled me to him and held me in his strong arms. I buried my face in his chest and bawled my eyes out. I was so glad he was there to hold me. I needed to be held so badly. I could tell that Ross was crying too. I could feel the sobs in his chest. He was so upset for me that he shed tears for me.

I clung to him. I needed him. I raised my face and looked into his eyes. I pressed my lips to his and kissed him. I didn't break the kiss, I just kept on kissing him, more and more deeply. I needed him. I wanted him.

Ross and I sank down on the bed. I pulled his shirt off. He pulled mine over my head. I kissed him, again, and ran my hands over his powerful torso. He took me in his arms and held me. He loved me. With fumbling fingers, I undressed him, and he undressed me. In mere moments we were naked on my bed, pressing against each other, kissing and loving each other.

Our hunger for each other was intense. I wasn't even quite sure I was fully human anymore. I was a wild thing. Ross and I writhed on the bed, making love. He was so beautiful, so loving, so strong. I felt safe with him. I loved him. We made love all night long, releasing all our pent up desires and pain. We made love over and over. I needed him, and he was there for me.

Ross gave me what I needed just then. He made me feel loved and secure, just when I needed it the most. He was so strong and confident. He seemed to have the very qualities I lacked. I clung to him and made love to him. He was so beautiful, so loving. I fell asleep in his arms.

Ralph

————————— ◆ —————————

The atmosphere at school changed. Word had quickly spread about Jordan and Corey Thomas. Instantly spread would probably be closer to the truth. Girls stopped approaching me asking for Jordan's autograph. No one asked me questions about Phantom. Most people seemed afraid to approach me at all. I had never been so miserable in my life. I was hurt and angry. I walked around like a wounded animal, dangerous and ready to attack any who drew near.

I knew Adam was just dying to taunt and torment me, but even he didn't dare. He'd had a taste of my fist and he knew I'd go nuts and beat him senseless if he started in on me. He knew as well as I it would happen.

People looked at me everywhere I went, although most looked away almost fearfully if I looked in their direction. The only ones brave enough to approach me were Chris and Denise. Our friendship protected them, but they still treated me cautiously. At lunch the first day after the news broke, they both sat quietly with me. They knew I didn't want to talk about it, so they were there for me, simply by being there with me. It helped, but not much.

Denise dropped by the house after school. I was down by the pond, sitting and thinking. My parents pointed her in my direction. They knew I was hurting, but they couldn't help me. There are some things that parents just can't fix. Denise approached me quietly. I knew it was her coming up behind me, even though I had not seen her.

"I don't want to talk about it," I said.

"I'll go if that's what you really want," said Denise.

I was conflicted. I wanted her to go, and I wanted her to stay. I didn't say anything. She sat down beside me.

"I've lost everything," I said.

"I know you are hurt, and you feel like you've lost everything, but you haven't."

"I've lost him," I said. Denise didn't know what to say to that.

"I can't believe…" she said. "Jordan was kind and sweet and loving, if it wasn't for that picture, I'd never have believed it."

"I still can't," I said. "It doesn't even seem possible, but there it is, he did it. He wasn't gone a week and he went out and found himself someone else. I knew it was all too good to be true." Tears were flowing from my eyes. "You know, I think it would have been best if I'd never met him, then I could keep on dreaming at least. I thought my dream had come true, beyond all hope, but instead, it's gone, he's gone. What am I going to do?"

"I don't know, Ralph, but you've got to just keep on going. You can't quit."

"I feel like it."

"I know. I can't really understand what you are feeling, but I know it hurts. I know you probably feel like you have nothing at all. I know this won't help much right now, but things will get better Ralph."

"You're right, it doesn't help," I said "but thanks for trying."

Denise looked at me with pity. She knew I was miserable and she wanted to help, she just didn't know how.

"I really thought he loved me. I just wanted someone to love, and to love me back." I cried some more.

Denise put her hand on my shoulder. I was glad she was my friend.

*   *   *

I still loved Jordan, but he had broken my heart. I loved him, and I hated him. No hate is so powerful as that that comes from love betrayed, and that's just what he'd done to me. My heart told me it could not be true, but reality told a different story. I took down my *Phantom* calendar and all my pictures of Jordan. Looking at them brought me pain. I put away all my *Phantom* CD's. Listening to them no longer took away my sadness and loneliness. Instead, it magnified it beyond belief. When I heard Jordan's voice, all I could remember is how happy I'd been, and how he'd destroyed it all. I didn't think I could ever forgive him for taking from me what I valued most of all—himself.

It had been little more than a day, but I felt like I'd been suffering for months, years even. I couldn't stand the pain. The worst of it was the loneliness. Jordan's betrayal had cast me into a void. When the one you loved with all your heart betrayed you, there was no trusting or loving anyone. I was so lonely I thought I'd die. Denise and Chris tried to reach me, tried to help, but could not. I was beyond any help they could provide, beyond any solace they could offer. What I needed, they could not give me.

*   *   *

The next day was a new high in lows. I felt so bad I thought I'd die. I wanted to die. It seemed the only thing that could ease my pain. If I could have willed myself dead I would have done so. I walked in utter despair. It was the worst time of my entire life.

Lance was at my locker again after school. He just stood a short distance away and gazed me at me. I knew he didn't love me. He just wanted me. I looked at him and saw the hunger in his eyes again. I was desperately lonely. I was vulnerable, afraid, and in pain. Lance kept looking at me.

"My parents are going to be gone again," he said, letting the implications hang in the air.

"Then let's go," I told him.

Jordan

◆

I woke up naked beside Ross. His long, black hair partially obscured his face. It flowed down over his chest. He looked so beautiful sleeping peacefully by my side. I felt calmer than I had the night before. I'd reached out to Ross, and he'd been there for me. I hadn't planned for us to make love, it just happened. I was hurting and I needed it, needed him.

I felt guilty, like I'd cheated on Ralph, but he wasn't my boyfriend anymore. He'd told me he didn't want to know me. He was gone. I couldn't stop loving him, however. I still wanted to be with him, spend time with him, make love to him. I was angry with him too. How could he push me away just because I'd helped a friend when he needed it?

Ross stirred and opened his eyes. He smiled at me.

"Good morning," he said.

"Good morning."

Ross sat up in bed beside me, pushing his hair out of his face.

"Are you okay?" he asked. "About… about what happened between us last night?"

"I… I don't know," I said sadly.

"Are you sorry it happened?"

"No. I needed you. I needed to be loved."

"I do love you, Jordan." Ross frowned. His expression didn't seem to match his words.

"What's wrong?" I asked him. He didn't answer for a good, long time. I turned and looked at him. It was obvious he was trying to put his feelings into words.

"You know how I feel about you. I wanted what happened last night. But now... This is going to sound just completely stupid after what we've just done, but... I'm not gay. I'm not even bi. I've never been attracted to another boy, except for you. I wanted last night more than you'll ever know, but... but I don't think I ever want to do it again."

He looked at me as if he feared he'd hurt me. He hadn't. Even though it didn't seem to make any sense at all, I understood. Real life was like that. It didn't always make sense. It wasn't all black and white, nothing was all good or bad. Maybe there wasn't even a gay, straight, and bi. It was all just labels for things that none of us could really understand. Reality was so far beyond any of us that maybe we'd never grasp it. I understood Ross though. I knew what he meant.

"I do understand, Ross. I can't explain how, but I do."

"I love you," he said. "I'm glad we shared last night. It makes me feel like I'm a part of you now, and that you're a part of me. I think that's what I really wanted with you, not your body, but to be a part of your soul."

I smiled at Ross. I knew just what he meant. I knew that we'd never sleep together again, but I'd always treasure what had passed between us. It had created a bond that would not break. I pulled Ross to me, and kissed him on the cheek.

We arose and dressed. It was late in the morning, but we decided on breakfast instead of lunch.

"How about French toast?" I asked.

"We're not going to Burger Dude," said Ross mischievously.

"No, we're going to cook it."

"You do know I can manage to burn orange juice?" said Ross.

"I know you're a bit slow, but I can help you."

"Hey!" yelled Ross, but he was laughing.

I found a big bowl and started calling to Ross for ingredients. He might not be much of a cook, but he was a good assistant. I did let him try to break one egg, but he squeezed it so hard when he tapped it on the bowl that it imploded, sending shell fragments flying. Ross spent a good deal of time picking them out of the eggs. After that I just had him hand me the milk, brown sugar, cinnamon, and other ingredients.

Ross was in an extremely good mood. He was smiling and tapping his fingers on everything, including my head. Our night together had meant a lot to both of us, but I think it solved some things for Ross. I think it made it possible for him to work out his feelings about me. We had taken things to the extreme, and now he was content to pull back from the far edge and enjoy a close, loving, but not physically intimate relationship.

I whipped up the batter as I thought about what the night before meant to me. It didn't solve things for me the way it did for Ross. The relationship that Ross and I had was cool, but that wasn't the relationship I was trying to work out. Despite everything, I still wanted Ralph. Ross was a great and dear friend, but he'd never be my boyfriend. Neither of us wanted that. It wasn't the relationship that was meant to be between us. Ross was extremely talented and virile in bed, but that would never happen between us again either. Ross was the best friend I had, but he was a friend, not a lover, not a boyfriend. Even after what Ralph had said to me, I still wanted him back. I grew sad at the thought, because he obviously wanted nothing to do with me.

I sliced the bread, heated up a big skillet, and dropped butter into it to melt. I soaked the bread a bit in the batter, and put it into the pan to cook. Ross sniffed appreciatively.

"That smells good, I'm hungry."

"I'm starving," I said.

"After last night, you should be. No wonder Ralph is always so happy." The smiled died on Ross' face. "I'm sorry, Jordan. I didn't mean…"

"It's okay. Sometimes I forget too. Sometimes I think everything is okay." Ross gave me a quick hug.

"Maybe you should call him," said Ross.

"He doesn't want to talk to me. He said he didn't want to know me. He's never been that upset before. There was hatred in his voice, Ross. He really hates me." Tears welled up in my eyes, but I forced them back down. "I wanted to explain, but he wasn't interested in listening. I've lost him. He's gone."

"I wish I knew who told him," said Ross.

"Me too. The only ones who could have told him just wouldn't do it. It's like a crime without suspects."

The French toast was done. We sat down at the table and began to devour it with lots of syrup and powdered sugar. Kieran came in just then and raised his eyebrow at us eating breakfast so late. It was now past noon. I did a double take and looked back at Kieran. He looked angry.

"What?" I asked. I wondered if he knew about me and Ross sleeping together and didn't approve.

"Sometimes I feel like I don't know you, Jordan," he said.

"What are you talking about?"

"How could you do something like that? I thought Ralph meant so much to you."

"Oh not you too!" I said. I wondered how he'd found out. Could he be the one who told Ralph? It didn't make sense. Nothing made sense.

"What? I'm supposed to approve when you go and cheat on the boy you said you loved?"

"I wouldn't call it cheating."

"You are unbelievable. There's a picture of you making out with him right on the front page and you say you weren't cheating? Does someone have to get a picture of you fu…"

"What picture? There's a picture?"

"Uh, yeah!" said Kieran sarcastically. "Isn't that what this is all about? You making out with Corey Thomas and doing God only knows what else with him?"

Ross and I just looked at each other.

"What are you talking about?" I asked, completely lost.

"This!" said Kieran, shaking a tabloid in my face. "This, Jordan! See it! Huh?" Kieran was pissed. I could tell he was extremely upset with me.

"Oh my God!" I said, looking at the paper. There, as clear as day, was a photo of me kissing Corey Thomas, but... but it couldn't be. "I don't even know Corey Thomas!" I cried out. Kieran looked like he didn't believe me.

"This is what the phone call was about?" asked Ross. "It wasn't about us?"

"About you two? What?" asked Kieran.

"Everybody just shut up for a minute," I said.

I looked at the photo. There it was, but I knew it couldn't be real. It just couldn't. I'd never kissed Corey Thomas. I knew I hadn't. I'd only kissed two boys in my entire life, and that was Ralph and Ross. Was I going crazy?

"It's a fake," I said. "It has to be." Kieran looked skeptical. "It makes sense," I said, turning to Ross. "No one who knew you and I kissed would have told Ralph. If they thought there was something wrong with it, they would have confronted us first."

"You and Ross kissed? You are turning into a real slut, Jordan." I knew Kieran was terribly disappointed in me. He never said things like that. I guess I'd have been disappointed too if I believed what he did.

"We kissed," I said. "But I only kissed Ross. I never kissed Corey. I never touched him. I've never even met him. Listen Kieran, you said you felt like you didn't know me, because of what I've done. Think about it, would I cheat on Ralph, would I?"

"Well it sure seems you did with Ross."

"Listen, Ross was upset. I did kiss him, but it wasn't like that. It wasn't sexual. It was… It was like a hug. But this thing with Corey, it never happened. You do know me, Kieran. You know I wouldn't do that. You know I love Ralph."

Kieran looked at me and I could tell he was beginning to believe me, despite evidence that clearly indicated I was guilty.

"But what about the picture?"

"It has to be a fake," I said as I looked at it. "I know it looks real, but it can't be, it just can't. I may be forgetful about some things, but I wouldn't forget something like making out with Corey Thomas. Come on. This is me, Kieran."

He looked me straight in the eyes and I looked back at him. It was as if we were communicating without speaking, perhaps we were.

"I believe you," he said, finally.

"How did they do it?" asked Ross, looking at the picture.

"Fuck!" I said. "Fuck!"

"Jordan," said Kieran, as if he were surprised at me. He probably was, I'd just used a word I'd never used around him before.

"This is what Ralph was upset about! It wasn't about us at all," I said, looking at Ross. "No wonder we couldn't figure out who told him, because no one did. No wonder he's so upset. No wonder he thought I'd cheated on him. You know what this means?" I said, looking at Ross excitedly.

"Call him," said Ross.

"Whoa, whoa, wait a minute," said Kieran as I was reaching for the phone. "You think he's going to believe you?"

I put the phone down. I just about felt like crying. Why would he believe me? I'd heard the hurt in his voice. He believed I'd cheated on him. He thought I had betrayed him. He wasn't likely to listen to reason, especially when I couldn't prove nothing had happened.

"Listen," said Kieran. "Let's call the management company. They obviously don't know about this photo yet or the phone would be ringing off the hook. We'll tell them it's a fake and let them go after the tabloid."

My mind was racing, but I tried to think logically.

"We should call Corey, too, or his agent or whoever," I said. "He'll know this photo is a fake as well as I do. I'm sure that whoever manages him will be just as interested to get to the bottom of things as our management company."

"That's right," said Kieran. "It will take a while, but we'll get this thing cleared up, Jordan. You just have to be patient."

"But every hour that passes is one more that Ralph will go on thinking I cheated on him and betrayed him. I can't bear to think of him in pain like that. I just can't!"

"Calm down, Jordan. We'll get this taken care of. Ross, toss me the phone."

Kieran walked away with the phone. He knew how to take care of things. I was so relieved I wanted to cry. I was so upset I did start crying. I felt like a huge weight had been lifted from my shoulders, but at the same time I was sick with worry over Ralph. No wonder he was so hurt. I knew what he was feeling. I'd felt it too. It was unbearable. I couldn't stand to think of him in pain. I loved him with all my heart. I wanted more than anything to just rush to his side, but I knew I couldn't do it.

Ross held my hand and patted it.

"Just hang in there, dude. It's all going to be okay."

"I hope so," I said. "I just hope Ralph will believe the truth. What if he doesn't?" I couldn't bear the thought.

"He will," said Ross. "He will."

I wanted to believe him, but I was too afraid to believe. Too much was at stake. Kieran came back a short while later. Ross left me with him, and quietly slipped out the door.

Ralph

————◆————

I lay in bed and stretched sleepily. I loved Saturday mornings, no school, no getting up early. It took me a few moments before I remembered the night before. I had an uncomfortable feeling about it. It hadn't been the same as it had been with Jordan. I almost couldn't believe I'd done it, but I had.

I felt somewhat violated, as if Lance had somehow taken advantage of me. Maybe he had in a way. I was in a vulnerable state when he seduced me. No, I couldn't lay anything on Lance. He'd seen what he wanted and had gone after it, but that was all. I was a big boy. I knew what I was doing. I needed someone to hold me, love me, and make love to me. It hadn't been like that, however. Lance had held me, but there was no love. We'd had sex, but we had not made love. What we did satisfied my body, but not my soul. It didn't fill the void. It was not as it had been with Jordan. I should have known that. I knew Lance didn't love me. I didn't love him either. Why had I done it?

I guess maybe I just needed to be with someone. I guess I just needed to pretend that someone loved me. It had worked, for a little while, but I was left feeling worse than I had before. Maybe I wanted to hurt Jordan too, the way he had hurt me. He'd never know about it, however. Everything he did might make the papers, but no one really cared what I did. Down deep, I didn't even want to hurt him. I still loved him. I couldn't shake it. Despite everything, that love was still there.

I felt dirty and nasty for what I'd done. I'd had sex with someone I didn't love. Lance was attractive to be sure, but I felt nothing for him. I just used him, and he used me. It just didn't feel right.

Mom walked into my bedroom.

"You need to get up dear, someone is here to see you."

Great, just what I needed, Denise or Chris coming over to ruin my decadent Saturday lie in. I slipped out of bed and into my clothes. I walked into the living room, and my jaw dropped open.

"Ross?" I said, incredulously.

"We need to talk," he said.

"What are you doing here?" I was so shocked to see him I almost thought I was dreaming. I might have even been more shocked than the day that Jordan first turned up.

"We need to talk," he repeated.

"Oh, yeah, sure," I said.

We walked outside and started down the hill.

"Um, does uh, Jordan know you are here?"

"No. I didn't want to get his hopes up in case I failed. He's in a lot of pain, Ralph, and he's very worried about you."

I scowled and started to say something sarcastic. Ross cut me off before I had a chance.

"Just shut up and listen," he said.

Ross started talking, and I listened. He talked for a good, long while, telling me things I found hard to believe. I finally interrupted him.

"Ross, I know you are a good friend to Jordan, and are trying to help. I'm not mad at you of course, but I saw the photo."

"The photo is a fake."

"That's very convenient to say," I told him.

"And very hard to prove," said Ross "but here's the proof."

He pulled two large photos out of an envelope he was carrying and showed them to me.

"The quality isn't very good. I had these faxed to me. A lot of people spent all night tracking this down, but I think you'll understand why it was worth it."

I looked at the first photo. It was an enlargement of the one I'd seen on the tabloid. There was Jordan, kissing Corey Thomas, for all the world to see. I looked at the next photo. There was Corey Thomas, making out with an actress I recognized. I stared at the photos. I looked at one, then the other.

"Oh my God!" I said.

"That's right," said Ross, "it's a fake. A very, very good fake, but a fake. This photo here," said Ross, pointing to the one of Corey and the girl, "is from a movie, I don't know which one. Someone has taken it, and altered it. I don't know where the photo of Jordan came from, but someone has put two photos together, undoubtedly on a computer. Two separate photos, a little magic, and voila, Jordan is kissing Corey."

"Then this means…"

"It never happened."

I started crying. I was so relieved and so happy I couldn't help myself. I just bawled. Ross smiled and drew me to him. He wrapped his arms around me and held me as I cried. As I cried tears of relief and joy, they turned to tears of sorrow and pain. I drew back and looked at Ross.

"I've done something terrible," I said. "Oh no, Jordan will never forgive me."

"I have some things to explain to you, too," said Ross quite seriously. He looked different when he was serious, kind of wise. "Some of it may hurt when you hear, but just listen okay, and let me explain?"

"Yes," I said, "if you'll do the same for me after." He nodded.

Ross and I sat down on the grass. He started talking. He told me how he felt about Jordan. He told me what happened out in L.A. at the side of the pool. Things began to fall into place. I understood how the misunderstanding between Jordan and I had occurred. When I called him upset over the photo of him and Corey, Jordan thought I was talking about him kissing Ross. No wonder he didn't understand why I was so upset. I was talking about Jordan and Corey, while Jordan was talking about himself and Ross. If only one of us had been more specific... There was no changing the past, however. Maybe that didn't matter, because we could change the present.

Ross kept talking, and his words became more painful for me to hear. When he spoke of sleeping with Jordan, I felt like a knife had just sunk into my chest. I just sat and listened, however, and when he was done, I understood. I understood everything, and it was okay. I held no blame in my heart for Ross, or for Jordan. I understood. I just hoped that Jordan would understand what I had done. I hoped that Jordan would forgive me.

"He will," said Ross, when I had finished telling him what I'd done with Lance and voiced aloud my hope that Jordan would forgive me. "I know he will," said Ross.

"How do you know?" I asked.

"Because love forgives," he said.

Jordan

———————— ◆ ————————

The phone rang. That was no surprise. It had been ringing constantly the whole day. The tabloid story had gained the attention of the real press, and they'd managed to track me down. There were a bunch of them outside the house, and they called and called and called. The press loved a scandal. The scandal was quickly turning back upon the tabloid, however. Our management company had already dug up proof that the photo was a fake. Corey's manager was going after the tabloid as well. It would be a legal mess for years. At least the story was getting out that I hadn't done what the tabloid said I did.

I looked over at Mike. He was talking to whoever was on the phone. Instead of the quick "No comment.", he was actually speaking.

"It's for you," he said.

"Hello."

"Hey dude." It was Ross.

"Where the hell are you?"

"Never mind that. I have someone here who wants to talk to you." I could hear him handing the phone to someone.

"Jordan?"

"Ralph? I was about to start crying. I think Ralph was too.

"I love you," he said.

"I love you too."

"I'm so sorry…" Ralph really did start crying.

"Ralph, Ralphie… it's okay. Let's talk."

I took the phone in the bedroom and we did talk, for more than three hours. I was both shocked and hurt to hear that he'd slept with that boy, but I understood it too. Ralph needed someone when he'd done it, just like I'd needed Ross. He thought I'd betrayed him when he'd done it, just like I thought he'd dumped me when I'd slept with Ross.

We talked and talked, and talked it all out. We shared our thoughts and feelings, holding nothing back. It was so good just to hear his voice. It was so good to be together again. I'd been miserable without him, but he was back in my life.

"Let's always talk things through, no matter what we think has happened, no matter what we think the other has done, okay? I don't want to ever go through anything like this again," I said.

"Yeah, me either. If only we'd done that this time."

"Yes, but let's not worry about that. It's over and we're back, and you know what?"

"What?"

"I love you more than ever, Ralph, if that's possible."

"And you know what, Jordan?"

"What?"

"I love you more than ever too, if that's possible."

We talked some more and by the end both of us knew that all was well between us. When I hung up I had a warm feeling in my chest. There was nothing like being in love.

Ralph

————————— ◆ —————————

It was nearly impossible to believe how things could change in less than a week. I almost thought about writing an essay for English on it and calling it "To Hell And Back Again". My life had been so wonderful, then it had all crashed down around me, then it was back and better than ever.

Jordan told me that he thought everything happened for a reason, that every event was meant to teach us something. Maybe what had happened was meant to teach me to always believe my heart and not my head. While I was writhing in agony over an imagined betrayal, my heart went right on loving Jordan. Somehow, it knew.

Some part of me wanted to hate Lance for the part he played, but if what I was coming to believe was true, then he was meant to play that part. As the days passed, Jordan and I talked on the phone a lot, and one of the things we talked about was Lance. I didn't know that Jordan kind of had the hots for him before we started dating. I didn't know he'd actually thought about doing with him the very things Lance and I had done. Jordan got a big laugh when he asked me how Lance was in bed and I told him I could describe it best in two words "premature ejaculation". It was wonderful that we could laugh about what had happened. We could do it because we'd been honest with each other about everything, and we understood.

Everyone, except Adam, seemed very happy that the whole Jordan/Corey thing was a fake, although one girl had told me she got a thrill about thinking about them together. I didn't share her opinion. I think a lot of the girls were relieved that the story wasn't true for fairly selfish reasons. There would be no autographs if Jordan and I broke up. I guess that little touch of selfishness was even okay, because it was born out of their love for Jordan, and their desire to be connected to him in some way. They got their autographs, Jordan sent me a ton of signed photos, some of him only and some of *Phantom*, signed by all the guys.

Jacob, the jock who asked for an autograph for his girl, was so thrilled when I got a signed photo of Jordan for him that he said he'd be my slave for life. I had the feeling that photo was going to get Jacob something he wanted very bad. At least that's the idea I got when he said. "Finally, all the waiting is over. My parents will be gone this weekend, and when I give this to my girl…" I wondered if Jordan would appreciate that he'd helped a sex-starved jock score. I had the feeling he'd laugh when I told him, and he did.

I don't know if it was because I was dating a celebrity, or because my classmates were just more accepting than I thought they'd be, but no one really gave me much trouble about being gay. I think most of it had to do with Jordan, both because he was famous, and because he was so good looking. I think it was harder for people to be down on me when my boyfriend was so famous, and so very cute. I'd also earned a reputation of being able to take care of myself. Part of that came from the day I belted Adam in the face, and part of it came from the way I just didn't take crap off of anyone.

The incident I liked best was when a boy came up to me in the cafeteria and started talking trash. Some girls were with me (they seemed to follow me around) and were glaring at him. Sometimes I felt like the girls were my own personal bodyguards or something. I didn't need them to protect me, however. I could take care of myself.

I let the boy talk trash for a bit, then I let him have it with just one phrase.

"You're just jealous because my boyfriend is way cuter than your girl-friend."

He didn't know what to say to that. He kind of sputtered and mumbled and then wandered off in confusion. The girls around me clapped, and agreed with me that Jordan was cuter than his girl.

I was about to die to see Jordan, but at least I could talk to him every day. He sent me a digital camera too, and we emailed each other photos every day, of each other, and things we were doing. It was awesome. It wasn't the same as being there with him, but it was pretty cool.

The best thing was a very early Christmas gift he sent me, it was a cam for my computer. He got one too, so we could talk and see each other. It was kind of choppy sometimes and didn't always work right, but it was cool to see him and talk to him at the same time.

The weeks were passing, and I couldn't wait. Every day that passed put me one day closer to being with Jordan again.

Jordan

———————— ◆ ————————

Ross, Kieran, and I had been making a lot of progress putting together songs for our new CD. In just a few weeks, we had three new songs finished and had several others in various stages of completion. I had one I'd been working on now and then, ever since the horrible days that had nearly destroyed my relationship with Ralph. I was stuck, however, and needed some help.

All three of us were in the makeshift studio on the lower level. We were just starting work and I thought it was a good time to propose a new song.

"Guys, I've got a chorus partly worked out. I want to see what you think of it," I said.

"Cool, let's hear it," said Kieran.

I started singing it Acappella, to let them get the words firmly in mind.

> Mis-under-stand-ing, *Right from the start.*
> Mis-under-stand-ing, *Tears us apart.*
> Mis-under-stand-ing, *Ruined my heart.*
> Mis-under-stand-ing, *Why can't you see?*
> Mis-under-stand-ing, *Should never be.*
> Mis-under-stand-ing, *Took you from me.*

"That's great," said Ross, drumming his fingers on his knee. I knew he was working out something for the song in his head.

"I like it," said Kieran, "but that's a lot of 'Misunderstandings' in a row.

"Yeah," I said. "I was thinking maybe we could split it, put a bridge between *Ruined my heart* and *Should never be.*"

"Yeah, that would work better," said Kieran. The *Mis-under-stand-ing* is good and strong, but too strong if it just keeps going. If we bridge it, we can use it to emphasize the rest of the song."

"Hey, here's what I was thinking of for the melody," I said, walking to the keyboard. I sang the words again, playing the melody that had been forming in my head.

"Oh! Dude! Dude!" said Ross almost before I'd finished. He ran over to the keyboard. "How about this over the top of it?"

Ross played for a bit. He wasn't as accomplished on the keyboard as he was on the drums, but he could play tolerably well.

"That's not a bad harmony," said Kieran.

I played with it on the keyboard for a while, seeing how I could mix in the notes Ross had played with what I already had in my head.

"How about this?" I said, and started playing. "No wait, this."

Kieran and Ross liked it, so we turned on a recorder and I sang and played the entire chorus.

After I'd finished, Kieran started singing softly out loud.

"The things you say, the things you believe, can change the world in your head."

Kieran started laughing.

"I don't think that's quite it, is it? It sounded better in my head."

"No, but I like the idea behind it," I said.

We kept working, throwing ideas back and forth, working out little sections that didn't fit together yet, and maybe never would. Ross hopped on his drums now and then, trying to find a beat, and sometimes just messing around. We all sang bits and pieces of what could go in the song, bouncing ideas off each other. It was the way we worked. Sometimes things all came together fast, and sometimes they didn't come together at all. By the time we were getting tired, we'd made some good progress on the song. It was far from done, but it was a great start on a song we'd only been working on for a few hours. If I had to evaluate our progress, I'd say we had it a little over half finished, although it was impossible to really say how close it was to done. Regardless, it was coming along fast. A lot of songs took way more work than that. I had a good feeling about this one. It wouldn't end up on the scrap pile. I sure hoped not, it had a special meaning to me that was obvious.

Ralph

◆

I shouldered my bag as I got off the plane. Christmas music wafted from the terminal. I smiled to myself, it was *Phantom* singing "White Christmas". Perfect. Waiting for me was a well dressed man that walked up to me as soon as I entered the terminal.

"Ralph, I'm here to take you to the house." I shook his hand.

Another guy walked up behind him. He looked suspiciously like a secret service man. He took off his sunglasses. It was Mike.

"Hey, glad to see you, Mike," I said, "but I don't need a bodyguard."

"Just following orders. Jordan wants to make sure you're safe."

"Well, at least you'll make me look important." I smiled.

It was true, people were already looking at me, no doubt wondering who I might be. Three girls stopped me before we'd walked very far.

"You're Jordan's boyfriend, aren't you?" one said.

"Yes." I grinned.

"Can we have your autograph?"

I signed pieces of paper they poked at me, trying not to laugh. I'd been asked to sign a few autographs now and then, but it always stuck me as funny that anyone would want my signature. Dating Jordan was my one and only claim to fame, but I guess that was enough for some people. The girls were really nice, and soon we were on our way.

It was just a few days before Christmas, but I sure couldn't tell it. I'd left snow behind in Indiana, but L.A. was sunny and warm. It almost didn't seem like I was on the same planet.

When I arrived at the house that Jordan was renting with Ross and Kieran, it felt a lot more like Christmas. All three of them were busy decorating a tree. Jordan dropped everything when he saw me, ran to me at top speed and hugged me so hard I thought he'd crush my ribs. I was hugging him back just as hard. I was so glad to see him, I nearly cried. We covered each other with kisses, barely aware that there was anyone else in the room.

Ross started making a coughing noise that sounded a lot like "horn dogs", although I couldn't be sure. I gave him a hug next. I'd never forget that Ross had flown all the way out to Indiana to patch things up between Jordan and me. I was sure Jordan would never forget it either.

I gave Kieran a hug too. It was so good to see them all, especially Jordan. A break was called in trimming the tree and everyone suddenly remembered somewhere he had to be, leaving Jordan and me alone. I don't know if it was something Jordan had planned, or if Ross and Kieran had simply decided to get out of our way. It is a good thing they did or someone might have got hurt.

Jordan took me by the hand and led me to his room. The door hadn't finished closing before we were ripping each others clothes off. I'm not speaking figuratively either, I actually ripped Jordan's shirt and he tore my boxers.

We sank down onto the bed, kissing and hugging each other. It was so wonderful to be with him, to be able to hug him and kiss him and touch him. I loved him so much it hurt. The phone calls had been wonderful, but they were nothing like being with him. I stared into Jordan's eyes hungrily.

"I want you in me," I said. I couldn't believe I was so bold.

Jordan and I made passionate, intense love until we heard the others return nearly three hours later.

We both came out of the bedroom, still dressing. Ross and Kieran started clapping for us.

"Damn dudes, I think that's a new record," said Ross.

Both Jordan and I turned a little red, and smiled.

It was about seventy out, but Kieran blasted the air conditioner, Ross made hot cocoa, we all put on sweaters, and decorated the tree. Christmas music was playing and it seemed like Christmas in Indiana, as long as I didn't look outside to see the bright sunshine and palm trees. I loved sharing those moments with Jordan. It just seemed so right.

When the tree was decorated and the cocoa consumed, we took off our sweaters and gave the air conditioner a rest. It was fun to pretend a while, but it was Christmastime no matter what the weather was like outside.

The doorbell rang and Kieran went to answer it.

"Oh!" said Jordan. "I almost forgot. I hope you don't mind Ralph, but we are having a visitor. Your arrival totally pushed him out of my head."

"I wonder why?" smirked Ross, then laughed.

Kieran led a boy about my age into the room. He looked slightly frightened and definitely nervous, but also extremely excited to be there.

"Courtney?" said Jordan, as he walked toward him.

"Hi. Yes, it's me."

"I'm so glad to meet you," said Jordan.

"Courtney?" I asked. "The boy from Texas?"

"Yeah," said Kieran quietly, "Jordan arranged for him to come out."

I smiled as I watched Courtney with Jordan. It was obvious that Courtney adored him. Jordan hugged him and he looked like he was going to die of pure pleasure.

Courtney looked at me a bit apprehensively. I think he was afraid I wouldn't like him because of the note he'd once given Jordan, telling him he loved him. I smiled, walked over, and shook his hand, then I hugged him too. I wanted him to be as comfortable as possible. I also wanted him to learn that being gay was cool, and not something that should make him ashamed. I know Jordan wanted that too. He'd wanted it ever since Courtney had passed him the note at the concert in Dallas. It had bothered Jordan that he'd missed his chance to help someone who really needed it. Now, Jordan would be able to make up for that.

Courtney was certainly happy for the moment. He sat there, apparently in awe of all of us. I knew how he felt. It hadn't been so many months before when I'd experienced a sense of awe every time I came into the presence of Ross, Kieran, and particularly Jordan. I'd come to know them all since then, and I knew they were human just like me, just like everyone, with problems, annoying habits, and the whole lot. I'd come to love them all deeply, Ross and Kieran as close friends, and Jordan as my soul mate. I loved sitting back watching Courtney. I know he was experiencing the thrill of a life-time.

That night, as I lay in bed beside Jordan, we spoke of Courtney, and all the other boys out there like him. Those boys were taught that there was something wrong with them; by parents, friends, politicians, religious leaders, busybodies, and fools. In reality, love was love and the sex of those in love was irrelevant. Love is the most precious and valuable thing in the universe, and should be honored and respected wherever it is found. Courtney, and boys like him, needed to learn how to trust their hearts and ignore the spiteful and foolish.

I turned to Jordan, he was so beautiful he made my heart ache. He was physically beautiful, but the real beauty came from inside. It was his soul that was truly beautiful. Looks faded, but the kind of beauty that Jordan had did not. I knew I'd always find him beautiful, even when we were both old men in our eighties. I was the luckiest boy in the world. I had a lifetime to spend with the one I loved.

*   *   *

It was just a few days until Christmas, but the guys still had work to do. The next morning, we all piled in a van and headed for a recording studio. I was excited because I'd never been in a studio before. Courtney was beside himself. He fidgeted constantly. He was almost as bad as Ross and his constant tapping.

While the boys were setting up, one of the sound technicians gave Courtney and me a little tour. There was a big room where Jordan, Ross, and Kieran had their instruments set up. It didn't look all that different from a setup on stage, except that everything was closer together. Behind a big glass window was the control room. I expected to see a lot of knobs and dials and things, but I wasn't prepared for what the control room really looked like. It was like stepping into Mission Control or something. Everywhere I looked there were gauges and whole banks of sliding controls. I didn't know the right names for any of it, but it looked so complicated that I didn't see how anyone could run it.

Chad was there waiting for us. If anyone could handle equipment like that, it was him. He greeted me and Courtney with his usual "Hey dudes!" Chad seemed right at home in California. I could almost picture him surfing all day, taking time out only to come in and help with recording sessions. He wasn't really a California surfer boy, but he sure looked and acted like one. At least he had the appearance and mannerisms of the surfer dude stereotype.

The guys ran a whole series of sound tests. It was much more involved than the sound tests before a concert. Jordan had explained why on the way over. At a concert, it wasn't necessary to be perfect. A live performance had its own energy. The crowd was not only listening to the music, they were a part of it. They could even interact with the guys. At a concert, fans could not only hear Jordan, Ross, and Kieran, they could see them. A concert was as much about performing as it was about music. Recording a CD was a whole other ballgame. There was no direct interaction between the guys and the fans. There was no energy

from a crowd. It was just the music. It had to sound just right. A flaw
that went unnoticed during a concert would stand out on a CD.

I began to understand the use of some of the sound equipment as the
boys ran through individual instrument and voice sound tests. I
watched as Chad and others carefully manipulated the sound boards.
Sometimes even the smallest adjustment seemed to make a big difference. There was an art to it. I realized that what Chad did took as much
talent as what Jordan and the others did. It was just a different kind of
talent.

Courtney and I watched as the boys sang one of their newest songs,
Misunderstanding. Tears welled up in my eyes as I heard it for the very
first time. I knew it was about the misunderstanding between Jordan
and myself, the one that had nearly destroyed our relationship. One of
the lines in the chorus, "...ruined my heart", brought back the pain of
those horrible days. I liked the song, well, loved it really, even though it
brought up painful memories. Everything was fine now, so it was okay.
It was a beautiful song.

It was kind of weird that I couldn't hear the boys, except through
speakers. They were just on the other side of the glass, but no sound
seemed to come through. I guess that was to keep the noise of the sound
booth out of the recording.

No actual recording took place for a long time. There was a whole lot
of setup up. I learned fast that there was a lot more work to recording a
CD than I'd thought. Like most people, I just thought singers went in,
sang a song, and it was done. Maybe they'd have to sing it more than
once, but I really thought it was pretty simple. I was wrong.

I was amazed that some of the tracks were recorded separately.
Separate recordings were made of just the lyrics and just the instruments. There were even separate recordings made of individual sections, like the guitar solo that Kieran had in one of the new songs. Then
there were recordings of everything done together. Chad told me that
when another musician laid down tracks for the album, he might come

in and do it on an entirely different day. I began to see why it took so long to record a CD. Even when the work in the recording studio was done, there would be tons of editing, mixing, and so on.

We were in there for hours. I made a run to Burger Dude and got us all something to eat. It was like old times on tour. No one recognized me as Jordan's boyfriend while I was out. There were a lot of stars in L.A., so I was definitely small potatoes. That was fine by me. I'd seen what fame was like for Jordan, and had a little taste of it myself now and then, and it was something I could definitely live without. I was actually thankful that I'd never be really famous. It would have been just too much to handle.

It was late when we left the studio. The CD was far from finished, but a good deal of work had been done. There would be other days in the studio, but not until after the New Year. The next few days would be as close to a vacation as was possible for the boys. I was glad. It meant I'd have a lot of time to spend with Jordan.

Jordan

◆

I wanted to spend as much time as I possibly could with Ralph while he was in Los Angeles. I knew he'd have to go back to Indiana shortly after New Year's. When we were away from each other, I missed him so bad it hurt. I couldn't even imagine how I'd managed to get by before he came into my life. It was like I wasn't whole, like a part of me was missing. Ralph had called us soul mates, and I know that he was right. I really felt that we belonged with each other, now, and forever.

I smiled when I thought of how Ralph and I had come together. It was so unlikely it nearly seemed impossible. It took an entire series of unlikely events, each one leading into the next. It couldn't have just happened. The odds against that were incalculable. It was meant to happen.

As much as I wanted to spend time with Ralph, I made sure to spend a great deal of time with Courtney too. I knew he was thrilled to be with me, but there was an underlying sadness and pain to him. I knew I could not solve all his problems for him, but I intended to do what little I could. I had a real chance to speak with him when everyone else went out for a day on the beach. Ralph normally stayed with me, but I think he sensed that Courtney needed to be alone with me just then. I loved Ralph for his compassion.

As Courtney and I sat talking quietly, I steered the conversation toward his problems with being gay. I could tell he had trouble discussing it at first, but he began to relax.

"You know that note you gave me really bothered me," I said. "Not for the reason you thought it would, but because you had such a low opinion of yourself. Courtney, you should never look down on yourself because you're gay. There is absolutely nothing wrong with it."

"I feel like there is," he said. "I hid it from everyone for a very long time, but I finally worked up the courage to tell my best friend. You know what he did? He called me a 'fag.'"

"I'm sorry."

"He really hurt me. I opened up to him because I was hurting so bad, and he just up and turned on me. He told my parents. He told the whole school. He told everyone. I thought he was my friend, but he outed me. He was even the worst of those that rode me for being gay. It hurt so much."

Courtney started crying. I sat next to him and held him. I hugged him to me.

"They call me names at school—"faggot", "gay-slut", lots more. Sometimes I feel like the whole school is working together to make me cry, but I won't do it. I won't give them the satisfaction. Most days, I go home and cry in my room after school, but I don't let them see it."

"You're very brave," I said.

"Brave?"

"Yes. I wonder how many of those that torment you would be able to hold up under all that."

Courtney shrugged his shoulders.

"My dad is about as bad. He doesn't call me nasty names, but he hints around that I'm weak, that I'll never be a man. It hurts."

"I'm so sorry, Courtney."

"Sometimes I just don't feel like I can make it. It's been better lately though. I couldn't believe it when I saw you on television, telling every-one you were gay. I really thought I was just dreaming it. You've always been my idol…" Courtney blushed and looked at me sheepishly before going on. "I've always thought you were beautiful, talented, and wonderful, but I never dared dream that you were gay. I just looked at you standing there and thought how I must be okay, because there you were, telling everyone you were gay. You were proud of it. It made me proud of myself too. What's wrong, Jordan?"

Tears were rolling down my face. I started crying. I felt so good just then that it made me cry. To think that I'd touched even one boy in such a way made my entire life seem worthwhile. I explained that to Courtney, and he smiled.

"Don't ever get down on yourself because you are gay," I said. "I know other people can make it hard. They'll call you all kinds of names and say all kinds of things about you, but it doesn't matter because they are wrong. They've put us down for centuries and mainly because they know they are wrong. It's just an excuse to be cruel and to try and hold us down. They know that most of the world's greatest artists, writers, and musician's have been gay. Did you know Michelangelo was gay? He was one of the greatest artists of the Renaissance, of all time, and he was gay just like us. Walt Whitman was too, and tons and tons of others. Even Alexander The Great was gay, and he was the greatest conqueror in the entire world. He was the very essence of all the things a lot of people say gays are not. People put us down because they are jealous. They know we have most of the talent and the intelligence. I'm not saying that non-gays don't have talent or anything like that, but I'm saying gays have more than their share. People treat us as if we were inferior, but that could not be further from the truth. If they justly stereotyped us, they'd have to admit that we are superior, if anything. That's why they work so very hard to put us down. They are afraid. They are cowards. If they could just let go of that, they'd see they have nothing to fear."

I stopped talking. I had really gotten up on my soapbox. I'd never said most of those things before. I wanted so badly for Courtney to see the truth, that I felt I needed to paint as accurate a picture as I could for him. I could tell I'd made him think. I could tell it made a difference.

Courtney and I talked on and on, about a great many things. We talked about what it was like for me to be famous and gay. We talked about Courtney and his parents. We talked about me and Ralph. I could almost see a change coming over Courtney as we spoke. I could almost see his opinion of himself raising. I was able to open his eyes and make him look at himself and see what he truly was, and that was a wonderful, beautiful, talented boy with a lot to offer the world. It was the most satisfying day of my life. It was more important than the concerts and the CD's. It was more important than the fame. It was even more important than the music itself. It was more important than anything.

Ralph

---◆---

On Christmas eve, Jordan and I sat around the tree and opened presents. Courtney had departed for Texas the day before, and Ross and Kieran had left to spend Christmas with their families the day before that. It was just me and Jordan. Mike was there too, of course, but he did so well keeping out of sight it didn't matter.

Jordan opened a sweater I'd bought for him. It was dark green and matched his eyes beautifully. I knew he'd look good in it. Of course, Jordan looked good in anything.

"I know it's too warm to wear it, but you'll be somewhere cold sooner or later," I told him.

I opened a box wrapped with brightly colored paper to find a big bunch of CD's. They looked like they had been privately recorded.

"Those are filled with unreleased songs," said Jordan. "Don't ever let them get away from you."

I couldn't believe he'd given me those CD's. There were fans who would have killed for just one of them. I couldn't wait to start listening to them.

We kept unwrapping presents. Finally, Jordan got down to the last gift I had for him. I couldn't wait to see how he reacted. He slowly ripped away the paper to reveal a plain, cardboard box that weighed practically nothing. He opened it up and drew out a small card with just two words on it—"I'm staying." He didn't get it at first, but when he understood, he jerked his head in my direction.

"Does this mean what I think it does?" A smile was already creeping across his face.

"Yes, I'm not going home after New Year's. I'm staying. If it's all right with you of course."

"Of course it's all right with me! But what about school? What about your parents?"

"I've got almost enough credits to graduate right now." I told him. "I can finish up here with a tutor, then go back and graduate with my class."

"You don't mind missing out on the rest of your Senior year?"

"I'm sure I'll be missing a few things, but I can't bear being away from you any longer. I belong here, with you. I love you and I don't ever want to be away from you again."

Jordan hugged me tight.

"I love you so much, Ralph! I was already dreading when you'd leave. This is the best Christmas present ever!"

We hugged and kissed.

"So your parents are cool with this?"

"Yeah, we discussed it, at length. Dad said I was old enough to make my own decisions. Mom said it was okay as long as I called her at least once a week."

"Oh Ralph! This is going to be so wonderful! We'll get you a tutor. You can study while I'm working, then we can spend all our free time together. Oh there is so much to see in L.A.! We'll go everywhere. There will probably be another tour next summer too, and then we can travel and… Well, it doesn't matter, just so we are together." Jordan hugged me close again.

*　　　　　*　　　　　*

At the very end of May, Jordan and I flew to South Bend, Indiana, by way of Chicago. For the first time I could remember, Mike wasn't with us. He wasn't too happy about that, but Jordan thought he needed a vacation. He was on the job 24/7, without letup. Besides, there was little danger where we were going. The worst that could happen was that we'd get mobbed somewhere, and Jordan doubted even that would happen. I liked Mike, but it was nice to be with just Jordan, instead of Jordan and his bodyguard. Three can definitely be a crowd.

We picked up our rental car and headed south to the little town of Verona. It was where Jordan's dad had lived, and died. Jordan had never been there so we decided to visit, before completing the journey home.

I looked at Jordan as he drove. There was a certain sadness to him. I couldn't even imagine what it must have been like to grow up without a father, without ever having seen him. Jordan's dad died without even knowing he was going to have a son. I wondered if his dad would have killed himself if he had known.

It only took us about an hour to reach Verona. It was a quiet little town, not unlike those near where I lived in the southern part of the state. We drove around for a bit until we found the graveyard.

Jordan and I walked among the graves. When we'd been searching a long time without luck, we spotted someone in the distance and thought maybe we could ask if he knew where the grave was.

We walked up to a very muscular, middle-aged man. He was kneeling in front of a tombstone, having just placed flowers there. When he looked up and saw us, his face went pale and he gasped. I guess he was shocked to see a rock star in a graveyard in Indiana.

"Excuse me," said Jordan, "but we're looking for a grave. Could you help us? It's my dad's." Jordan was very emotional. I think speaking of his father, and being right there in the very graveyard where he was buried, was unsettling for him.

"Your father?"

"Yes, his name was Taylor Potter."

The man gasped again and held his hand to his heart. I was afraid that he might be having a heart attack or something.

"Taylor Potter?" he said, as if he couldn't believe what he'd heard.

"Yes," said Jordan, eyeing him.

The man swallowed hard.

"He's buried right here," he said, moving aside to reveal a tombstone. I read the name upon it. It said *Taylor Potter*. There were fresh flowers on it, and on the grave beside it. The tombstone on the other grave read *Mark Bailey*. Whomever the man was, he'd just put flowers on the grave of Jordan's dad. Jordan realized this as quickly as I did.

"Did you know my dad?" he asked.

"Yes, yes I did, but I never knew…" He paused for a long time before going on. He looked like he was in shock. "I never knew Tay had a son. You look so much like him. When I saw you, at first I thought… Well, I thought you were him."

That explained his reaction when seeing Jordan. It wasn't because he was a rock star at all.

"I'm Ethan," said the man.

"Jordan."

"Ralph."

We all shook hands. Jordan and Ethan were gazing at each other. I could well understand why. Jordan apparently looked just like his dad, and Ethan was a man that had actually known Jordan's father. It was amazing that they were in the same graveyard, at the same time. Then again, maybe it wasn't so amazing. Everything happened for a reason.

"Could you tell me about him?" asked Jordan. "Anything, everything. I don't know anything about him, except that he killed himself." Jordan looked at the grave beside that of his father. "This must be his boyfriend's grave."

"You know?" asked Ethan.

"Yes, my mom told me. She dated my dad in high school, before he and his boyfriend were found out. She was horribly upset and hurt, but later she understood."

"Your mom's name was Stephanie, wasn't it?"

"Yes, it was, well, it is. She's still alive."

"Yes, I remember when Taylor dated Stephanie. That's when he and Mark had 'girlfriends' to help hide that they were boyfriends."

"Can you please tell me about him?" Jordan seemed almost desperate.

"Of course, I'll tell you everything I know."

Jordan smiled and there were tears in his eyes.

"My truck is parked over there. Why don't I wait for you, then when you are finished here, you can follow me home. It's going to take a long time to tell you all about your father."

"Okay, yes. Thank you so much! You have no idea what this means to me."

"You take all the time you want. I'm in no hurry and, to be honest, I need a little time to recover from the shock of meeting you. I can't believe how much you look like him," said Ethan. "I just can't believe it." He walked toward his truck, shaking his head.

Jordan turned his attention to his dad's grave. He sank down on his knees and started crying.

"Dad…" he said, but then his sobs kept him from speaking more.

"Do you want me to go?" I asked. "Do you want to be alone?"

Jordan looked up at me and smiled through his tears.

"No, stay with me." He reached up and took my hand, and I kneeled down beside him.

"Dad, I don't know where you are now, but I wanted you to meet someone. This is my boyfriend, Ralph, and I love him very much. He means everything to me. I know you understand." Jordan looked over at Mark's grave for a moment, then turned his attention back to Taylor's grave. "I wish I could have known you. There were so many times I needed my daddy when I was growing up, but it's okay Dad. I know you didn't leave me on purpose. I just know you wouldn't have left me if you'd known about me. I bet you'd have been a great dad. Well, anyway, I just wanted to say that I think of you often, and I love you Dad."

Jordan started crying again and I held him. I knew how very difficult this must be for him. He laid the flowers he'd brought beside those left by Ethan, then leaned over and kissed his dad's tombstone. We stood, then Jordan kneeled and placed flowers on Mark's grave too.

"I don't really know anything about you at all, Mark, but I know you loved my dad, and that's enough for me. I think of you as my dad too. I wish you were both still alive. It would have been so wonderful to have had two dad's. Maybe I could have even lived with you. I'm sorry you had to go, but somehow I know you two are together, and someday me and Ralph can be with you too. Don't worry, we don't plan on coming soon. Things are better now than they were in your time for boys like us."

Jordan kneeled down and kissed Mark's tombstone too. He stood and looked at both graves for several moments, then we turned and walked away. Jordan still had tears in his eyes. I did too. Soon, we were following Ethan's pickup to his home.

"I guess you think I'm pretty silly, don't you?" said Jordan.

"No, not at all."

Jordan looked at me and smiled. He knew I meant what I said.

Before we knew it, we'd stopped near a big farmhouse. There was a large barn and several outbuildings. Fields of corn went off into the distance as far as the eye could see. It reminded me a great deal of home, except it was a working farm and the house was a whole lot bigger. Ethan got out of his truck and led us inside.

We walked into a large kitchen. I heard china shatter upon the floor when we'd barely stepped in the door. There was another middle-aged man standing there, staring at Jordan in shock. He'd dropped the coffee mug he'd been holding and it had broken. He quickly turned to Ethan with a question in his eyes.

"Nathan, I would like you to meet Jordan. He is Taylor's son."

"Son!?" said Nathan. If anything, he was more shocked than Ethan had been.

"Yes, I know it's quiet a surprise, but it's true. One look at him should tell you that."

"You look exactly as I remember him," said Nathan. He seemed to recover his senses. "I'm sorry. I didn't mean to stare. It's just that this is quite a shock. I'm very glad to meet you Jordan. I'm Nathan." Jordan shook his hand.

"I'm Ralph," I said, "Jordan's boyfriend."

I'm not quite sure why I quickly announced I was Jordan's boyfriend. I guess I thought it was safe since Ethan and Nathan obviously knew Jordan's dad was gay. Jordan and I were probably the most openly out couple in the whole country, so saying it out loud wasn't that big of a deal. It didn't seem to bother Nathan in the least. He just smiled and shook my hand.

"Nathan is my boyfriend," said Ethan. "We've been together since we were younger than you."

"That's really cool," I said, looking at Jordan and smiling. I was thinking about us still being together when we were their age, and older.

Nathan got us all soft drinks and made us sandwiches while Ethan began to tell us about Jordan's dad. I really liked Ethan and Nathan and I felt completely at home sitting there in their kitchen.

"What was my dad like?" asked Jordan. My mom never told me much about him. I think remembering him made her sad."

"He was beautiful," said Ethan, "and I'm not just talking about his looks, although he was about the most beautiful boy I'd ever seen. You look just like him." That made Jordan blush a little. "So much like him it's uncanny. He was very sweet, and very kind, quiet too. He was the sensitive type and I believe he even wrote poetry, although I never had the chance to read any of it. I actually knew Mark, his boyfriend, better, but I was around Taylor quite a lot.

"He was very athletic. He played soccer. In fact, he and Mark were the center forwards for the high school team. They rarely lost a game. Taylor was a jock, but not one of those stuck up ones that thinks he's hot. Taylor never seemed to realize he was beautiful. Both Tay and Mark were very modest and as nice to everyone as they could be."

"He sounds wonderful," said Jordan. "I wish I could have known him."

"He would have been very proud of you. I'm sure he would have been very happy to have such a wonderful son."

Tears were welling up in Jordan's eyes and one rolled down his cheek.

"I wish he hadn't died. My mom was very nice, but so often I needed a dad," said Jordan. "I know how he died, but I understand. I'm not angry with him or anything. I just wish…" his voice trailed off.

"I think if he'd have known he was going to have a son, Taylor would not have taken his own life. He would have stayed around for you, no matter how hard things were on him. He was like that, always thinking of others, instead of himself."

Jordan smiled, but then his expression grew serious, almost fearful.

"I'm not sure if I want to know this, but what happened, what made him…kill himself?" asked Jordan.

"Well, the thing that made him snap was when his dad threw him out of the house. He'd been forbidden to see Mark, but he went right on doing it anyway. His dad tossed him out for it, and said some very horrible things to him. Most of what drove him to it, however, took place before. Everyone at school was pretty cruel to Taylor and Mark. Well, not everyone, but most. And then there were guys like me…" Ethan stopped speaking for a moment. "I was there. I saw what was happening, but I was too afraid to help. I was too scared to stand up for them as I should have. It's something I've always regretted. I always talked to Mark and Tay. I sat with them at lunch. I tried to help them out by just being their friend. I should have done more, but I just wasn't strong enough at the time."

Jordan reached out and took Ethan's hand.

"I'm glad my dad had a friend like you," he said. "I'm sure you did everything you could. Sometimes doing what's right is hard. I know. I've made mistakes. I haven't always done what I could have to help someone, but I'm doing better. I know you helped my dad as much as you could, and I'm very grateful."

Ethan smiled, although his eyes were filled with tears.

"I don't think you'll ever know how much that means to me," said Ethan.

I could tell that Ethan must have cared about Taylor and Mark very much. I wondered what it was like for him, finding out that Taylor had a son, after all these years.

A blond boy about our age came down the stairs and walked into the kitchen. He stopped dead in his tracks and just gawked at Jordan.

"Oh my God!" he said, staring at Jordan. At first I thought he was shocked because Jordan looked so much like Taylor, but then I realized the boy was too young to have even known Jordan's dad. He was also staring at me with the same shocked expression.

"I can't believe it! Jordan is in my house! Oh my God! Jordan is in my house!"

Ethan and Nathan were staring at the boy as if he'd lost his mind.

"Do you know who this is?" the boy said excitedly.

"Uh, yes, but how do you know him?"

"Everyone knows him! He's a rock star!" The boy turned to me. "And you're his boyfriend, Ralph! I can't believe you guys are here!"

Ethan and Nathan both looked back at Jordan. I could tell they had no idea he was famous.

"A rock star?" said Ethan.

"Gee Dad, have you been living under a rock or what?"

I smiled at that.

Ethan looked perplexed.

"Hold on, I'll be back in a sec," said the boy, and ran back upstairs.

"That's Nick, our son, we adopted him not long ago," said Ethan.

Nick was back in a flash.

"Here," he said shoving a CD into Ethan's hands.

"Well I can't believe it, Taylor's son is a rock star. Oh how I wish he could have lived to have seen that," said Ethan.

Nick was so worked up we had to stop talking about Jordan's dad for a while. Nick took us upstairs to see his room. There was a big *Phantom* insignia poster on the wall. On the shelf, Nick had almost as many *Phantom* CD's as I owned, and that was saying something. Nick was so excited he could hardly stand it.

Jordan was extremely nice to him. Nick pulled out a huge scrapbook of *Phantom* photos and clippings and asked Jordan if he'd autograph a photo for him. Jordan signed photo after photo, the insignia poster on the wall, and even the wall itself. Nick was delighted. I had Nick write down his address, and told him we'd send him tickets and backstage passes for the next tour. That way he could meet Ross and Kieran too, as well as see *Phantom* live.

We went back downstairs and ate sandwiches, while Ethan talked more about Taylor, and Mark. Tears welled up in Jordan's eyes when Ethan gave him a photo of Taylor and his boyfriend. I almost gasped when I looked at it. No wonder both Ethan and Nathan had been so shocked when they first saw Jordan. Taylor looked exactly like him. I would have believed it was a photo of Jordan if I didn't know better. The other boy was very handsome and athletic looking. Both boys were smiling and had their arms around each other. I knew that Jordan would keep that photo forever.

It had grown late and Ethan and Nathan insisted that we stay the night. Normally, we wouldn't have dreamed of doing something like that, especially since we'd known Ethan and his family for only a few hours, but this was different.

Nick absolutely insisted that we take his room and sleep in his bed. He stayed and talked to us a bit while we were getting ready for bed. He gawked when Jordan took his shirt off. I smiled. Nick was absolutely drooling over him. I had no doubt that Nick was gay too. That's probably why Ethan and Nathan had adopted him. Jordan noticed Nick staring and Nick turned red.

"I'm sorry, but I'm a huge fan of yours, and I kinda… Well, I have crush on you." The expression on Nick's face clearly said that he couldn't believe he'd admitted that. Jordan smiled at him.

"Well, I better go and let you guys sleep. Just don't leave in the morning without saying goodbye!"

"We won't," said Jordan. Nick smiled and left.

Jordan and I crawled into bed. He rested his head on my chest.

"I can't believe this," he said. "I never dreamed I'd meet someone who actually knew my dad. It's just so incredible. I couldn't have wished for anything more."

I held him close while he talked about his dad. I knew how very much all this meant to him. He was discovering his past. We snuggled together and soon fell asleep.

*   *   *

Ethan and Nathan made us all a big breakfast the next morning. After we were stuffed, they took us around town showing us all the sites. Nick went with us too, of course. Ethan pointed out where Jordan's dad had gone to school, the fields on which he'd played soccer, the little restaurant he'd eaten in, and even the house he'd lived in. Jordan was keenly interested in everything.

After we returned to the farm, Ethan insisted we stay for lunch before we departed. Another boy of about our age arrived and Nick introduced him as his boyfriend Sean. He was very nice, and they were so cute together. When lunch was over and it was time to leave, I found I didn't want to go. I don't think Jordan did either.

"I have something else for you," said Ethan. "Good thing I recently made a copy." He opened a drawer and pulled out a big manila envelope. He pulled out a thick stack of typed pages. "This was written by your father's boyfriend. It tells all about how they met and what happened to them, right up until the end. I'll warn you now, some of it will be very hard for you to read. Some of it is unpleasant. Parts of it make me cry to this day. It will tell you much about your dad though, even more than I can."

"Thank you so much," said Jordan. "How can I ever repay you for this?"

"How about by keeping in touch? I'd like to know what Taylor's son is doing."

"Certainly!" said Jordan. "You feel like family." Ethan smiled.

"You make sure to come back and visit us," said Ethan, as we all stood by the car a few moments later.

"Oh we will. We definitely will," said Jordan, and I knew he meant it.

Jordan gave both Ethan and Nathan a hug and thanked them once again for everything. Nick and his boyfriend hugged Jordan too. Both Jordan and I were smiling as we pulled away. Jordan had come looking for his father's grave, but he'd found a whole lot more.

*   *   *

In early June, Jordan sat in the audience and watched as I received my diploma. It felt so odd to be leaving high school behind, even though I hadn't actually attended high school in months. There was a finality to it, however, that was bittersweet. It was a little frightening knowing that I'd be out in the world, instead of the smaller, more secure world of high school. It wasn't too scary, however. I'd already been out in that world with Jordan, and I knew I'd do just fine.

After graduation, the whole Senior class headed out to our farm for a huge graduation party. That farm had never seen such a crowd. A lot of people that had nothing to do with my class were there too. There was no keeping them away. It didn't matter. All was well.

Phantom performed at the party. Having a rock star boyfriend definitely came in handy when it came to entertainment. I don't think any of my class would have dreamed that *Phantom* would be performing at their graduation party. Then again, none of them would have ever dreamed I'd be dating Jordan. Sometimes I felt that life was a dream. Mine had become so wonderful that there was little else to explain it. In the end, it didn't matter. I didn't try to analyze it. I just lived it.

Jacob was there with his girlfriend of course. I made sure to bring Jordan over and introduce them. Beth just about died when Jordan leaned over and gave her a kiss on the cheek. He talked to her for quite a while and she ate it up. Jacob wasn't jealous in the least. He knew Jordan was not after his girl. When we were alone later, Jacob leaned over and said, "Thanks dude, Beth is so hyped now. She's gonna be a wild girl tonight." He arched his eyebrows and I knew what he meant. I'd have to tell Jordan he'd helped Jacob score again. Those poor straight boys needed all the help they could get.

The party lasted well into the night. The boys sang song after song, performing far longer than they did at any concert. Ross was a wild boy, of course. He was the life of the party. He was also a big flirt. One of the girls was brazen enough to ask for his shirt. He pulled it right off his back and gave it to her. Some of the other girls just about passed out when they saw him shirtless. Ross has a pretty nice build and they were drooling. Ross loved it. He didn't even bother looking for another shirt.

Kieran wasn't as wild as Ross, but he had his own little harem surrounding him and I could tell he liked it. Everyone was pretty calm. There wasn't any pushing and shoving. I think they all knew they'd have plenty of time to talk to the guys. Jordan was the real center of attention. He and I sat on a table together, holding hands, for the longest time. My classmates kept coming up and talking to us, shaking his hand, asking for autographs. It was a blast.

What I liked most about the evening is that no one gave me and Jordan any crap. We sat there holding hands and no one said anything about it. Even Adam kept his mouth shut. He didn't get near Jordan. I think he was a little afraid of him. Adam actually seemed to be having a good time. He seemed almost nice. I wondered if maybe he hadn't wised up some. I hoped so, for his sake.

It was late before everyone was gone. We were hard pressed to find places for everyone to sleep. The crew had flown in for the party, so we didn't even have the bunks on the bus. Besides, me, Mom, Dad, and Jordan, there was Ross, Kieran, Mike, Shawn, Rod, and Chad. There were sleeping bags everywhere.

Jordan and I crept out late at night and sat watching the reflection of the moon on the pond. We held hands and just enjoyed each other. I felt so lucky to have someone that I loved so, who loved me back. It didn't have anything to do with Jordan being a rock star either. I'd have loved him if he worked in a car wash or a fast food restaurant. I'd have loved him no matter what.

I loved feeling his hand in mind. I loved knowing that I'd never have to leave his side. We'd found each other, and I knew we'd never part. Jordan leaned over, kissed me deeply, then whispered in my ear, "Do you know that I love you?"

The End

About the Author

◆

This is the fifth novel published by Mark A. Roeder. His novels have been reviewed in such publications as XY Magazine. To date he has written and published *Ancient Prejudice Break To New Mutiny, Someone Is Watching, Someone Is Killing The Gay Boys of Verona, A Better Place* and *Do You Know That I Love You.* He lives in a 150 year old log cabin in the rolling hills of Southern Indiana and has one of the largest collections of boyband CD's in the world.

Read more about the author's novels at his official website http://kclark.net/markroeder/